BLOOD MAIDENS

A Selection of Recent Titles from Barbara Hambly

The Benjamin January Series

A FREE MAN OF COLOR
FEVER SEASON
GRAVEYARD DUST
SOLD DOWN THE RIVER
DIE UPON A KISS
WET GRAVE
DAYS OF THE DEAD
DEAD WATER
DEAD AND BURIED *

The James Asher Vampire Novels

THOSE WHO HUNT THE NIGHT
TRAVELING WITH THE DEAD
BLOOD MAIDENS *

* *available from Severn House*

BLOOD MAIDENS

Barbara Hambly

This first world edition published 2010
in Great Britain and in the USA by
SEVERN HOUSE PUBLISHERS LTD of
9–15 High Street, Sutton, Surrey, England, SM1 1DF.
Trade paperback edition first published
in Great Britain and the USA 2011 by
SEVERN HOUSE PUBLISHERS LTD.

British Library Cataloguing in Publication Data

Hambly, Barbara.
  Blood maidens.
  1. Vampires–Fiction. 2. Saint Petersburg (Russia)–
  Fiction. 3. Russia–History–1904-1914–Fiction.
  4. Horror tales.
  I. Title
  813.5'4-dc22

ISBN-13: 978-0-7278-6947-0   (cased)
ISBN-13: 978-1-84751-280-2   (trade paper)

All Severn House titles are printed on acid-free paper.

Severn House Publishers support The Forest Stewardship Council [FSC],
the leading international forest certification organisation. All our titles that
are printed on Greenpeace-approved FSC-certified paper carry the FSC logo.

 Mixed Sources
Product group from well-managed
forests and other controlled sources
www.fsc.org Cert no. SA-COC-1565
© 1996 Forest Stewardship Council

Typeset by Palimpsest Book Production Ltd.,
Grangemouth, Stirlingshire, Scotland.
Printed and bound in Great Britain by
MPG Books Ltd., Bodmin, Cornwall.

For Gillyflower

Special thanks to the folks on my blog for their help and advice with research directions: Mosswing, Moondagger, Dorianegrey, ann mcn, redrose, mizkit, and shakatany.
Couldn't have done it without you.

ONE

Fog muffled the sound of screaming.

James Asher lengthened his stride, keeping close to the gray wooden wall of the workers' barracks. The smell of churned dust and cordite – the smell of burning – grated in his nostrils, drowning those other smells that told him where he was: latrines, curry, chickens . . . *Where is the fog coming from?* The answer held the key to what was happening that night, if only he could find it. *The Molopo River never fogs like this . . .*

The ground underfoot jerked with the impact of artillery shells.

He was in a part of Mafeking he'd never seen before, and he would have taken an oath he knew every block and street of that dusty mining-town. Close to the slums where the families of the Boralong workers lived, he could hear them screaming: children and women terrified by the rain of death from the night sky. *I have to get there. I have to find . . .*

He couldn't recall what or who he had to find this time.

I have to stop them . . .

He turned a corner, felt pavement underfoot. Tall brick buildings now hemmed him in: the offices of the mining companies, the first-class stores where their ladies shopped for British fashions. He wasn't sure how he'd gotten there, it was nearly impossible to orient himself, but through the gritty gloom he saw buildings burning ahead. A lapdog scuttled by him, crying in terror. Another shell hit, closer, shaking the world. Fire in a window nearby showed Asher something on the pavement of the alley ahead of him: a thin glistening stream of flowing blood.

The breath seemed to lock in his lungs. *Dear God, how many are dead?* The coppery reek penetrated even the choke of the smoke. The blood lapped thickly against his boot toe, widening as it flowed, ruby reflections in the flame. He looked up the alleyway and saw gruesome little lakes among the fog-wet cobblestones, losing themselves in that inky canyon.

He followed, keeping to the wall. The screaming, and the earth-shaking hammer of the Boer artillery, swelled, then faded as the fog grew thicker. He could still smell the river and the smoke of the city burning, but as the alleyway narrowed around him he thought, *This isn't Mafeking. This is London.*

I'm dreaming.

The reflection brought him no comfort. It only meant that anything could lie beyond the darkness. All the things he had seen and done, in Africa during the fight against the Boers, in the Balkans, in China – in all those places where his Queen had sent him in the course of twenty years' clandestine service – gave him no reason to think that whatever awaited him would be anything but appalling.

In waking life he'd seen blood flow down streets like this, and not in single modest gleaming ribbons barely an inch wide.

He turned a corner, his hand to the wall to guide him. This was definitely London, a small square somewhere near the Tower and the docks. Against the firelit brume he could just make out the tower of a crumbling pre-Wren church; the spire had been damaged, and he dimly descried darker night through the holes. There was a street lamp – not the new electric, but the outmoded gas variety – but its glass was broken, its flame quenched. Before one of the houses a candle-lantern hung on a rusted bracket, and its feeble light somehow showed him that a lake of blood extended most of the way across the square.

In the doorway of the tall and lightless house, Don Simon Ysidro stood beneath the lantern, waiting for him.

'James.' The vampire's habitual half-whisper still came to him, clearly audible above the falling of the shells, the screams of the dying. 'We must speak.'

Asher said, 'Go to hell.'

His eyes opened in the dark. His face was washed in sweat and he was trembling.

Go to hell . . .

He didn't even need to hear what he knew Ysidro had replied to that remark, because he knew that the dream had been the vision of exactly that.

Not the Boers shelling Mafeking. Germans bombing London. He'd seen the stately Zeppelin airships, silent as clouds above

Lake Constance, and the plans to convert them to aerial transports to dump high explosives on cities. He'd seen the stockpiles of weapons – those of the Germans, the Austrians, the French and the Russians and the Turks. He'd seen the Kaiser's armies on review, rank after gray goose-stepping rank marching down Unter den Linden, and the way the eyes of the German officers had glittered at the thought of leading their unbeatable forces to carve themselves 'our proper place' in Europe and the world.

The lake of blood was a puddle. The stream, only the drip of a pinprick, compared to what was coming.

I have to get there. I have to stop them. I have to find . . .

He made himself draw breath; made himself let it out. For his superiors in the Department, there was always one last thing to find, so that he – James Asher, New College Lecturer of Philology – could stop whatever horror was next around the corner . . .

But somehow it always turned out to be just something that the Army thought it needed to get a few points ahead of the Germans, in that endless competition for who had the most powerful weaponry, the most enormous battleships, the most terrifying strength.

Why Ysidro?

Asher lay in the darkness, listening to the rain. As if the deafening blasts of the artillery had been real – real tonight, not real twelve years ago – Lydia's peaceful breathing seemed loud in the stillness. She lay curled against his side like a child, her head on his shoulder, the thick braided silk of her long hair dark in the night light's tiny glow; it was red as henna in the sun. She had not resumed her nightdress after making love, in spite of the chill of the spring night, and around her bare throat glinted the links of the silver chain that she never took off.

Because Ysidro is a vampire?

Asher dared not shut his eyes again, fearing he would slide back into the dream at the point at which he'd jerked free. Fearing he would see that slight form again, standing in the doorway beneath the lantern bracket; the thin face that had once been handsome, the long colorless hair, wispy as spider silk. The curious, bleached-yellow eyes that caught reflection like a cat's.

Do I dream of him because Ysidro has killed – in the course of three hundred and fifty-plus years of hunting the living for sustenance – *without remorse and without hesitation probably enough men, women, and children to populate Mafeking two or three times over?*

Asher's hand moved to touch, above the points of his collarbone, his own chain. The smooth silver links seemed to bind him – and Lydia – to secret knowledge, secret dread. As his fingers brushed the metal they also touched the scars that tracked his jugular and carotid from ear to shoulder, as they marked his arms to the elbows.

Because to my subconscious mind – as this Freud fellow in Vienna would say – Don Simon Christian Xavier Morado de la Cadeña-Ysidro represents Death?

Asher hoped so.

He didn't want to consider the alternative explanation that might be true.

Wanwei Village. The Shantung Peninsula. Night's humidity a stifling cloak; thrumming cicadas and croaking frogs a mask for those other sounds he thought he heard, in the scrim of trees that bordered the rice paddies.

The not-quite-audible creak of felt boots on broken branches. Voices breathing a dialect he only barely understood. The vertiginous uneasiness at being unable to interpret those unspoken signals that he saw pass from peasant to peasant during the day – impassive faces, non-committal bows – because he understood only isolated fragments of the fathomless culture that lay beneath the surface.

The Germans who were building a naval compound in Tsingtao thought he was a German and would shoot him out of hand if it came to their attention that he wasn't. But outside the compound it didn't matter if he was German or English or American or French.

He was *fan quai*, a Long-Nose devil. With the fall of darkness, those silent, dutiful peasants rose as one, to close in on a lone foreigner like sharks.

Wanwei village had been deserted for years. The largest of the two-room huts still had the shutters to its windows, though the roof was half gone. Barred moonlight through the rafters showed him the cold brick platform that had been the stove, some broken baskets and jars. Everything smelled of mold and rats' mess . . . and blood.

He was dreaming again.

Asher looked around him, knowing how the actual night in 1898 had ended and not wanting to go through it again. In moments – he knew – the shadows of men would appear above the rafters: local adherents of the Society of Harmonious Fists, dedicated to the elimination of the whites who had raped the Chinese way of life, sold them drugs at gunpoint, insulted their faith and their families and now sought to carve up their country in the name of Christianity and progressive civilities of modern trade. If he could find some way to get out over the hut's rear wall before they came . . .

But the moonlight faded, turning a ghastly greenish-yellow. Instead of guerrilla fighters, something like a mist began to ooze into the hut with a thick movement not like other mist. Wisps of it burned Asher's throat and eyes, gagging him with a smell like concentrated mustard. He'd heard of this at the Foreign Office, this new weapon the Germans were developing, poison gas that would leave a man paralysed and blind . . .

There was a door at the rear of the hut, (*why wasn't it there in June of 1898?* he wondered), and when he dodged through it he found himself at the base of what appeared to be a stone stair, winding up into a tower that was certainly no part of the hut he'd just come from. The gas trickled in under the door into the tower, and he didn't hesitate, fled up the stone stairs where the smell of blood grew stronger and stronger. A sliver of moonlight showed him a running line of blood, trickling down the stairs.

It has to be coming in from somewhere . . .

The gas was rising behind him. The Foreign Office reports said that the gas was heavier than air, and he told himself he had to be able to out-climb it eventually. But the moonlight blinked out around him, and he was groping his way in blackness, choking on the stench of blood and poison. The stairs ended, and there was no door after all, only a stone wall. He could see nothing and didn't know whether this was because the tower was windowless or whether the gas had blinded him. He dropped to his knees in the darkness, pawed at the edge of the floor – *the blood has to be coming in from somewhere . . .*

He could find no crack, no join. Only the stickiness

gumming his hands, hot and fresh as if just pumped from a wound. The gas seared his throat, and he stood, groping desperately at the wall in the blackness—

And very softly, a voice whispered in his ear. 'James,' it said. 'We must speak.'

'He can do that.' Lydia returned to the breakfast table with a cup of coffee, an egg and toast on a pink-and-green china plate and a second muffin for him. The note of remote disinterest in her voice didn't fool Asher for one single second. 'When he decided I needed a chaperone, if I was going to travel with him to Vienna to find you last year, he – he used dreams to summon one.'

And killed her when he was done with her, Lydia did not add, though she kept her wide, velvet-brown eyes on her egg as she tore her toast into tiny fragments and dabbled them in the rummelled-up yolk – fragments that she set on the edge of her plate, uneaten.

Asher knew the signs and wished he had not needed to bring up the vampire's name with her.

She had loved him.

Asher suspected – watching how his young wife now carefully arranged her coffee spoon, egg spoon, and knife so that they made a precisely symmetrical pattern where they rested on the edge of the plate – that she loved Don Simon Ysidro still.

It is our lure to be attractive, Ysidro had told him, when they had parted in the stillness of the Hagia Sophia in Constantinople. *It is how we hunt. It means nothing.*

This Asher knew. His own emotions had been scalded by his relationship with the vampire Countess of Ernchester: he knew what Lydia had gone through. Though she was no longer the sheltered girl who'd scandalized her family by marrying a man a dozen years older than herself – and an impoverished lecturer at that! – he knew that in many ways, her absorption in medical research had continued the emotional insulation that her father's fortune had begun. She was still far more conversant with the endocrine systems of human beings than she was with their behavior, lives, or souls.

Loving Ysidro – and finding the body of that poor companion lying drained of blood on her bed – had torn her apart inside. For nearly eighteen months now Asher had watched her shut herself into the dissecting rooms of the Radcliffe Infirmary, retreat into the Radcliffe Camera's shelves of medical lore, and conceal herself in her study here on Holywell Street as she penned concisely-reasoned articles about experimental procedures and pineal secretions. He had thought she was coming out of it last September – not quite a year after they had returned from that terrible journey to Constantinople – when, he suspected, she had conceived a child . . .

A suspicion confirmed when she had miscarried at the end of October, returning to her silence and, for a time, passing into a remoteness that had terrified him. She had done her best to comfort his grief, and had seemed to be forcing herself through the motions of being comforted, but he knew there was a part of her that had retreated too far to be touched.

Only at Christmas – at long last – had he heard her laugh unaffectedly for the first time; had he heard her get into an argument, as she'd used to, with one of her stuffier Willoughby cousins about whether or not cats had souls. Christmas night, she had woken up in the darkness and wept in his arms. At New Year's, on the way home from dinner with her uncle, the Dean of the College, she had asked him, 'What will you do with this year, Jamie?' and he'd heard in her voice that she didn't mean his students or his research into obscure legends or Serbian verb-forms.

For three months, it had seemed to him that he watched green shoots peeping hesitantly from the cracks in a sheathing of stone.

Now, at the mention of the vampire's name, the guarded silence was back.

Speaking carefully – as if she were carrying fragile glass – he replied, 'I know. It doesn't mean I'm going to obey him.'

Her spectacled glance touched his very briefly, then dropped quickly to the rearrangement of the silverware. 'Not even to see what he wants?'

'I know what he wants. He wants me to do something for him that he cannot do himself because of what he is.'

She moved the coffee spoon to a more precise angle, as if she would not even think of what they both knew. For all their powers over the human mind, the Undead were powerless to

save themselves from daylight. They both had seen the blazing
horror when the first touch of sun ignited vampire-flesh. For
all their great strength – Asher had watched Don Simon Ysidro
bend forged steel in his skinny fingers – vampires could not
touch silver without sustaining corrosive blisters and sometimes
weeks of illness. And for all their conditional immortality, the
Undead were at the mercy of their need to hunt, their need
for the physical nourishment of blood, and for the psychic
rejuvenation that could only come with the death of their
victims.

'At a guess,' said Asher in a more normal tone of voice,
and scratched one side of his mustache, 'he either wants me
to use my connections in the Foreign Office to learn something for him, or he wants me to accompany him on a journey.
Almost anything else, he can trick or buy or blackmail the
living into doing, as he tricked poor Miss Potton into being
your companion, and blackmailed me back in '07. And I resent
having my personal nightmares used as set decorations for
his threats.'

Her long, slim fingers hesitated over a millimeter's alteration
in the placement of the egg spoon. Then her mouth quirked
and she scooped the silverware together, set it in deliberate
disarray on the edge of the plate, and looked back at him
again, her old matter-of-fact self. Against the wan, wet daylight
of the windows – it was bitterly cold that March of 1911, and
the wind whipped the bare branches of the garden willows –
her carnelian hair had the ruddiness of the fireplace coals, and
her round spectacle-lenses glinted as bright as the silver toast-
racks. 'Are you expecting a threat?'

It was Asher's turn to look aside from what he did not wish
to see. Was Ysidro fishing in the nightmares that had pursued
him for a dozen years only because the vampire knew how
to twist compliance from unspoken fears? Or did those visions
spring from his own too-informed knowledge of what a modern
war would bring?

He didn't know.

'If it weren't important,' she went on, with the calm logic
that sometimes made her such a disconcerting companion, 'he
would never have tried to contact you, you know.'

Asher knew she was right. Knew, too, that his first instinct
– to protect her from her memories of the vampire – had been,

at least in part, a smokescreen. The other person he wanted to protect was himself.

Tiredly, he said, 'It's always important, Lydia. Every time the Department chiefs asked me to risk my life for Queen and Country, it was always because it was the most vital thing in the world and they were relying on me. And it always ended in death, or betrayal, or me doing something to someone that I would *never* have done – would never have *considered* doing – if it were not the most vital thing in the world.' He sighed bitterly, as if trying to flush from his lungs the smells of blood and mustard gas. 'I got tired of it, Lydia. And I grew frightened because I was starting not to mind. And now my tea is cold,' he added, and she laughed and went to the sideboard for the pot. 'I didn't mean you should fetch it—'

'Josetta and I are going to a lecture on ancient Egyptian medical texts after I'm done at the dissecting rooms.' She named her closest friend, who had been the Literature mistress at one of her very expensive boarding-schools, and poured his tea. 'So this is the last you'll see of me till evening.' She set the teapot back on its little spirit-lamp and shook down the layers of lace-edged sleeve-ruffles to cover her hands, like a thin red-haired marsh-fairy inexplicably playing dress-up in a Worth suit of hunter-green wool. Hesitantly, she added, 'You aren't angry at Don Simon, are you, Jamie?'

He raised one eyebrow. 'Should I not be angry at a man who has murdered hundreds of people, only that he himself might continue to live beyond mankind's allotted span? No,' he added, seeing the troubled look that returned to her eyes. 'I'm not angry. He's helped us in the past – and whatever he wants of me may be desperately important – but that doesn't mean that he isn't dangerous in himself. Every time I or you or anyone crosses his path – crosses the path of *any* vampire – we take our lives in our hands.' He removed the cup from her grip, and his fingers closed around hers. 'If I knew where to write to him, I would send him a polite note telling him I'm not for hire this week.'

She smiled, her quicksilver beauty piercing his heart as it had when she'd been sixteen and he, her academic uncle's guest at croquet parties at Willoughby Towers, with not the slightest hope of ever being more than a family friend who might one day be invited to see her wedded to someone else.

Then she sobered. 'Just be careful, Jamie.' She removed her spectacles – God forbid cab drivers, or her best friend, should see her in them – and stowed them in their silver case. 'If it's important, I don't think he's going to take no for an answer.'

'He'll have to.'

But, with a sinking heart, Asher guessed that his wife was, in fact, correct.

TWO

'Lydia?'

The shadows of the stairwell swallowed up the sound of her name, and in the silence of the house – death-still but not empty – Asher thought, *This is a dream.*

Anger flooded him, at the knowledge that he had stood here once before.

A foggy evening in the autumn of 1907. The house chill. The clip of hooves in Holywell Street loud in the silence. Standing in the front hall in his dark academic gown, Asher knew that if he went downstairs to the kitchen he'd find Mrs Grimes, Ellen the maid, and Sylvie the tweeny – who had married the butcher's son last year and been replaced by the equally feckless Daisy – crumpled asleep at the table, like a tableau in a cheap melodrama . . .

And upstairs, Lydia would be lying unconscious on the divan in the upstairs parlor, fingers clasped around her spectacles where they rested upon her breast and hair hanging in a pottery-red coil to the floor. Don Simon Ysidro would be sitting at Asher's desk, just out of the line of sight of the door, long hands folded, like a skeletal white mantis awaiting his prey. 'My name is Don Simon Xavier Christian Morado de la Cadeña-Ysidro, and I am what you call a vampire.'

And despite half a lifetime of research into the folklore of a dozen cultures, Asher had not believed him until he had listened to his chest with Lydia's stethoscope and satisfied himself that his uncanny guest had neither heartbeat nor breath.

He whispered, 'Damn you—' and strode up the stairs.

But when he threw open the door of the upstairs study, the

divan – though it was back in the same position it had been in, that evening four years before, visible through the half-open connecting door – was empty. No whispered suggestion, as there had been on that occasion: *I can kill your wife, your servants, and all those you care for, if I choose . . . if you do not do as I say.* The lamp on his desk was lit, but no slender gentleman sat there, with his long white hair hanging to his shoulders and his eyes like crystallized sulfur, and the faint lilt of archaic Spanish still lingering in his soft voice.

The papers at the desk had been splattered with droplets of blood.

And in blood was written – *on Lydia's stationery, damn his effrontery!* – in a sixteenth-century hand:

James,
We must speak.

It took Asher a day to find the court he had seen in dreams.

He knew it would be near the river, in the medieval tangle of streets that had been spared by the Great Fire. He knew it would be towards the east, between Whitechapel Street and the filthy, sprawling mazes of the docks. He knew to look for the half-ruinous spire of a pre-Wren church and a small, oddly-angled square surrounded by houses of blackened brick and ancient half-timbering: homes that must once have been the pride of wealthy Elizabethan merchants, but were now given over to sailors' boarding houses and the tenements of the poor.

The March afternoon was arctic, and by three – when he finally identified the place – fog was rising from the river, mingling with the mephitic stinks of coal smoke and outdoor latrines. Shadowy figures stumbled on the worn cobblestones of the alleys, or clustered around the glowing stoves of the chestnut vendors, their coughing like that of the restless ghosts Odysseus had encountered on the banks of the Styx—

Bodiless, until you gave them blood.

Ysidro wouldn't make his appearance until the sun was out of the sky.

Having located the square, Asher repaired to the nearest public house for a surprisingly good dinner of bangers and mash. The stevedores, thieves, whores and toughs who populated the Fish and Ring on Marigold Walk neither troubled

Asher nor indeed seemed to notice him. Oddly for a man who was routinely shown off by his students to visiting Americans as the quintessential Oxford don, Asher had perfected the appearance of the equally quintessential out-of-work laborer. Had he not been a chameleon, he supposed, he would not have lived to the age of forty-six as a Secret Servant of the King.

When full dark came, he paid his two bob and made his way back to Felmonger Court.

In his dream that narrow, crooked space had been empty – to say nothing of awash with a lake of blood. In waking reality, at six o'clock on a raw spring evening the place swarmed with ragged children, rolling hoops and throwing rocks and calling to one another with piping ghostly voices in the fog. Slatternly women spoke to Asher from the dark-ness of alleyways as he passed. Men jostled past him, reeking of tobacco and gin and garments years unwashed, seeking only the relative shelter of overcrowded rooms and a few hours' kip before returning to their work. Somewhere an old man's quavery voice wailed, 'Scissors, brollies, fix 'em all, fix 'em up—Scissors, brollies . . .'

Contrary to the assertions of Bram Stoker (Ysidro had informed him) and most other writers on the subject, vampires lived primarily on the poor, whom no one would seek to avenge or even locate if they should disappear. As he crossed the court, Asher scanned the darkness (the street lamp really was broken), wondering which whore, which child, which gin-fuddled drunkard would fail to come home that night, always supposing he or she had a home. Wondering if Grippen – the Master Vampire of London – or one of his fledglings was watching those huddled bundles of rags from the shadows right now, choosing a victim . . .

Though, of course, it was no more possible to see Grippen when he hunted, than it was to see smallpox or cholera or starvation, before they struck.

And it crossed Asher's mind – not for the first time – to wonder if it was Ysidro at all who had put those images in his dreams, and not Grippen or one of the others, who considered that one mortal who knew how to find vampire lairs – one mortal who truly believed that such creatures existed – was one mortal too many.

Then beside him a gentle voice said, 'James. 'Twere good of you to come.'

He felt the hair on his nape rise as he turned. 'Had I a choice?'

'My dear James.' The vampire regarded him without change of expression, a stillness that had nothing in it of the immobility of a corpse. The death was inside and had happened long ago. 'One always has choices.' They passed from beneath the dim and greasy glow of a window; shadow veiled Ysidro's thin face once more. The hand that closed on Asher's elbow was light as a girl's, though the fingers could have crushed the bone. In the mouth of an alleyway, rank with sewage and dead fish, a woman's voice purred, ''Ere, gents, ever 'ad the two of you turned off at once?'

Ysidro responded politely, 'There is nothing we have not had, Madame, my friend and I,' and they kept moving, deeper into the darkness.

Asher felt icy water slop against the outside of his boots, and then the plank of a makeshift bridge vibrated underfoot. He caught a glimpse of water below them in the shadows. They turned twice right, then left, Asher counting strides. He felt Ysidro's mind press on his own, a sort of sleepy uncaring, and he fought it . . . *three, four, five, six* . . . Another right, the creak of a hinge, and a cold up-rushing stench of mice and mold.

Stairs going down. An old kitchen at the bottom. A lamp on a wooden table, its dim glow barely outlining a dusty rummage of burst sacks and broken bins around the wall. A door on the facing wall; the smell of more water beyond.

'Not my primary residence.' Ysidro brought a slat-backed chair for Asher and perched himself, straight as if with the boning of a court doublet, on the table beside the lamp. 'Mistress Lydia is entirely too clever in the study of deeds of conveyance. I trust she is well?'

'She is well, yes.'

Ysidro's silence lasted a few moments longer than it had to, the only indication that he had met – much less traveled with, or loved, or deliberately deceived – Asher's young wife. It was only with careful attention – vampires relying as they did upon the misdirection of human perception – that Asher could see the frightful scars that Ysidro had taken on his face and throat in Lydia's defense and his own. Undead flesh healed slowly, and differently from that of living men. After eighteen months, the marks still stood out like ridges of dried sticking-plaster on the colorless flesh. *How long would it – did it – take vampire flesh to heal?*

Lydia would have asked outright.

He remembered her silence and the words she would sometimes cry out in sleep.

Or maybe not.

'Yourself?'

'I'm well,' said Asher. 'You?'

'Is this politeness?' Ysidro's head tilted a little to one side. 'Or do you truly wish to know?'

Asher considered for a moment, then said, 'I don't know.' And after another moment, 'I truly wish to know, Don Simon.'

'Another time, then.' Ysidro drew a folded paper from the pocket of an immaculate gray coat – only a vampire could have worn such a garment in the East End and remained un-noticed – and passed it across.

It was in English:

> *St Petersburg*
> *3 February 1911*
> *Dearest Simon,*
>
> *Forgive me my long silence. At this season of the year one is much abroad, and a letter filled with the minutiae of ballet and opera, scandal and politics, creeps towards its conclusion on my secretaire . . . but this is a matter that cannot wait.*
>
> *Some few years ago you wrote of a scientist named B—, who sought to learn what wasn't his business for the benefit of King and Country—*

Asher glanced sharply at the vampire's inscrutable face. 'Does she mean Horace Blaydon?' He named the researcher who, four years before, had sought to distill vampire blood in order to produce the powers of the Undead in a living man: to create a hybrid, able to walk in daylight as well as darkness and to touch silver as casually as steel. A man who held vampire powers without vampire limitations. A man who would use these abilities in the fight that all men knew was coming, against Germany and its allies.

An immortal who would strive selflessly for King and Country. As Asher had striven, not caring who suffered in consequence.

Ysidro's assent stirred nothing more than the lids of his yellow eyes.

> *Without your account of the matter I doubt I would have attended to what I heard – who DOES listen to scientists when they prose on about their research at soirées, for Heaven's sake? But there is a German doctor here whose studies strike me as remarkably similar, and last night at a Venetian breakfast at the Obolenskys', in flight from the Grand Duke George (the most SHOCKING bore in the Empire, I assure you) I entered the conservatory to see our Teutonic student of blood and folklore in deep conversation with one of us.*
>
> *What should I do, dear friend? As you know, King and Country has not been a matter of concern to me for many years, and yet . . .*
>
> *The Kaiser is such a NOXIOUS little toad, I find I cannot stomach the thought of him stamping into Whitehall in his big boots after all, shouting orders. One must draw the line somewhere.*
>
> *Is this Professor A— of yours still alive somewhere? Might he be persuaded to give his assistance again? Or did Grippen kill him?*
>
> *And if so, what course do you advise?*
>
> *Until eternity,*
> *Irene*

Horace Blaydon.

Asher still had nightmares about Blaydon's son Dennis, and what injections of that distillate had done to him.

As he had said to Lydia, *it was always because it was the most vital thing in the world* . . . And he had meant what he said.

But, to the marrow of his bones, he knew immediately that he would – he must – go to St Petersburg and find that *Teutonic student of blood and folklore* . . .

Carefully, he said, 'And what did you advise?'

One of us, she had said. *Is this Professor A— still alive somewhere, or did Grippen kill him?*

He knew he had come within a hair's width of it.

'I telegraphed her at once, for more information.' Ysidro took the paper from his fingers, refolded it. Like everything else about him his gloves were expensive and perfect: gray French kid at half a crown a pair.

'What did she say?'

'I have had no reply. This was over five weeks ago – their third of February being what we know as the seventeenth. Lady Irene Eaton disregards all things in this life that touch not upon her comfort, her *toilettes*, or her safety . . . yet as much as her own comfort, she prizes her opinions. And though she has not set foot upon English soil in nine decades, she disdains the Prussians as upstart barbarians well deserving of a putting-down. I do not think she would neglect a reply that would bring about their discomfiture.'

In the silence that followed, the only sound was the hissing of the lamp wick as it burned, and once, the scrabble of a rat in some upper chamber.

One of us . . .

I entered the conservatory to see our Teutonic student of blood and folklore in deep conversation with one of us.

Against red anger as Asher recalled the friends he had betrayed – or killed – for his country's sake, he remembered clearly Horace Blaydon's unshakeable conviction that he understood enough about vampires to be able to control the thing he had made. The unshakeable conviction of every Foreign Office official Asher had ever met: that they knew exactly what they were doing and could guide the results at will. Presumably, those who worked for the Auswärtiges Amt in Berlin felt the same.

Will all great Neptune's ocean wash this blood clean from my hand?

The lake of blood he'd seen in his dream had not been from Ysidro's kills, he realized, but his own. Kills he had undertaken at the behest of men who'd sworn they knew what they were doing. And he, poor fool, had believed them.

He looked up, to meet cold unhuman eyes. 'I take it you want me to go to St Petersburg?'

'My dear James, the Master of Petersburg would devour you between the station and your hotel,' the vampire replied. 'I would have you accompany me.'

'How soon?'

'Monday, if all can be ready.'

Willoughby would be livid at the thought of having to find someone to cover the final lectures in folklore and philology with the end of term coming up. On the other hand, the Dean of New College had always irritated Asher with his constant winks and nudges, and hints that he understood that his Lecturer in Philology had not *really* severed his mysterious ties with the Foreign Office . . . The man was going to get him killed one of these days.

He was aware he was being regarded, beneath those straight white lashes – *Curiosity?* Had Ysidro thought he would refuse in the end? That he would put up more of a fight?

Or had the vampire merely expected him to display more anger, on Lydia's behalf?

'I'll leave it to you to make the arrangements,' Asher said. 'You know what you'll need – and I am given to understand that there are . . . *accommodations* in every city for those who hunt the night.'

What could have been a smile touched one corner of Ysidro's fanged lips. 'I would not go so far as to say so. You yourself must know that every city contains *accommodations* for any with specialized requirements – and a good deal of money. It is merely our business to know what these are. We who hunt the night must needs know all we can about those with whom we share our domain: killers and lovers, thieves and spies. Do you know Petersburg?'

'I was there about seventeen years ago. Yourself?'

Ysidro made a move of his head – *No.* 'It is far to travel, for the Undead, and perilous.' He looked as if he would have said something else – spoken of why it was that Lady Irene Eaton had called him '*Dearest Simon*', and how an Englishwoman had come to be made a vampire in that gilded arctic Venice—

—And in that moment's inattention, the vampire reached out and touched his mind, and Asher came to himself again, breathless with shock, on the pavement of Praed Street across from Paddington Station. He looked around him, a little wildly, though he knew perfectly well that he wouldn't see Ysidro walking away through fog and gaslight and jostling crowds . . .

But late that night, when the scene replayed itself for him in dreams, it seemed to him that, the moment before he woke

up again, in his open-eyed trance he saw Grippen, the Vampire
Master of London, watching him from a mist-choked alleyway,
with his fledglings gathered around him, their eyes gleaming
in the dark.

THREE

They reached St Petersburg in two days.
Asher had been clean-shaven during his earlier visits
to Germany, and bearded in South Africa. The night
before his departure for London he shaved the top of his head
and dyed his remaining hair and mustache a streaky black, which
sent Lydia into fits of giggles. Still, it made him feel a little
safer when they changed trains – with a mountain of luggage
including Ysidro's double-lidded coffin-trunk – in Berlin.

Abroad, men in the Department called it.

*In enemy territory, even if the King has a treaty with
whoever's in charge where you are.* To the Department, *Abroad*
was, by definition, always enemy territory.

And many, many people knew him in Berlin as the Herr
Professor Ignatius Leyden . . .

Some of whom might have been wondering why the Herr
Professor had so suddenly dropped out of sight after the South
African war.

Ysidro left their first-class compartment some miles outside
of Berlin – it was dark by that time, the train drumming full
speed through the dreary wastes of Prussian pine-forests and
gray little Prussian farm-villages – and it wasn't until after the
cab ride from the Potsdamer Bahnhof on Königsgrazerstrasse
to the Settiner Bahnhof on the other side of the river, the inspec-
tion of travel papers, and the St Petersburg train's departure
shortly after midnight, that he came silently into the compartment again and settled down with a copy of *Le Temps*.

'Was the Master of Berlin aware of you?' Asher set aside
his own paper, the *Norddeutsche Allgemeine Zeitung*, remembering the masters of other cities he had met: the brittle and
vicious woman who ruled the Paris nest; the dark and frightening shadow he had so narrowly escaped in Vienna.

The bleached horror in Constantinople that still sometimes burned in his dreams.

Compared with those, the chance of a brush with someone in the Auswärtiges Amt who might remember his face paled into a momentary contretemps.

'I spoke with none.' Ysidro turned a page. 'And as I am not such a fool as to hunt upon ground not my own, I think that the Master of Berlin only watched my passage, if so much. He has the reputation of remaining like a spider in his cave, unless one draws his eye. All know this to be unwise.' He folded the newspaper. 'I was not aware of his attention.'

'And your friend in Petersburg,' asked Asher, after a long hesitation – *did* one speak words of reassurance to the Dead? – 'will you be able to find her through her dreams, once we've reached that city? Learn what happened to her, and why she has not written?'

Ysidro was silent for so long that had he not known the vampire as he did, Asher would have taken the lack of reaction as a snub. The vampire absorbed the newspaper as he would have savored a zabaglione at the Savoy, with a delicious slow sensuality, as if he could taste the minds and hearts of those whose stories he pieced together. At length he said, 'I don't know.'

'She was not vampire when you knew her in England, then?'

'No.'

'Then she is not your fledgling?'

Ysidro looked up for a brief instant, and it seemed to Asher as if – for the space of a single wingbeat of the Angel of Death – he might have replied. Then he only said again, 'No,' in a voice remote as the arctic ice.

So we may not have her help in learning WHICH German scientist is allying himself with the Undead, Asher thought. *Nor in knowing how far things have progressed, and in what direction.*

A few hours later, blackness still lying over the Baltic forests, Ysidro handed Asher a slip of paper bearing two addresses, and a draft on the Crédit Lyonnais for five thousand francs, then silently vanished into the corridor again.

At five minutes to eight in the morning, with dirty snow still blotching the streets and breaking ice bobbing in the steely canal below a rampart of dreary apartments, Asher stepped

off the train at the somewhat confusingly-named Warsaw
Station in the Russian capital. Cab drivers and porters swad-
dled in sheepskin clustered around bonfires built on the street
corners; the air reeked of charcoal, burnt bread, and the frowst
of unwashed wool. Little drifts of Russian, French, German,
and Polish seemed to move like clouds above the muffled
figures hurrying along the station platforms, and Asher felt
the queer bristling surge of excitement that was only half fear.
  Abroad.
  Where everything was brilliantly focused, every color vivid
and every scent the scent of peril. Where every sound was
significant and the blood in the veins felt charged with electricity – only in fact, reflected Asher ruefully, what the blood
was charged with was adrenalin, which Lydia had informed
him was a common glandular reaction to stress.
  He recalled what it had felt like to love being Abroad.
  For two days he'd been reading *War and Peace*, so that
enough of his rusty Russian had come back to him to engage
porters and summon a cab. It was Lent – not, Asher knew,
that that would slow St Petersburg society down much, with
the exception of the Tsar and his pious Empress. As the porter's
wagon slithered and skidded its way towards the first of the
addresses, a small town house near the Smolny monastery,
the carriages and motor cars of the rich passed them in the
foggy dawn-light, homeward bound from the usual very un-
Penitential Petersburg parties. Against the silvery morning
grayness, the painted plaster of the town's buildings stood out
like spring flowers – pale greens, lemon yellows, cerulean
blues – all trimmed with white like the frosting on Rococo
pastries. Bureaucrats, clerks, and middle-ranking Army officers already clogged the flagways, hurrying – Petersburgers
were always hurrying – with the purposeful stride of men who
fear to be seen by their superiors as less than passionately
dedicated to the welfare of their pettifogging departments,
bearing from one office to another an endless round of Russian
paperwork. Overhead, the seagulls mewed eerily in the raw
mists.
  The city hadn't changed.
  Asher had the trunks disposed in the rather shallow – but
pitch dark and windowless – cellar of the town house, locked
the house thoroughly, summoned another cab, and betook

himself to the second address, Les Meublées L'Imperatrice Catherine on the Moyka Embankment. There he took from his carpet bag garlands of dried garlic and wild roses – plants universally recognized as causing severe discomfort to the Undead – done up in netting, wreathed the windows in them, and slept until ten, when he had arranged for the concierge's servant to bring up breakfast and draw a bath. He did not sleep particularly well.

It is not often that we travel, Ysidro had told him once; *we whom the sun's slightest ray will ignite to unquenchable fire. A vampire traveler is always the portent of disturbance and change. Claims to territory among the masters aside, we all of us hate change.*

Hence, Asher reflected, the dispatch with which Ysidro had parted company with him in Berlin. His own experiences with the master vampires of Paris and Vienna had taught him that they were likely to kill an interloping vampire's human companion out of hand – either to limit the information about their existence that might be spread abroad, or merely to let the interloper know that no intruders would be tolerated.

With luck, Ysidro would locate the Master of St Petersburg and square things before the sun rose tomorrow.

For himself, Asher had his own masters to locate.

His time in St Petersburg had been too long ago for him to be sure of finding any of his old contacts at the Embassy itself. Given the current state of international affairs, that elegant mansion on the Neva Embankment would be watched, as a matter of routine, by German eyes – and, in any case, after the South African fiasco he was never quite certain what the Embassy boffins would do with any piece of information he gave them. Instead, after a late breakfast of coffee and rolls, he made his way to the rather seedy district north of the canal, where a man allegedly named Hervieu kept a tobacco shop on a side street.

'Good Lord, Asher, it's never yoursel'!' the allegedly Swiss proprietor exclaimed, after the only other customer had left and the usual preliminaries of enquiries for Virginia cigarettes had been exchanged and vetted.

Asher winked at him behind his pince-nez. 'The years have been hard ones . . .'

'Hard years, my arse,' retorted Hervieu, whose baptismal name had actually been McAliester. 'Not so hard, or they'd have made you near as bald as mesel''.' He ran a hand over his slick pink dome. 'Here's you wi' a head of hair a schoolboy would envy! I heard ye'd quit the Firm.'

Asher looked him straight in the eye. 'You heard correctly,' he replied, putting great significance into his tone. 'I have had nothing further to do with Whitehall, nor do I wish to.'

'Ye've come to Petersburg for your health, then?'

'I have.'

'Aye, well, winter in the Arctic circle's a good time for that. Where you staying?'

'You can leave a message for me at Phlekov's.' Anyone who worked St Petersburg quickly learned that half the stationers', cafés, and news-stands in the city were operated by petty bourgeoisie who for a few kopecks would act as mail drops for the Devil. Phlekov's on the Voznesensky Prospect was far enough from the Imperatrice Catherine to give Asher a good chance of observing if he'd picked up a follower. But even the Germans hadn't the money to keep an eye on every letter drop in the city. 'I've told them my name is Weber.'

Hervieu didn't trouble to ask what name he'd told his landlords. He'd been in the Department a long time.

'Who's in charge at the Embassy?' Asher asked, and for a few minutes he slipped comfortably back into the old shorthand: what's the new chief like? Who have the Germans got in town these days? Are the Russians any more efficient than they were back in '94? (*What a hope!*) Secret police as much a nuisance as ever? Is a Revolution still being plotted, or did that fizzle out when they got a Duma? He dared not ask after German scientists – God knew what ham-fisted enquiries would be launched by the Department or what the results would be – but it was good at least to check the territory.

'What do things look like from London?' the tobacconist asked in return. 'I get word from the Embassy, but wi' censorship, an' all the diplomats bound and determined not to speak a word agin' the Old Country, I've always got it at the back of my mind to wonder if I'm bein' lied to.'

'They're idiots,' said Asher harshly. 'And you are being lied to. We all are. Britain builds a new class of battleships, so Germany's building them too. Germany gets nine-inch guns, so France must have them or die. And to everyone who points out that a war between our coalition and their coalition is going to be Armageddon – like no war ever seen before – we get only, *Well, we must protect our interests abroad,* and – God help us – *Dem Deutschen gehört die Welt . . . The world belongs to Germans.* It's the Germans who've said, *We want territory even if it belongs to foreigners, so that we may shape the future according to our needs,* but it might as well have been Asquith and those imbeciles in Parliament. *War makes mankind strong,* and *God save us from a world without the manly training of combat*! And if you want peace – or talk about how to avoid this *manly training* – you're a Socialist or a degenerate, or in German pay. Sorry,' he added, shaking his head. 'Coming through France and Germany always affects me—'

'It's readin' all them newspapers.' Hervieu laid a comforting, red-furred paw on Asher's hand. 'Of course the lot of 'em are barkin' daft, but you'll never convince 'em of it . . . and lied to or not, as long as the Germans are comin' at us, for whatever reason, you know we'll fight. So what can we do?'

Asher whispered, 'What indeed?' He grasped Hervieu's hand. 'Thank you.'

'Anythin' else I might need to know?'

'Not that I can tell you right now.'

The bright-blue eyes looked sharply into his for a time, hearing the gaps in his information, but understanding as only the Crown's Secret Servants could or did. 'For King and Country, then.'

'For King and Country.' Asher sketched a salute at the older man, pulled his fur-lined hat close over his naked scalp, and stepped out of the frowsty little shop into the cold, silvery glitter of the street.

What can we do? Asher stepped out of the way of a peddler like a giant ball of old clothes, who bore like a battle standard a pole bedecked with gaily-colored mittens. The words were the wheel on which Asher's soul had been broken. Yet it was good to know that at least someone from the old Department knew he was in town – and would make enquiries if he didn't report himself in. In an odd way, he felt himself again.

The distaste at traveling with Ysidro – at knowing who and what he was – shifted its perspective, though did not become any easier to understand. Did the fact that the vampire took his victims singly while the governments of Germany and England and France proposed to do so wholesale alter the sin of their deaths?

Or make partnership with this man more, or less, foul than partnership with the Foreign Office?

He didn't know.

For King and Country.

Asher hated the words.

FOUR

At seven Asher changed his shirt, donning beneath it the little forearm-sheathe he'd had made for him in China, though instead of the hideout knife he'd worn in those days, he equipped it with a silver letter-opener, sharpened carefully to as much of an edge and point as the soft metal would take. He found a café near the Engineering Academy that served a dinner of zakuski, borscht, and smoke-flavored caravan tea for a rouble. An old-style porcelain heating-stove blazed at one end of the little room, but near the windows it was like sitting outside on a sharp spring morning in Oxford – yet Asher chose one of the small tables there and watched the passers-by in the square before the Mikhailovsky Palace in the chilly evening light. Schoolgirls with long fair hair hanging out from beneath hats and scarves brushed elbows with the ragged women who worked in the sewing factories and cigarette factories and factories that made boots for the army. North of the river – what was locally called the Vyborg-side – and east of the handsome houses of St Petersburg's eighteenth-century core, these factories ringed the city, turning out guns, battleships, uniforms, tents, and buttons for the biggest army in the world. Between, behind, around the factories lay the slums: the largest, the filthiest, and the poorest in Europe.

Asher wondered if they had changed as little as the city's center had, in the seventeen years since he had been here last. Street after unpaved street of squalid tenements, the slums sprawled into what had been the countryside, the air above and the dirty snow underfoot reeking alike of coal smoke and sewage. Even here you could smell it.

And within that ring of squalor were all the offices of the government's thousand petty bureaux – offices of the Church, offices of the regulation of each province, offices of the railroad and of Army procurement and of the regulation of schools and the regulation of finances and the regulation of Jews. Clerks in tight-buttoned coats shivered like Bob Cratchit as they scurried to catch trams, trailing banners of smoky breath. Students lurking along the pavement pushed crudely-printed handbills into their hands, for a rally or a revolution. Elderly men hawked hot pies, cups of tea, aprons, scissors, umbrellas, second-hand shoes. Gray-faced shadowy men from the Third Section took surreptitious notes on everything they saw.

Daylight dwindled. By ten it was dark, and Asher made his way to the chilly electric glitter of the Nevsky Prospect, which led towards the river.

'I have spoke with the Master of Petersburg,' stated Ysidro's quiet voice at his elbow. 'Neither he nor any of his fledglings has seen the Lady Irene since the full moon of February.' His words laid no cloud of steam in the ghostly bluish light of the street lamps, and he spoke as if of a stranger.

As if he had not come eighteen hundred miles, at risk of his life, to learn her fate.

'And the man she saw at the Obolenskys', before she disappeared?'

'Count Golenischev – the Master of Petersburg – was certain that none of his fledglings would have the poor taste to do anything with a jumped-up German tradesman but drink his blood, if that, nor the temerity to attend a ball at the Obolenskys' or anywhere else without him – Golenischev – at their side. And he knew of no living man or woman, he said, with whom she associated, as the Undead sometimes do. Like us all, she was a watcher in the shadows.'

'Do you believe him?'

Ysidro considered the matter. 'I do not disbelieve,' he said at length. 'There is very little, you understand, that the Kaiser or any other monarch can offer a vampire master that it would be safe for that master to accept, and he seemed ready enough to tell me what he knew. I did not say 'twas a scientist or a doctor that we sought.'

'Have we permission to visit her residence?'

'We have.' With a gray-gloved fastidious finger, Ysidro touched the lap robe in the smelly little box of the cab they hailed, but forbore to take advantage of it. Asher suspected that the same would have been true even had the vampire not been impervious to the freezing night.

'When she had been missing a week,' Ysidro went on, slipping one narrow shoulder from beneath the strap of his heavy satchel, 'Golenischev broke into her house, but found, he said, no trace of violence or misfortune or indeed of anything amiss. He holds it more probable that she has simply gone to the Crimea, as many of the Petersburg nobility do, both living and Undead.'

'But he does not know this for certain?'

'No.'

'She is not his fledgling then either?'

'The Lady Irene was something of an outsider here.' Ysidro's yellow gaze rested on the distance beyond the frost-rimmed window-glass, as if it could follow those shadowy forms that hurried, late and shivering, along the wide thoroughfare. 'She came to Russia after the defeat of Napoleon and was made vampire by the former master of this city, who had the misfortune to perish while in the Crimea some sixty years ago. The peasantry there are more primitive than the inhabitants of Petersburg or Moscow, and more ready to act upon their suspicions.' He did not sound particularly grieved at this circumstance.

'Some masters will feel it, when a fledgling is destroyed,' he went on after a moment, and his voice, thought Asher, hesitated fractionally over the words. 'Not all; certainly Grippen does not. And Golenischev is young in his domination of this city and was chosen by his own master for his money and connections rather than his brains. The Lady Irene, though the elder, never challenged him for supremacy. Nor has she had the temerity to make fledglings of her own.'

'As you have never challenged Grippen for mastery of London?'

The yellow eyes regarded him for a moment behind straight white lashes, then moved: a dismissal. 'Grippen is a Protestant.' The contempt in his voice implied that this explained everything – *or anything*, reflected Asher, exasperated. That question settled,

Ysidro went on, 'The Petersburg nest is in any case not a large one, owing to the awkwardness of there being two months of the year wherein it is impossible to hunt, and two more in which one hunts at one's peril. Here we are.'

They stepped from the cab in a handsome street of town houses and small town-palaces, not far, Asher judged, from Ysidro's own temporary residence. A row of town houses graced one side of the street, as in a London court; on the other side, a couple of small free-standing villas stood in their own walled gardens. Lamps burned in a porter's lodge at the far end of the way. The others stood dark.

The vampire shouldered his satchel, crossed the pavement to the end house of the row, and drew from his coat pocket a modern brass Yale key. The house was set high above what seemed to be a shallow basement, owing – Asher guessed – to Petersburg's marshy water-table. The steps ascending were marble, alternating black and pink. A woman passed on the pavement, huddled in the skimpy and faded clothing of the poor, and looked up as Asher happened to turn his head. He saw her make the horned sign for the aversion of evil, followed up quickly with the Sign of the Cross. She was still crossing herself as she hastened away.

Ysidro closed the door behind them. Unshuttered vestibule windows let through a daub of reflection from the gas lamps on the pavement as the vampire produced two small bullseye lanterns and a box of matches. 'Would the Lady Irene not have shuttered the windows if she were going to the Crimea?' Asher inquired as he followed Don Simon into the hall.

'Given the numbers of the poor in Petersburg – curse or no curse—'

Asher hadn't thought the vampire had noticed the woman on the street.

'—I would assume she would have taken such a precaution. Irene was most assiduous in the protection of her property, particularly of her jewels.' The vampire shut the slide on his lantern and held it low, careless of the beam of its light, but Asher raised his, so that the narrow shaft of brightness gleamed across a suggestion of porphyry inlay, colored marbles, gilded atlantes along the wall. Oriental carpets scattered the floor: Persian and Turkish and Aubusson stacked one on the other, so that the exquisite Chippendale furniture seemed to wade hock-deep in the colored pile. The drawn curtains were moss-colored velvet, tasseled and corded with plum and gold. A silver samovar the size of a steam-engine boiler caught the light, its surface thinly frosted.

'And what are the chances that it was the Count himself that Lady Irene saw at the Obolenskys'?'

'Slender.' Ysidro crossed the hall, passed through the dining room that opened from it. A mahogany table that could have seated fifty. Flowers only a day or two old: she must have some arrangement with day servants that had not been cancelled. 'He was at a masked ball at the opera that night, he says, with two of his fledglings – who might also have been lying, 'tis true. Yet something in the way he spoke of Germans – whom he holds in contempt, as many Russians so sapiently do – sounded genuine.'

Evidently, the day help's ministrations didn't extend to the kitchen quarters. These had been disused for decades, every shelf and cupboard bare. The front of the house was for show, Asher thought, or perhaps to satisfy the desire of its inhabitant for an echo of what it had been to be human. There was a boiler, and coal enough that My Lady could bathe. 'There is little, as I said, that the Kaiser can offer a master vampire, particularly of a city like Petersburg, where the slums are vast and neither the government nor the owners of the factories themselves inquire what becomes of the poor.' Asher's footfalls echoed like the drip of far-off water. Like Virgil's in the *Inferno*, Ysidro's weightless tread left no mark upon the silence. 'The Russians of the countryside believe in the vampire. Here in town, they are told that there is no such thing, and indeed they have learned that to complain is to bring oneself to the attention of the Third Section, which is never a good idea.'

He led the way down the stairs from the kitchen. Lantern held high, Asher followed, though he did not expect to see anything but a hidden chamber and an empty coffin – the first things the Master of Petersburg would have checked, notwithstanding his certainty of an early departure for the Crimea.

Estimating the dimensions of the basement by those of the house above – something one did a lot of, working for the Department – Asher guessed where a chamber had been walled off it even before Ysidro went to the entrance, which was concealed behind stacked boxes that it took a vampire's preternatural strength to shift. When Ysidro pushed them aside – they had frozen to the floor, owing to the swampy dampness of the semi-subterranean room – and unlocked the narrow door they covered, the coffin was seen to be open and empty when the lantern beams pierced the utter darkness of the bricked-shut room.

No sign of burning or of blood on the extravagant white satin of the lining. Nothing in the room, save the ice that sheeted the floor bricks. No surprises and no information, though Ysidro stood for a time, running his hand along the satin, as if he would have asked a question of the darkness, or looked for some message written upon it.

Then he turned and soundlessly left the room.

Asher followed. 'Was Lady Eaton the wife of a diplomat? Or simply an unfortunate traveler, such as yourself?' Ysidro's sidelong glance reflected the lantern light like a cat's. 'I don't imagine,' Asher went on, 'that when you left Madrid in 1555 to attend your King's wedding to the Queen of England, you counted on meeting a vampire in London and finding yourself obliged to remain there for the next several centuries.'

'No.' The tiniest ghost of an expression – wry? half-amused? – pressed itself like a needle scratch into one corner of the vampire's lips, and the shadow that had settled on him as he stood beside the coffin seemed to retreat. 'No, I did not.'

In the drawing room, Ysidro opened the drawers of the baroque desk – a stupendous confection of ebony and mother-of-pearl – and turned one thin shoulder, very slightly, to block Asher's view as he drew forth packets of letters. He went on, 'I have since learned that there were vampires aplenty in Madrid, and in Toledo also, which was my home. I could as easily have been taken there, given my carelessness at walking abroad nights. Perhaps in Madrid and Toledo it was guessed that I should be missed.'

Past his shoulder Asher glimpsed the handwriting, a fine sixteenth-century court-hand. Packet after packet of letters, carefully bound in ribbons. Now and then Don Simon would glance at a date: April of 1835. November of 1860. Asher himself had not yet been born. He glimpsed his birthday, of the first year he'd been sent to that horrible school in York, the year his parents had died: like the scent of old patchouli unexpectedly encountered. Ysidro had been writing a letter on that night.

'She was the wife of a diplomat, yes,' went on the vampire, flipping open one drawer after another, like a man seeking some further prize. Smaller packs of letters, with addresses in different hands, he dropped on the corner of the desk for Asher to take: bills, invitations, a memorandum book, household expenses. 'She was not happy in her marriage and so took a good deal of pleasure, I think, in making her husband the first among her victims. This is not uncommon. Nor is it uncommon to take – or to ask one's master vampire to take – the bereaved husband or wife or lover as a fledgling also, under the mistaken impression that they will provide one with company in eternity.'

'Mistaken?' Asher stowed the correspondence in the pockets of his heavy black greatcoat, sat on the edge of the desk as Ysidro moved around the study's rose-and-gilt Louis XVI paneling, tapping and probing for sliding panels or other secret caches. While he watched Don Simon, he kept an ear towards the stairway and the street. The last thing he needed was to be taken up by the Petersburg police for burglary.

'The husband or wife or lover in question seldom truly wishes to become vampire.' Ysidro finished his circuit of the room, glanced back over his shoulder as he picked up his lantern again by the door. 'Usually they have not the will to survive the transition – the giving over of their soul, their consciousness, to the master vampire, to be held within the embrace of his mind –' his long hand closed illustratively on itself, like some strange colorless plant devouring insect prey – 'and returned to the body after the body's death. Or else they simply do not make good vampires and get themselves killed very quickly. By that time –' and his dry, soft whisper was dust falling in a room long closed – 'the vampire who wished to bring them with him – or her – into Eternity has usually lost interest in them. Love might conquer Death, but it seldom transcends the selfishness necessary to accept killing others to prolong one's own life.'

He passed through the door into the oval central hallway of the main floor, mounted the curving stairway to the dark bedrooms above.

A velvet-festooned cavern of a bedroom, then a dressing

room nearly as large – cupboard after cypress cupboard, mirrors dimmed with frost. Ysidro opened them, one after another, checking shelves and corners. Still searching. And to judge by the places he looked, it was for something small.

All the gowns were this year's style, subdued pinks and silvers succeeding the dim mauves and mosses of a few seasons past. Such detail was something else one learned in the Department, even if one had not the delirious privilege of being married to Lydia. The hats on the shelves were the newest monstrosities from Paris. The colors – as far as Asher could tell by lantern light – favored an English rose. 'If she was going to the Crimea,' he remarked, 'she didn't pack anything suitable to wear there, unless she had a completely separate summer wardrobe beyond what's here. Will there be luggage in the box room upstairs?'

'I misdoubt Golenischev gave the matter a thought.'

Absorbed in his search, Ysidro did not turn. Seemingly out of nowhere, it crossed Asher's mind that there might be a photograph of Lady Eaton in the bedroom and he went to look – later he could not imagine he could have been that stupid. As he crossed the dark chamber to the dressing table beyond the bed something in the air oppressed him: not a smell, but a sense of suffocation that made him pull his scarf from his throat despite the cold. Even so that sense of heaviness did not leave him, but grew. Not giddiness, but—

A cold hand clamped over his mouth and jerked his head back, while another ripped his collar aside; the grip that closed over his arms was like a machine in its strength. Had the vampires that closed in around him been less greedy – or less determined to teach Ysidro a lesson – he knew they could have slit his throat with their claws and left him dead on Lady Eaton's pastel Axminster carpet in less time than it would take for Ysidro to know what had happened . . .

But they wanted to feed.

And Asher had walked into vampire nests before.

He jerked his hand hard, dropping into his palm the silver blade from its arm-sheathe, and struck backward with it into the vampire who held him from behind, even as he felt the cold touch of an icy forehead against his jaw. A woman screamed in pain. The triple and quadruple coils of silver chain around his throat under his collar were enough to burn any vampire's lips and hands. For a blurred second he fought to keep his mind clear, and he twisted – more by instinct than by thought – against the grip on his elbows as it loosened. Someone struck him across the face with a violence that nearly broke his neck, and he slashed again with the knife, knowing the unhuman speed of his attackers—

'Drop him!' Ysidro's voice was a silver whip.

Asher hit the floor, too stunned for a moment to breathe.

'Get back.'

They stepped aside, shadows in the crooked reflection of his fallen lantern, eyes like animals shining out of the dark. Asher managed to get onto one knee and set the lantern upright – no sense in bringing the St Petersburg Fire Brigade to complicate matters. He pressed his hand to his throat, then pulled off his glove and did so again. Attack, defense, release had occupied seconds. It was only now that he began to shake.

'And did Count Golenischev neglect to mention my visit this evening?' asked Ysidro in his deadly-soft voice.

'Golenischev can go fuck himself,' retorted a young man in a rough jacket. He wore a straggly beard and the rather nautical-looking cap of a student, and he held his hand pressed in agony to a bloody stab-wound in his thigh. Ysidro had spoken in French, but the student had snapped his reply in the proletarian Russian of the factories and the streets.

There were three of them. One – a woman of the same student type, short and thickset with a mouth like an iron trap – turned towards the dark door at the far side of the room, and Ysidro said, 'Stay.' He neither raised his voice nor moved, but she turned back, as if he had laid one of those steel hands on her shoulder. Asher could see where the silver of his neck chains had welted her lips. Her eyes mirrored the lantern light. Asher had never seen such an expression of sour hate.

Even with his life hanging in the balance, Asher couldn't imagine either her or the student being invited to a party at the house of the highest aristocrats in Russia.

The other girl with them might have been though. She was tall and slim and fragile-looking, with fair hair coiled on the top of her head like a dancer and a dancer's way of holding herself.

It was she who said, 'Golenischev has no command over us,' and there was shaky defiance rather than confidence in her voice.

Ysidro said nothing for a time, only regarded them with that cold calm. The male student almost shouted, 'Golenischev is an aristocratic pig, a bourgeoisie fat-cat who lives from the sweat of the working man.'

Asher was tempted to inquire when had been the last time the young man had either worked or lifted a hand to assist the Revolution, but didn't. Nor did he dare move a finger towards the sharpened silver letter-opener, which lay on the blood-daubed carpet a yard away.

'I take it,' said Ysidro at last, 'that there are two masters in Petersburg?'

'There are not.'

Asher had heard nothing in the house below, but in the dark of the doorway he saw gleaming eyes and the blur of faces untouched by sun. He knew which of the four newcomers had to be Count Golenischev, for the man had the calm arrogance of one who has ruled over the lives of peasants on his estates from infancy. *There is little the Kaiser can offer the master vampire of any city.* This man clearly considered the lives that he traded for his own survival his due – and had, just as clearly, been made vampire by his own master, as Ysidro had said, for his money and connections rather than his brains – a criterion he seemed to have used to select his own fledglings in his turn. Three more of them followed Golenischev into the room like hunting dogs.

'Ippo,' said the Count to the student. 'You will beg Monsieur Ysidro's pardon.' He looked young – no vampire Asher had ever seen appeared more than forty – and as suave and soigné as a Frenchman in his well-cut London suit. 'You, also, Marya, Olyusha—'

'I spit on Monsieur Ysidro!' proclaimed the student. 'And I spit on you.'

For a moment Golenischev only stood looking at the fledgling, anger blazing in his pale-blue eyes, and his beautiful lips in their gold frame of Prince Albert twisted with fury. Then – with a violent motion, as if dragged by some unseen hand – the student Ippo dropped to his knees, then to all fours. Sobbing curses, he crawled forward and lay on his belly to

kiss Ysidro's boot. The three fledglings who had come in with
Golenischev only watched this humiliation, but there was
something deadly in their silence, volatile anger shimmering
on the edge of open defiance. As silently as humanly possible,
Asher edged away from the remaining two rebels. If any of
the newcomers joined their rebellion – if the situation snapped
suddenly out of control, as situations had a way of doing –
the rebels probably wouldn't strike either the Count or Ysidro
. . . but they would certainly turn on him.

And as his back touched the wainscot of the wall behind
him, he felt the panel sink slightly and shift.

The two women repeated Ippo's performance, the dancer
Olyusha weeping with anger, the student Marya screaming
obscenities and thrashing her head back and forth like an
unwilling dog on a chain. Ysidro watched them both without
even an expression of boredom, as if nothing in the human
world touched him any longer. Perhaps, thought Asher, it did
not – though he wondered if the Lady Irene Eaton's master
had ever forced her through a performance like this. And
whether she had written to Ysidro about it.

'You would like to bite him, wouldn't you, Marya?' mocked
Golenischev. 'Ah, look at her! What a face, eh? Go bite Ippo,
Marya. Go on.' Her face demonic, the woman crawled inch
by inch to the student – *had they been lovers?* Asher wondered
– seized Ippo by the ears and began to tear and worry at his
face and hands with her teeth.

'Bourgeoisie scum!' Ippo screamed at the Count. 'Lackey
of the ruling classes—'

'Don't give us that "ruling classes" drivel, Ippoliton
Nikolaivitch.' One of the fledglings who had followed Golenischev
into the bedroom spoke up, a stooped man with a face of ground-
in sourness. 'You care no more these days about the workers
than I care about the Russian Empire anymore. I think the last
time I saw you at a Party meeting you killed a shop girl as she
came out and went down an alley on her way home.'

'Now hear me,' said Count Golenischev, when the last of
the three rebels had done their homage and knelt, heads to the
floor, in the near darkness of the failing lantern-light. In a
single move – the terrifying movement of a vampire, that
blanks the mind until the cold grip falls – the Count was
beside Asher, catching his arm and pulling him to his feet like

a policeman manhandling a beggar child. 'Your friend Prince Dargomyzhsky cannot protect you, and when I catch that wretched traitor I will show you just how powerless he is. If you touch this man –' he pushed Asher a little towards them – 'if any harm comes to him – you will find out just what that traitor's protection is worth. I have given my word as a nobleman of the Empire that it shall be so.' He inclined his head graciously to Ysidro, then thrust Asher in his direction with a force that – had Asher not been determined and ready for something of the kind – would have thrown him to his knees.

The Count turned back to the culprits, Asher already forgotten – a side issue in what was clearly an ongoing contest of wills. 'Whatever the Prince has told you, you three are mine. And if you need that proved again –' he stepped forward to chuck the furious Marya under the chin, to flick his claw-like nails over Ippo's torn and gory face – 'I will be most happy to oblige.'

Asher woke – suddenly and with the sensation of having fainted, though he knew this was not the case – standing outdoors in the bitter night alone.

FIVE

To Professor James C. Asher
c/o Hoare's Bank
English Embankment
St Petersburg, Russia

Oxford,
April 5, 1911

Dearest Jamie,
    Did you arrive in St Petersburg safely? Was the journey frightful? Does this railroad (or is it a factory?) that Uncle William wanted you to look at actually seem to be a safe investment? One hears such horrid reports

of Russian inefficiency, and it is a tremendous lot of money – and besides, you know how Uncle William is.

While you are in St Petersburg, would it be possible for you to look up a few of my colleagues there? I've enclosed letters of introduction, but I'm sure at least Dr Harbach should remember me from when he was last in England; what I am chiefly interested in is opening a correspondence with specialists in blood disorders, as I am rather puzzled by some of my own findings here. (I won't trouble you with the details, but they seem anomalous to say the least.) These gentlemen would be:

Dr Immanuel Grün, on the Nevsky Prospect,

Dr Wilhelm Harbach, on the Admiralty Prospect,

Dr Emrich Spurzheim, on Karavannaia Street near the Fontanka Canal (or is it a river?),

Dr Benedict Theiss, on Samsonievsky Street,

Dr Richard Bierstadt, on Italianskaia Street,

and Dr Johann Leutze, also on the Nevsky Prospect.

A Dr Ludwig Spohr has offices on the Tverskaia in Moscow (such names they have!); also in Moscow are Dr Kaspar Manteuffel (on Nikitskaia), Dr Klaus Holderlin (also on Tverskaia), and Dr Reinhold Preuze (whose direction I could not find, but I believe it is in Moscow also.) Two others – Dr Richard Franck and Dr Emil Bodenschatz – are listed as having worked in Russia in the past, but I can find no mention of whether or not they are in St Petersburg now.

All are specialists in blood chemistry. I hope you can find one of them, at least, who shares your interests in folklore!

And good luck with Uncle William's factory (or is it a railroad?).

All my love,

Lydia

Rain whipped with gray violence against the study windows. Lydia sealed the envelope, dug through the frothy chaos of her desk drawer for a stamp (*so THAT'S where I put those notes about nervous lesions!*), then settled back in her chair, looking out at the wet-dark wall of the New College, at two young men (students unwilling to get their gowns soaked?) scudding along Holywell Street like outsize black leaves.

Thinking about Don Simon Ysidro.

She knew she ought to go up to her bedroom and sort all those issues of *Lancet*, the *British Journal of Medicine*, *Le Journal Francais Physiochemique* and several German and American periodicals back into their respective boxes for Mick to return to the attic. Knew she should re-copy into a more readable form the notes she'd been making for the past three days, almost non-stop, on all those articles by German blood-doctors working in Russia. But she didn't. She didn't move.

A poulterer's wagon passed along the street: *clip-clip-clip*. A woman held onto her hat against a gust of wind, her other hand firmly gripping that of a wrapped and cloaked and scarved and booted little boy. Lydia closed her eyes, took off her spectacles, wondered if the child she had lost last year would have been a girl or a boy.

Don't think of that. It wasn't meant to be.

The wind rested, then flung handfuls of rain at the window again.

Don Simon . . .

Not that, either.

It is only fascination.

He said so himself.

She pressed her fingers to the bridge of her nose.

Vampires hunt by making you trust them. Why else would someone go down a dark alley with a complete stranger in the middle of the night?

The sensation she had of breathlessness – of piercing grief – at the recollection of those calm yellow eyes, that soft voice and the cold touch of his hand, were no more than the reaction to a period of excitement and danger that had ended in tragedy.

Like Jamie, she would not be drawn back.

For Jamie, it was different. He had sickened at the Department's deceit, at its demand that he hold himself ready to harm anyone who came between himself and his duty, but she knew he was very good at what he did. She had never felt sure of her footing in the vampire's presence, never known whether what she was doing was right or wrong.

In the Department, Jamie said, it was always very clear.

You had to keep yourself alive by whatever means you could, until whatever information you were seeking had been safely turned over to your chiefs. You didn't look past that. It was why so many men, though they might hate what they did, could not imagine living in any other fashion.

'You always have to be seen to be going where you're going for a reason,' he had explained to her once: the reason that she had surrounded her list of German blood-doctors with made-up persiflage about Uncle William's fictitious Russian railway investments. In Russia, everyone's letters were opened by the Secret Police, and no one thought anything about it. 'Nine people out of ten aren't going to ask themselves, *What's a Dutch philologist doing receiving letters from London?* Or, *Where does Herr Professor Leyden go when he disappears like that . . .?* But that tenth person – or whoever he or she talks to – is the one who can get you killed.'

Get you killed.

Jamie.

That had been back in the days when she'd been a school-girl, visiting her uncle in Oxford and playing croquet with a small army of young gentlemen waiting with barely-concealed impatience for the heiress to the Willoughby Fortune to be brought 'out' so one or another of them could marry her and it . . .

And with one of her uncle's scholastic colleagues, who turned out not to be nearly the dry middle-aged academic he appeared to be.

After her second meeting with him, she'd started making notes of his journeys and destinations, and comparing them with places mentioned in the newspapers. She had finally gotten up the nerve to ask him, as they'd hunted for a lost ball in the long grass by the river, 'Professor Asher . . . *are* you a spy?'

His eyes, when he'd looked swiftly sidelong at her – such surprisingly bright brown eyes – had registered no surprise.

It was then – or maybe she'd known it already – that she'd understood that she loved him. Not as a schoolgirl, but as the woman she only just realized she would one day become.

Don Simon . . .

'Ma'am?' Ellen stood in the study doorway, a tray in her

hands. 'I've brought you a cup of tea, ma'am. You didn't so much as touch your lunch.'

'I'm so sorry.' Lydia smiled, put her spectacles back on, and looked around rather vaguely for space on the desk.

Ellen carried the tray to the occasional table by the fireplace, permitting herself a tiny sidelong grin of her own. She'd been the nursery maid at Willoughby Court and had spent a good portion of her life since that time wading after her mistress through a morass of books, papers, journals, discarded social invitations and milliners' silk samples, trying to get her to remember to eat regular meals or go to bed on time.

'Now, don't you worry, ma'am.' Ellen knelt to stir up the blaze – which, Lydia became aware, had sunk almost to ashes while she'd been sorting through the last of the information to prepare her report. 'You know Mr James's starts. He'll find this cousin of his, never fear.' That was the story they had given her. It had had to be a good one, for Asher to leave this close to the end of term. 'No need to starve and worry yourself into a thread paper.'

'No,' agreed Lydia. 'Of course not.'

'I just wish that cousin – what was his name?'

Lydia shook her head. She hadn't her husband's ability to keep track of long, consistent lies, and she knew better than to pull a name out of the air. Ellen's memory was surprisingly good, and she was more observant than she seemed. 'He told me, and I simply can't remember right now.'

'Harold, I think he said,' provided Ellen, straightening up. 'I just wish this Harold person hadn't gone to some Godforsaken corner of the world . . . You remember how ill Mr James was, when he came back from Constantinople of all places . . . And as cold as it is, too. May I take that to the post for you, ma'am?'

Lydia obediently handed her the letter and settled by the new-made fire, grateful for its warmth. Without her spectacles the blaze had a gently blurred light, comforting as the gray afternoon drew in.

She remembered how ill Mr James had been when they'd come home from Constantinople, after the horrors of that city: after the death of the Master of Constantinople, and of the vampire couple who had been James's friends.

Get you killed . . .

She closed her eyes again. Saw Don Simon as she'd seen him first, in the dark of Horace Blaydon's bricked-up cellar, a cool disheveled rescuer bending down to kiss her hand. *I am at your service, Madame . . .*

And later, when James had gone off into what she had belatedly realized was a trap, and she'd sought out the vampire in his crypt beneath his London house . . . The light of her lamp falling through the crypt bars, illuminating his long hand with its gold signet-ring in the shadows as he slept.

She loved James, as strongly and fiercely as ever. James was real – the man in whose arms she lay at night. The father of the child she hadn't borne. The man who'd wept beside her in that awful darkness of loss, when she herself had not been able to weep.

Simon . . .

What I feel for him isn't love . . .

Then why does it hurt so much?

Both James and Don Simon had told her that vampires could tamper with the minds of their victims, with their perceptions and their dreams. She had seen how Ysidro – the oldest and strongest of the London vampires – had searched the dreams of that great city, when he had found himself seeking a female companion for Lydia who would be willing to drop her livelihood and her hopes of ever finding another position, at twenty-four hours' notice, and leave the country to meet in Paris a woman she didn't know . . .

She had seen how he had insinuated himself into Margaret Potton's dreams, not asking her, but making her believe that it was a sacrifice she wished to make.

Because Margaret Potton loved him.

Because he made her love him. He had seen the image of romance in her dreams and had clothed himself in those garish melodramatic hues.

For three nights now – since Jamie had gone away – Lydia had dug through her medical journals, checking names, checking facts, checking letter columns for addresses . . . only so that she would not dream of Margaret Potton lying dead and bloodless on her bed.

Or at least cut down the number of hours per night that she did.

Her heart had screamed at him, across Margaret's body, *How could you?* But her mind told her, with simple matter-of-factness, *How could he not?*

He was a vampire. Because she, Lydia, had insisted that she would not accept his protection unless he abstained from killing – abstained from the psychic feeding on his victims' death from which he derived his own mental powers of illusion – he had been starving. And poor besotted Margaret had told him more than once that she was his to use as he pleased, even unto death.

That was love.

Why do I care?

Why do I hurt?

Why do I hurt so BADLY?

The memories of all those nights of talk – over cards, over bank ledgers, over the investigation they had done together; in train carriages, in the latticed window-bay of a house in Constantinople, in the fog before the skeletal black-and-white stones of the Vienna cathedral – they should be nothing.

That sense she had had of dealing not with a vampire, but with a man – wry and clever, brilliant and maddening, a scholar and a sometime poet and an observer of three and a half mortal centuries of folly – would not leave her, and the intensity of it filled her with shame.

None of it is true. It's only another illusion. He is no more than the cast chrysalis of his former shape. There was nothing inside him but darkness and the hunger for another's death.

It is our lure to be attractive. It is how we hunt, he had said to James. *It means nothing . . .*

She wondered why the knowledge didn't make her hurt less.

Ellen's heavy tread in the hall. Lydia sat up quickly, realizing with a start that it was dark, her untouched tea was stone cold, and that she had done nothing for three days about the article for *Lancet*, which was due on Thursday . . .

'Here we are, ma'am,' said her handmaiden proudly and held out an envelope to her, smudged and dirty and dotted with Dutch stamps. 'I told you he'd be well.'

Rotterdam
4 April, 1911
Best Beloved,
All well so far.
J.

Lydia put on her spectacles, checked the date, then went to
the globe in the corner – she never could remember where all
those little countries were, between France and Germany. He
must have written this in the train station (the paper certainly
looked like something one would find in a public waiting-
room!), before boarding the train that would take him into
Germany.

She made herself beam for Ellen, but when Ellen was gone
she read the note again, then took off her spectacles and sat
for some time in the amber gloom.

She did not believe in a God of miracles.

It was as unreasonable to pray for one as it would have
been, for instance, to feel love for a man who to her certain
knowledge had personally murdered – at the lowest possible
computation – well over thirty thousand men, women, and
children, one at a time, presuming the abstemious rate of two
per week for three hundred and fifty-six years . . .

God, please bring him home safe . . .

SIX

B ecause man does not exist in a vacuum – and because
Asher guessed that the *dvornik*, or concierge, of the
Imperatrice Catherine was probably being paid by
someone on the staff of the German Ambassador, as well as
by the local Secret Police, to note the arrivals and departures
of foreign visitors at this unfashionable time of year – on the
following morning he carefully re-shaved the top of his head,
touched up the dye on his hair and mustache, reread the
Editorials page of the copy of the *Chicago Tribune* that he
had brought with him, and paid a visit to the Ministry of
Police. Though the Ministry had been folded into that of the

Interior some years previously, the Chief of Police still ruled St Petersburg from the ill-famed building on the Fontanka Embankment, and Asher had little trouble presenting himself as Mr Jules Plummer of Chicago, in outraged and affluent pursuit of an absconding wife.

'I heard she'd come here, and I don't want to make trouble,' he announced, in a loud voice and grating Middle-Border accent that no one would have associated with the soft-spoken Lecturer in Philology of New College, Oxford. 'But I won't be made a fool of, either, damn it. The man she ran off with claimed he was a Russian Count, and I know he had letters from St Petersburg, so here I am. Damn all women, anyway. Bastard probably lied, but I'm here to make a start.'

Needless to say, no member of the extremely wealthy Orlov family (Asher spelled and pronounced it Orloff) had been anywhere near Chicago that the police knew about – and the movements of the near-royal Orlovs were well known. 'Knew it,' growled Asher, and he gave the rest of his report to the bored functionary with just enough impatience, condescension, and arrogance not to get himself arrested as well: a good defense, he had found, against recognition by those who might have last encountered him as the self-effacing Professor Leyden.

In a major capital, in a time of increasingly murderous international affairs, the Auswärtiges Amt was likely to send in its most experienced men. One couldn't be too careful.

That done, he took a cab across the river to the Kirov Islands and inquired, of the footman in powdered wig and blue-and-burgundy livery who answered the door of a particularly splendid palace, if Prince Razumovsky was in town at this season. The footman replied in impeccable French that this was in fact the case, contracted (for two roubles) to take up M'sieu Plummer's card and inquire if His Excellency was, in fact, at home, and left Asher in a drawing room that made the Lady Irene Eaton's town house look like an East End tenement. Returning, the footman implied that it was a shame that his master would lower himself to speak to an American, particularly at this hour of the morning (it was one in the afternoon), but that he would. Please come this way, M'sieu.

The Prince looked up from his desk as Asher was shown in, without the faintest trace of recognition. As soon as the door shut behind the footman, Asher removed his pince-nez, relaxed from his American strut into his usual posture, and said, 'Your Excellency?' in his normal voice.

The golden giant's face transformed. '*Jamie?*'

Asher put a finger to his lips. Prince Razumovsky had a voice like an operatic basso.

'Good God, man!' The Prince came around the desk, grabbed Asher by the shoulders, and kissed him on both cheeks. 'Where is it that you've sprung from, eh? I thought you had—'

'I have,' said Asher, holding up a warning finger. 'I'm in Petersburg on a private matter, Your Highness. Not even my own Department knows I'm here.'

'And your beautiful lady—'

'Is at home.'

'Just as well.' Razumovsky shook his head. 'Lent in St Petersburg . . .' He shuddered theatrically. 'I couldn't interest you in coming to the Theosophical Society's charity ball at the Winter Palace tonight, could I? The two Princesses of Montenegro are trying to catch the final contributions before everyone makes their escape for the Crimea . . . It will be a horrific crush – every charlatan in the city, and everyone in the city who wishes to be on the good side of their Highnesses.' The Prince stroked his splendid mustache. By *everyone*, Asher knew he meant the two or three thousand (out of a population of a million and a half) who were fashionable in their professions, or in the highest levels of the government bureaucracy.

'I should be honored, Your Excellency.' Asher inclined his head, glad that he had thought to pack evening clothes. He had first encountered Razumovsky not in Petersburg, but in Berlin, when the Prince had been in charge of collecting the day-to-day information of the Foreign Bureau agents there: the clerks in the defense ministry who had blotted their copy-books; the officer on the Kaiser's staff who was living beyond his means and wasn't averse to having his gambling debts paid, no questions asked. The tiny details of which nine-tenths of good intelligence work consisted. While he would never have expected the aristocratic diplomat to assist him in anything against the interests of the Russian Empire, he knew he could trust the man as a friend.

There were few in his own Department in Petersburg that he knew to that extent.

'Excellent! *Wunderbar*!' The Prince waved him to a chair beside the stove – a monument of colored tiles and gold – and rang the bell. 'One can only endure so many platitudes about the Serbian situation or communications with the dead – both of which topics seem to suffer severely from lack of hard information. You'll have tea with me, Jamie—?'

'Mr Plummer. And perhaps it's best that I don't. There isn't anyone in town from Berlin, is there? Or who was, for instance, in South Africa—?'

'Or China? Or Vienna? Or Bosnia? Or Mesopotamia—?'

'Who told you about Mesopotamia?' returned Asher with a grin, and Razumovsky shook a finger at him.

'Nobody can remember all the faces, Jamie. Not you – and not them. So far as I know, all the good folk over at the German Embassy are the ones who've been there since Tsar Alexander was on the throne – or Catherine the Great, for that matter. Now tell me how I can help you in this "private matter" that's brought you eighteen hundred miles from your beautiful Madame Asher at a time when Germany is boiling to conquer Morocco and revolution is threatening to sweep the world—'

'Not my business,' said Asher firmly, and he accepted the tea – in a silver-mounted glass, with a lump of sugar, and stronger than most coffee in England – that the liveried footman deigned to offer him on a tray.

The Prince waited until the servant was gone before he asked, more quietly, 'And what is your business, Jamie? It is a long way to come at this season, and that is the truth.'

'I don't know what is the truth,' replied Asher, just as softly. 'And the information I'm looking for is going to sound insane to you.' He was silent for a moment, debating how much he might ask without triggering a Russian investigation – and how much would be in the report he'd asked Lydia to compile and send to him, which should arrive, he hoped, within days . . .

The very word 'German' – especially coupled with 'scientist' – was likely to start the Third Section asking questions . . .

and might lead to his own deportation. Instead, he asked, 'Can you speak to the police – or perhaps to the Okhrana – and find out if there have been cases here in Petersburg of what has been called spontaneous human combustion?'

Razumovsky's eyebrows mounted halfway up to his hairline. 'Like in Dickens?'

Asher nodded. 'As in Dickens.'

'Why—?'

Asher lifted his hand, shook his head. 'For the moment, it's what I need to know,' he said. 'It doesn't have to be proved, only reported. I'm looking for one within the past two months.' *If you can't start at one end, start at the other . . . at least until Lydia's report arrives.*

The Russian was silent for a moment, blue eyes narrowing. Asher wondered if he – or anyone – had heard or read reports of what had been found in the old palace in the ancient section of Constantinople, from which he and Lydia had emerged on a winter morning in 1909: four or five charred bodies, consumed almost totally with no evidence of pyre or combustibles. The Turkish government had hushed the matter up, and it had been lost in accounts of the larger rioting that had swept the ancient city that night.

But as his friend – and as an agent of the Tsar – Razumovsky would certainly have looked up the reports.

But the Prince said only, 'Well, if it is spontaneous human combustion you seek, my friend, the Theosophical Society ball tonight is the place to hear all about it. And about poltergeists, levitation, falls of live fishes, and frogs found alive in impenetrable hollows of rock. The Montenegrin sisters cannot get enough of this sort of fare. Every scientist who makes his living attempting to develop teleportation or to explain mysterious monsters in Scottish lakes shall be there—'

'And I will be urging them on to unfold themselves to their utmost.' *And perhaps asking them whether they specialize in diseases of the blood as well.*

'Then you will doubtless be the most popular man at the event. Most of these "scientists" won't even listen to one another.'

'But I would also like to hear,' said Asher, 'what the Okhrana has to say about it.'

'You can ask them tonight yourself.' Razumovsky grinned again. 'They, too, will be there in force.'

With a further assurance from Prince Razumovsky that any unspecified 'trouble' Asher might happen to find himself in during his stay in St Petersburg could be referred to the Prince's department in the Ministry of the Interior, Asher took a cab back along the Kamenno Ostrovsky Prospect to the city again. The day was freezing cold but clear, and in the fading light the Islands still retained the fairy-tale air of a place and time long separated from the nascent Twentieth Century; the woods and birch groves of aristocratic private estates, the little wooden *izbas* that mimicked peasant simplicity, all seemed like something glimpsed through a magic mirror. A glimmering quality of Once Upon a Time.

The world that children grew up in? Asher leaned his head back against the dirty squabs of the cab, remembering the cottage his aunts had had in the Kentish countryside, the sweetness of the woods beyond their garden. The world where something new and beautiful is waiting beyond the next turn of the path, under the next mushroom? *Is that why it fascinates us so? Do we chase folk tales and fairy gold, when what we really want is our childhoods back, when we were safe and loved?*

When the world was a safe place to live in, because we knew no better?

Back when we hadn't learned about things like poison gas and bombs?

Through the leafless trees the Gulf seemed to glitter, a hard green-black flecked with white. Behind the mossed-over gargoyles and granite lions of porters' lodges, Italianate palaces of yellow, pink, and green showed up as bright as the flowers. They would be glorious inside, Asher knew, with polished stone of a hundred colors, with ebony and gilt, and with French marquetry and Chinese silks: every rouble of it contributed against their will by peasants in a thousand dreary hinterlands villages, and by workers who were shivering themselves to death in those dreary miles of tenements and factories within walking distance of this magical place.

The cab dropped him off at the gardens of the Tauride Palace. He walked to the house where the Lady Irene Eaton had lived.

Though the days were lengthening, the light was fading fast. Over breakfast, and during his various cab-rides, Asher had read steadily through all the more recent missives in the packets Ysidro had given him: so far, Golenischev seemed to have been accurate in his statement that she had no living acquaintance whose communication went beyond the superficial. Yet Ysidro had been searching for something. He walked around to the mews behind the row of town houses, scaled the back gate and passed through the bare garden – simple hedges that a jobbing day-gardener could tend, and a good deal of pavement – and found that the lock of the kitchen door, like that of the front, was a modern Yale model, a good fifty years newer than the house.

The dimness inside was disquieting. He had not had the impression that Golenischev and his fledglings had taken over the lair – not if there was a suspicion that Lady Irene had met with some ugly fate – nor had they seemed to think the rival master, Dargomyzhsky, would be in residence. Nevertheless, the place made his scalp prickle, and he guessed that the St Petersburg vampires kept an eye on it after dark. Who had she brought here, he wondered as he climbed the wide swoop of the stairs from the front hall, that she wanted to impress with her Greek statuary, her brocaded curtains? Was it she who had played on the great golden concert harp that stood in the music room? Or did one of those cat-eyed forms he'd glimpsed in the darkness behind Count Golenischev last night have conversation with her, beyond the hunt?

'For many of us, everything becomes the hunt,' Ysidro had said to him, one of those nights on the Nord Express, with the flat chessboard of Holland flickering past the windows like the Looking-Glass Country in the dark. 'Some take pleasure in hunting in teams – picking victims to share, two and three in a hunt . . . planning the where and the when.' Long white fingers shuffled cards; the vampire would play solitaire for hours, of an insane complexity that Asher was often unable to follow. 'You understand, there is not much challenge in killing the poor. And most vampires come to understand very quickly that the rich – even those sleek arrogant merchants of whom this world produces so many in these degenerate times – even if they are hated, they are missed.

Those who live forever find that forever includes many, many hours of waking that must be filled.'

He had laid out the cards, two and three decks of them, his movements so quick as to baffle the eye; less a game of solitaire than what appeared to be meditations on mathematical permutation and principle. Asher had wondered how many of those endless hours of waking Ysidro had filled with the handling of these pasteboard generators of random numbers.

'So we hunt. And when we meet, we speak of the hunt. Those of us who once read books, or wrote poems, or made music, or played chess, or studied languages, mostly find that these things pale to insignificance beside the immediacy, the urgency, and the intimacy of the hunt. It is what they spend their nights looking forward to, or back upon. The world becomes blood and fear and power.' He scooped the cards together again, long pale hair half hiding the face that was itself a concealment, then dealt them out again. Lydia had told him that Ysidro had taught her to play the old-fashioned game of piquet, but she would never teach it to him. Ysidro had done so, the first night of their travels together. 'For many, there is nothing else.'

From Lydia, who had traveled in Ysidro's company from Paris to Constantinople, Asher had also learned enough to guess that Ysidro was not one of those who had forgotten the challenges of chess, the joys of reading, the challenge of learning new languages. There were books, she had said, in at least twelve tongues in his house somewhere in the mazes of the East End by the river, and three chessboards.

The library in Lady Irene's house was wide-ranging, and Asher noticed nearly two shelves of books on mathematics, on computation and calculation, and on the theories of music and numbers. But when Asher touched the red calfskin bindings, the gold-stamped spines, he found the leather dry, the tops of the pages dusty. No books lay on the tables of purple bloodwood and pale yellow tulipwood. In the study he opened the desk drawers, empty now save for dust and old pen-nibs. The ink in the old-fashioned standish was fresh; the pens had been much used. When he passed through the music room again he touched the strings of the harp and found them red with rust.

The gorgeous carpet in the bedroom was splotched with the drying blood of the two vampires, Marya and Ippo, where the Count Golenischev had made them maul one another. Was that why he had never made a fledgling? . . . *The giving over of their soul, their consciousness, to the master vampire, to be held in his mind . . .*

Asher could not even imagine the kind of intimacy that would engender, the naked soul held in the embrace of the naked soul. It reduced the consummations of the wedding bed to the level of a gloved handshake.

Knowing Lydia would never forgive him if he didn't, he went back down to the study to find a clean piece of notepaper and an envelope, and returning, used his penknife to crop a few inches of blood-soaked carpet-pile for her to examine . . .

If I survive to hand it to her.

Those two lost revolutionaries – for whom the Revolution had faded before the lure of the hunt as surely as had the Lady Irene's love for the harp – were not the only thing Asher recalled of last night. His knowledge of human nature told him – if Marya's animal glare had not – that it was he, who had only been fighting for his life, against whom their hatred would turn. They had been brought down before a human.

If they thought they could kill him without Golenischev finding out, he was a dead man.

His blood sample collected, he turned to the corner where he had been thrown. Pressed his hand to the lower panel of the wall, and felt it give.

The moveable panel was a simple one. It didn't take much probing along the ornate scrollwork on its edges to find the catch. The compartment behind, barely five inches deep, contained stacks of banknotes, a thick glass bottle containing an aqueous solution of silver nitrate – evidently the Lady Irene had no more trust in her vampire colleagues than Asher did – a revolver loaded with silver bullets, three different sets of identity papers, and, in an envelope at the back, another envelope, yellow with age, addressed in Ysidro's spidery hand.

Asher collected everything, tucked it into his satchel, closed up the panel, and got out of the house as quickly as he could.

At no point had he seen, or heard, or sensed in any fashion that anyone else was in the house or that the house was being observed . . .

Yet he got into the cab that he hailed, and left the Smolny District behind him in the cold spring twilight, with a sense of having escaped just in time.

In his chambers at the Imperatrice Catherine, he sat in the bow window overlooking the river and read Ysidro's letter to the Lady Irene Eaton.

London
May 10, 1820
My Lady,
I received your letter.
And I read in it that which fills me with horror.
DO NOT DO THIS THING. I beg of you, in the name of the love that I bear you. In the name of the love that you bear for me, do not do it.
When we parted, you asked of me that which I would not do – and despite my pleadings, despite my most desperate efforts to explain my refusal, though you said that you understood, I think that you did not and do not.
You said that I would live forever, while you as a living woman were doomed to die. Yet I do not live forever. I do not live now (as I told you then, you shaking your head, eyes shut), and death changes things. Death changes all things. And Un-Death the more so than Death, for in Death memory survives untainted by future change.
You do not think that you will change, but you will. I have seen hundreds pass this gate of blood into the world I now inhabit, and I have not seen more than four or five who did not turn into the Grippens of the world, who did not turn into the Lottas and the Francescas at whom you stared with such fearful interest when at my side you heard the chimes at midnight: who did not become, in truth, demons who live only for the kill. I have seen scholars turn from their books and artists from their easels; I have seen mothers who sought this state

the better to aid their children turn from those children in boredom, once they had passed the gate that you knocked upon, with such desperation, the night of our parting.

I love you because you are who you are, Lady. To see you lose the self – the Lady – that I love, to see you turn from your music and your love of learning and the joy you take in your pets, and become as I am, would be infinitely worse than to lose you, whole and yourself, to death, even to death of withered age.

I write this as I read how you have met the vampires of St Petersburg – how you followed on from what I had told you of the London vampires, and those of Paris . . . and I am filled with horror and with dread.

I know you, Lady. And I very much fear – knowing your courage, and your determination, and your love – that you write to me not waiting for my reply.

The world does not need another vampire, Irene. The world – and I – needs you as a living woman.

If you have not gone unto these vampires of the North to ask to be changed by them, do not.

If you have done so already, I write to you with the gravest foreboding that I will never look upon your face again.

Ysidro

SEVEN

T he Theosophical Society's charity ball was held – in the absence of the Imperial Family, who hadn't lived in the Winter Palace in years – in one of the Palace's larger halls: a jaw-dropping barn of crimson curtains and golden columns that looked as if it could have swallowed Westminster Abbey whole. Even Ysidro – who gave the impression that the destruction of the planet would not discompose him – paused for a moment on the threshold and said, in his soft expressionless voice, '*Dios.*'

Asher hid a grin. 'Travel is broadening,' he observed, and

the vampire's pale-yellow glance flicked sidelong at him, then back to the gilt-trimmed ceiling, to the ocean of humanity swirling around the refreshment tables at the far end of the room.

'As is longevity,' returned Ysidro. 'Each time, I delude myself that I have beheld the limit of money wasted by rulers in praise of their own glory, yet I am humbled anew. 'Tis enough to make one believe there is a God.' And he moved, like a slim impeccable specter in black and white, ahead of Asher into the enormous hall.

'At least I won't be called upon tonight to confirm some would-be adept's visions of fairies at the bottom of her garden,' murmured Asher as he followed in the vampire's wake. 'Which seems to be part of the job, if one lectures in Folklore . . . Not to speak of being dragged to seances by that imbecile cousin of Lydia's, who regards me as the local expert on things that go bump in the night. I didn't think there were this many True Believers to be found in any European city . . .'

'As I say, 'tis only that you lack three centuries' experience in the matter.'

'Nor do I want it,' replied Asher firmly, and received – to his surprise – one of Ysidro's fleeting, unexpectedly human smiles.

'It has its compensations.'

Asher checked his steps, halfway across the acres of crowded parquet that separated the doors from the buffet: '*Are* they real?'

Ysidro turned back. Around them, ladies in satin gowns cut to the nipples – in the fashion of St Petersburg – and wan-looking gentlemen in evening dress or, in some cases, extravagant silk versions of 'the raiment of the people', chatted at the top of their lungs in French or Russian about apports, apparitions, ectoplasmic manifestations, or railway shares . . .

'Are what real?'

'The fairies at the bottom of the garden. I've studied accounts of them going back to classical times without ever for a single instant believing that any had actually been seen – precisely as I studied accounts of vampires.'

'The difference being,' said Ysidro, 'that vampires are not supernatural. We are merely rare, and intelligent enough – for the most part – to keep hidden from the eyes of our far-more-numerous prey. Regarding the fairies at the bottom of the garden, I have on the subject no more than any man or woman in this extremely noisy room: an opinion. Which is, that while I can not deny that some persons may actually have seen elemental spirits, even as some persons may have held converse with ghosts, I deeply doubt that *all* those who claim such experiences have actually had more than delusions.'

Asher grinned again at the phrasing of the statement. '*Have* you ever seen fairies?'

'Would they make themselves visible to a vampire?'

Ysidro turned away, and Asher reflected, *Touché*. And touched, in the pocket of his extremely American tuxedo-style jacket, the letter from Lydia that had been waiting for him earlier that evening on his return from Lady Irene's. Then he squared up his shoulders and reminded himself that everyone in the room was an effete superstition-ridden non-Protestant and he was an American, by God, and the match of any bunch of sniveling Russkis.

He strode to the reception line and was introduced to his hostesses, the Prince of Montenegro's twin daughters, who had both married cousins of the Tsar; they were dark-eyed, elegant women of roughly his own age, dressed with a lavishness that Englishwomen reserved for Court presentations. Prince Razumovsky managed to appear, like a smiling green-uniformed genie, just as Asher reached the front of the line, and he added a few words praising Mr Plummer's open-mindedness and large holdings in shipping and packing-house stocks. This guaranteed Asher a steady stream of company for the evening: aristocrats – male and female – bored with the 'stifling conventions' of the Orthodox Church and eager to 'explore the realms that so-called modern science has claimed do not exist'; pasty, intense scions of the vast class of professional bureaucrats who for centuries had administered the Russian Empire, brimming over with love for 'the *real* Russia, the *true* Russia of the villages, which understands its own heart'; charlatans – native, foreign, or of totally indeterminate nationality – who gripped Asher's elbow or shoulder, as if to draw him by force through the Gate of Enlightenment, and gazed into his eyes, saying, 'I can see you are a seeker after Truth . . .'

And I can see YOU are about to pick my pocket.

He wondered if any of these individuals had battened upon Ysidro, and with what result.

In the cab on the way to the palace, after he had briefed his companion on the names of doctors he was to listen for, he had brought up the subject of Count Golenischev: 'Is there a chance we'll encounter him tonight?'

'I doubt it.' Elegant in evening dress, Ysidro had folded his gloved hands, like an ivory statue against the lights of the Embankment.

'And his rival for mastery? Prince Dargomyzhsky?'

'I think had it been Dargomyzhsky whom Lady Irene saw, Golenischev would have named him, if only to cause him grief. Therefore I assume that the Prince was also at this opera ball on the night of the Obolenskys' affair. Golenischev is vain – foolish, too, particularly in his choice of fledglings – yet, to remain master at all, he must have learned that we are safe only so long as we are invisible. These people here tonight, above all, are the ones no vampire in his right mind would speak to: people who both believe that a vampire could exist and possess sufficient social standing to gain a hearing from the powerful. It is only our good fortune,' Ysidro had added drily, 'that no one believes *them*.'

Indeed, once within the hall, Asher was not surprised that Ysidro became, if not literally invisible, at least profoundly unseen. Was this, he wondered, because the vampire was not quite capable of making his scarred face look completely human? Or did he simply wish to avoid the conversation of four thousand people who talked of nothing but the mysterious rain of fish that had fallen on Olneyville, Rhode Island, in May of 1900, or of whether 'star jelly' (whatever that was) was extraterrestrial or supernatural in origin? Four women and one man told Asher about the ghosts in their houses. An earnest-looking woman in her sixties wearing diamonds that could easily have purchased New College and the souls of everyone employed there held Asher's hands in hers and told him about the fairies she had seen at the bottom of her garden. Asher achieved his gravest expression and exclaimed, 'You don't say!'

And three people, herded in his direction at various times in the evening by Prince Razumovsky, told him all about Spontaneous Human Combustion. 'That woman in France in the 1700s, now, she was only one out of many, stretching back to Biblical accounts!' asserted an earnest dark-eyed woman whom Asher guessed – from the estimated cost of her dress and jewels – to be the wife or sister of an upper-level bureaucrat in one of the Ministries. 'Science *conspires* – positively *conspires*! – to keep these things from us, Mr Plummer, for fear of creating a panic. But I myself have heard – from a dear friend whose word can be *entirely* trusted! – of an actual case that a friend of *his* was acquainted with, in Kiev . . .'

'It's true,' boomed a stubby little gentleman with round heavy-lensed spectacles, like a slightly overfed gnome. He – in common with a number of the men present, though Asher had noticed that the genuinely Theosophically-minded guests tended to be women – had chosen to wear, not formal evening-dress of white tie and tailcoat, but 'the raiment of the people': i.e. a loose blouse such as the peasant men wore, baggy trousers, and boots, the difference being that 'the people', in their desolate villages, generally didn't have their blouses and trousers tailored for them out of heavy Chinese silk.

'It is as much as my reputation at the University would be worth, were I to write up all I have found,' went on the gnome, gripping Asher's sleeve in a way that hinted at the flight of his former auditors and wagging a finger in his face. 'Yet evidence points definitively to the truth of such accounts. Not in India or Mexico, mind you, but here in Petersburg! Only this past September, in Little Samsonievsky Court, the *dvornik* of one of those tenement buildings found a charred heap of ashes in one of his rooms, burned so hotly that the whole of a human body was consumed, save for the shoes . . .'

'There was a rash of such happenings,' broke in the bureaucrat's wife, 'four or five, in those horrible little streets around the Kresky Prison and the train station. And always the same! The oily yellow deposits on the walls, the blue smoke in the air . . .'

'You don't say!' exclaimed Asher, switching to English from the sixth-form French in which he had been laboriously addressing his informants.

'There were other such burnings – or findings of burned bodies, with no sign of combustible materials – between

August and October, all about St Petersburg,' added the gnome, poking Asher's waistcoat with a stumpy forefinger. 'Now, scientists would tell you that these were all in the Vyborg-side – the most appalling slums in Petersburg, Monsieur Plummer – and that the poor are all much addicted to the consumption of vodka. Ergo, these were all poor drunkards whose clothes had been soaked with the stuff and who had lit themselves on fire smoking American cigarettes. But, I ask you, *all* of them? I have heard at least seven different accounts . . . Is it reasonable that seven people – one of them a young girl, to judge by the size and style of her shoes . . . shoes, moreover, not such as a factory girl would wear – *seven* of them, would all soak themselves in enough vodka to consume not only the flesh but the bones as well?'

'But what does it mean?' asked Asher.

'They are signs of the End.' The bureaucrat's wife spoke with a trace of indignation in her voice, as if Asher surely had no need to ask. 'Signs of the coming of the Antichrist—'

'Oh, nonsense!' retorted the gnome, instantly defensive. 'Great God, woman, have you learned nothing about the ageless cycles through which this universe passes?' He turned back to Asher, face ablaze with eagerness. 'It is mere proof that the universe is entering a Realm within the Abyss of Eons wherein the boundaries between the natural and supernatural world shift and grow indistinct. We of the Circle of Astral Light have found arcane hints at such things in ancient writings, which cannot mean anything else! Entities from other Realms—'

'Can you persist in clinging to Science,' demanded the woman, 'with evidence of the Day of Judgment – of fire raining from Heaven with the sounding of the First Trumpet of the Seventh Seal – staring you in the face? Can you *be* so blind?'

Asher stepped back out of the conversation – both other participants had apparently forgotten his existence already – and a cool thin voice at his elbow said, 'It was not Little Samsonievsky Court, but Samsonievsky Alley . . . and, so far as I can determine, all those seven accounts can be traced back to only one.'

Asher turned to meet pale eyes behind heavy spectacles, a gray little man who reminded him indefinably of Count

Golenischev's cold-faced fledgling. Prince Razumovsky, hovering behind him, lifted his eyebrows, but this signal wasn't necessary. Okhrana – Secret Police – emanated from the little gray gentleman like the clanging of a warning bell. Asher immediately became as American as possible, bunched his eyebrows together and exclaimed with naive eagerness, 'You sound like you know a lot about it, Mr—'

'Zudanievsky,' Razumovsky introduced. 'Gospodin Alois Zudanievsky, Mr Jules Plummer, of Chicago—'

'Mighty pleased to meet you, sir.' Asher shook hands like a pump handle.

'His Excellency tells me you seek information about the phenomenon of Spontaneous Human Combustion.' Curiosity flickered in Zudanievsky's winter-colored eyes. Asher was familiar with the expression, from having worn it himself, and with just that caution about letting too much interest show. *And why would this person be seeking information about that?*

Asher nodded. 'There's so much hearsay, and this-person-I-talked-to-said-this, and when you get to the bottom of it, it all happened where nobody could verify anything. And I'm looking for an actual case. An actual event.'

'Are you a journalist, Mr Plummer?'

'No.' He rubbed the side of his nose. 'Fact is, Mr Zudanievsky, the man I'm looking for – for personal reasons . . .' He made a gesture, as if shooing those reasons aside. 'One of the few times I had a conversation with him when he wasn't lying – or I don't *think* he was lying – was when he spoke of such an event having happened to his sister, this past fall. He seemed to think there was a plot of some kind, but I don't know the nature of it.'

'And what was your friend's name?'

'He said his name was Orloff,' said Asher gruffly, mindful that the first thing Zudanievsky was going to do was check the police report he'd submitted. 'I've found out since that was a lie. But I had reason to think he came here to Petersburg.'

'I would be extremely grateful,' put in Razumovsky, 'for any help that you – or your Bureau – could extend to my friend Plummer in his inquiries.'

Zudanievsky inclined his head to the Prince in a bow that was almost burlesque. 'Such assistance as I can give will be my pleasure, Excellency.' Even in formal dress he looked gray, like a dust-colored spider; his face was the face of the man, Asher realized, that he himself had quit the Department rather than become. *The man who will do whatever his government requires of him, without asking why, and not even take pleasure in it.*

'Do you know the Bureau Headquarters, on Kronverkskiy Prospect? Across from the Fortress . . . If you would give this to them –' Zudanievsky produced his card – 'and ask to see me at . . . one o'clock tomorrow? I will show you what we have.'

Asher presented the policeman with a card of his own, even as one of the twin Grand Duchesses clasped him by the arm and haled him away to introduce to a spiritualist who was collecting funds to establish an Institute for Research into the Supernatural in Chicago – an exercise in its way more trying than the conversation with Zudanievsky, since Zudanievsky hadn't asked him anything about that city, which Asher had never visited in his life. Supper was served at midnight in a nearby hall – Lenten fare of caviar and Norway salmon, and a thousand sorts of mushrooms and pickles – and, in another hall, chairs had been set up before a grand piano played by a young man of extraordinary talent to whose efforts barely a third of those present actually listened. In addition to conversation, it seemed to Asher that there was a great deal of flirting going on, far more openly than would be the case in London. (*'Dearest, in the middle of the day? With her* husband, *of all people?'*)

He drifted from group to group, vexed with the necessity of keeping his ears open for gossip rather than for the music. *For King and Country,* McAliester would have said, damn him . . . He asked names, dropped hints, mentioned a cousin who was a specialist in diseases of the blood – and mentally sifted endless rivers of persiflage infinitely less interesting to him than the entertainment that his conversational partners so totally ignored. He reminded himself that the Kaiser was seeking to enroll a vampire in some fashion in his arsenal of weapons . . . and that the American he was supposed to be wouldn't have been able to tell a Debussy concerto from 'Way Down Upon the Swanee River'.

But most of what he heard concerned the more prominent

table-tappers and spirit-summoners then operating in
St Petersburg, including one whom he recognized as having
been exposed as a fraud in London. He listened with assumed
fascination to accounts of people who had disappeared in plain
sight of crowds – though not generally in cities where it was
possible to investigate thoroughly – or of objects apported
from distant locations by spirit mediums, including bona-
fide sparrows' nests that had miraculously, but not provably,
originated in China . . . Not to speak of assignations,
contretemps, affaires and alliances of an altogether less exalted
nature . . .

And in the middle of an account from the Grand Duchess
Anastasia herself, of a giant wheel of light seen by the crew
of a Swedish fishing-vessel in the middle of the Atlantic Ocean
only the previous year, past Her Highness's shoulder he saw
a face that he knew.

Berlin.

Ice water could not have doused him so chillingly.

I've seen that man in Berlin . . .

Rissler, his name had been. A young man, tall, stooped and
colorless, with prying discontent in his blue eyes . . . It was
the way he stood and his bitter expression, as much as anything
else, that had brought him back to Asher's mind. He'd seen
him come and go half a dozen times from the Auswärtiges
Amt in the Wilhelmstrasse; a clerk, Asher recalled. He had
only known his name because he made it his habit to know
the names and faces of everyone connected with the Foreign
Service. One simply never knew.

Asher excused himself to the Grand Duchess, followed the
German clerk's lean, drooping form as he made his way down
the length of the hall with a small plate of caviar and toast
points in one hand, a glass of champagne in the other.

First assignment abroad? He hadn't been one of the men
assigned to running foreign agents, at least not in 1896 he
hadn't. Even now, he didn't have an experienced agent's
walk or manner – he hadn't even made an effort to alter his
appearance, still wearing his flaccid mutton-chop whiskers
and anemic mustache. Did those idiots in the Wilhelstrasse
really think nobody noticed what the lesser clerks looked
like?

So there must be something only he could do – perhaps

he was the only one who spoke Russian or knew what star jelly was.

With all the gossips and assignees flirting and chatting along the sides of the hall among the ostentatious golden pillars, it was a simple matter to follow him down the hall, and remain out of sight . 'Dear Monsieur Plummer—' A slim hand in an eighteen-button kid glove fastened itself to his elbow. 'You really *must* permit me to introduce you to one of our most *devoted* seekers after truth! Madame Anna Vyrubova, Monsieur Plummer of Chicago—'

Asher bowed to the other Grand Duchess – the Grand Duchess Militsa was the one with the emeralds and the Grand Duchess Anastasia wore the rubies – and to the round-faced, plump little blonde woman she had in tow, keeping his eye on the retreating mutton chops. Fortunately, Rissler – or whatever he was calling himself here – was tall . . .

'*Chicago!*' Madame Vyrubova squealed, clasped plump hands in an ecstasy of delight. 'All the way here from the United States!' She seized Asher's fingers like an excited schoolgirl. 'How do you like Petersburg, *cher* Monsieur?'

'Excuse me, Highness,' said Asher with a bow and a glance towards Rissler, who had reached his goal: a large and handsome gentleman, whose dark hair and close-trimmed beard were streaked with white. 'But could you tell me who that gentleman might be over there? The one whose sinister minion is handing him the champagne?'

Both women looked. 'Oh, my *dear* Mr Plummer.' Madame Vyrubova dimpled mightily. 'Dr Benedict Theiss! You must *indeed* possess Second Sight! "Sinister minion" is *precisely* how I would describe Monsieur Texel! Because one sees in his eyes, you know – dreadful, *shifty* eyes! – that whatever he *says*, he hasn't the *slightest* belief in dear Dr Theiss's theories about the deeper powers of the World Soul . . .'

'He is a German,' remarked the Duchess dismissively – sparing Asher the trouble of surreptitiously double-checking Lydia's list for the name. In any case he remembered it clearly, and the address, on the Samsonievsky Prospect, the main avenue of the Vyborg-side.

'Now, don't speak of Germans in that horrid superior tone of yours, Militsa! Dr Theiss is a German, and he has a mind *most* open to the influences of the Unseen worlds. A veritable exile, Monsieur Plummer,' the little woman sighed. 'A tragic case, indeed. I quite *weep* when I think of it . . . Though I do weep very easily, Mr Plummer. All my friends say that I am too sensitive. He was a young man, you know, when that *horrible* Bismarck swallowed up his country into that *awful* German Empire of theirs . . . He left, rather than be ruled from Berlin, and never went back. And Bavaria still is a separate country, you know, Militsa! So Dr Theiss isn't *really* a German! He does such unselfish good, you know,' she added, turning back to Asher and clasping his hand, 'working with the poor in the slums!'

'That is true,' the Grand Duchess allowed, her distaste at the man's birthplace melting into a forgiving smile. 'Shall I introduce you, Monsieur Plummer? I fear you'll find our Annushka exaggerates his belief. Benedict is a scholar of folklore, but, I fear, a sad skeptic. These scientists! They cannot truly *give* themselves, as one must, in childlike faith . . . Or perhaps the overdevelopment of the cranial nerves blinds the Inner Eye to True Sight . . . Indeed, it might be simply that his clinic devours all of his energy and time. It is, as Annushka says, tragic.'

'I'd be honored,' said Asher. 'Always ready to hear what a skeptic has to say – I have to wonder about any argument that can't stand light shed on it from both sides.'

'*Exactly* what I always say!' cried Anna triumphantly, bouncing on tiptoes like a child. 'One must keep an *open mind* . . . Oh, excuse us just one moment, Monsieur, there's General Saltykov-Scherensky wanting to . . . We shall be back . . .'

Asher, who had been to enough diplomatic receptions to know that any hostess was completely incapable of making it ten feet without being interrupted or sidetracked, melted into the crowd.

'Dr Benedict Theiss.' Ysidro materialized at Asher's elbow, as Asher himself stepped into the niche formed by the gilt-sheathed pillars along the wall. 'And none other from Mistress Asher's list, so far as I can tell, here tonight.'

'It may be that none of the others operates a charity clinic in need of donations.' Asher angled his head slightly to look around the pillar at the expatriate Bavarian. 'The man with him was a clerk at the German Foreign Office in Berlin.'

'Was he, indeed?' The vampire regarded doctor and minion like a snake contemplating crickets. 'It may be that a visit to this clinic is indicated, to see what is there to be seen. Will you speak with him?'

'I think not tonight,' said Asher. 'I want to hear what Razumovsky has to say about him, and possibly one of my friends in the Department here, before I let him see me to recognize me again.'

'Then I shall await you outside. Whether or not he is the man Irene saw, the odds that you shall find *two* German scientists accompanied by agents of the Auswärtiges Amt here tonight are in the order of nine hundred and fifty thousand to one.'

'I'll bid goodnight to Prince Razumovsky.'

'He seems to be much taken with an extremely handsome Baroness, but have it as you will. I doubt he will notice if you disappear.'

Ysidro moved off. Asher looked around for the Prince – who did indeed seem to be making what might in another man be interpreted as a proposal of marriage to a slender dark woman in a dramatic pink gown on the other side of the hall – and was starting in their direction when a hand was laid on his arm.

Asher had smelled the man coming before he was stopped by him; he turned, startled and repelled. Even among the occasional non-bathers that one found in any large gathering – and Asher had learned that aristocratic rank was no guarantee against personal eccentricity in that area – this man stood out. His 'raiment of the people' was costly silk, but the hand on Asher's arm was dirty, the nails long and broken; the face he found himself looking into, a peasant's bearded face.

Except for the eyes.

'Who is that?' The man's coarse peasant Russian was as startling in this upper-class milieu as his goatish smell. 'That one that you spoke to?'

Asher shook his head. 'I don't know.'

'Keep from him.' The peasant turned his head, pale eyes – gray and mad – following through the crowd although Asher himself could see no sign of Ysidro. 'Flee him. Do you not see what he is? Darkness burns around him, as light burns around the faces of saints.'

'And have you seen,' asked Asher, 'the faces of saints?'

The peasant looked back at him, startled, and his eyes were human again. Maybe they always had been. Then, framed by the long greasy mane of his hair, he broke into a grin. 'We have all seen the faces of saints, my friend.'

Close by, Annushka Vyrubova paused in conversation with two uniformed Guards officers, caught sight of them, and smiled in adoration. 'Father Gregory—' Arms outstretched, she hurried towards them in a frou-frou of dowdy lilac silk.

'Watch yourself, my friend.' Father Gregory made the sign of the Cross before Asher's face. 'Go with God's blessing. For I promise you, if you see that one again you will need it. That is one who cannot endure the light of day.'

EIGHT

On the way along the Nevsky Prospect in a cab, Asher recounted where and how he had seen Herr Rissler – now, apparently, Monsieur Texel – before. 'That's another piece of information that I shall keep to myself for the time being,' he added, drawing the cab's lap robe more closely around himself against the night's brutal cold. The local population didn't appear to mind. Carriages passed them as if it were four in the evening instead of four in the morning, and in the windows of elegant apartments above the marble-fronted shops, lamps still glowed through the raw Neva fog. 'It was a joke in the Department, how obvious it was when the Okhrana started following one of us: one chap used to send his mistress's footman out with hot coffee for them on cold nights. By Lydia's list, there are nearly a dozen German specialists in blood disorders operating in Petersburg alone. It won't take our vampire long to find another, once he learns one is blown.'

'In truth,' Ysidro murmured. 'Even allowing for the fact that some of those dozen may be in Petersburg because they cannot stomach the Kaiser and his aims, as Theiss apparently claims to be. At least we know in which direction we should be looking at the moment . . . if this Theiss is indeed the man Irene saw.' He folded his gloved hands, relapsed into silent consideration of those muffled figures on coachman's boxes and footman's perches, those jewel-box windows.

'I'll vet the others.' Asher drew from his pocket the solid little pack of visiting cards that had been pressed into his hands in the course of the evening, at least half of them bearing scribbled invitations to tea, seances, soirées. 'It shouldn't be difficult, the way these people talk about each other. I'm booked for luncheon with the Circle of Astral Light on Friday . . .'

Yet in his heart he knew this was only caution. A clinic on the Samsonievsky Prospect . . . An ideal cover. *Is Rissler – Texel – his only henchman?* Any of the men in that enormous gold-and-crimson hall might have been German agents also. *It was purely chance that I recognized Texel . . .*

Would the AA send more than one agent?

They would if they believed Theiss. If they believed they could have at their call a shadow agent whom no sentry could stop, no picket see.

A German doctor here whose studies strike me as remarkably similar, the Lady Irene had written.

As if Asher had spoken her name, instead of merely thought it, he became suddenly conscious of Ysidro's silence. Without turning from his contemplation of the street, the vampire said, 'It is absurd to suppose that, were she still able to do so, the Lady would not feel my presence in Petersburg and contrive to get in touch with me. This policeman you spoke to – I commend your accent, by the way – said there had been ashes found, and a woman's shoe.'

'In the autumn,' said Asher quickly. 'Your friend's letter was written in February.'

Ysidro turned his head, the tiniest human flex to his brows: evidently surprised, and – surprisingly – touched, at the offer of comfort. 'Such being the case,' he said after a time, 'whose, then? Golenischev spoke of no such loss among his nest.'

'And, in any event, it wasn't our pro-German Undead, either. Would Golenischev have lied? Or would the girl have been a fledgling of this Prince Dargomyzhsky they spoke of?'

'Had she been, I cannot imagine Golenischev would not have thrown the fact at his little rebels last night, in the midst of all that drama and blood. And while we who hunt the night distrust our own kind, 'tis almost unheard of for a vampire to kill another vampire or engineer his death.'

'Would Lady Eaton have written to you, had one of the Petersburg vampires come to grief? Or of the rebellion in the Petersburg nest?'

The slight tilt of the Spaniard's head would, in another man, have been sharply raised eyebrows, an elaborate scoff, and – in the case of the fragile old Warden of New College – an upflung hand and a disbelieving cry of, *My DEAR Asher—!* 'She had little use for the other vampires of Petersburg,' said Ysidro, as the breaking ice on the Moyka flashed below them, jeweled by the reflected lights on the bridge. 'Never in her letters to me did she so much as mention the names of Golenischev's fledglings. And the letter she sent me at the time of the assassination of the present Tsar's grandfather made no mention of the event, and she only touched upon the rioting here six years ago insofar as it inconvenienced her hunting.'

His scarred forehead tugged into the tiniest ghost of a frown, and for an instant Asher recalled the rusted harp and the long-dried leather of those book covers, a library of mathematics and scientific theory that had not been updated in the course of nearly a century.

'As to this traitor to the ranks of the Undead, and whether Golenischev is lying for some reason – and indeed whether this division in the Petersburg nest has any connection at all to the conference that Irene saw – I suspect that, for answers, we will be obliged to travel to Moscow, to ask these things of the vampires there. Can you be prepared to leave tomorrow night – this coming day's night? There is a train at midnight, from the Warsaw Station.'

Which should arrive – Asher did some rapid mental calcu-lation – at two the following afternoon. 'I'll be there.' Arguing with Ysidro was a waste of time at best, when he had made up his mind. 'Is there anything about this journey that I need to know?' The scars that tracked Asher's throat and forearms under the protective silver chains had been acquired the first time he'd gone to Paris with Ysidro.

'The less you know the better.' The cab squeaked to a halt by the lodge of the Imperatrice Catherine; Asher stepped down, letting Ysidro pay. 'Vampires have preternatural skill in knowing when the living are on their track. I think it best, after you have left my trunks at the address I have hired for myself, for you to go directly to your own rooms and remain there.'

'I agree,' said Asher. 'And does the Master of Moscow speak French?'

Ysidro's eyes narrowed – he had clearly heard something about the Master of Moscow – but an evening in the company of the Petersburg vampires, and another strolling among the *haut ton* of the Theosophical Society and its hangers-on, had probably led him to believe that most Russians spoke French ... Which, Asher was well aware, was not the case. Upper-class Petersburgers did – in many cases, better than they spoke Russian.

But Moscow wasn't Petersburg. Its master, Asher was uncomfortably aware, might well be some bearded boyar who had defied Peter the Great and considered French merely the language of Napoleon's vanquished troops.

'I shall remain at your lodging,' said Asher, 'and trust that if it so happens that you do need my services as a translator, you'll protect me from the consequences of overhearing the conversation.'

For King and Country? To keep the horror of the falling bombs, the slow-oozing gas, in his dreams, where it had lurked for a dozen years?

Or for the friend who had written, 'By the love I bear you ...' to a woman who had disappeared?

'I will do all within my power –' there was no trace of the usual light irony in Ysidro's voice – 'to keep you from harm. I thank you,' he added, almost hesitantly, 'for your assistance in this matter. The Lady Irene—'

Asher thought, later, that the vampire had been about to speak of just why it was that he had come nearly a thousand miles to the Arctic circle – that he was about to admit that it had little to do with the governments of the world availing themselves of the services of vampires. Instead, there was one of those disconcerting moments of mental blindness, from which Asher jerked, blinking, a minute – or two minutes – or five minutes – later, to find himself alone on the flagway before the handsome bronze doors of the Imperatrice Catherine, with no Ysidro in sight.

As he climbed the steps to where the *dvornik* waited by
the open door (doubtless noting when Jules Plummer came
in, for the benefit of the Secret Police), Asher wondered if
Ysidro – raised in Toledo at the height of the Counter-
Reformation – believed in Hell.

'One reads of cases now and then.' Gospodin Zudanievsky's
French was not the pure unaccented Parisian of French
governesses and expensive education abroad, but sounded, to
Asher's trained ear, like a painstaking schoolboy familiarity,
built upon by years of dealing with foreign visitors to the
Russian capital. All sorts of inflections cluttered it: Italian,
German, English, American. He longed to sit the policeman
down and take notes.

The corridors of that solid brick edifice across from the
Peter and Paul Fortress had not changed since '94. They still
stank of smoke and sweat and the lingering back-taste of
mildew. Cheap pine tables narrowed the hallways, heaped with
the decades-deep backlog of Russian paperwork – forms,
reports, permissions, requests for permissions, requests for
further information before permission could be granted . . .
When last Asher had been brought this way, there had been
no Entente Cordiale between the Queen's Empire and the
Tsar's. He spent an extremely unpleasant seventy-two hours
in a small chamber in the basement before the Okhrana had
finally believed his totally mendacious story and let him go.
He knew how close he'd come to never being heard from
again.

Had Zudanievsky been with the department then? He didn't
recall the man, but nevertheless increased his swagger and his
drawl. 'Well, what I always think is, like Hamlet says, there's
more things than meet the eye.' He puffed on his very American
and extremely foul-smelling cigar. 'Things that can't be
explained. I admit, a lot of 'em are total horse-hockey. That
woman in Paris they always talk about, back in whenever it
was, seventeen hundred and something . . . You can't tell me
it wasn't her husband that soaked her in gin and lit a match.
But some of those others . . .' He shook his head. 'I just don't
know.'

'And this Orloff—'

'Or whatever his name was.'

'Precisely. He said that a relative of his—?'

'His sister,' agreed Asher somberly. 'He told my— Well, I happened to be party to a conversation where this kind of thing came up, and another of the folks there kind of scoffed at it, and he said no, that it really could happen because it *had* happened. His sister caught fire, he said, out of the clear blue, with no fire in the room nor nothing to burn, and she sure wasn't no drinker, the way some of these poor folk here was. He said the fire was so hot it burned up even her bones. He said— He was damn shook up about it. You could see it. Now, I've traveled some, and I do know how much fuel it takes to make a fire that hot and reduce a grown woman's body down to nothing.'

'And did he say,' inquired Zudanievsky, pale eyes sliding sidelong to Asher behind the fish-eye spectacles, 'if his sister had been involved in any . . . any curious activity, prior to her immolation?'

'Is pourin' vodka over her own head what you're talkin' about?' If he could have kept his heart from beating quicker at the question he would have – the policeman had the look of a man who could have heard such a thing. *Curious activity???*

They turned a corner and passed through a narrow door. Asher felt his hair rising on the nape of his neck at the smell of the low-ceilinged corridor, dingy with gaslight and seeming to sweat fear from its walls. The stair they'd taken him down was at the far end . . . But Zudanievsky turned almost at once and unlocked a little office.

'Nothing of that kind.' There were shelves in the room and boxes on the shelves. Zudanievsky lowered the gasolier down closer over the central table – battered, stained, with the air of careless uncleanness so familiar in the offices of Russian police – then fetched a stout tin lock-box from a shelf. 'Was Devushka Orloff mixed up in any club or organization, in the months before the . . . incident? Did her brother ever mention the Circle of Astral Light, or the Cult of the World Soul?'

Asher laid his cigar on the edge of the table. 'Now, that I don't know. It was only the one time he talked about this, and he was a little drunk – and, like I said, his name might not have been Orloff. He did say he hadn't seen much of her . . .'

'Hadn't seen much of her? Or hadn't seen her at all?'

Asher pulled a face of mild frustration. 'You know, if he said it I just don't recollect. This conversation was about six months ago. He said, *I hadn't seen her*, but I don't know whether that meant he was away, or she was away, or they just wasn't speakin'—'

'How old was the girl?'

Asher shook his head once more.

'And did he say he was in the same house with her – the same building – when she burned?'

Asher considered the matter – trying to look as if he were calling back the conversation, but in fact debating what would sound the most convincing – then said, 'It sounded like it. I got that impression, but to be honest, I don't recall what he said that led me to think it. Why d'you ask, sir?'

Zudanievsky lifted the lid of the box. It contained about a quart of grayish dust, mixed with chunks of what Asher recognized as teeth and bone. On top lay a little oilcloth packet, wrapped loosely enough that he could see a pair of brown, low-heeled pumps inside.

'Since midwinter of 1908, seventeen young men and women have disappeared from the slum district north of the river called the Vyborg-side. Seventeen.' The policeman produced a magnifying glass and a pair of forceps from one pocket, held them out to Asher, and reached up to angle the gasolier so that its light fell more clearly into the box. 'It is one of the most vile slums in Petersburg. People vanish there all the time. They freeze, they starve, they get drunk and fall into the river . . .' The policeman's cold, pale eyes rested consideringly on Asher's face.

'It's the factory district, isn't it?' Asher frowned as if he'd barely heard of the place.

'One of them. Factories, tenements . . . hovels that would disgrace a Chinese village.' Sudden anger, startling after the man's flat calm, flared in the policeman's voice. 'And they wonder why the strikes start there, why the riots start there, why half the troublemakers in Petersburg come from there . . .' His mouth pinched up, as if catching back unwise words, tucking them away where his superiors might not come upon them.

With the same gray evenness, he went on, 'But these who have been disappearing are young: thirteen, fourteen, fifteen years old. Some of the boys were care-for-nothing toughs who worked at the armaments factories; some of them were good little lads who slaved in the navy rope-works and brought their paychecks home to *matyushka*. A couple of the girls were part-time streetwalkers, and others did nothing but look after their baby brothers and sisters all day and take in sewing for a couple of kopecks at night.'

Asher put on his gloves to pick up the shoes, turned them over in the gaslight to look at the soles. 'New,' he murmured. He turned back the uppers as far as they'd separate, took off his pince-nez to examine the lining through the magnifier. 'Was the flesh in them consumed?' The lining was stained and discolored, the leather barely charred. *A vampire. Either Golenischev was lying, or . . .*

Or what?

'Yes. Not as badly, and all of the bones survived.'

Asher – reaching for one of the teeth with the forceps – realized he had slipped for an instant back into his true self, set the instrument down, picked up his cigar, and frowned as if he hadn't the slightest idea what to make of it all. 'Lordy.'

'Did your Gospodin Orloff ever say what his sister's name was?'

'Not that I recollect, sir,' Asher scowled for a time at the boxful of ashes, filled with the calm familiar chill of the chase that had made Abroad so delicious in the early days. Like putting together a glass jigsaw-puzzle that could explode in your hands. Then he glanced at his companion from beneath heavy brows and asked, 'What do you make of it, Mr Zudanievsky? I can't see no factory girl wearing that shoe.'

'No – they generally do wear hand-me-downs from their mothers and sisters. Yet it is not an expensive shoe. It's the sort of thing factories turn out by the thousand.'

'The girl could have stolen it, if she worked where they made 'em. I take it she was no relation to anyone who lived in the building where she was found?'

'Not that anyone knew of. The room was only empty by chance, because the old man who'd died there a few days before had died of scarlet fever, and the fear of contagion was still fresh. Generally, there are people renting sleeping space even on the floors of the hall.'

Asher chewed silently on a corner of his mustache. There were tenements in the East End of London of which the same could be said. He was aware of Zudanievsky watching him again, sizing up this 'friend' of Prince Razumovsky's for whom it behooved him to do a favor.

'Seventeen?'

The policeman led him to a map on the wall, the loop of the Neva and the maze of streets interspersed with the dark blocks of monasteries, churches, factories, railway stations . . . and, towards the islands of the gulf, the wider open spaces where those graceful palaces stood among the birch groves, behind their walls and their lodges. Those private fairylands and 'peasant' dachas where the pillows on the simple beds were wrought of China silk.

As Zudanievsky had said, *And they wonder* . . .

'The black pins mark where the boys lived, who have disappeared,' said the policeman. 'The red pins, the girls. Those are the dates written in beside them.'

Asher was silent, studying the penciled marks. Even given a major war between Undead factions, this didn't sound like anything any sane vampire would do. 'Between March and May,' he said at last. 'A few in the summer months, but nothing after the first of September – not last year, nor the year before.'

'What does that say to you?'

Asher considered the map, seeking a pattern and finding none. 'Longer daylight hours? They could walk farther?'

'So I thought.'

'And these are all? None from other districts?'

'None,' said the policeman. 'They are children who would not be missed. Or rather, children who are missed by people whose missing children do not matter.'

'Except to yourself?'

'It isn't my business.' The set of Zudanievsky's mouth belied the words. Asher guessed that this was something he had been told, by someone he had asked. 'The first one wasn't, nor the second, nor the third . . . But when eight go missing, and then nine . . . Then people become angry. Stories start to circulate – ridiculous stories, but dangerous. *Then* it becomes my business.'

Silence again, the two men considering the scatter of red and black. Like droplets of blood and beads of night.

'And this year?'

'One,' said Zudanievsky. 'Last week. Evgenia Greb, fifteen years old. She worked in a boot factory near the artillery depot. On the fifteenth of March—'

Asher, startled, mentally readjusted his calendar to the Julian.

'—she simply didn't come home.'

'Has anyone spoken to her family? Her friends?'

Zudanievsky sniffed. 'Those who would ask them would get no answers, because people in the Vyborg-side know who half of our informers are . . . and the other half dare not ask, for fear of being revealed for what they are. I hoped we'd be lucky, this year . . . I understand you've purchased a ticket for Moscow tonight.'

'Just making enquiries about Orloff or . . . or someone else I'm looking for.' Asher knit his brows and made a dismissive little gesture, trying to look like a man who wasn't perfectly aware that the Okhrana knew all about his allegedly absconding wife. 'I should be back Monday. I'm not sure where I'll be staying, but if another of these young people disappears – or if you learn anything further about this poor girl – I'd be grateful if you'd leave me word at my rooms. I'm at the Imperatrice Catherine – though I suppose you know that already?'

The policeman made a little bow, like a fencer acknowledging a hit. 'Anything to oblige a friend of the Prince, Gospodin. I shall indeed send word.'

NINE

Ysidro was waiting on the platform of Warsaw Station when Asher arrived at half-past eleven. Wordlessly, he slipped a luggage claim-ticket into his hand in passing and vanished at once into the little knots of students and workers, functionaries and their wives, who milled about in the cold, talking, checking tickets, giving last-minute assurances of love to Cousin Volodya in Bologoe . . .

Outside the station, murky fog-banks drifted in the streets, thick with the smells of sewage, coal smoke, and the sea.

The vampire did not enter their first-class compartment until the train had passed beyond the ghastly ring of wooden tenements, unpaved streets, and mephitic factories that encircled St Petersburg's exquisite eighteenth-century heart, and was on its way south through the darkness. It crossed Asher's mind that Ysidro – Count Golenischev's reassurances of support notwithstanding – might feel himself to be Abroad as well.

As he set up the tiny ivory pieces of his traveling chess-set, the Spaniard listened with interest to Asher's account of his visit to the Okhrana. 'No wonder Golenischev's fledglings are uneasy,' he murmured, when Asher had finished. 'We – the vampire kind – find profoundly unsettling these rumors that fly among the poor. Such panic can stir up the police and waken street mobs and riots. 'Tis no mischance that none of the Paris nest survived the Revolution. Even without open violence, tales of that kind cause the poor to watch one another more closely and to take greater care of themselves. When this killer of whores whom the newspapers called the Ripper walked London's streets, tavern keepers and dock hands took it into their heads that he must have a "lair" somewhere, and groups of them developed an unhealthy interest in the cellars of empty buildings, and town houses whose inhabitants did not show themselves by day.'

Asher turned from the pitch-black abyss of the window. 'I wonder the lot of you didn't do something about Jolly Jack, then.'

'We did.' Ysidro adjusted the frosted-glass shade of the lamp over the compartment's narrow table and moved his knight. He always, Asher was amused to note, chose the black figures: Spanish, stained ivory, and extremely old. 'What these disappearing children – or for that matter the burning of this vampire girl whom Golenischev did not think to mention to me – have to do with our German scientist's friend, I know not. Yet it is clear to me that all is not – *stable* – in Petersburg.'

'Could vampires exist in Petersburg that Golenischev doesn't know about?'

'Only if they did not hunt. And if one is not going to hunt, why risk travel to a different city?'

'To see a doctor?' Asher moved his knight out of the trap Ysidro was closing upon it and perceived, in a single irritated glance, that in the next three moves he would be checkmated and there wasn't a single thing he could do about it.

'Golenischev informs me that the Master of Moscow is one of the old nobility,' Ysidro went on. 'Molchanov – an old long-beard, Golenischev calls him. These days he lets his acres to bailiffs to farm and himself dwells in Moscow, though he will return for a week, or perhaps two, to his ancestral lands, sleeping in the old chapel there and never showing himself to his tenants, nor laying hand upon them, Golenischev says. Will you have tea?' A bearded little man with a crooked back, old enough to be Asher's father, had tapped at the door, bearing a tray of steaming glasses. Ysidro gave him two roubles extra and received the man's blessing with unmoved countenance.

'They do not know that their Baron is the same man for whom their fathers worked, and their grandfathers,' the vampire went on, when the man had gone. 'Yet he has paid to bring a schoolteacher to the estate and gives generous dowries for the young girls in his villages when they wed.'

'Kind of him.' Asher doggedly shifted a pawn. He was coming to know some of his companion's pet moves and, more, coming to learn how the vampire played, with the whole of the game and all its myriad possibilities existing in his mind before his thin fingers touched the first piece.

'Were Baron Molchanov kind, I doubt he would have remained Master of Moscow through the French invasion and the burning of the city. Yet he knows that which apparently eluded your Mr Stoker in his so-interesting novel: that a vampire lord who preys upon his own peasants is doomed to swift discovery and death. 'Tis difficult for our kind to hide in the countryside. Even Golenischev, who has never set foot upon his own acres, takes care to keep his peasants content and in his debt, lest he should need the services of one to pick up a wagonload of boxes from the station one day, while the sun is high, and leave them in a dark room at the man's town palace without asking too many questions. Check.'

Asher thrust down the urge to throw the nearest bishop at his companion's head.

Towards morning Ysidro disappeared, leaving Asher to get a few hours of sleep as the train rolled through the dreary blackness of an endless plain. As they left the sea the clouds thinned, and waning moonlight painted the bulbous domes of country churches, the snow thick upon the fields. For a long while, it seemed, a single lamplit window burned in the distance – *what are they doing awake at this hour?* The train stopped at Tver and Klin, low wooden buildings dimly descried through the gloom and an occasional bearded peasant moving about the frozen streets as light struggled unwillingly into the sky. Waking, Asher took another cup of tea and turned in his mind all that Ysidro had ever told him of the Undead and all he had learned of them in his studies of folklore and legend. What could the Kaiser offer a vampire that would counterbalance the terrible risks of setting off organized hunts for their lairs by a population convinced of their existence?

'Tis almost unheard of for a vampire to kill another vampire, Ysidro had said . . . yet Asher felt almost certain that even as the vampires of London had attempted to kill him, Asher, rather than have him assist Ysidro in searching for the creature that was killing *them*, so they might very well kill a vampire who threatened to break the secrecy that was their strongest protection.

Was that what had happened last autumn? Had the girl, whoever she had been, come to Petersburg with Theiss?

Yet would they not have killed Theiss, rather than the girl, if they'd found out?

He reached in his pocket for Lydia's letter, but brought out, instead, the one he had found in Lady Irene's house.

Lady, I received your letter . . .

Why had she not gone back to London after the Master of Petersburg had died?

Had she been ashamed to face Ysidro? Or had it only been that she could find none to accompany her on the journey?

Had her memories of England – wind and meadowlarks on the high downs, and the sound of Oxford church-bells – rusted like the strings of her harp? Withered like the bindings of the mathematics books in her library, until there had been nothing left but the hunt?

Dearest Simon, forgive me my long silence . . . a letter filled with the minutiae of ballet and opera, scandal and politics, creeps towards its conclusion on my secretaire . . .

Would he miss them, those letters filled with the minutiae of ballet and opera, scandal and politics? Asher recalled how Ysidro had thrust thick packets of his replies to those letters into the pockets of his coat and cloak . . . To burn? To reread? Would one who had lost all capacity for caring – one for whom all the world had reduced itself to the passion of the hunt – care about what he had written to one who now would no longer write?

Asher closed his eyes . . . and woke sharply with the jostle of the carriage wheels over the points, a woman's voice in the corridor complaining, '—and if that coachman of his is drunk again I *swear* I shall tell him to send the man packing!' in bad provincial French.

Ysidro had given Asher an address on the Ragojskaia Zastava, on the outskirts of Moscow: a small town-house, built early in the century upon what looked like the ruins of a convent and set in its own walled grounds. Stone lions the size of sheepdogs guarded its little gate, and Asher half-expected to see the hairy shadow of the Dvorovoi – the Slavic spirit of the yard – lurking in the dusk. If Ysidro did, in fact, find himself in need of a translator, Asher guessed that the Moscow vampires would sooner come to an isolated structure than to a terraced house or a rented flat. Still, when the Spanish vampire emerged from his locked, double-lidded trunk with fall of darkness, bathed and changed clothes and disappeared into the night, Asher unpacked those dry net-wrapped swags of wild rose and wild garlic with which he'd filled his luggage and made the bedroom that overlooked the gate as secure as he could, given who he was dealing with. He slipped his little silver sleeve-knife into its holster and satisfied himself that it would drop with a twitch of his wrist into his hand.

The day help had left a meal of soup and *pirozhki*. Asher ate it by lamplight – Moscow's gas-company mains did not extend so far, and of course there was nothing of electricity here – in the breakfast room that overlooked the barren garden and wondered if the first buds were on the willow branches in his own garden at home and what Lydia was doing tonight. Despite the snow, and the crushing cold, the days were lengthening, and he knew with what swiftness the spring would come.

His body had settled very quickly back into the strange rhythms of Abroad: sleep a few hours here, a few hours there; quick wakefulness; eat when and how he could, with little sense of hunger between-times. He carried up the small samovar to his room and made tea by the dim amber gloom of the lamp. Then he turned the flame down, so that only the little burner of the samovar pierced the dark like a tiny unilluminating star, and sat beside the bedroom window, gazing into the night.

He was still wide awake at two when he saw them. Nearly a dozen, they came at a sort of drifting run from the direction of the tram stop, pale faces like ghosts where the clouds cleared a little and the moonlight broke through.

He hadn't thought there would be so many. None of them bothered with the gate. They sprang to the top of the wall like cats: a couple of students, like the ill-fated Ippo and Marya in Petersburg; a couple of well-dressed gentlemen and youthful-looking ladies in dark gowns of another year, silken skirts billowing when they sprang down into the garden. Long hair floated loose like cloud rack. Even the attenuated glimmer of the cloud-crossed stars made their eyes seem to glow.

Ysidro must have come through the gate, though Asher hadn't seen him do so . . . *Can even the other vampires follow, when he moves?*

He stood on the graveled walk, diminutive beside a heavy-shouldered man in countrified tweeds, like a character out of Tolstoy, bearded and bear-like without seeming in the slightest bit clumsy. A young woman stood between them, ivory pale in a colorless satin gown, her long hair loose upon her shoulders like a schoolgirl, speaking to each in turn. Evidently Ysidro had found a translator, and that, Asher thought, was just as well. Curious as he was about the Master of Moscow's patterns of speech and inflection – as a philologist Asher would have given almost anything to hear how Russian had been spoken in the seventeenth century – but he knew the knowledge would have cost him his life.

So he watched from his window, and now and then Molchanov would turn his shaggy head and glance in his direction, as if he knew perfectly well that Ysidro couldn't have gotten to St Petersburg, and then to Moscow, from London without a human escort . . .

And knew perfectly well that humans were nosy, even to the point of peeking through the doors of Hell.

The clock downstairs chimed the quarter hour. As if they heard it, the vampires swarmed the garden wall again, leaping down – cloaks, hair, dresses billowing – on the outside. The moon struggled like a drowning swimmer from the clouds, and Asher saw the garden was empty. The Master of Moscow, the pale beautiful woman, Ysidro . . . They were all gone. He waited, listening for footfalls he knew he wouldn't hear, until outside the door of his room he heard Ysidro say, 'James?'

Only then did he get to his feet and remove the protective swags of garlic and whitethorn, stow them in his suitcase again, and open the door.

Asher realized he was shaking. The fire in the stove had burned to ashes, unnoticed.

'You are cold.' The vampire crossed to the samovar, filled a silver-mounted glass with steaming tea.

Asher turned up the lamp. 'Just glad you found someone else to talk to our friends.'

'As am I.' Ysidro knelt to open the stove's shining grate, added a log and stirred the fire, its orange light painting the illusion of life on his thin features. 'I was invited to go hunting, in what remained of the night – would I dine with them, they asked. I replied I would sup when I returned to Petersburg. This satisfied them, though Molchanov suggested that he could find me an escort back, should harm befall you here.'

Asher stood by the window for a time, the tea glass cradled in his hands. Guessing what would have happened, had Ysidro gone hunting with the fledglings, while Molchanov remained behind. Now that the vampires were gone, he found he could not stop shivering. 'What did you tell him?'

'That I had need of one who could speak both English and Russian. He cautioned me against employing a man with brains: *Get a good, stupid peasant*, he said – through the lovely Xenia, who is certainly stupid enough to suit him to the ground. *They're loyal, and they don't ask questions. You can't trust a city man. Like weasels, they always think they know best*. I did not ask him how he came to know what weasels think. I never met a master who did not consider himself more intelligent than any man living.' Ysidro brought up a chair to the stove and, after a glance at Asher, silently, brought from the window the chair in which Asher had watched and placed it by the open grate as well.

Then he sat and folded his long, white hands. 'I have now learnt all that gossip can tell me of the Petersburg vampires,' he said. 'No inconsiderable matter, given the fewness of hours in the night that can actually be spent in the hunt and the length of years in which human minds – whom immortality renders no less human – have nothing to occupy themselves with except gossip.'

Asher hid a smile and took the chair opposite him, as if he had been a living friend. 'You behold me agog.'

'I fear you will be less so,' responded the vampire politely, 'when you learn that you and I will be obliged to continue our travels together through Europe for some weeks yet. It appears that the rivalry between Count Golenischev and his brother-fledgling Prince Dargomyzhsky – both fledglings of the same master who made the Lady Irene vampire – has been complicated still further by the presence of an inter-loper, a vampire who came to Petersburg about two years ago. For years the Count and the Prince each have attempted to gain Irene's support, but she kept apart from them both – regarding both as imbeciles, an evaluation I find it difficult to contest. The interloper – whom Molchanov simply referred to as a German, meaning in Old Russian simply a foreigner – he called you one, too – sides now with one, now with the other—'

'And now with the actual Germans?'

'That, neither Molchanov nor any of his fledglings could

say. They do not, you understand, travel abroad themselves. Like all Muscovites they regard Moscow as the heart and center of the physical and spiritual universe, and Petersburg as a sort of corrupt excrescence, necessary only to maintain a contact with the tradesmen of the West. And it is a long distance,' he added. 'A vampire alone might be able to travel from Moscow to Petersburg in two days in midwinter, could he find secure lodging in Bologoe. Myself, I would not care to try. Petersburg has always had a very small population of the Undead, and its masters have tended to be those who had not the strength to establish themselves elsewhere.'

'And this vampire girl who perished in the autumn?'

'He knew nothing of her. The Lady Xenia – our fair translator, who corresponds with Golenischev – assured me that Golenischev knew nothing of her either. Had he done so, he would have attempted to recruit her, not sought to do her harm; doubtless Dargomyzhsky would have as well.'

'Either they're all lying . . .' Asher set his tea glass on the raised stone of the hearth on which the stove stood. 'Or what? What *could* the Kaiser's government offer a vampire? Power? I'd think that given the weakness of the local master, in St Petersburg that wouldn't be much of a consideration. Food? God knows, the city has the biggest slums this side of India, and even the families of those who disappear don't dare ask questions. What else is there?'

'That,' Ysidro replied, 'is what we must travel to discover. To Prague – to Warsaw – to Köln – to Frankfurt – to Munich . . . and to Berlin.'

Mrs L.M. Asher
Holywell Street, Oxford
    Uncle William's stocks prospering no danger there stop yet your husband has fallen dangerously ill advise come at once stop contact Isaacson in Petersburg stop
    Don Simon

TEN

A sher sent the telegram – signed with Ysidro's name – to Lydia from Moscow's Kursk Station, just before boarding the ten a.m. train. Further conversation in the small hours had only confirmed Asher's conviction that it would be best to move their departure forward to daylight, an opinion in which Ysidro concurred. 'Molchanov has many fledglings,' the vampire remarked an hour or so before it grew light, as he packed clothing, toiletries, clean shirts – he was as fastidious as any dandy Asher had ever met. 'His mistrust of Western "cleverness", as he terms it, outdistances any consideration of what he would do were a foreign vampire to become stranded in Moscow because his servant had met an unfortunate end. Besides, he can think of no greater felicity than to be obliged to dwell in Russia for the rest of eternity. I think it were best, were neither you nor I in Moscow when darkness next falls.'

'I'm not going to argue with you there.'

It would take Lydia, Asher calculated, three days to reach St Petersburg. Profoundly as he missed her, the thought of her coming here – crossing the paths of the vampires, as he had warned her not to do back in the smug safety of Oxford – filled him with dread. Yet if he and Ysidro were to trace the St Petersburg interloper – to find his name, possibly his former nest, and any account of his intentions, resources, and contacts – they would have to seek him in Germany: and Ysidro being what he was, there was no question of either he, or Asher, undertaking the search alone.

What an unaided human could do to locate the interloper in St Petersburg, Lydia knew well how to do. She had tracked down vampire lairs before and knew what to look for, not only in the numbers in bank records – in property transfer dates and the names on accounts – but in the more subtle realms of gossip, rumor, and newspaper reports. She might not know the Triple Entente from the Triple Alliance, or be able to recall the name of the Prime Minister or what party he was in, but a girlhood in upper-class London society had given her a talent for sorting usable information from the persiflage of gossip, for asking the right questions, for listening to what people said when they forgot that anyone was listening, and most of all for sniffing out where money was.

And a lifetime of using precisely those unobtrusive skills in the name of Queen and Country had taught Asher that gossip and listening, sorting chance remarks and poking into peoples' financial records, generally yielded better results than hair's-breadth escapes after stealing secret plans.

How long the interloper planned to remain in Petersburg, Asher did not know, nor where he would go from there; he was acutely conscious that this might be their only chance to scotch the alliance between vampire and Kaiser. Yet, every time Lydia tampered in the business end of the affairs of the Undead, it was like watching her dart across a den of sleeping lions.

'Razumovsky can get her whatever bank records she needs,' he had said, looking up from the telegram form at Ysidro, who was perched on the corner of the gilt-and-malachite desk in the town house's tiny library. That was at six a.m., the first whispers of dawnlight not far off. Razumovsky – as Lydia would know from the duplicate address-book he had left with her – was the man he meant by *Isaacson*; any reference to Uncle William's railway shares was the tag that meant, *The following sentence is to be disregarded, it's only for show.* 'If our interloper is German, he'll deal with German banks. And I trust that neither of our St Petersburg rivals has the sophistication to realize that Lydia will be a threat.'

'They are Russians.' A world of conquistador scorn glinted like a single pale star in Ysidro's colorless voice. Ysidro himself – upon learning how Lydia went about comparing wills and property records, payments from one bank account to another, and clandestine transfers of stocks and bearer bonds – had rearranged his own living arrangements to preclude such investigation. For a man who had died in 1555 he had become surprisingly conversant with such modern conveniences as telegraphs, foreign bank accounts, and consolidated private holding companies with headquarters in New York.

'Moreover, they will themselves soon depart for the Crimea, for Odessa or Kiev. Within a month our interloper will have

the city to himself, though how this could profit him I know
not. For nigh on two months he will be a prisoner, and the
cellars of the town are shallow and damp. 'Twere best, I think,
did you not meet with your lady, save by daylight.'

'That's another statement I'm not going to give you an argument about.'

They departed Moscow by the ten o'clock train that same
morning: an express, roaring through a flat world of fields
where bare ground was only beginning to show. Asher closed
himself into his first-class reserved compartment, and slept –
the light, wary sleep of Abroad – and dreamed, uneasily, of
an endlessly huge railway station with golden pillars between
its platforms, like the Admiralty Hall in the Winter Palace.
He and Lydia sought one another, leaping onto trains to avoid
some frightful peril, riding them to terminus and then coming
back in the hopes of finding one another before whatever it
was – faceless, silent, smelling of rotten blood – found them.

When he climbed the steps of the Imperatrice Catherine at
nine thirty that night, the dvornik handed him a note, the glue
on its envelope surprisingly intact.

> *Jules Plummer*
> *L'Imperatrice Catherine*
> *26, Moyka Embankment*
>> *There has been another burning.*
>> *Zudanievsky*

'I told you!' Ellen's voice cracked in real distress. 'I said,
didn't I, ma'am, that if Mr James went off looking for that
cousin of his, and in such terrible weather – and to Russia,
of all the heathen places! – didn't I say he'd come down ill,
as he did before?'

'Indeed you did.' Lydia folded up the telegram, her heart
beating fast.

Not because she believed for one instant that Jamie was ill,
of course.

Don Simon . . .

Ysidro.

She set the yellow paper down, aware that it gave away
how badly her hands were shaking. Ellen peered at her, thick

untidy brows drawing together: 'Now, ma'am, don't take on so,' she said, her own anxiety shoved abruptly aside. 'I'm sure it's not so bad as this Mr Simon seems to think. He'll be all right.'

'Yes, of course.' Lydia smiled up at the bigger woman, realizing – from the cold of her hands and feet, and the expression on Ellen's face – that she must have gone pale.

'It's probably just a chill.'

'I'm sure it is.' She took a deep breath. 'Would you have Mick bring down my luggage from the box room? I think there's a train to London this evening.'

'And then what?' demanded her servant. 'Us arriving at all hours of the night and having to find a hotel . . .'

Lydia opened her mouth, shut it, then managed to say, 'Yes, of course.' *Us*. The inevitable taboo against young ladies traveling alone . . .

Margaret Potton's face rose before her, huge blue eyes blinking behind thick spectacles beneath the eaves of her outdated hat.

Don Simon told me I'd find you here . . .

Ysidro had announced, *I will not have you traveling alone abroad like a jauntering slut*, and, disregarding Lydia's protests, had coolly gone about recruiting a respectable female companion for her.

A companion he had killed, because by journey's end Margaret Potton had known too much about vampires – and about him.

And because she'd bored him. Guilt seared her, at the knowledge that this was true. She blinked quickly . . . though not quickly enough to keep Ellen, misinterpreting, from laying a hand on her shoulder and saying, 'There, there, ma'am, he'll be all right.'

She took another breath and patted the big, rough hand where it lay among the lace of her tea gown. 'Thank you,' she whispered. Ysidro liked her – *loves you*, her mind whispered, though she pushed the thought violently away (*such creatures don't love . . .*) – among other reasons, because of her intelligence that matched his own. He had chosen Margaret because she was stupid. Had made her fall in love with him because she was lonely . . . and had disposed of her like an ink-stained glove because she was clingy, uninteresting to him, and awkward in her jealous love. Because she was everything that Lydia wasn't.

And Margaret had known it. Their journey together had been punctuated by a dozen jealous scenes that had left the wretched little governess in tears.

And, after all that, Ysidro had killed her.

In what she hoped was a normal voice, Lydia went on, 'You're quite right. We'll pack tonight, and you'll come with me as far as London tomorrow morning. There are bureaux in London where one can hire a gentlewoman companion – I would never *dream* of taking you so far from your family, and into danger of sickness—'

'I'd be all right, ma'am.' Ellen sounded deeply dubious, however, about the whole idea of travel beyond the English-speaking world. 'If you'd rather I went . . .?'

'Dearest, I wouldn't.' Lydia pressed her hand again and manufactured a dewy smile. 'Besides, Mr Hurley would never forgive me if I were to take you away.' She named the keeper of the local pub on the corner, a widower with a handsome mustache.

Ellen bridled like a coy percheron. 'Go along with you!'

Lydia finally got her out of the study, so that she could look up who the blazes Isaacson really was, whom she was supposed to find in St Petersburg. When she saw that it was Prince Razumovsky she felt profoundly cheered, as if she'd seen the Russian diplomat's handsome, gold-bearded face in a crowd. Thus she ascended to her packing with a lighter heart: tea gowns, day gowns, evening dresses, walking dresses . . . The white-and-green shoes would go with the lavender carriage-suit, but not the blue-and-white, so she'd better take the blue half-boots also . . . Would the camel-hair coat be warm enough or should she take the gray fur? Both, to be on the safe side . . . *How cold did it get in St Petersburg in April?* Oh, and hats . . . and Fischer's book on the chemistry of proteins . . . and that remarkable treatise on radiography by Curie, and the last four issues of the British Journal of Medicine, and the little set of picklocks James had gotten her and made her learn to use . . . What color gloves would go with the cinnamon-red walking-suit? *Dear me, I seem to need another trunk . . .*

But whenever she paused in her laying-out of petticoats

and blouses, stockings and corsets among the froth of lace on the bed, silence seemed to flow into her room like deadly black water. And though the evening was barely come, she closed the curtains, as if she feared to look out into the darkness and see a pale shape in the gathering mists, watching from across the road with eyes that reflected the light of her bedroom lamps.

'Where was this one found?' Asher stirred the debris in the tin box with the long-snouted forceps Zudanievsky had handed him, mentally identifying the fragments among the grayish dust. Teeth, a heat-warped wing of pelvis, an exploded skull that had shrunk to the size of an orange. Toe bones and finger bones better preserved, as if the body had burned from the breast and belly outward. No corset bones or lacing tips, but the melted remains of steel shirt- and trouser-buttons: the victim had been a boy. The smell of ash filled the little room, almost drowning the building's other stinks.

'An old carriage-house on Stone Island.' Zudanievsky marked the place with a yellow pin on the map. It was across one of the river's lesser branches from the slums of the Vyborgside, less than a mile from the dun-colored brick monolith of the Okhrana headquarters. A distance easily walked. 'Would you like to see the place?'

'I would. And the attic where the girl was found last autumn, if it wouldn't be a trouble to you.'

The policeman shook his head. 'It would be my pleasure, Gospodin. You returned earlier than you had thought – did you find what you sought in Moscow?'

'Not a thing.' And, remembering that he was an American in quest of an absconding wife, 'But I think there's got to be a connection. This Orloff – or whatever his name really is – said as how he thought someone had murdered his sister, had somehow caused this to happen to her . . . I just can't imagine how, or why.'

Behind the thick lenses of his spectacles, Zudanievsky's pale eyes rested briefly on his face. They were heavily lined at the corners, and smudgy looking, as if he'd slept badly. 'There are many mysteries associated with this case, Mr Plummer. Some of them are not my affair. Others, my superiors tell me, are not my affair, except insofar as they are making the poor in

their slums angry and afraid – and that the Prince has seen
fit to order me to assist you in all that you would ask. I live
in hope that you will find some meaning in these disappear-
ances – these burnings – that you will be able to share with me.'

Asher replied, with proper American heartiness, 'That I will
certainly do.'

'Very good, then. Let us see what there is to see.'

It was considerably less than a mile from the Kronverksky
Prospect to Stone Island, and even in the afternoon's sleety
rain, the streets of Apothecary Island that lay between bustled
with shabby women heavily wrapped, with peddlers of dolls
and hot tea and chestnuts, with soldiers from the barracks
nearby. The property where the carriage house stood was
typical of the neighborhood, walled and quiet, as if there
weren't factories and a shipyard and street after filthy street
of run-down tenements nearby.

The house – low and Italianate and painted robin's-egg blue
against the bleak grayness of the day – had been shut since
Twelfth Night with its widowed owner's departure for her son-
in-law's home in Moscow. No straw lay on the brick floor of
the ornate carriage-house. The gray light that filtered through
the louvers in the window shutters, the panes of the high
lantern-dome of its echoing ceiling, showed Asher a low-slung
victoria carriage – open to better show off Madame's gown
when she went driving through the Botanical Gardens on a
summer afternoon – a handsome German brougham, the
lacquer of which gleamed with polishing, and a closed sleigh.

'The ashes were found in this corner.' Zudanievsky signed
to the caretaker who had admitted them to open the building's
shutters, then led Asher to the corner farthest away from them.
'As you see, he gathered together all the carriage rugs he could
find here, to sleep on—'

The remains of them – corners and edges surviving around
a gruesome central crater in which the very bricks had been
cracked with the heat – lay there still, disarrayed by the men
who'd shoveled the ashes into that locked tin box. Asher stood
gazing up at the ceiling lantern, whose unshuttered panes
would admit moonlight in any city less consistently overcast
than St Petersburg . . .

And had to close his mouth, hard, on the first thought that
came to his mind:

No vampire would sleep in this place.

Zudanievsky said, 'Yes?' as if he'd heard the clanging of words unsaid.

'Nothing.'

Asher thought of the secret chamber beneath the Lady Irene's town house, the medieval crypt where Lydia had once tracked Ysidro, the lightless vaults of the Constantinople vampire lair. The double-lidded travel coffins; the locked, barred, bolted, hidden hideaways of every vampire he'd ever encountered.

And, more than those, the close, cautious, wary turn of mind that vampires developed, and the single-minded obsession with absolute control of their environment. For vampires, everything that was not about the hunt was about making sure that no possibility existed that the slightest touch of the sun's light could reach them, could ignite their friable flesh and terminate their fragile immortality.

Twenty years in the Department had effectively pulverized Asher's boyhood faith, but the recollection of Oxford discussions of God and Eternity returned to him, and he wondered if this were some sly jest by Whoever might be in charge of the Universe: that, in order to live forever, the vampires must surrender everything that made the world desirable. Their immortality depended upon shrinking their lives down smaller and smaller, until all that existed was the craving for a truly inviolable coffin, and blood to drink.

There were men – not vampires – he knew in the Department whose whole lives had become about hedging their world with safety precautions, about watching for enemies or possible enemies or the possibility of perhaps a possible enemy knowing where they might be . . .

He passed a hand over his bald-shaved head beneath the fur of his hat.

He was one of them.

Which was how he knew, looking about him at the open vastness of the carriage house – the broken-in glass of a nearby window showing him where the boy had entered the place – that whatever else that boy had been, he had not been a vampire.

Or not one that any master had ever trained.

And why make a fledgling, only to let him die the moment

he went outside? Particularly if the master would feel – as some masters did – the agony of that blazing death?

Light – gray and weak with the rain, but glaring after the filtered gloom – splashed into the carriage house as the caretaker opened the first of the shutters.

A spontaneous mutation? Asher shivered at the thought. Yet how else would a vampire come into being, who did not know even that terrible First Principle of survival?

Was that what Theiss was doing? Creating vampires? But why do that, when he had a vampire associate?

Or did the interloper refuse, like Ysidro, to create fledglings?

But, in that case, why associate with Theiss?

And where did the Kaiser and Herr Texel come in to it?

Zudanievsky knelt on the other side of the burned scatter of rags, lifting each charred hunk of fur and carefully stowing it in the rucksack he'd brought. 'When was the body found?' Asher inquired, and the policeman replied:

'Saturday evening. The caretaker found it. The ashes were already cold. I ordered all to be left as it was, save the ashes themselves, knowing you would wish to see the place undisturbed.'

'Thank you.' Asher looked around the cavernous chamber, as more and more light came in with the putting back of the shutters, and noted the well-kept glint of the sleigh runners, the bright sparkle of silver mountings within the brougham. No sign of restraints that might have bound a doomed vampire, of ropes or chains . . . Not that ropes would hold the Undead. Or chains, unless they were either damned thick or coated with silver. 'Did you search the room?'

'I had not time for more than a quick – what would you call it? A brush-over? Like the maid who shakes out the antimacassars when she has not time to beat the carpets. It was near darkness when I got here, and I knew I would return with you. What *is* this that we behold?' The policeman squatted back on his heels, as Asher began his own process of lifting, shaking, folding the scorched and fragile furs. 'What is it that you expect to find, Gospodin? *What is it that you know about all this*, that you exhibit neither disbelief nor even surprise?'

'If you will excuse me,' said Asher evenly, answering in French although the policeman had spoken the last sentence in Russian, 'my Russian is not so good.'

Don't you try to trap ME with an old ruse like that, Gospodin.

'Pff!' Zudanievsky waved a gray-gloved little hand. 'The wife and Monsieur "Orloff" and his sister . . . and that is all that you will tell me?'

'It's all that I know.' Asher folded his arms around his drawn-up knee, faced the policeman across the cracked and blackened bricks. 'Have you never met an American before who believes that there is more in Heaven and Earth than are dreamt of in the philosophies of so-called "scientific minds"?'

'I have. And I pray to Saint Joshua, who looks after the affairs of such as you and I, to deliver me from Americans who believe in ectoplasm and teleportation . . . Yet seldom have I met such an American who has made his own fortune in railroads and packing houses.'

'Come to Chicago,' retorted Asher with a grin, 'and I'll introduce you to a hundred, Gospodin. D'you plan to arrest me for it?'

'I should.' Zudanievsky returned the grin, that gray feature-less face suddenly looking like a wicked little elf. 'Just to see what consul you actually go to.' He pushed his spectacles straight on his nose. 'But through my skin – and after thirty years of chasing revolutionaries and anarchists who turn out to be police spies themselves – through my skin I feel that you know the truth of things that other men do not even believe in, and that if I had you thrown out of the country, I would get no answers . . . And these poor luckless boys and girls would continue to disappear.' He turned back a fold of blanket, where a forgotten dust of ash and bone lay in a little heap. 'And worse, I think. Here,' he added, and at the sharpness of his voice, Asher unfolded his long legs and crossed to him in a stride.

Zudanievsky sat back, a tin box in his hand, of the sort that English rum-toffees were sold in, slightly larger and thicker than the palm of a man's hand. He shook it, and something thudded and clicked faintly within. As Asher knelt beside him, the policeman opened it.

It contained two severed fingers of a woman's hand. Well-kept, well-manicured, clean and without calluses, one of them circled by a pearl ring. All this Asher noted in the second or two between the opening of the box to the daylight and the moment when the fingers burst into searing and unquench-able flame.

ELEVEN

'**A** pearl ring,' Ysidro said.
'A baroque pearl, shaped like a tiny snail-shell, about two-thirds the size of a pea. The band was plain gold—' Asher reached for his waistcoat pocket, and the vampire made a movement with his long fingers. *No need.*

'I gave it to her.'

Silence then. The brocaded curtains, and the double-glazing of the windows, cut out the noise of night traffic on the Moyka Embankment, so that the sitting room, with its tufted red velvet chairs, its prosaic dark furniture, seemed cut adrift from the world. After a moment Asher said, 'It doesn't inevitably mean she's dead.'

'She has been dead since 1820,' replied Ysidro calmly. ''Tis kind in you to speak words of comfort, if such be your intent,' he added, raising his head to meet Asher's eyes. 'But a man who would study the flesh of vampires would be safest to do so using the twice dead – the truly dead – rather than one who might yet escape and demand an accounting for her missing fingers. And a vampire working in partnership with such a man would never permit a potential rival to come within that man's orbit. No,' he said. 'She is truly dead at last.'

Would he have sighed, Asher wondered, had he breath himself?

Asher recalled the untouched books, the rusted harp-strings. Would he – James Asher – continue to love Lydia if she ceased to study her experimental notes in bed, ceased to read the *Lancet* as if it were Dickens, ceased to love her friends and take her accustomed delight in the incongruities of the world?

Yes. In the months after the miscarriage of their child, she had laid down all of those things and retreated into some zone of grief as still and colorless as the Neva ice. Through his own grief, he had waited for her, patiently, knowing she must one day emerge. In time she had, as the ice had broken from the river and now was gone.

But I'm not a vampire myself. Nor is she.

'Did you see the place where the other one – the girl – burned up?'

Asher shook himself sharply free of his thoughts. Wondered how much the vampire had read of them.

'As Zudanievsky said, it's an attic on Little Samsonievsky Alley. Only fear of the Okhrana kept the manager from bringing in new tenants before this: there were three families of them waiting in the stairway with their dishes and bedding as we came out. There wasn't much to see. But I'll swear no vampire would have taken refuge there. The window is small, but it's unshuttered and uncurtained. Nobody could think the place wouldn't be light with the coming of day.'

Ysidro sat with hands folded before his lips, elbows propped on the arms of his chair, before the sitting-room stove.

'I asked you about fairies, back at the Theosophical Society ball,' said Asher, as the silence lengthened. '*Are* there other creatures – supernatural or merely rare – who share this . . . this photopyroactivity with your kind?'

'If they burst into flame with the mere light of day,' replied the vampire, 'I should say they would be rare indeed, especially were they not intelligent enough to know to go to ground where it is safe. Yet by the clothing found – the girl's shoes, the boy's buttons – these were human beings. And, I should say, probably two of the boys and girls who disappeared.'

'Is there any possibility – any at all – that this is a spontaneous mutation? That for some reason certain people are . . . are becoming vampires . . .' He hesitated, hearing the preposterousness of the idea even as he said it.

'Without masters? In truth, James, I know not. But I have never heard of such, and for three hundred years and more I have studied the nature of our state with great attention. No . . . There have been those – your old friend Blaydon among them – who sought to develop a vampire hybrid who would have the vampire's powers but none of his weaknesses. Yet who would develop a creature with the weaknesses but none of the strengths?'

'Benedict Theiss, it looks like,' murmured Asher. 'I'll set Lydia to finding what she can about the man when she gets here. Razumovsky can get her into this Circle of Astral Light that Theiss seems to favor . . . or one of his mistresses can. Behind that innocent air of hers she's very good at picking out the names of people's contacts – fitting together who goes where with whom. If I asked Zudanievsky or my friends at the Department to look into him and by some chance the man turns out to be a perfectly innocent soul who only seeks to alleviate the sicknesses of Petersburg's poor . . .'

'A man who employs a clerk from the Auswärtiges Amt,' responded Ysidro drily, 'is not perfectly innocent. Yet personally, if Theiss and this man Texel find themselves locked up in the Peter and Paul Fortress, I would rather not remain in Petersburg into June trying to find who our interloper next contacts. Theiss at least we know about. This most recent girl who disappeared—'

'—knew nothing, spoke to no one, and never had a friend outside her family circle, to hear her mother tell it.' Asher rose from his chair and crossed to the samovar, poured himself tea. The long walk in the rain, coming directly after three days of train journey, had left him feeling fatigued and old. There was no real rest Abroad, and he knew the coming journey would be worse.

'You should have seen their eyes when I asked them questions. Always checking the expression on Zudanievsky's face, or glancing at each other: *Is this safe to say? What do they want to hear? Will things be better or worse if we tell them that?* In England, if you poke your nose around the East End with *copper* written all over you like a music-hall poster, they'll play dumb, but they won't be scared like that. Not scared for their lives.'

'Inconvenient.' Ysidro sounded politely bored. He was a Spanish nobleman: the rights of the poor had never interested him as a living man, and he clearly had not the slightest concern about them now that he was dead.

Terrified of their betters is the way the poor should be. He's probably going to go out tonight and kill Evgenia Greb's mother for his supper.

As the vampire rose to go, Asher drew from his pocket a small wrapped bundle of pink tissue-paper and held it out. After the slightest of hesitations, Ysidro took it. He didn't unfold it, as if he felt through the tissue the slightly deformed gold, the heat-cracked pearl. Only slipped it into his pocket, as he had slipped her letters.

'I thought you might want it.'

''Twas kind.' Ysidro swung his cloak over his shoulders, though the bitter night held no chill for such as he. 'Yet did I concern myself with the impedimenta of those whom once I knew, no house could contain them. Mistress Asher will be here on Thursday?'

'There was a telegraph from her at the bank, sent from Paris this morning.'

'I trust—' The vampire stopped himself, a mistake in speech so unusual for him that Asher knew what he had been going to ask.

In an even voice, he replied to the unspoken words. 'I do not know whether Lydia travels alone or not. I hope she has the good sense to bring Ellen with her – and I hope I may assure her when she gets here that Ellen has nothing to fear from yourself.'

'As you and I shall be departing on our own travels the day after Mistress Asher arrives from hers,' responded Ysidro, 'I believe you can make that assurance.'

'I understand,' went on Asher, 'that about the other Petersburg vampires, you can offer no guarantees.'

'There are no guarantees regarding anything in this world, James. Neither for the living, nor for the dead.'

Then he was gone. Asher felt the cold pressure of the vampire's mind on his and resisted it as well as he could, so that he saw his visitor actually go to the door, open it, and let himself out. A convenience, he reflected, in getting past the *dvornik* unseen, anyway . . .

He draped windows and doors in their shrouds of garlic and white thorn and went to bed. Arctic spring sunrises aside, it had been three very long days.

There was, of course, no question of Mr Jules Plummer of Chicago going to the station to meet the red-haired wife of a New College Lecturer in Folklore upon her arrival in the northern capital. On Thursday, the thirtieth of March by Russian reckoning, Mr Plummer went instead to the palace of Prince Razumovsky on Krestovsky Island, and having let himself onto the grounds with the key the Prince had given him, walked through the birch groves and woodlands, where the first of the spring's buds were beginning, to the *izba* near the riverbank where the Prince's guests sometimes stayed.

The servants there bowed to the honorable Gospodin – there were four of them: a cook, two maids, and a young man from the Prince's stables who looked after the garden – brought him tea, and went about their work of cleaning and tidying, and shortly after noon the jingle of harness and the crunch of carriage wheels sounded in the drive. Lydia sprang from the low barouche without waiting for the assistance of the Prince's liveried footman and threw herself into Asher's arms. 'It's all right,' she whispered, when after the first delirious kiss he raised his head to see the Prince handing another woman out of the carriage. 'I've told her my name is Berkhampton and that you're my husband, and anyway she's going home in the morning. Mrs Flasket,' she introduced, 'this is my husband, Silas Berkhampton. Mrs Flasket was kind enough to agree to accompany me here at the very last minute . . .'

'My dear Mrs Berkhampton.' The stout, square-faced widow made a close-lipped friendly smile that did not quite conceal protruding front teeth. 'For thirteen years now I've made it my business to be company for ladies who find themselves in need of it, and in the course of that time I've seen every shabby boarding establishment south of the Thames. An offer to accompany someone to St Petersburg was like a chance to run away with the gypsies.' Her dark eyes sparkled. 'I shall very much take my time going back.'

'*Brava.*' Asher bent over her black-gloved hand. If he knew Lydia, this woman would have a generous amount over her train fare.

'And now,' declared Mrs Flasket, 'His Excellency has offered to show me a little more of the estate.'

Razumovsky, resplendent in the London-tailored morning-dress he wore when not in uniform, bowed to her as if to the Empress. 'If you are not too fatigued, Madame . . .?'

'Your Excellency, I must be dead before I would pass up the chance to go riding in a carriage with a Russian Prince! *Â bientôt*, ma'am . . .' She twinkled and waved.

'*Â bientôt.*' Lydia returned the wave, smiling, as the Prince helped Mrs Flasket – bursting with energy in the dark costume of second-mourning widowhood – into the carriage again.

Asher glanced back at the *izba* behind them, but the servants had all mysteriously disappeared.

The carriage was yet not out of sight behind the brown-and-silver screen of trees as he scooped Lydia up into his arms.

'*Silas*?' he asked later, as he was lacing up Lydia's corset again.

'I've always liked the name. It's very American.' She groped around blindly for her spectacles on the table by the bed.

'Ah sure 'preciate the compliment, ma'am,' he replied, in an exaggeration of Jules Plummer's Midwestern accent, and ducked as she threw her comb at him. 'Will it cause talk for you to stay here without a companion?' he added, in his own voice. The clouds had broken, and the silvery afternoon light that Asher always associated with St Petersburg had given way to a thin, sweet sunlight. The birch trees outside the windows, with their tight bronze buds, their tiny cones, seemed clear as something etched on glass. It was unbelievable that the filthy attic he'd seen, with its burned floorboards and its stink of poverty and despair, lay less than a mile away.

'I asked Prince Razumovsky that.' In a soft billow of padded silk, Lydia crossed to the dressing table. 'He said that in Petersburg society nobody would raise an eyebrow if I was staying here openly with a male dancer from the Ballet Russes and two captains of the Imperial guard. I'd be received every-where – except, perhaps, by the Empress. He said he'd get his sister to take me shopping to put me *bien à la mode*—'

Asher rolled his eyes in a caricature of an aggrieved husband, which made her laugh. Since it was her family money, he had always taken the position that it was none of his business what she did with it or what she wore, which included hats that resembled coal scuttles and ornamental parasols scarcely larger than sunflowers. He settled against the pillows, tucked his bare feet under the furs, and watched his wife as she undertook her painstaking ritual of skin cream, astringent, rice powder, carmine, talcum, cologne water, tiny touches of mascara, and thirty minutes of braiding, pinning, swagging, studying, orna-menting, demolishing, and redoing the astonishing beauty of her cinnamon-colored hair – removing and replacing her spec-tacles every few moments all the while. Had she just emerged from a wallow in the stable midden she would still have outshone Helen of Troy, and it never ceased to amaze him that she saw nothing of this: only the size of her nose, and the waif-like thinness of her cheeks.

How could the words of your stepmother and your nannies have had such force that you've believed yourself ugly ever since?

In a smaller voice she asked, 'Do you leave tonight?'

'At a quarter to midnight. Ysidro says that it is vital that we arrive in daylight, and that we never meet once darkness falls.'

Lydia appeared for a time to concentrate all her attention on the score of tiny pearl buttons that closed the transparent lace of blouse and collar over the silver that ringed her throat. 'And I'm to find who Theiss associates with – particularly anyone with the social peculiarity of never being seen by daylight?'

'If you can. Though I can assure you now that half the young dandies and three-quarters of the ladies of Petersburg society never go to bed until dawn and aren't out of doors until the sun is going down, so there's a good chance they've never noticed if one of their number is strictly nocturnal or not. That's where the bank records come in.'

She smiled. 'I don't need bank records for that, silly.' And her smile faded. 'You'll be careful going through Germany?'

'I won't stir a foot out-of-doors once the sun is down. It's not quite a day and a half to Warsaw,' Asher went on, as lightly as if they both did not know why it was so vital that none of the vampires in the cities they would visit should learn where Ysidro's human partner could be found. 'We'll reach Berlin at noon on Wednesday – I hope and trust – and with luck be gone from there just after dawn on Thursday. I have no desire to be in Berlin a moment longer than we have to, and even then, it's too long. Right now my one prayer is that whoever this renegade fledgling is, he or she isn't from Berlin. I don't want to have to stay long enough to search for vampire nests, with or without the cooperation of the local master. Being picked up by the Berlin police for burglary would be all I need.'

'Don Simon would get you out of trouble –' she turned from the mirror, short-sighted brown eyes filled with the fear she ordinarily hid – 'wouldn't he?'

'He would,' said Asher grimly. 'But if the hue and cry resulting from the murder of two or three stray *polizei* lasted until daylight, *I'd* then be hard put to protect *him* long enough to get us both to the Polish border. Right now I'll settle for hoping that the situation doesn't arise.'

Her voice deliberately off-hand, she went back to her scrutiny of her eyelashes. 'I would think Don Simon would be more subtle than to leave official corpses lying about.'

'As would I. But accidents happen – and the spy who doesn't take that into account is the spy who doesn't make it back to home base in one piece and with the goods in his pocket. I hear the silent whisper of invisible minions setting out luncheon, and something tells me His Excellency keeps a high standard in the way of cuisine.'

Ever tactful, Prince Razumovsky did not return to the *izba* until well into the afternoon, having kept Mrs Flasket entertained at a luncheon of their own at his palace. Lydia meanwhile met and completely charmed the servants – one of whom, Alyssa, the senior maid, spoke excellent French – while they unpacked the companion's luggage in the smaller chamber that Mrs Flasket would occupy for one night before returning to England.

'She really is an excellent companion,' said Lydia, as through one of the wide windows they observed Razumovsky and the widow emerge from the woods that almost completely hid the little cottage from the palace. 'She's read everything from Plato to penny dreadfuls, can argue any political question backwards and forwards – once I'd assured her she didn't have to keep up a flow of chat on the train, I don't know *how* many newspapers she read . . . She can even keep track of what's going on in the Balkans, and nobody I know but you can do that! And she knows about fashion and cricket and how to care for lapdogs, enough to at least keep up small talk about it for hours, if small talk is what you were paying her for. I've written her a recommendation for my Aunt Louise in Paris—'

'I've met your Aunt Louise and that isn't a kindness.'

'Well, no, but she does pay very well for the boredom and abuse she serves out, and poor Mrs F. is very much in need of a job. And I think she'd enjoy living in Paris. And she's

the most tactful creature in the world. It's the one thing Don
Simon did teach me, you know,' she added, with that slightly
forced note her voice took on when she spoke the vampire's
name. 'That whatever you need in any city in the world,
there's someone you can get to do it, if you have enough
money.'

She half-opened her lips then to say something else – about
Ysidro, Asher thought – and then closed them as the Prince
and the companion crossed the covered veranda, stomping
mud and gravel from their shoes. The only snow that remained
was on the shady side of the trees. It would probably freeze
again that night, Asher judged, seeing how Razumovsky's
breath smoked in the deepening slant of the light. But in a
week the birch trees would begin to leaf.

'I expect you had best be going,' said Lydia softly.

'I had, yes.' He laid his hand over hers. He wanted to remain
with her the way a drowning man wanted breath, with the
whole of his flesh and being. Yet he remembered the cold grip
of the vampire Ippo's hands on his arms, the flickering pale
ghosts of the Moscow vampires as they leaped weightlessly
to the top of the wall . . .

And he would have thrown himself into the teeth of a
threshing machine before he would have given any of those
creatures – who knew him, who had seen his face – the slightest
hint that there was someone in St Petersburg to whom he,
Ysidro's human servant, might tell secrets.

'Be careful,' she said softly, as he brought up her fingers
and her palm to kiss, memorizing the touch of them, knowing
he'd want that memory in the days ahead. 'Tell Ysidro— Give
him my best.'

'I will.' Seeing the trouble in her eyes, he added, 'He understands, you know.'

'I know.' She nodded slightly. 'I'm glad he does,' she added.
'I – we – owe him a great deal, and I don't want him to think
I'm ungrateful for his protection of you. And of me, for that
matter. It's just that – I don't ever want to see him again.'
And she took off her glasses, lest Razumovsky and Mrs Flasket,
opening the door with laughter and jokes, should behold her
in them.

TWELVE

They left St Petersburg at just before midnight. First light showed Asher the trackless, boggy forests of the Baltic plain through the window of the first-class compartment. Ysidro had vanished some time before that, and Asher slept for a few hours in the very handsome wagon-lit provided by the Russian Imperial Rail Service, then woke to a view substantially the same. Gray-trunked pines with sodden snow still around their feet; the far-off glint of lakes; sometimes the blunt gray walls of ancient fortresses that spoke of terrible medieval wars that English schoolchildren never heard of. Then more trees.

'I take it,' Ysidro inquired on the following night, when at last the northern twilight had shimmered out of existence, 'that the Polish tongue is not one of your accomplishments?'

'You are correct. But, even more so than in Russia, the Polish aristocracy are more fluent in French and German than in the language their own peasants speak. At least in some circles in Russia, it's fashionable to know a little Russian.'

Ysidro dismissed the entire Slavic race with a single movement of fine-cut nostrils. 'It were best, then, that you do not see the Warsaw vampires at all. Molchanov and Golenischev spoke of them with contempt, but that may have been because they were Russians, speaking of a conquered people. Will you be in danger on your own account, in that city?'

'I have a good book,' replied Asher, 'and a secure room to read it in. Much as it would interest me to view the city again, I have learned to take no chances whilst Abroad.'

As in Moscow and St Petersburg, Ysidro had arranged for his own lodging in an antique but well-kept town house in the Old City and for Asher's in a *pension* not far away. Asher saw their considerable luggage, including Ysidro's enormous coffin-trunk, brought to the town house, and he remained there through the long spring day, reading *Les Miserables*, napping, playing the piano in the parlor – old tunes from childhood, a practice he found soothing on the occasions that his motorcycle was unavailable to him – and watching the street below. At eight – the sun westering in the high northern sky – he departed, got himself a café dinner in the Ulica Senatorska, and was in his own *pension* room while twilight lingered yet over the red-and-gold steeples of the town.

Abroad, he had learned long ago to see cities in terms of danger and safety – zones marked clearly on a mental map – and in terms of the likelihood of encountering an enemy, or the occasional necessity of a quick escape. There wasn't a city from Petersburg to Lisbon that he could not traverse unseen by the local police, if need be. As a young man he had loved the cities of Europe for their beauty and their age, for palaces and parks, for the astonishing variety of passers-by and peddlers' cries and the many-colored torrents of languages that flowed like streams along the cobbled ways. He had been sorry – more profoundly sorry than he had realized at the time – when he'd become aware that this love for these places was fading into the instinctive wariness of the Job.

Perhaps that loss had let him fully comprehend the regret in Ysidro's voice, when the vampire had spoken of those for whom all things had become matters of indifference, except for the Hunt and the Kill.

He had not known, he realized now, when he was well off, with only that loss to mourn.

Since knowing the vampires – knowing that they were real – the cities of Europe had changed for him once again. They had become places where the danger was not only real, but unfathomable. He found he could not pass an ancient church without wondering what might be sleeping in its crypts – what would wake with fall of dark; could not cross the old stone pavements without seeing them as only a brittle crust above an abyss of demons.

Demons who now threatened to emerge and become part of the politics of blood and iron.

How could I have left Lydia alone in such a place?

Yet he knew that she was no safer in Oxford, if one of the London vampires should decide to run the risk of Ysidro's formidable wrath and put her out of the way. The journey up from London was a short one.

Don't think of it. He closed his eyes, rested his forehead on the window's dark glass. *The sword was offered you one more time, and you grasped it, of your own free will. You accepted the Job, yet again . . .*

Because he knew in his heart that he could not have done otherwise.

Somewhere, there is a German scientist working with a vampire. And you need a vampire to help you destroy the threat of what that scientist will unleash on the world.

But he had to sit for some time, hearing the clacking of traffic in the darkness below, before the red-hot knot of fear loosened a little in his chest and he could go back to the long-ago sorrows of Jean Valjean.

When full daylight was back to the sky, he returned to the town house and found on the piano seat two tickets for the 11:52 express that night to Berlin.

'Nothing.' The vampire slid shut the door of the first-class compartment as the lights of Warsaw were swallowed behind them in darkness and mist. 'No fledgling has left this nest. Nor, they say, have they heard of any such in Gdansk, a city whose master spawned the Master of Warsaw. They are blockheads,' he added, in the tone of an entomologist identifying a common species of bug. 'Arrogant and intolerant.' Considering Ysidro's heritage of Reconquista and Inquisition, Asher did not think the Spanish vampire had a great deal of room to talk.

As he had when they had passed through Berlin on the way to St Petersburg, Asher found himself prey to the conviction that all the men who'd associated with him as the Herr Professor Leyden in the various cities of Germany during the early nineties had foregathered in the Empire's capital and were all looking for him – a conviction upon which he was hard put to close his mental door so that he could behave normally. From long experience – his own, and the observed behavior of others – he knew how difficult it was to act 'naturally,' whatever 'naturally' might be; how fine a line separates an ordinary American accent from an assumed drawl that practically shouts to the observant ear, *Ah-all am a fake!*

He had seen more than one Department novice stopped by the police, essentially, for overdoing a disguise to the point where it was obvious that it was a disguise.

It was difficult not to keep checking the shaven skin of his head, to make sure that he'd gotten every last millimeter of stubble. Even after decades of the Job, he felt the impulse to reassure himself of his appearance at every reflective surface he passed, though this behavior was among the first things he looked for in men he suspected of playing for the Opposition. It was like not scratching an itch.

He remained indoors at Ysidro's elegant rented apartment through the daylight hours, and at his own hotel from sunset on, jotting notes in a personal code as to the addresses of these temporary nests. One never knew when the smallest trifles of information would become critical to one's survival: like Lydia's artless queries over tea and shopping, about who might be a 'special friend' of whom. It was from addresses and street names that recurred, names or even initials that repeated, as much as from property that changed hands suspiciously or not at all, that Lydia was able to put together the location of possible nests.

He slept for a few hours and dreamed of bombs falling on London, though the man who stood in the doorway of the lightless house by the lake of blood wasn't Ysidro, but Benedict Theiss.

When the sun rose at six he returned to Ysidro's apartment with two porters and a cab, to load up the luggage there and make his way to the Anhalter Bahnhof. By two that afternoon they were in Prague.

'Princess Stana –' Prince Razumovsky bowed deeply as their hostess crossed the tiled conservatory vestibule – 'might I present Madame Asher of England, the wife of an old friend? Madame Asher, Her Royal Highness Princess Stana Petrovich Njegosh of Montenegro.'

'*Enchanted.*' The dark lady wearing – even to Lydia's short-sighted gaze – rather more jewelry than Englishwomen would have donned in the afternoon, over rather less bodice, held out a lace-mitted hand and, when Lydia would have curtseyed, laughed and tugged her up again. 'Silly miss! Here we are all just women who share a passion for the spiritual evolution of the Soul of Humankind.' She pressed Lydia's hands between her own. 'And its physical well-being,' she added, with a smile at Razumovsky. 'How mysterious is the bond that binds the flesh with the spirit, the physical heart with the soul that dwells within! Dearest Andrei –' she put her arm through the Prince's – 'tells me you are a physician yourself, Madame . . . Such a formal title, *Madame*! Might I call you Lydia? So much more *natural*! And please do call me Stana! Andrei tells me you research the blood, the way dearest Benedict does . . . Madame Asher—'

While she had chatted in her soft alto voice she had been leading them deeper into the jungles of fern and orchids, towards the men and women gathered around three small tables of white wickerwork in a sort of crystalline rotunda of foliage and glass.

'—please allow me to present Dr Benedict Theiss.'

The gentleman into whose affairs Lydia had come to St Petersburg to inquire was, so far as she could tell, almost exactly Jamie's six-foot height, with thinning dark hair and a close-clipped, square-cut beard that made a rectangular frame for his rectangular features. He wore a camel-colored tweed suit and a gentleman's cologne scented with sandal-wood and lemon; his big hand within its worn glove was firm and strong. After disowning any true knowledge of blood chemistry: 'It's the glandular secretions that are my specialty, but I was fascinated by the similarity of some of your theories about proteins . . .' Lydia steered the conversation to his clinic in the Vyborg-side slums with the hope of learning something of its funding, and was quickly, and rather disconcertingly, struck with the man's compassionate anger when he spoke of the lives of the poor.

'By and large, the rich don't care,' he said, in a deep, quiet voice that Lydia guessed would have won him his fortune as a nerve doctor to wealthy female clients. 'So long as their factories and their tenement properties turn a profit – present company of course excepted,' he added, with a bow in the direction of Her Royal Highness and Her Royal Highness's equally dark, bejeweled, and Royal sister, 'it doesn't concern the Semyanikovs and the Putilovs and the other owners of property how they live – these people who work for sixteen hours out of twenty-four making boots or guns or lace; these people who sleep two families to a room in chambers I wouldn't house a dog in. They don't see them. I don't think most women who buy lace think that someone had to make that lace, much less that that someone might have a sweetheart or a mother or

a younger brother whom that someone loves as dearly as the
Madame getting into her motor car in the Bolshaya Morskaya
loves her *own* sweetheart or mother or brother.'

At one of the other little tables – an extravagant Lenten tea
had been spread in the fashion of a bistro, among the banks
of hothouse aspidistra and tubbed orange-trees – a man spoke
in Russian, and turning her head, despite her lack of spectacles Lydia saw at the other table the man who could only be
the one Asher had described to her from the Theosophists'
Ball, the silk-clothed peasant who had seen Ysidro when Ysidro
did not want to be seen. He was among a group of ladies –
an impression of gorgeous colors and the susurration of costly
silk – and she could tell by the way they jockeyed each other
for position close to him that they hung on this bearded man's
every word.

One of them – a stout little woman in garish pink who was
sitting on the peasant's knee – looked over at Lydia and translated, 'Father Gregory says, you get these same rich people
out into the country, and suddenly the peasants on their estates
are their friends.'

Lydia was close enough to Theiss to see by his wry sidelong smile that he had no great opinion of Father Gregory.
But he replied with a sigh, 'Father Gregory is quite right, alas,
Annushka. It is fashionable in certain circles to know the
names of your coachman's children and to toss the cook's
little girl candy . . . to show how close one is to the soil, I
suppose.'

But when Annushka in pink translated, the Father shook
his head – Lydia could almost hear the greasy locks of his
hair rattle – and objected:

'No, Father Gregory says that it is the city itself that blinds
men to the joys and griefs of their fellows.'

So earnest was the translator's voice that Dr Theiss said
gently, 'Perhaps the good father is right, Annushka. I am not
a countryman myself.'

As the other ladies of the Circle of Astral Light came over
to be introduced, Lydia found, rather to her surprise, that
Razumovsky – at a fern-bowered table a little distance away,
deep in a flirtation with his hostess – had been absolutely right
when he'd said that her staying unchaperoned at the *izba* on his
property wouldn't make the slightest difference to St Petersburg

society. In London she would have been looked at askance, if she was admitted to the house at all. Here, under the aegis of Razumovsky and his equally tall, equally golden-haired sister Natalia – who greeted her with kisses like a long-lost sister – she found herself accepted, sympathized with (*'That GHASTLY long journey from Paris, my dear, I can't IMAGINE how Irina Muremsky DOES it every year for dress fittings . . .'*), invited to a dozen soirées, dinners, and teas (*'No dancing, I'm afraid, dearest, it IS Lent . . .'*), and introduced to Father Gregory Rasputin (*'My dear, a most extraordinary man . . . a genuine saint . . .'*), though the look Father Gregory gave her when he kissed her, peasant-fashion, on both cheeks was one of the least saintly Lydia had ever encountered.

'He does that to everyone,' giggled plump Annushka.

Evidently, Father Gregory was on his best behavior, for beyond that, for the most part, he sat listening to the conversation – the bulk of which was in French – or trading remarks with his own little cluster of devotees in Russian and consuming caviar with his hands. But when Theiss drew Lydia into speculation about the crossing-over point between the psychic and the physical, the Princess Stana said, 'Perhaps we might ask Father Gregory, since he has within his flesh the power to heal,' and the peasant considered for a time the questions Lydia asked.

At length he shook his head and replied – Annushka Vyrubova translating: 'You look in the wrong place for answers, beautiful lady. I know not whether God sends His healing through my soul or through my flesh, and it doesn't matter.'

'It might,' responded Lydia, 'if by knowing how it is done, you can learn to be a stronger healer, or a better one.'

Father Gregory's mad gray eyes smiled gently into hers. 'Always learning. Beautiful lady, has learning given you that which you desire most in the world?'

And Lydia knew, to the core of her heart, that he meant, *Has it given you a child?*

And felt her eyes flood with tears. At the miscarriages, at the hopes raised and hopes defeated. At the shamed suspicion that she was too flawed to conceive, a suspicion she hid even from the man she loved . . . and at showing it to this smelly stranger with fish eggs in his beard.

As if they had been alone, he laid a grubby hand to her cheek. '*Matyushka*,' he said. 'You learn, the way I sin, because we cannot be other than we are. God knows what He needs you to do . . . And you will have His gift, when the hour is right.' His brows pulled together, and he began to say something else to her, but just then the Princess's sister came rustling over in a pearl-sewn cloud of aubergine-colored taffeta, demanding something in voluble Russian, and Father Gregory turned to her with hands outstretched.

'If you indeed learn the way Rasputin sins, Mrs Asher,' remarked Dr Theiss drily, 'your store of knowledge must be formidable indeed,' and Lydia, remembering the insistent kisses the holy man had given her, burst out laughing.

'Tell me, Doctor,' she asked him. 'How did you come to St Petersburg? I believe His Excellency said you were from Munich?'

Something changed in Theiss's eyes, their warm hazel brightness clouding. 'I was born in a city called Munich, yes,' he said slowly. 'A city which no longer exists. In a country called Bavaria, which is as . . . as gone from this world as any of those Vedic kingdoms these ladies –' he nodded slightly in the direction of the group around Rasputin – 'speak of as having once existed, eons ago in lands now at the bottom of the sea. My country wed herself to Prussia the way a young girl will throw herself into the arms of a bad and violent man, and it is . . . just as painful to watch, for those who love her. I see where Prussia is leading this German Reich of theirs, and I shudder for my country. I am sorry,' he added at once, pressing her hand. 'I did not mean—'

Lydia shook her head. 'You sound very homesick.'

'Only a fool wants to go back to the land of childhood . . . Or perhaps it is the longing for the certainties of childhood that makes a man a fool. I have work here – vital work . . .' His face saddened at some recollection.

'His Excellency has spoken of the good you do at your clinic.'

'Ah – the clinic.' He smoothed the white streaks that marked his beard on either side of his mouth. The note of regret did not leave his voice. 'His Excellency is too kind. At the clinic, I plow the sea. The work there is endless – and soul-breaking. There was a time when I thought I should never be able to return to my true work.'

'Have you been able to, then, Doctor?'

'Thanks to these ladies—' His small gesture took in his hostesses, mutually enraptured in Annushka's account of a seance at Madame Golovina's. 'One does what one can. I'm happy to say that now at least I can afford an assistant, my good Texel, who is there now.'

'Might I visit your clinic? I must say,' she added, following his gaze, 'I would be extremely curious to test our friend Father Gregory's proteins, if he is supposed to be a healer. It might be enlightening to see whether such a talent is indeed embodied in the chemistry of flesh or blood, since I find it difficult to believe it would be in his soul . . .'

'I think you would find,' smiled Theiss, 'that his flesh is as base as his instincts, and that the healing he does comes from the miraculous powers that imbue the minds of his subjects, rather than his own. The human mind is an astonishing thing, Mrs Asher, a thing of miracles – as is the human flesh that the rich, and the rulers of this earth, treat so casually. We are capable of astonishing things, without any need of a fake holy man from Siberia.' He lowered his voice conspiratorially and glanced towards the two princesses. 'But, I beg of you, don't tell Their Royal Highnesses I said so.'

And yet, reflected Lydia, if Father Gregory Rasputin was merely reading what he found in the faces of those who believed in him, he was reading very accurately indeed. For as she shivered in her gray furs on the shallow steps above the courtyard, waiting for the Prince's car to be brought around, Annushka Vyrubova emerged from the palace doors and rustled up to her side.

'Please forgive me, Madame Asher – and please, please understand I would not ask this, except Father Gregory was so deeply troubled by it . . .'

If he asks me for an assignation, what do I say? Lydia blinked uncertainly at the chubby little blonde woman in the dowdy pink gown. Two of the male members of the Circle of Astral Light – young officers in the Tsar's elite Guards regiments – had already taken her aside and let her know that they were interested in beginning *affaires* with her, on what seemed to Lydia to be extremely short acquaintance . . .

'He asks, who is this man that you love, who walks in the . . . in the darkness.' Annushka seemed to be fishing to translate the man's peasant Russian into proper French. 'He said he's seen him – the man with the dark halo—'

While Lydia was still staring at her in shock, the holy man himself ducked and slithered through the group around the door and strode over to them in his heavy boots. '*Tyemno-svyet*,' he agreed, and he made a gesture around his own head and shoulders, as if trying to describe an invisible aura.

'Dark light,' Annushka Vyrubova corrected herself painstakingly. 'He asks, who is this? He has been here, he has seen him at the Winter Palace . . .'

Lydia shook her head, knowing that he meant Ysidro – for her husband had told her of Rasputin's words at the Theosophist Society Ball . . . *I can't let him connect me and Jamie through Ysidro* . . .

Who is this man that you love, who walks in the darkness . . .?

. . . this man that you love . . .

'*Smotritye!*' insisted Father Gregory, pointing. '*Tam!*' And followed this with a flood of Russian, soft-voiced and urgent, as Lydia turned in time to see a woman get out of a motor car at the foot of the shallow steps: so insistent was Father Gregory's voice that, after a quick glance at the group around Razumovsky and the princesses to make sure no one was looking, Lydia whipped her spectacles from her handbag and put them on—

'There is another one of them,' translated Annushka, obviously tremendously worried about either the vehemence – or the outrageousness – of her friend's contention. 'He asks – Father Gregory asks – what are these things that look like men and women, that walk in the dark light? I'm *so* sorry,' she added at once. 'Father Gregory is a visionary, he sees into the souls of men . . . and women, too—'

'*Tyemno-svyet*,' insisted the holy man again, pointing to the woman over whose hand, now, Benedict Theiss was bending in a sort of affectionate punctiliousness.

A beautiful woman in her mid-thirties, clothed in a sulfur-yellow Worth ensemble that must have cost at least two hundred pounds. The thought flashed through Lydia's mind, *Of course she'd wear a veil if she's a vampire* . . . only to be dismissed. *It's five in the afternoon, for Heaven's sake . . . .!* The sun stood high in the Arctic sky.

'He asks, do you not see?'

The woman put back her veil – champagne-colored point-lace that wouldn't have stopped a glance, let alone sunlight – and readjusted the stole of red-and-black sables that hung over her shoulder to her heels. A determined oval face, a firm chin, pale as new wax in the spring sunlight.

'She is another of them,' translated Madame Vyrubova, glancing worriedly from Father Gregory's face to Lydia's, and back to the courtyard as Dr Theiss helped the woman in yellow into the sleek red touring-car, removed his hat to climb in after her. 'What are they, these demons who wear darkness like a garment, to walk among men?'

Lydia said, breathless, 'I don't know. I have never seen that woman in my life. I – I have no idea what Father Gregory is talking about.'

And, thanking her stars that Razumovsky's motor car had drawn up into the place left by the red touring-car as it drove away, she almost ran down the steps, so swiftly that the chauffeur was hard put to open the door for her in time.

THIRTEEN

Asher had always loved Prague. He'd visited it in the early eighties as a student, fascinated by the ancient walls and cobblestone streets of the Bohemian capital, and had felt himself drawn to the profound sense of mysteries that clung to its crumbling university. Though rational by nature, he had returned again and again in his studies to the sense that the city was a threshold – *praha*, in Slavic – to those strange pre-Christian beliefs that even then were his deepest joy. From Prague he had trekked to the nearby mountains a dozen times, to study curious verb-forms – in Slovak, Czech, Serbian and dialects even more obscure – and even more curious beliefs, in out-of-the-way valleys and villages where the Slovak had lived cheek-by-jowl with the Turk for half a millennium.

If any town in Europe would have vampires, he knew it would be Prague.

Ysidro had taken a house in the Old Town that had the look of having originally been a gatehouse to some larger structure. There was a crypt down below, lightless as the pit of Hell, where Asher paid his porters to deposit the trunks and luggage. The journey from Germany into Bohemia had taken only hours, and he had not seen his traveling companion for a day and a half. Only the presence of the train tickets, and the Prague addresses jotted on a slip of notepaper in the Berlin apartment, had informed him that their quarry was not in the German capital, and that they were moving on.

His own temporary residence, on the other side of the river in the Lesser Town, had some extremely Elizabethan inequalities of floor level between parlor and bedchamber, and a lack of both heating and plumbing that reminded Asher strongly of his student days. As he walked back across the great bridge in the chilly spring twilight from an afternoon spent in the paneled book-room of Ysidro's rented nest, he considered turning his steps towards what had been the Ghetto and calling on one of his old mentors. Only the remote possibility that some connection might be established between himself and Ysidro by the local master kept him away.

Yet he sat for a long time in the window of his *pension*, watching the dark street, the starry blackness above the town's steeples, after the city's lights winked out.

> *James,*
>
> *For three years past, the Master of Berlin has sensed the coming of an outsider to that city, six or eight times in a year: subtle, clever, and unseen. Because this outsider does not hunt, he has not seen him, or her. Yet he is aware of the presence, and aware when that presence departs, after a stay of two nights or three.*
>
> *I still seek the Master of Prague.*
>
> *There is a strangeness in this city. For your life, do not be on the streets when darkness falls.*

'Are there vampires in Prague?'

'James.' Old Dr Solomon Karlebach ducked his head a little – a habit Asher remembered from his student days – and peered at his former student from between spectacle rims and those astonishing eyebrows. These days the expression of his mouth was more than ever concealed by the flowing Assyrian beard. 'And you a man of science.' The old man – and he'd been old, Asher reflected, when he'd first met him twenty years ago – hadn't seemed in the slightest surprised to see him, when one of the great-grandchildren of the household had brought him down to the parlor to greet his guest. Even the fact that his former student was now three-fourths bald and embellished with black American side-whiskers and a pince-nez didn't seem to faze the scholar, who had not the least trouble seeing through the disguise.

'True science lies in keeping an open mind.' Asher obeyed the old man's gesture and seated himself on one of the faded chairs with which the parlor was so superabundantly provided. With the curtains drawn to muffle the noise from the narrow street, every object in the room seemed to be the same indeterminate shadow-color, even as he remembered them. White-lace antimacassars still blotched the gloom like mammoth bird-droppings. Half a dozen lampshades, each trimmed with glass-bead fringes, provided a queer glittering quality to the darkness, galaxies of nearly-invisible stars. 'At least so you were always telling me. I have recently wondered if there were some reason behind your certainty.'

'Ah.' The old Jew settled back in his velvet chair (red? purple? brown?) and stroked his beard. His advancing age showed itself most in his hands, which Asher was distressed to see were so twisted with arthritis that the growing yellow claws on the last two fingers of each had left scars on the flesh of the palms. 'And something has happened recently, which has caused you to wonder?' His dark eyes went to the window, as if to satisfy himself at the thin slit of light still visible between the panes of the shadow-color brocade.

'Are there vampires in Prague?'

'The world is full of vampires, Jamie.' Karlebach turned and smiled at the grandson (or great-grandson) who brought in a silver tray with tea on it, served in the Eastern fashion, in ornamental glasses fitted into silver holders, with a little dish of sugar chunks to suck it through. When the boy left: 'Not all are Undead.'

'I know that.' Asher thought about his Chief at the Department, thanking him for saving the South African assignment by killing a sixteen-year-old boy who had been a friend to him, then passing without pause for breath to the next mission he wanted him to undertake.

'*L'chaim*.' Dr Karlebach saluted with his tea glass. 'And I think – from the scars on your neck and the silver chain I see under your right shirt-cuff – that you know yourself about the ones who are. So tell me what you really want to know, Jamie. About the vampires? Or the Others?'

Asher sipped his tea. '*Others*?' He had already seen, when his host had lifted his glass, that Dr Karlebach wore silver chains around his wrists – and probably his throat – as well.

Karlebach's beard shifted a little with his smile. 'Tell me why you ask.'

'I can't.'

'Ah.' For a time the old man studied his face with sudden sadness in those sharp dark eyes. 'So you have become their servant, Jamie? Don't trust them, my boy. Whatever they have told you—'

'I don't.'

But he did, in a way. Even though he was aware that Ysidro had tricked him, as vampires do, into participating in his search for the Lady Irene . . . his concern about the Kaiser, bombs, and poison gas being minimal at best.

And he could see that Karlebach read his trust.

The old man sighed, a tiny breath stirring the extravagant white mustaches. As he had sighed, Asher recalled, when he had told his mentor that he was going to work for the Department. 'Very well.' The deep, rusty voice rumbled over the clipped vowels and sing-song consonants of the Austrian German that the Kaiser and his followers in Berlin would barely have recognized. 'I don't know who – or even what – the Others are, but I think the vampires fear them. Certainly more than they do any of the living. I have never heard mention of them anywhere else; only in Prague. I've seen them – the few times I *have* seen them – near the bridges, and on the islands of the river. They're hard to spot. If you don't go looking for them, you are generally safe.'

'Are they a kind of vampire?'

'They kill.' The old man sketched a small gesture with those yellow-nailed hands. 'I think not so frequently as the vampires do, but also not so carefully. Sometimes two and three men in a month, then nothing for years. Sometimes they will kill a vampire: open its crypt, and summon rats – with whom they have a . . . a *kinship* – by the thousands, to devour it while it sleeps.'

Asher was silent, appalled. Was this what Ysidro had meant by his warning? Or – given the deadly squabbles within the vampire community itself – was there a factional war in Prague too, complicated by the presence of beings that neither side could control?

I still seek the Master of Prague.

There is a strangeness in this city.

'Jamie.'

He was aware how long he'd been silent, wrapped in the shadows of his thought. Old Karlebach was still watching his face, reading him as he'd always been able to read him.

'Don't bargain with them, Jamie,' said the old man again. 'Don't help them, don't believe them, don't let them live one moment beyond what it takes to destroy them safely. No matter what they tell you, about why it is so necessary that you help them do whatever it is they're asking you to help them do. They are lying.'

'Is it that obvious?' Asher tried to speak lightly, but the recollection of how Ysidro had manipulated his dreams stung him still. He found himself, too, extremely conscious that the stripe of light between the curtains had gone from gold to pallid gray and would soon be gone.

'I have studied them.' His teacher sighed again and shook his head. 'Seventy years I have watched them, not believing at first, then believing – and fearing. I have read each book, each manuscript, each monastic record and fragment and gloss the length and breadth of Europe, and I know, as well as any living man knows, who they are and what they do. And how they do it.' His eyes were on Asher, as if he knew all about his dreams of coming war.

'Have you met them?' But he already knew the answer to that. Beneath that flowing ocean of beard, did his teacher bear scars of his own? 'Do they know of your . . . researches?'

'Oh, yes.' Karlebach folded his misshapen hands.

'And in your researches,' said Asher, 'have you ever heard of vampires coming into being without the infection from another vampire?'

The old man frowned, startled and disconcerted by the idea.

'Never.' He shook his head, white hair glinting under the black velvet of his cap. 'Such a creation would never survive the dawnlight, without a master to instruct it . . .' His dark eyes narrowed. 'Is that what you seek?'

'It's one of the things we're seeking.'

'*We.*' Karlebach pronounced the word as if it were worm-wood on his tongue. 'I wish you could hear how you just said that. They're seducers, Jamie. When they need the living – and they often do – they whisper in your dreams, and you find yourself going where you dreamed of going, and doing what you did in your dream—'

As poor Margaret Potton did . . .

And myself.

'Do you think the only kind of seduction is the sort that warms the loins? That is the simplest – the most basic . . . Else why did Dante place the Circle of the Lustful at the top of Hell, just within its gates? Everyone stumbles into that circle sooner or later. It's big. But, as well, they seduce through the intellect, which thinks *it* can best judge the circumstances of whatever the particular instance is that the vampire presents. They cause you to think that you're doing your duty – to country, to love, to a friend, even to God – when in fact you are only doing exactly what the vampire wants you to do. Am I right?'

For a long while Asher did not reply, thinking of the ribbon of blood flowing down the streets of Mafeking in his dream. Of the slim shadow of Ysidro by lantern light, on the other side of a lake of blood. Of the pearl ring Ysidro had given to the woman he had loved. Then he said, 'You are right.'

'It is *all* seduction. For all their strength they are fragile creatures, brittle as handfuls of poisoned glass. You *have* become the servant to one of them, haven't you? His day man – like the shabbas goy my granddaughter employs to light the fires in the stoves here on the Seventh Day, so that her husband will remain holy and yet have warm feet.' The luxuriant mustache moved again in a wry smile.

Asher sat silent, knowing that what his teacher said was right. A whisper out of shadow: *James, we must speak . . .*

He knew what the old man was about to say.

'They kill those who serve them.'

'I know that.'

'And those to whom they speak.'

'Which is why –' Asher glanced at the window, aware that the room was now almost dark – 'I should go.'

'Not for my sake.' Dr Karlebach waved dismissively. 'They know all about me . . . But, yes, for your own. Where do you stay?'

'Across the river. In the Leteriská . . .'

'Be careful when you cross the bridge. It's early enough . . . You're not going to kill him, are you? Your vampire.'

'Not now,' said Asher. 'No.'

'Because he's made you think you can't.'

The old man shook his head, got to his feet, and, when Asher did so, too, gripped his arm briefly, as a man will touch a friend whom he knows to be making a tragic mistake. Then he crossed to a cabinet – a towering marvel of black carving and hidden drawers looming in the shadows – and unlocked one of its compartments, bringing out a small tin of what looked like American snuff and a leather band studded with tiny silver disks. He took Asher's hand – even stooped with age he was nearly Asher's height, still bulky and strong – and slapped the tin into his palm. 'I misspoke myself when I said that the first circle of Hell is Lust, Jamie. Wider still is the outermost circle, the most deadly, the circle of indifference. That state when you are not thinking of anything in particular . . . perhaps you are a little sleepy – I can see that you are short of sleep, traveling with this creature – and off your guard. This will keep you alert. Rub it on your gums, like the Americans so disgustingly do. But only a very little. *Vehrstehe?*'

Asher opened the tin and sniffed: the smell was sharply unpleasant and nothing like tobacco. The tin had once actually contained American snuff: *Leidersdorf's Nic Nac Fine Cut Chewing*, it said.

'And put this on.' Karlebach unbuckled the band. Near where it fastened, Asher saw there was a small turn-screw that operated a tiny pair of hidden jaws – like a miniature instrument of torture on the inside of the leather. When twisted, the jaws would extend and bite into the flesh of the wrist. 'If you need more than my little powder to keep yourself awake. Pain will usually serve against the vampire, though not always. The best remedy against the vampire is distance – the more of it, the better.'

Silently, Asher held out his wrist and helped the crooked fingers affix the buckle tight.

'Thank you. More than I can say. If there is anything I can do to repay—'

'There is.' Karlebach put both hands on Asher's shoulders, looked hard into his face. 'Don't let this thing live. Kill it. Else you take his sins upon yourself. Every kill he makes henceforth will be upon your head as well as his. God has put this opportunity into your hand, James. Tomorrow morning if you can—'

'I can't.'

'So it would have you think. So *he* would have you think – for they are as human as we are, and as mortal . . .'

The dark eyes held his for a long moment more, under polar-bear brows. Distantly, the clock in the bell house was striking nine. 'Go with God, my old friend. Because you're going to need His help. And Him, too, you should think perhaps to repay.'

As Asher passed beneath the gothic tower that guarded the Old City end of the bridge he thought he saw movement beyond its shadow, but when he reached the spot, beside the stone railing past the first of its aisle of statues, there was nothing there. He leaned over the lichened rail, saw dark water gleam below him in the gaslight. A thug, a pickpocket, lurking out of sight now that the day's traffic of omnibuses and peddlers' carts was gone?

Or something else?

A kinship with rats, Karlebach had said. *I have never heard mention of them anywhere else; only in Prague.*

They kill. Sometimes they will kill a vampire . . .

. . . summon rats by the thousands . . .

A species of vampire? Asher drew back from the rail, continued across the bridge. Found himself holding to the center of the way as much as he could.

A variant form of the bacillus by which, Lydia had theorized, human flesh was altered, one cell at a time, into cells that did not decay with age, but combusted with the touch of the sun's light?

He thought about the envelope in his luggage, containing snippets of the Lady Irene's bedroom carpet, stiff with dried vampire blood. *Marya's and Ippo's* . . . He could still see their faces, distorted with hatred, for him and for their master. For years, Lydia had spoken of getting her hands on vampire blood to study, though not – Asher was acutely aware – since the death of Margaret Potton in Constantinople. He wondered now if she would welcome the sample. *One would have to handle it very carefully, of course, lest there be an accident and you infect yourself*, she had said . . .

And then what? If your body was infected with the tainted blood – if indeed it was a bacillus – but you had no master vampire to gather your mind and soul into his own, to preserve it during the death of the body . . . would you simply die? Was that what had happened to those poor children in Petersburg?

Or had it been something else?

He was acutely grateful for the dim lights of the Lesser Town's cafés, for the presence of street vendors, students, flower sellers and knife grinders who set up shop in the angles of those cobblestoned ways, as he climbed the stairs of his *pension* and locked himself in.

He left the lamp burning beside the bed as he slept.

FOURTEEN

The woman kept repeating something that Lydia knew could only be, 'Will he be all right? Will he be all right?' but since she was speaking Russian it actually could have been anything. It didn't matter. The tears of anxiety running down her face, the way her stooped thin body trembled in the awkward circle of Lydia's arm, made translation supererogatory. Annushka Vyrubova, on the woman's other side, murmured softly in Russian, comforting words, while at the battered table of the clinic's curtained-in consulting-room, Dr Benedict Theiss unwrapped the gory wad of torn pillowcases from around the young man's hand and examined the fingers that were left.

Lydia whispered in French, 'What happened?'

'An accident in the factory,' Madame Vyrubova whispered back. 'They've stepped up the production quotas because of the new battleships, and the poor boy had been working since eight last night. No wonder he didn't get his hand out of the press quickly enough . . .'

Despite the morphia – the first thing Theiss had administered when the young man had been half-carried into the clinic by his mother and brothers – the patient screamed, and on the bench between Lydia and Madame Vyrubova the mother cried out in anguish, like an echo. The bleached canvas curtains of the consulting 'room,' only slightly higher than a man's head, hung partly open, and past them the clinic – which had the appearance, in the thin clear sunlight of the first springlike day, of having begun life as a small factory itself – was filled with a commingled reek of blood, carbolic soap, and unwashed clothing and bodies, a combination of stinks that, despite herself, Lydia hated.

In her years as a medical student she had worked at hospitals, sustained through clinic duty only by her stepmother's smirking assurances that, 'You'll hate it, dear, you know . . .'

Well, of course someone has to see to the poor things, but I don't see why it has to be you . . . That had been her Aunt Faith. And, *Darling, I know it's* bien à la mode *to take an interest in the poor, but surely one day a month at a settlement house – Andromache Brightwell knows a PERFECTLY clean and decent one – would do* . . .

After which, of course, Lydia had been completely unable to protest that she, too, disliked the stinks and the wastefulness and the sense of speechless futility that filled her in the face of poverty. It had been impossible to admit that she did not share the usual womanly motives of her stepmother's friends who went in for nursing the 'less fortunate', as they were politely called . . .

She couldn't tell them – the aunts who had raised her, the exquisite slender woman that her father had married the year Lydia was sent away to school – that what she sought was knowledge of the human body, of those squeamish fascinating details that women weren't supposed to know about or want to know about. *A thing of miracles*, Benedict Theiss had called the human body . . . Tubes and nodules, nooks and crannies, nerves and bones and the secrets hidden in the marrow . . . Blood and spit and semen, why and how. Working in the clinics was a stepping stone to the end that she sought, which was research for its own sake – knowledge for its own sake – the pursuit of goals far beyond the tying up of a drunkard's bruises or the Sisyphean labor of primary care for the poor.

The big clinic room had recently been painted a dreary shade of beige, and there were about two dozen people on the benches at one end, men and women – several with children clustered around them and babies slung in shawls at their bosoms – in the faded, mended, ill-fitting and unwashed garments that people make do with when every available penny is being spent on rent and fuel and food if it could be afforded. They were thin, in the way that even the poorest of the London denizens of settlement houses and clinics were not: thin and wary, like animals that have been frightfully abused. Lydia recalled the streets she and Madame Vyrubova had been driven through, to come to this dingy yellow-brick building on the Samsonievsky Prospect. Even through the comforting blur of myopia, it was clear to her that these slums were worse than anything she'd ever seen in London, grown up like oozing sores around the factories.

'Please forgive us for interrupting you,' said Lydia, when Dr Theiss had finished his task and washed his hands – he was reaching for his frock coat, hung on its peg, as if to get himself ready to welcome his visitors. She held up her hand. 'Don't. I shouldn't have asked to come.' Though it had been, in fact, Madame Vyrubova who'd suggested it. *Of course dear Dr Theiss will be delighted to receive us. He always is . . .*

He probably always was for this dumpy little woman who was said to be the best friend of the Empress and almost a member of the imperial family.

'I see now you have many more important matters to attend to.'

Madame Vyrubova looked surprised at her words – it had probably been a long time since anyone had professed matters more important than her warm-hearted desire to make the world a better place – but the physician's hazel eyes thanked Lydia's understanding. 'It's kind of you to think of me, Dr Asher. Yet I know you spoke, when last we met, of my research, and one could not be other than delighted to take a moment's rest when our Annushka has come all this way to visit.' He took Madame Vyrubova's hand and bowed deeply.

'Texel—' At the lifting of Theiss's voice, the man Jamie had

identified as an agent of German Intelligence came through
the door of the wooden partition that divided the great whitewashed brick room. 'Is there tea? Thank you. Would you
please let my friends know –' his gesture took in the men and
women waiting on the benches – 'that I must perform the
offices of society for ten short minutes, and then I will return?'

'*Bien sûr*, doctor.'

Lydia struggled with the impulse to slip her spectacles from
her beaded handbag and sneak a better look at the man, who
at that distance was little more than an impression of stooping
height, arms that seemed slightly too long, skimpy mutton
chops hanging on his jaws like socks on a clothesline, and
thin fairish hair slicked unappetizingly to a dolichocephalic
skull. Even his voice was thin, with a nasal quality to it and
– though Lydia's ear for accents was not nearly as good as
her husband's, especially not when everyone was speaking
French – an inflection that differed from Theiss's. As Theiss
led them through the doorway into a laboratory – and thence
to a chamber beyond it, barely wider than its window, which
served as a sitting room – she inquired, 'Mr Texel also a
physician, I think you said?'

'A medical student.' And, with a humorous half-smile: 'And
one, I suspect, who blotted his copybook a little with the
Kaiser's police. He's an Alsatian, from Strasbourg; he came
to me at first only because he needed the work. Yet he has
found – as I have – the profound ease of heart that comes
from working towards the good of one's fellow man.'

Or he says he has. Anyone else might have doubted James
Asher's ability to remember the face of a man he'd seen on
three brief occasions seventeen years previously, but Lydia knew
her husband's memory for faces and details was as extraordinary as his ear for accents and did not doubt for a moment that
it was the same man. For Dr Theiss, with his dislike of the new
German Reich, a detail about 'blotting one's copybook with
the Kaiser's police' – if worked artfully into the conversation
– would be an infallible Open Sesame to trust . . . Was Alsace
one of those places that Germany had taken away from France?
Lydia recalled her friend Josetta had mentioned something about
it, and she tried to remember what.

'I beg you will excuse me for intruding on your work,' said
Lydia, as the scientist poured out tea for the three of them,

where the window's sunlight made small lace patterns on tablecloth and dishes. 'It truly is unforgivable of me. But I read your article on serums in the blood, and I'm afraid I allowed my own enthusiasms get away with me. How on earth do you manage to continue your researches, with the volume of work you do here?'

And who is giving you the money to do it?

'There was a time when it was impossible.' Theiss smiled at her. 'But now, thanks to Madame –' he nodded at Madame Vyrubova and saluted her with his cup – 'who put me in contact with some most generous patrons . . . That was how it was that I was able to hire my good Texel in the first place; and, of course the donation of this building – and of another excellent laboratory facility not far from here – was of inestimable assistance. And I must admit,' he added ruefully, 'that my soul is so insufficiently evolved that I *did* grudge not being able to pursue my own researches, for so many years . . .'

'Oh, Professor—' simpered Madame Vyrubova.

'It was the profession's loss,' said Lydia. 'Yet this most recent article of yours . . . I thought it showed signs of a completely new direction in your researches . . .'

It was a shot in the dark, because Lydia had barely skimmed Theiss's latest work – published eighteen months previously in the *Journal des Medicins* – but Theiss beamed like an author whose more subtle themes had been applauded. Lydia put on her spectacles, and with Madame Vyrubova tagging politely on their heels, was taken on a tour of the laboratory next door, which was obviously – to her trained eyes – set up for experiments involving the meticulous testing, filtering, distillation and chemical analysis of the various components of blood.

'Oh, I covet your microscope,' she cried jestingly, and Theiss responded with a gallant little bow, hand over heart, as if he, like she, found relief in being able to talk with someone else who understood the quest for knowledge for its own sake. It was a relief, Lydia reflected, only to talk with another physician. Much as she enjoyed the stylish social rounds she'd been taken on by Razumovsky's sister (*'Call me Natalia Illyanova, darling, Madame Korova sounds so formal . . .'*) in her quest for information about people who were never seen by daylight, she found the constant attempts of the young Army officers and members of the Court to get her into bed wearing in the extreme. The upper social circle of St Petersburg was just as gossipy as that of her London relations, but far more heated: everyone – with the exception of Madame Vyrubova, who seemed to be oblivious to it all – appeared to be engaged in adultery with everyone else.

And as Jamie had said, NONE of them seemed to go to bed before dawn or to rise before dusk. If it weren't for their bank accounts she would suspect them all of sleeping in coffins.

By contrast, like herself, Benedict Theiss was a researcher in his heart. Perhaps, reflected Lydia, it was why she found the man so enormously sympathetic – had it not been for the presence of Texel in his household, and the monk Rasputin's disconcerting reaction to the lady in the red touring-car, she would have concluded that there was nothing to investigate. When Theiss spoke of working far into the nights, of the limitations of working with very small sample-groups (*how small?* Lydia wondered), of the difficulties in obtaining the absolutely most up-to-date journals – which were censored, like everything else in Russia – she found herself in danger of forgetting all that Jamie had told her about the scheme to ally a vampire with the German Reich.

Even now she found herself wondering, *Was Jamie wrong?*

'Ach—' Theiss looked at his watch. 'Please, please excuse me, dear ladies . . . It is just that my unfortunates out there, they wait so long and so patiently, and there are so few to succor them . . . Texel!' He raised his voice only slightly, but the younger man appeared at once in the doorway. 'Texel, would you please continue to give Dr Asher a tour of my experiments, and explain to her whatever she wishes to know? Texel has been of invaluable help . . . Thank you, Texel . . .'

He clasped his assistant's hand as he hurried out to his patients once more.

'I'm fascinated by the filtration process that Dr Theiss is using.' Lydia smiled across at the glowering Alsatian. 'Is that a dilute alcohol solution across plaster of Paris, as Pasteur did?' The addition of spectacles to her perception hadn't altered it: there was still an air of meagerness about the assistant, far deeper than form or face or hair. As if everything about him were begrudged and produced as cheaply as the market would bear. His replies to her questions were short and uninformative

– on two occasions going so far as outright lies, when she asked him, with an expression of *naïveté*, about processes that she herself already knew about.

What would Jamie make of the man's accent? Was it really from Strasbourg? Jamie could place anyone in Oxford – scholar, servant, or shopkeeper – within ten miles of his or her birthplace after five minutes' conversation, and according to him, regional dialects in German were far more pronounced than in England, almost separate languages. Would that show up in the French they were speaking? Evasions aside, it didn't take someone of Jamie's talents at observation to notice that the equipment in the laboratory was all new, and all of the same degree of newness: bought within the last year and a half.

And none of it cheap. Had that been one of the wealthy patrons Madame Vyrubova had introduced Dr Theiss to? Princess Stana, or that frightful Madame Muremsky, who would go on and *on* about the Slavic Race's unique position in the History of the Cosmos?

Or someone a little less disinterested?

And how might she ask, without word of it getting back to the vampire in question, that someone was on his trail?

'I'm sure I have bored you ladies long enough,' Texel concluded, with his tight manufactured smile, and herded them towards the door. 'Poor Madame Vyrubova, I can see you yawning . . .'

'Not at all!' lied the little lady gallantly. 'Indeed,' she confided to Lydia, 'I have frequently thought that *dear* Dr Theiss should make a scientific examination of Father Gregory's brain. Such *genius*! Such God-given ability must surely have refined and altered the very substance of his tissues . . . Many and many a time he has cured my *terrible* headaches, and the dear Empress's, too, with just a touch . . . And sometimes with only a few words over the telephone . . .'

Lydia was just removing her spectacles as they stepped through the door into the clinic – even if these people were factory workers and stevedores, she wasn't going to exhibit herself to them looking like a goggled stork – when she saw Dr Theiss deep in conversation with the woman in the stole of black-and-red sables who had picked him up in her red touring car at the Princess Stana's less than a week ago.

Lydia quickly put her spectacles back on. There was no mistaking that fur – it must have cost hundreds of guineas – nor the woman's height and bearing. *Dark light*, Rasputin had said . . .

These demons who wear darkness like a garment, to walk among men . . .

She is another of them . . .

Who is this man that you love? The man with the dark halo . . .

Lydia drew a shaky breath. Whoever she was, today she was wearing a Doucet suit of sage-green and gold, which set off her honey coloring without shouting, *I cost more than this building!* Which, of course, M'sieu Doucet's suits did . . .

What was it Don Simon had said to her, one of those evenings on that long, frightening journey to Constantinople? That even fairly modest investments could accrue a phenomenal amount of interest in two centuries?

Theiss led the lady in the sables to one of the benches, where a young man got to his feet. He was clearly a boy from the countryside, recently come in, like so many, for work in the factories: thin, dark-haired, and shy in his faded peasant trousers, his countrified boots and striped red-and-blue shirt. The boy started to bow awkwardly, but the woman in green took his hands, shook her head, said something that made the youth look quickly around him, as if fearing they had been overheard.

'Who is that?'

Interrupted in her encomiums of Father Gregory's holiness and healing skills, Madame Vyrubova looked. 'Oh, that's Petronilla Ehrenberg.' By her tone, it was someone she had met in society at least once or twice. 'One of dear Dr Theiss's most generous patrons. I cannot *imagine* why *dear* Father Gregory spoke of her as he did the other day. He is a visionary . . . though she *is* a little *outré*,' she added, her brow puckering like a gossipy schoolgirl's. 'I understand she does not go into society much – a widow, I believe. One seldom sees her, but I know that she does great good for the poor. It was she who paid for this building, you know, and I believe for the other laboratory facility dear Dr Theiss spoke of.'

'A compatriot of Dr Theiss?'

'Now, I *hope* you're not going to be like so many people and think all Germans are like those terrible Prussians! She is *perfectly* civilized. Just don't let her talk to you alone—' Madame Vyrubova dropped her voice as Dr Theiss came towards them, followed by the lovely Madame Ehrenberg. The Russian boy, still standing beside his bench, gazed after her like one struck by a vision. 'She has a positive *mania* about St Michael and St George, and will talk your ear off about them if you let her. She has spoken about founding a nunnery devoted to their veneration—'

'Rather like my cousin Bertie's fixation with Joan of Arc, I suppose.'

'Oh, you poor *dear*! My Aunt Catherine had a fixation or an obsession or whatever it is that they call them, about . . . *Dear* Dr Theiss!' She held out her hands to their host. 'We came to bid you farewell – that is, if dear Madame Asher has seen all that she wishes—?'

'Thank you.' Lydia clasped the scientist's hand.

'It has been my pleasure . . . So much so that I have entirely forgotten my manners.' He smiled again, his shy, self-deprecating smile. 'First I neglect my visitors, then . . . Madame Ehrenberg, may I present Dr Asher, a fellow scientist and physician from England?'

'Scarcely a scientist,' denied Lydia quickly, seeing the flicker of steely wariness in the other woman's green eyes. 'That is, I do medical research at the Radcliffe Infirmary. On glands, you know.'

'How wonderful!' Madame Ehrenberg had a deep voice for a woman, soft and velvety; tall like Lydia, in her neat subdued symphony of green and gold – her hands, even, were gloved in green kid. 'A thousand times I've read of such things in the newspapers – of women studying medicine, or the law, or some such thing, in England . . . I'm afraid you may find even St Petersburg very behind the times, so far as the rights of half the human race are concerned . . . Or,' she added, with a glance around her, 'considerably more than half. I read, only the other day, how it is research into the glands that will, one day, open the doors of immortality to the human race.'

Lydia had read that, too – half-cocked articles in the penny newspapers, extolling mysterious 'distillations' and 'infusions'

taken from the glands of monkeys and pigs, to 'rejuvenate'
the aged indefinitely. But only the aged who were wealthy,
as far as she could ascertain.

'At the moment,' she said tactfully, 'I'm afraid I pursue far
more pedestrian goals, like working out the relationship of
the various elements of the glandular system . . . One can't
perceive much until one knows what one is looking at, and
at the moment we know so little.'

Thus, chatting of commonplaces (*'IS that a Doucet?'*), the
three ladies were conducted to the doors of the clinic, which
opened into a grimy little court off Samsonievsky Prospect.
Smoke from the Putilov armaments works turned the chilly
sunlight a sickly yellow, burning Lydia's throat and lungs.
Other stinks mingled with it, as bad as the clinic they had
just left: choked sewers, overflowing latrines in every tenement yard, a dead horse somewhere nearby. As Madame
Vyrubova's car was brought up, M'sieu Texel opened the
clinic doors for them; turning back to clasp her host's hand
once more, Lydia – still wearing her spectacles – saw that
the young Russian boy to whom Madame Ehrenberg had been
speaking had followed them to the door, his young heart in
his eyes.

He will dream of her tonight, thought Lydia as she got into
the car.

As it pulled away – and Madame Vyrubova returned to her
earlier topic of Father Gregory's miracles and the dozens of
other miracle workers (*'Many of them* quite *dishonest, I'm
afraid . . .'*), who moved through St Petersburg society, it
occurred to Lydia what it was about Madame Ehrenberg that
had troubled her so.

It was something she would not have noticed, she realized
– turning in her seat for one last look at Dr Theiss and Madame
Ehrenberg in the grimy sunlight before the clinic doors – had
she not spent many weeks in the company of Don Simon
Ysidro.

She couldn't have sworn to it, but she was almost certain
that Madame Ehrenberg had not been breathing.

FIFTEEN

'What happened in Prague?'

'Why is it that you assume that anything did?' Ysidro took his accustomed seat, across from Asher, in the Royal Bavarian State Railway's immaculate green plush first-class seats, and withdrew from a pocket his deck of cards. Saxony's forests swallowed the lights of Dresden. The vampire's long fingers, with their pale strong claws like lacquered ivory, shuffled and cut, shuffled and cut, like some delicate machine, while his colorless eyes held Asher's.

'It seems to have taken you three nights to make contact with the master there.'

'The vampires of Prague are not like vampires elsewhere. The Master of Prague misses no fledgling, has heard naught of any who has made it a habit these three years to travel to Berlin. This means nothing,' he added, dealing out the cards between them. 'Fire from Heaven might rain upon Berlin and every other city in Germany, and the vampires of Prague would make little of it. They are old.'

His mind on the vampires of Prague, Asher didn't see him move. But he seemed to jerk awake after momentary sleep to find his left hand prisoned in a cold grip like a machine. With a long nail, Ysidro moved Asher's sleeve up to show Dr Karlebach's silver-studded leather band. 'That is new,' he observed.

'A toy. To keep me awake if I need it.' *Not that it did me any good a second ago, damn him . . .*

Ysidro's grip tightened warningly. 'There is a shop in Prague that sells such toys?'

'There is.'

He won't break the bones, Asher told himself. *He can't as long as he needs me . . .*

He kept his eyes on the vampire's, and his jaw ached with the effort not to cry out in pain.

'The vampires of Prague,' said Ysidro, 'sought from me assurance as to when I would kill you and your lady.'

His voice held steady with excruciating effort, Asher said, 'How do they know about Lydia?'

'They know of no man who can be trusted to serve, who is not threatened through the safety of his wife.'

He wanted to ask, *What assurance did you give?* but knew if he tried to speak he would probably scream.

Ysidro let go of his hand. There was silence for a time, save for the clacking of the train wheels, the light flutter of the cards as the vampire resumed shuffling them, and Asher's hoarse breath. 'I do not keep you in ignorance from malice, James,' Ysidro said after a time, 'but to guard you from what would be your death.'

'Were that entirely so,' Asher returned, a little surprised that he could speak at all, 'you would content yourself with a verbal warning, now that we're nowhere near Prague.' Across the little railway table, the vampire's face was expressionless. 'Neither you nor I knows what's afoot or what's involved with this . . . this interloper in Petersburg, who might or might not be the same as the interloper in Berlin. Neither you nor I know what piece of evidence will unlock the puzzle. Nor do either of us know how high or how deadly are the stakes. It may be that this interloper's contact with Benedict Theiss is only the tip of an iceberg, the visible tenth of a danger more perilous and vast, which we have no concept of . . . and may not ever see, if we continue to hide facts from one another.'

That said, he at last trusted himself to sit back a little and carefully flex his fingers, which he was astonished to find able to move at all.

'Whatever it is,' he continued, 'I think we both agree that whatever it was that Lady Irene learned, no league between a vampire and *any* human government – whether that government is part of the Triple Alliance or the Triple Entente or outside them both like the Americans – can come to good.'

Ysidro nodded – what, for him, was a nod.

'I know about the Others in Prague—'

'You did not meet them?' Only the half beat of quickness gave away the Spaniard's concern.

'Do you think I would have survived a meeting?'

'No.' The pale brows flexed, infinitesimally. 'I don't know. To the best of my knowledge – or the knowledge of the vampires of Prague – they make no bargains with men.' He dealt the cards, gathered them up; dealt and gathered again. 'I take it you spoke with the Jew near the Spanish Synagogue?'

'I did,' said Asher. 'He told me to kill you without delay. He told me also that, like you, he has never heard of vampires generating spontaneously. And yet they – and you – and the Others – must have originated somehow.'

'The Others are a variety of vampire,' said Ysidro, 'in that, according to the Master of Prague, the first of them were made as vampires are made. This was five hundred years ago, in the time of the Great Plague. But whether the Plague had aught to do with this matter is not written, perhaps never known. The vampires of Prague have long tried to destroy these crea-tures. They were humans once, these things – like the vampire, the transformation seems to render the organs of generation otiose. But in all the years of observing them, the vampires of Prague have not seen how this condition is transmitted. They do not appear particularly human.

'I had wished,' the vampire went on, with a slight hesita-tion in his whispery voice, 'to have spoken with Mistress Lydia of these things. 'Twould have been useful, to hear her opinion as to whether this agent of the blood, as she deems it, which transmits the vampire state from master to fledg-ling, can undergo mutation and create a sport or changeling unlike its progenitor. The matter would interest her vastly, I think.'

'Perhaps too much,' said Asher, with a wry twist to his mouth.

In his companion's eye he saw Ysidro's amused recogni-tion of exactly what risks Lydia was likely to run in pursuit of such knowledge. 'You have reason.' And, somewhere in the back of those sulfurous pupils, Asher thought he saw regret as well.

'In any case,' pursued Asher, 'we know the . . . the agent, whatever it is, of vampirism in the blood does mutate. When Horace Blaydon tried to create a serum that would make an artificial vampire, it turned his son into a monster. Whether that was because he did not understand something in the process that turns a human into a vampire—'

'More than likely,' murmured Ysidro. 'We do not ourselves understand it. Oh, we know how it is, that a man or a woman becomes physically vampire,' he added, in response to Asher's raised brows. 'And we know what must be done to preserve the fledgling's soul and keep the life from winking out during that process. We know that the blood of humans or animals will sustain vampire flesh, but that only the paroxysm of energy released by human death will renew our abilities to manipulate the human mind. But why this should be, and by what mechanism we drink that death and turn it into powers of our own – how it is, that without the kill, we cannot hunt, nor defend ourselves from those who hunt us – these things are hid from us. Even as it is hid from you, why it is that humans love, and die inside without loving.'

His hands grew still and he pressed the palms together, long fingers extended like a parody of prayer, and rested his lips against them, yellow eyes momentarily dreaming . . . *Of what?* wondered Asher.

Of the friend whose capacity for loving he had once treasured, ninety years ago?

Or only of whoever it was – in Dresden or Prague or Berlin, whore or bootblack or back-alley drunkard – whose life he had most recently drawn to feed the energies of his own wary mind?

Every kill he makes henceforth will be upon your head . . .

Three mornings had come and three sunsets had bled away to darkness, and Asher was no closer to any decision about his traveling companion – whose life rested in his hands with every sun that rose – than he had been in St Petersburg or Oxford or back in London four years ago.

They need the living, Karlebach had said. *They often do . . .*

You HAVE become the servant to one of them, haven't you?

Had Ysidro guessed, four years ago after Horace Blaydon's death, that he might need a servant again?

'So whoever our interloper is,' Asher said at last, 'he – or she – isn't from Prague . . . and apparently couldn't be one of the Others. And I presume is not from Dresden either?'

'They are a parcel of provincials in Dresden,' retorted Ysidro. 'I doubt there is one among them who could find St Petersburg on a map.' He gathered up his cards again.

By morning, when the train pulled into the München Hauptbahnhof, the bruises on Asher's hand, left by the vampire's fingers, had turned nearly black.

*   *   *

Following the incorporation of the Kingdom of Bavaria into the German Reich – after the mysterious death of its penultimate Wittelsbach monarch and the hasty incarceration of that unfortunate young man's brother, both mad as bedbugs – the city of Munich was, for all intents and purposes, as dangerous to Asher as Berlin. He spent Tuesday, the twenty-fifth of April, reading newspapers and pacing the small baroque town house that Ysidro had taken on a narrow court off Sebastiens Platz, and, to judge by the train tickets he found there on his return the following morning, Ysidro had had no information from the local master. Asher duly summoned a cab and porters, loaded up Ysidro's many trunks, and took the noon train for Nürnberg.

The sun was westering over the old university town when the train arrived. By the time Asher had installed the luggage and coffin trunk in the cellar deep beneath the half-timbered town house to which his papers directed him, the shadows were long in the cobbled streets. He found his own residence, a *pension* on the other side of the river in the shadow of an ancient church tower, and listened to the bells of the town at intervals through the night. Nürnberg had something to it of the shadowed atmosphere of Prague: an uneasy sense of gothic secrets and occult studies that Asher would have unhesitatingly pooh-poohed before he had met Ysidro . . . or spoken to Solomon Karlebach.

Most of the vampires he had met had been creatures of the last few centuries, fascinating to him as an historian of folklore and as a linguist – if terrifying – but human: the links that bound them to their former humanness plain to see. The single vampire survivor from the Middle Ages that he had encountered had been mad – how long could a human mind remain sane, in the circumstances imposed by the vampire state?

He wasn't sure, and he didn't think Ysidro would give him a straight answer on the subject.

That vampires became more acute, and more powerful, with age was another disturbing reflection, and as he crossed the bridge to the house on the Untere Kraemersgasse in the gray twilight of pre-dawn he was prey to the uneasy sensation of walking into a trap. The train to Frankfurt would leave at seven. No vampire could survive the dove-colored dawn-light that filled the streets at five, but who knew at what hour they slept in their coffins?

The fact that upon his arrival at Ysidro's rented nest he found, not train tickets, but a note from Ysidro, saying, *There are others with whom I must speak*, did not improve his mood. The newspapers he had read through yesterday's long afternoon were filled with speculations about the delicate balances of power between the ancient empires of Austria and Russia and the new Reich of Germany: Serbian states demanding independence from their Austrian rulers, German populations insisting upon reunion with the German Homeland, the Russians threatening the Austrians on behalf of their Slavic Serbian brethren . . . *Can't the Undead, even, keep themselves out of factional fights?*

He spent the ensuing day back at his pension beside the old church tower, organizing his memoranda about every house where Ysidro had stayed – the baroque town-palace in Warsaw, the fifteenth-century crypt at Prague, and the current half-timbered house on the Ludwigstrasse – and mailed it to himself, care of his bank in Oxford. During his days with the Department, he'd maintained his own private list of safe houses – and rentals, the owners of which would ask no questions – in every city in Europe. At a guess, though, Ysidro had more money at his disposal than the Department ever had.

The following morning at seven, he – and presumably the coffined Ysidro, though he and the Spanish vampire were careful not to meet in any city where the Undead had their dwelling places – were on the train for Frankfurt. After twenty-four hours in that city – noon on the twenty-ninth of April – they moved on to Köln on the Rhine: once a Free City of the Empire, then French, and now, to the vengeful fury of every red-blooded Frenchman living, German again.

And coming into the old stone house in the Ältstadt on Monday morning, Asher found on the harpsichord there a stack of envelopes, torn open and empty of letters, all bearing the address of Petronilla Ehrenberg, Heilege-Ursulasgasse, Neuehrenfeld . . . a village on the outskirts of Köln.

All were from someone named Colonel Sergius von Brühlsbuttel, of Charlottenstrasse, in Berlin.

Beside the envelopes lay a pair of train tickets. Asher sighed.

'It would have to be Berlin.'

SIXTEEN

The train for Berlin would leave at a few minutes to one. Asher stood for a short time, turning the envelopes over in his hands. Expensive paper, stiff and watermarked – at least three shillings a packet – and good quality ink. In keeping with the 'von'. Almost certainly a Prussian *Junker*. And from contact with him – over a period of two years, ending in April of 1910 – this Madame Ehrenberg had gone on to St Petersburg and Benedict Theiss, presumably with M'sieu Texel in tow.

Had the Köln vampires been with Ysidro, when he'd searched Petronilla Ehrenberg's house?

And if they had, had their presence – or simply a lack of training in the secret arts – kept Ysidro from making a thorough search? Asher reached into his jacket to touch the envelope still tucked into the secret pocket in its lining, the last letter that Ysidro had written to the Lady Irene Eaton in her days as a living woman . . . the letter she had kept, not in her desk with the others, but behind a wall panel in her bedroom. Would Ysidro have searched further, had he not been interrupted by the arrival of the Petersburg vampires? Would he have known where to look?

The tram that Asher took out to Neuehrenfeld was filled with laborers heading to work on the newest installment of fortifications that the Kaiser had ordered to defend the city against France's inevitable attempt – once The War that everyone was expecting got started – to retake it from the Germans who had seized it from them. Asher listened to them, the desultory complaints about the military, bellyaching about one's wife or one's children, and, *Have-you-got-a-cigarette?* in the sing-song Kölsch dialect. Some of the men joked with the charwomen and laundresses on their way out to the homes of the wealthy in that stylish suburb, the cooks who lived in town with husbands who kept taverns or drove cabs. They stayed on as the men got off, the men making their way towards the embankments of torn-up earth, the mountains of brick and concrete where the guns would go. As he watched them clamber over the muddy earthworks, Asher wanted to scream after them, *You don't understand what it will be like . . .*

But it wasn't they who would have the power to do anything. In another few years, it would be they, he thought, who would be manning those emplacements against the oncoming French. Who would mow the Frenchmen down like wheat before the Reaper's scythe.

He closed his eyes. *And it's up to me, to make sure they – and the people who live after the war – don't have officially-sanctioned vampires to contend with as well.*

Petronilla Ehrenberg's house reminded him a good deal of Lady Irene Eaton's: opulent, discreet, set back from the tree-shaded semi-rural roadway behind a high wall. Easy to hire servants to come and clean in the daytime; a pleasant place in which to maintain a night-time life. He put in three-quarters of an hour just observing the street, the neighborhood, and most especially the patrol patterns of the local constables. The last thing he needed was to be arrested in Germany within half a mile of a major military fortification against the French.

He let himself in with his picklocks, through the rear door.

It took him just under ninety minutes to find what he sought.

If the woman was working with German Intelligence, they would have given her advice on where to conceal things . . . If they had, she hadn't taken it. He found none of the usual safes and sliding panels of which the Auswärteges Amt was so fond. But he'd had experience enough with amateur agents to have learned all the myriad places where financial documents were likely to be kept – from loose floorboards under corners of rugs, to trunks tucked away in the attic. And financial documents would mean a box. *Thank God it's not a railway ticket I'm looking for, or a lost will, like a detective in fiction.* And she would have taken into account that whoever cleaned the house was there when she was unable to supervise . . .

That probably meant purpose-built concealment.

After investigating the floorboards of the attic – à la *The Sign of Four* – and the darker nooks among the rafters there, he worked his way systematically down the attic stairs, then those of the third floor, which were uncarpeted. The stairs from the second floor to the third were ill lit and covered with cheap drugget, and he checked top and bottom steps first . . . and found the drugget at the top was not nailed, but held in place with a batten, screwed only at the ends.

The cache was under the hinged second step, neatly folded in a couple of boxes that had once contained shoes.

No bank books – she'd taken those with her. But banking records, going back for decades, detailing property transfers, deeds of gift, investments . . . all those things whose counterparts Lydia was searching for, even now, through the records of every German bank in St Petersburg that Prince Razumovsky could bribe or command. The first box held the older records, commencing in 1848, probably shortly after Petronilla Ehrenberg became vampire – only the name she used then was Petra Ehrenberg. In the 1870s, she'd transferred everything to a 'niece' called Paulina, and it was as 'Paulina' that she'd bought this house, which was deeded – along with other properties in Köln and elsewhere, and considerable railway and shipping stock – to 'Petronilla Ehrenberg' in 1896.

In the second box he found more recent records, pertaining to a dozen trips to Berlin between October of 1907 and April of 1910. In November of 1909 – when winter would reduce the daylight there to a few hours around noon – there had been a trip to St Petersburg, followed by the purchase, through three sets of agents, of the deconsecrated monastery of St Job, on the north bank of the Neva, at that city's edge. At the same time she had bought a town house on Sadovaia Oulitza – not very far from the Lady Irene – and started to purchase rental property in the Vyborg-side, including a small building described as a 'former factory' on the Samsonievsky Prospect. There was also the counterfoil for a Deutsches Bank draft of fifty thousand francs, to Dr Benedict Theiss.

The last purchases recorded in the shoebox were made in April of 1910. That was about the time, Asher recalled, that the Master of Moscow had said that the 'interloper' had appeared in St Petersburg, to complicate further the squabbles of the vampires there.

Why St Petersburg? Because Theiss was there? He selected the documents pertaining to the Russian city, and a few others, then replaced the shoeboxes, the tread of the step, the drugget, and the batten, gathered up the oil lamp he'd brought with him from downstairs, and descended to tidy up after himself and take his departure. *Or because the vampires of that city were at war with one another and could be skilfully played off against one another by an interloper . . .*

But how had she known that? As far as he could tell, the Russian capital was the only other city she had visited besides Berlin, either in Russia or elsewhere. Had that been the choice of her Berlin spymaster von Brühlsbuttel? And if so, was it a coincidence that St Petersburg was one of the few cities in Europe in which an interloper could establish herself? Or had he – or she – known about the quarrel between Golenischev and Prince Dargomyzhsky, and if so, how?

Ysidro might know, if any of the other vampires had contact with German Intelligence. The twelve fifty-eight train – he glanced at his watch, and then at the daylight in the windows as he finished tidying away all trace of his visit – would reach Berlin before full dark fell in that northern city. Asher tried mentally to calculate how much light would linger in the sky at nine thirty – too much for stars to appear, which probably meant it would not be safe for vampires, even those as old and as tough as Ysidro. It was going to be a very close race, upon arrival in Berlin, to deliver coffin and luggage to that jewel-box eighteenth-century apartment on the Potsdamer Platz and get the hell away before the local vampires were up and around. Presumably, Asher reflected, he could write a note on the train and leave it lying on top of the pile before he ran for it.

When he returned to Ysidro's town house in the Ältstadt he parceled up the papers, and he posted them to Lydia at Prince Razumovsky's when he went out to find a cab. With solid information about St Job's and the house on the Sadovaia Oulitza – both purchases employed the Deutsches Bank as an agent – it shouldn't be difficult for Lydia to track Petronilla in St Petersburg, and so have information about her where-abouts by the time he himself returned there.

Dealing with Sergius von Brühlsbuttel in Berlin would be another matter. Arriving at the Kölnischer Bahnhof, Asher turned the matter over in his mind as he paid off the porters to take the trunks to the baggage area. He had the sense of working one of those schoolboy conundrums about the fox, the goose, and the bag of corn: if he and Ysidro spoke to the man together, it would bring him – Asher – to the perilous attention of the Berlin vampires; yet he doubted Ysidro had enough knowledge of the inner workings of the Intelligence game to be able to spot evasions and lies.

Under the high, glass-and-iron roof, the train platforms seethed with activity: three officers in gray jackets detraining yet more workers for the fortifications, wandering parties of lost American tourists – in clothes like those they couldn't be anything but Americans – and the usual confusion of hawkers selling newspapers, candy, ginger pop, pinwheels. The officers glared at a priest in black clericals – though Lutheran Prussia had annexed Catholic Köln nearly a century ago, the religious hatreds persisted. A stout English female tourist – surely none but an Englishwoman would presume to lecture a fully-uniformed German railway conductor – was insisting upon an explanation about something, red-backed guidebook in hand.

And yet, he thought, the Prussian officer would have to be dealt with quickly. Even twenty-four hours in Berlin was too long – the chances that someone would recognize him, among all those he'd known in that city, were simply too high. Asher stopped to buy a newspaper, trying to sort out in his mind some way of speaking with Ysidro tonight . . .

'Herr Professor Ignatius Leyden?' A hand fell on his shoulder from behind.

If they know my old alias they won't be alone.

It was the first thought that went through his mind. And then, *They'll search the trunks.*

But he was already moving as he thought. Like the bacillus that turned mortal flesh to vampire, once the Department was in your blood, there was no returning to what you had been. In the same motion he struck aside the gripping hand, swept the foot out from under the nearest policeman (*I was right, he isn't alone . . .*), and dodged between the other two and into the thick of the crowd.

People were shoving, shouting, demanding what was going on, and Asher ducked behind a news-stand, then walked – unhurriedly, he'd put distance between himself and those who knew what he looked like – to the nearest barrow of luggage, and behind its shelter slit open two carpet-bags (the first

contained a woman's dresses), and pulled out a man's gray
tweed jacket. It didn't fit, but the color was different from his
own; he transferred Ysidro's letter to his trouser pocket, stuffed
his jacket into the bag, discarded his hat . . .

They were searching the trains.

It was nearly one. The train would be leaving in minutes. *Just
get the luggage loaded. If he wakes in the left luggage shed in
Berlin he'll emerge knowing something went wrong . . .*

Asher started towards the train, but saw the police already
aboard it. Others were converging on the platform. *What I
need is a porter's uniform* . . . The midday crowds were too
thick, and half the width of the station separated him from
the porters' rooms, he'd never make it . . .

Then he saw, striding along the platform with a paper cone
of peppermints in her hand, a familiar dumpy figure in black.

'Mrs. Flasket!'

'Why, Mr Berkhampton!' Her toothy smile sparkled with
pleasure. 'Are you also on your way to Paris? What on earth
is the commotion—?'

From his trouser pocket Asher produced the train ticket,
the baggage checks, and nearly every franc and rouble he had
taken from Lady Eaton's secret cache. 'Will you go to Berlin?'

'I beg your—'

'Now, this minute, on that train.' He pointed. 'It leaves in
two minutes. When you reach Berlin, hire a cab and a porter
and take this luggage –' he slapped ticket, checks, and money
into her surprised hand – 'to this address.' He added the papers
Ysidro had left beside the stack of envelopes that morning.
'See that every single trunk is safely bestowed there – they
can just be left in the front room, just not piled on top of one
another – and then lock the door, get out of the building as
quickly as you can, and don't go back there again, ever. Will
you do that?'

'Mr Berkhampton.' Honoria Flasket's heavy eyebrows pulled
down sharply. 'There are over ten thousand francs here—'

'Will you do it?'

'Of course. But—'

'Go. You can't be seen with me. Those are the trunks there,
those buff ones with the brass. There are four of them, one
is extremely heavy. Get them to Berlin.' He gave her a little
push in their direction, then immediately walked away.

To her credit, she strode off in the direction of the trunks, without looking back.

God loves an Englishwoman.

Asher glanced towards the great doors that led out onto Opladenerstrasse – he knew he could get a later train to Berlin; he had left himself just enough money for that – but he saw the police, accompanied now by two railway officials and two of the artillery officers he'd seen earlier, heading towards the baggage shed as well. Just for an instant he heard Solomon Karlebach whisper in the back of his mind, *Kill him*, even as he heard the crash and roar of long-range artillery pounding Mafeking, smelled the sour mustardy stink of the yellow gas that had filled his dream . . .

Saw the bank-draft counterfoil transferring fifty thousand francs from the account of the vampire Petronilla Ehrenberg to that of Benedict Theiss, *Teutonic student of blood and folklore* . . .

He walked back along the platform, as if trying to look inconspicuous, and someone shouted, 'That's him.'

He ran, not fast, and they were around him. He heard the train whistle scream from the Berlin Express, and the chief plain-clothes policeman said, 'Somebody see if he has luggage . . .'

There was nothing for it. Asher turned in the grip of the man who held him and smashed his fist into the man's jaw with the whole of his strength.

SEVENTEEN

'You are certain you'll be well here?' Prince Razumovsky leaned one powerful shoulder against the carved pillar of the veranda, a rough mosaic of green uniform and gold sun-splashes: beard, buttons, the braid of his sleeves. What was it, Lydia wondered, that drew male Russian aristocrats to wear uniforms whenever they could, even if they weren't serving officers? A craving for brilliant plumage instead of the proper blues and grays and browns to which Western Civilization had condemned men, poor things?

'Perfectly, thank you, Prince.' She folded her hands on the neat piles of account books before her. 'You've left me more than ample entertainment—'

'And you truly find this perusal of dry numbers entertaining?'

Does he really think the idea of having affaires with half the Imperial Guards officers would amuse a woman? Well, she reflected, *it certainly seems to amuse his sister . . .*

'Oh, absolutely! It's a puzzle, like an egg hunt at Easter – or—' She gestured, trailing the edge of her sleeve lace through the wet ink-line on her notes. 'Or like analyzing the results of a series of graduated filtrations. Figuring out what things mean, or what they *could* mean—'

'I think it a great shame,' said the Prince, stepping around the wickerwork table to take and kiss her hand, 'that your husband will probably never permit you to work for our Third Sector.' With startling suddenness, spring had come to St Petersburg; though the weather was still sharply chill, Lydia found the sea air sweet and the touch of the sun on her face a blessing. Beyond the veranda's carved railing, the woods were tender with new green.

'I will give your very best wishes to my mother,' the Prince continued, 'who I suspect only wants to lecture *une Anglaise* on the spiritual virtues of living in the Russian countryside – not that she herself could tell a mushroom from a birch tree – and your excuses, and will return in no more than a week. And, of course, if your egg hunt palls, by all means walk up to the house and telephone Annushka or Ninochka or Sashenka –' he named several of the ladies whom Lydia had met through the Circle of Astral Light – 'and make them take you to tea at Donon's. Sashenka –' that was a very dashing, raven-haired Baroness whom Lydia suspected of being one of her host's mistresses – 'at least won't try to involve you in conversations with the dead.'

'It isn't the seances I mind.' Lydia reflected that conversations with the actual dead had been, in her experience, far more interesting than the ersatz variety moderated by mysterious individuals with names like Oneida and Princess Golden Eagle. 'In fact, I found Madame Muremsky's most instructive, though they did become quite annoyed when I insisted on wearing my spectacles and asked about why the lights had to be out – unreasonably so, I thought.' She dabbed a corner of her blotting paper at the inky disaster on the page, then gave it up. She hoped one of the maids up at the main house could deal with the sleeve lace.

'But the religion does trouble me. It's not that I *am* religious,' she hastened to add, reading the shift of Razumovsky's shoulders, the tilt of his head – for of course she had concealed her spectacles under a pile of Deutsches Bank credit transfer records the moment she'd glimpsed the Prince's refulgent form beyond the trees – and guessing that her words had touched a chord in his own thoughts. 'But it seems to blind them so. To render everything into black and white, so that anything that claims to be holy they automatically assume is *all* good, straight through, and has no . . . no patches of fallibility—'

'Like our friend Rasputin,' said the Prince, a little grimly. 'Who seems to be one entire patch of fulminating fallibility . . . Did he make an attempt on your virtue before he left town?'

'Oddly enough, no. I mean,' she added, 'not that it's odd that a man wouldn't, because plenty of men don't . . . but, honestly, so many of the gentlemen in society here *do*! And they seem so surprised when I'm not interested – and why would I be? I scarcely know them!'

Razumovsky laughed. 'Ah, Madame, in Petersburg society that doesn't matter.'

'So I've deduced,' said Lydia. 'Which seems so *odd* to me . . . And it does make me wonder about what Father Gregory gets up to, if he's considered excessive by comparison. It must be dreadfully fatiguing. But I think he's on his best behavior when Madame Vyrubova is around.'

The Prince grunted. 'You're in a small circle indeed, then, Madame. They are bored, you understand,' he went on after a moment, and in his voice was not the impatience Lydia had often heard, when men said that of upper-class women. He propped his boot on the seat of the other chair, leaned his forearms on his thigh. 'Bored and discontented, and indeed why should they not be? After Easter one goes to the Crimea; in the summer one visits one's country estates; in August one goes to one's Polish estates, for the hunting . . . In September it is either back to the Crimea, or to Monte Carlo or Nice or Paris, before the Season opens here in Petersburg. And in all of those places one sees the people one knows from Petersburg

or Paris or Vienna: one dances the waltz, one goes to the
Opera. If you're a girl – like my sisters, God help them, or
my poor wife –' this was the first the startled Lydia had heard
of this lady – 'one waits out one's time until one is old enough
to put one's hair up and be fitted for evening dresses and go
dancing and gambling, in order to get married to a man who
loses what interest he had in you very quickly—'

Softly, Lydia said, 'I know. All my life, when I was a child,
and in school . . . It's as if one is being swept away by a
flooding river – at least, I suppose it is, though I've never
actually *been* swept away by a flooding river . . . But so often
I felt as if I were fighting a current that was too strong for
me. And, instead of trying to help me, all the people on the
river bank were trying to push me back into the water. Except
Jamie.'

Razumovsky was close enough that she could see, as well
as sense, his smile. 'Except Jamie,' he said.

'But the thing is,' Lydia went on, 'it doesn't have to be that
way. That's the troubling thing about it. Not the religion –
because I should imagine, in all the centuries of the human
race, that God has seen so many varieties of religious sensi-
bility that He's past being surprised by anything – but the
waste of minds and energy that could better be used at actually helping the poor, instead of . . . of trying to get in touch
with the dead, or find out how many civilizations of hyper-
sentient spirits rose and fell on this planet in the dark abysses
of time before humankind evolved.'

The Prince's smile widened to a grin at this description of
some of the articles of faith among the devotees of Astral
Light, and of dozens of other occult societies in the city. Then
he sighed and shook his head. 'But religion is a thing that
they can master without education, you see,' he explained. 'To
which, God knows, few girls of my class have access, for all
the expense of Swiss boarding-schools and Madame Dupage's
Exclusive Establishment for Young Females, Rue St Honoré
. . . And, as you say, while the current of dress fittings and
dances and beaux sweeps them away, their parents and friends
and everyone whom they speak to is standing lined up on the
riverbank pushing them back in. So those without a Jamie to
pull them out when they were— How old were you, when
you met him?'

'Thirteen,' said Lydia. 'Sixteen, when he helped me swot for my exams to get into Somerville, but he'd been helping me find tutors and things for a year before that. I always knew I wanted to be a doctor, you see.'

'Thirteen,' said Razumovsky, and his handsome face was sad. 'And now those young ladies are twenty-seven, twenty-eight, and they have not had educations and can not marshal either the mental discipline or the informational knowledge to take pleasure in— What did you call it? Analyzing results? Their souls are ravenous, and they do not know for what. And, here in Russia, religion is not like religion in England . . . or anywhere else in the world, I think. Here in Russia, fairies and devils are as real as angels – and angels are as real as one's village priest. Here in Russia – perhaps because of the long winters, or the vastness of the land – one feels the Other World is very close. Have you not sensed it, when you sit on the veranda here in the twilight? Have you not felt that if you walked a little way down the path –' he nodded towards the graveled way that led back into the woods, towards the birch groves and the river – 'that you might meet bathhouse spirits, or swan maidens, or a kobold carrying a load of magical sticks? Russia has not been civilized for very long,' he added gently. 'For good or for ill, these things still lie very close to the skin. And now I am late!'

He straightened as the blue-and-burgundy form of a servant – by his walk and bearing, Lydia identified Jov the butler long before the man came close enough for her to make out his long, wrinkled face – appeared on the pathway. Razumovsky flung out his arms. 'I come, I come! See how I hasten—'

'It is my duty to preserve your Excellency from a beating at your mother's hands,' returned Jov with a grin. Like most of the Prince's upper servants, he spoke excellent French. 'And to save myself one, for not hastening your Excellency to his train. Madame Asher would not be persuaded to visit the Dowager Princess at Byerza? Madame,' he added, turning to address her – a dapper, elderly man with enormous grizzled side-whiskers that reminded Lydia of James's current disguise. 'Be assured that I speak for all of us when I say, do not hesitate to issue the smallest of commands.'

'Thank you.' Lydia got to her feet, extended her hands to the Prince. 'And thank you, Prince—'

'Andrei,' he corrected her. 'If Madame will be so kind. Until Monday next, then.' He kissed her hand again and was gone, disappearing among the bare silvery trees.

Lydia returned to her wickerwork chair and drew her shawl around her again, but for a long time she did not return to her systematic examination of Deutsches Bank property transactions over the past five years. Instead she sat, turning over in her mind what the Prince had said about the ladies of her acquaintance. From informants about possible partners and patrons of Benedict Theiss, they had become friends, some of them . . . On the previous Friday she had accompanied Natalia, and the Baroness Sashenka, and several others of their circle, to the night-long services of the Orthodox Good Friday; and had gone with them again the following night, praying and standing and praying and standing and singing and inhaling incense, and had seen the ecstasy of Easter on the faces all around her . . .

And had been propositioned four times at the Pascha breakfast after the Easter morning services, once by the Baroness's husband. She didn't doubt the sincerity of their beliefs, and yet – how easy it was to believe one was engaged in some vital quest for knowledge, when all one was doing was chasing phantoms in a dream . . .

If one could only figure out, she reflected, retrieving her spectacles from beneath the pile of her notes, *which was the phantom, and which the reality.*

Else why was she trying to trace money sent from a dead man's bank account in some unknown city, to purchase property in a place where even the Undead were unable to walk for two months of the year? *Which makes a good deal less sense*, she sighed, *than attempting to have a straightforward conversation with one's deceased Uncle Harold, something which at least has the virtue of repeated anecdotal evidence.*

She dunked her pen in the inkwell, found her place again, and continued with her notes.

'I want to see the American consul.'

'Not the British consul?' The interrogator was an elderly man, almost a caricature of a Prussian Junker: tall, fair, and with the contempt of one who has grown up knowing himself to be the ruler of every human being around him, outside his own family.

'I tell you I don't know who the hell this Professor Leyden is that you keep saying I am. My name is Plummer, and I'm from Chicago—'

'Then why did you assault the officers sent to apprehend you at the Bahnhof?'

Because I knew damn well my story wouldn't hold up for ten minutes. 'I told you, I thought he was this rat-bastard German named Speigel who's been followin' me ever since I come to Köln, swearin' I'm the man who meddled with his sister, the ugly cow—'

'And how long has that been?'

'Two days.'

'And you did not report this to the police?'

'Mister –'Asher poked his finger at the officer in his best imitation of an American engineer he'd known in Tsingtao – 'you know goddamn little about Americans if you think we run snivelin' to the cops every time a man leans on us for one thing or another. We take care of our own problems.'

Behind thick pince-nez, the interrogator's blue eyes narrowed. 'Evidently. Yet none of this explains why you then assaulted the police officers a second time on the platform, when it was amply clear to anyone but an imbecile that they were the police and not civilian attackers.'

'Well, maybe by that time you put my dander up.'

And thank God everyone from Land's End to Yokohama knows Americans think elevated dander a perfectly appropriate reason for taking on six policemen and two officers of the artillery.

He was taken back to his cell. There were two other men in it with him, one a laborer from Saxony on the Neuehrenfeld gun emplacements, the other an elderly Frenchman who persisted in shoving, cursing at, and haranguing the Saxon about Alsace-Lorraine and the foul attempts by the Germans to spy out the secrets of the French Army and then corrupt the populace with lies about the efficacy of that Army to defend *La Patrie.* Asher, whose whole body ached from the fracas at the Bahnhof, wished he could unobtrusively kill them both.

Grated windows gave onto a minuscule areaway about two feet below the level with the Rathaus courtyard. When the endless day ended and darkness finally fell, Asher wondered if Ysidro had emerged from his coffin before the train stopped in Berlin, and if Mrs Flasket had gotten herself away safely. How soon would the vampire become aware that he, Asher, was not in the city with him? And what would he do then?

A jail officer brought food: bean porridge in cheap tin bowls, water, and bread. Men talked in other cells, desultory abuse in five separate varieties of Rhineland German. The gray-haired Frenchman – for the dozenth time – ranted at the Saxon about *l'Affair Dreyfus*, despite the fact that the Saxon knew not a single word of what was being said to him. As silence gradually settled on the cells, Asher unobtrusively flipped open his box of 'snuff' and rubbed some of it on his gums.

It might be morning before Ysidro realized that, in the parlance of the Department, plans had come unstuck. But growing in the back of his mind was the uneasy vision of Petronilla Ehrenberg's handsome town house in Neuehrenfeld . . . and the recollection of the fact that, because of the shortness of time before the departure of the train, he had not searched it from top to bottom. If she slept there, she would have kept her coffin in a crypt or sub cellar, like the one beneath Ysidro's rented nest in Prague or the one in Lady Eaton's shallow cellar in Petersburg.

And he had no assurance that some other vampire had not been sleeping in that crypt, aware of him – as he knew vampires were sometimes aware – in its sleep.

Towards dawn he slept, and save for those intervals when his two cell-mates so infuriated one another as to attempt to settle European politics between them with fists, he dozed on and off through most of the day. When he asked the guard if the American consul had been contacted, the man said he didn't know, and in truth Asher knew this was a hazardous ploy at best. America, greedily snapping up every territory it could lay hands on in the Pacific and the Orient, had little use for Europe. Its Presidents tended to appoint as consuls personal friends whom they considered deserving of four years' paid holiday in Europe, or useful political supporters, ditto. Considering the strategic position of Köln on German's defensive line, the Americans were more than likely to wash their hands of him with Pilate-like speed . . .

And, of course, for the same reason, the Department – if he were willing to condemn himself in advance by asking for the British Consul – would do likewise.

He dreamed that night of Lydia, as he'd dreamed of her in China and later in Africa, in the years between his despairing realization that he loved that budding girl as a man loves a woman, and his return from Africa to find her disinherited and able – for all her family cared – to marry a poor man after all.

Lydia in white gauze and a wide-brimmed hat, with her red hair down her back . . .

Lydia glancing sidelong at him beneath those long dark lashes and saying, *You really ARE a spy, aren't you?*

Lydia . . .

He jerked awake with a gasp, but the cell was empty save for his snoring comrades. Under the dim flicker of the gas beyond the bars, the corridor lay shadowed but still.

On the second day – Tuesday – the American Consul visited him, and it quickly became clear that this square-jawed, disapproving banker with an insanely spreading beard wanted nothing to do with wild Midwesterners who got into brawls with the German police on railway platforms. 'You understand my position, I hope, Mr Palmer,' said Mr McGuffey, in his dry New England accent, and folded plump clerkly hands. 'I will, of course, cable Chicago at once to confirm your bona fides, but if you are as you say you are, I'm sure all these matters can be straightened out.'

The following morning Asher was taken from his cell to the office, where the same interrogator as before informed him – with a telling glance at the brown stubble that was ghosting visibly back into existence on the shaved top of his head – that a telegram had been sent to the Auswärtiges Amt in Berlin, and that he – Professor Ignatius Leyden aka Jules Plummer of Chicago – was facing a military court and a charge of espionage.

EIGHTEEN

And there it was.

Lydia thumbed the tightly-folded packet of counter-foils for the third time, seeking a note of explanation, but found none. Jamie must have parceled this up in a terrible hurry, not even to have enclosed word of where he'd found all these things. Knowing Jamie, she guessed he'd burgled Petronilla Ehrenberg's house . . .

She wondered if he'd burned it down afterwards, to cover his tracks. It would be like him.

It appeared that Petronilla Ehrenberg owned property on the north bank of the Neva across from Elaghinskoy Island: the former monastery of St Job. Lydia's sense of St Petersburg geography was good enough by this time to place it, on the outer edge of the grimy ring of factories that surrounded the city, within walking distance of the Vyborg-side slums. There was also a town house on the Sadovaia Oulitza in the Smolny district, as well as the 'small factory building' at the familiar address on Samsonievsky Prospect.

And she's clearly found a woman willing to serve her, to BE Petronilla Ehrenberg by daylight. That must have been what Rasputin saw.

She shuffled the stiff law-hand documents into chronological order, noting names, dates, bank-account numbers.

Juggling identities was nothing new for a vampire. Petra Ehrenberg – the real Petra Ehrenberg, who had become Undead in 1848 – had taken over the name and identity of her 'niece' Paulina, and then made a new identity as Petronilla years later. Did the woman she had spoken to at the clinic – this green-eyed woman in the Doucet suit and sables who flirted by daylight with Benedict Theiss in Petronilla Ehrenberg's name . . . Did she realize that it was the custom of vampires to murder their servants when they were done with them? *Or does she think she'll be the exception to that rule?*

For a moment, the recollection of Margaret Potton lying dead on their bed in Constantinople overwhelmed her: the waxen face, the blue eyes staring, the mouth agape, as if she'd died gasping for the oxygen her lungs were no longer getting . . .

If I pound on her door and tell her, thought Lydia, *she'll only turn that information over to the REAL Petronilla, hiding in her dark crypt somewhere . . .*

She knew from her dealings with Margaret and Ysidro how intransigent the victim of that seduction could be, when asked to consider any explanation other than the one that the vampire had planted in the victim's dreams.

Besides, I promised Jamie that I wouldn't.

Lydia took some deep breaths. It was a few minutes before Margaret's image retreated.

But what I CAN do is have a look at the place.

Unlike many so-called 'country dachas' on the properties of the rich, the cottage behind Razumovsky's palace really was a cottage. True, its four rooms were furnished more like a rustic stage-set for a pantomime fairy-tale than the dwelling of actual peasants, but at least it didn't have its own ballroom and marble-tubbed baths, like the 'cottage' owned by the Baroness Sashenka's husband. Lydia sought out Rina – the sturdy little cook – in the cellar, a gloomy rabbit-hole beneath the kitchen, which was, like every cellar in St Petersburg, as damp as a well; she'd never gotten used to the high-handed way the Petersburg ladies had of leaving the servants to guess whether they'd be in for dinner or not. Rina's French was limited to '*coq au vin*' and '*Joyeaux Noël*', but Lydia had made notes for herself of important phrases in Russian, such as, 'I will not be here for dinner,' and, 'Please ask Sergei to draw me a bath.' (A European bath was also different from a Russian bath, which was what was known in England as a Turkish bath, more or less. Even in Turkey, Lydia had not had a Turkish bath, and she was not sure – despite the languorous urging of Razumovsky's sister Natalia – that she felt up to utilizing the log-built banya at the end of the graveled path near the river.)

Dinner having been arranged for, Lydia changed her lacy 'at-home' gown for a very dashing carriage-dress, a Paquin medley of dark and pale greens that Natalia had supervised the purchase of ('*Those English things make you look like someone's virgin sister, darling . . .*'), made sure she had her little packet of picklocks buttoned to the lower edge of her corset, then walked the fifty yards or so through the woods to the stables, which rose, like a minor Versailles of gold-and-cream-colored stucco, before one reached the Razumovsky palace itself. Ivan – the only member of the stable staff who spoke French – chided her like a good-natured father for not having sent one of the maids with an order to get the carriage ready and bring it to the *izba's* door, but let her sit on the bench in the yard to watch the harnessing-up. 'I should send you back to the *izba*, to wait like a respectable lady, Gospozha,' said the coachman with a grin, as he re-emerged from his private door a few moments later, very trim and un-Ivan-like in his conservative 'day' livery of maroon piped with pale blue. 'What would His Excellency say, eh? Now, where is it that you have the wish to go?'

It was clear to Lydia that the Monastery of St Job had originally been built in the countryside, a mile or two back from the Neva, at some point early in the preceding century, when St Petersburg had been much smaller and the world much cleaner; Lydia was not in the slightest surprised that the monks had moved out. A factory producing rolling stock for Russia's railways stood a hundred yards away, drearily excreting smoke that yellowed the air and made Lydia's eyes burn as Ivan steered the team among the oozing ruts of the unpaved street. From the gates of the factory, from the doorways of grubby taverns or the steps of those endless, rickety wooden tenements, bearded, filthy men in faded clothing watched the gleaming vehicle pass with eyes that smoldered with resentment. As the brougham approached the dreary wasteland of railroad spur-lines and factory sheds that covered what had once been the monastery's orchards, a child ran from an alley and flung a handful of horse dung at its shining side.

'Are you sure of your directions, Gospozha?' asked Ivan doubtfully, leaning back to the communicating window.

Though considerably intimidated at the thought of getting out of the carriage, Lydia replied firmly, 'I'm sure that it's the Monastery of St Job that I was asked to inquire at.' *I have walked into vampire nests and survived rioting Turks in the back alleys of Constantinople*, she told herself. *Each of those men has a liver, a spleen, two kidneys, two lungs . . . I've taken apart the corpses of men like them and they all look the same inside . . .*

The coachman shook his head and said something in Russian. Ahead of them, in the midst of a rut-creased field of waste ground, the old monastery's walls rose, soot black and leprous with lichen and decay. A couple of men – bearded bundles of rags – crouched beside a fire built on the other side of a muddy lane nearby, but no one and nothing seemed willing to go anywhere near the walls themselves. There had apparently been a lane leading to the gates at one time, but it was barely visible, as a series of gravel patches and potholes in the gluey muck. The gate itself – old wrought-iron in a strange severe pattern – was backed with sheet iron, both forbidding and unspeakably desolate.

'Gospozha—' Ivan protested, as at Lydia's signal he reined to a halt.

'It's quite all right,' said Lydia firmly. She removed her spectacles and stepped down, gingerly holding up her skirt hem. 'I'm just going to have a look round.'

'There is no one here, Gospozha.' The coachman flung his arms wide in exasperation. 'You can see, the place has been deserted many years.'

'I was told there was a man living here that my husband wished me to find.' Lydia had found – she did not know why – that the fabrication of a mission undertaken at a husband's behest made more sense to most men than a woman under-taking action on her own. 'I may have been misled, but I do need to at least knock on the gates.' Across the unpaved lane, and beyond the corner of the walls, stretched several more acres of waste ground, in places fenced with boards, the torn-out sections of which showed a gaggle of makeshift huts at the far side – apparently deserted – and sheets of water and mud. In the grimy light – it was seven in the evening, but the sun stood disorientingly high in the sky – it looked ghastly beyond description, but not actively menacing. 'Stay here with the carriage, if you will, please.' She turned her back on Ivan's arguments – and he couldn't really follow her if he ever expected to see horse or carriage again, in this neighborhood – and, holding up her elegant skirts, she approached the squat arch of the gate.

It was, as she had expected, locked. What surprised her a little was that the lock was new – she put on her spectacles again once she was close – the steel bright and unrusted. There was little rust on the iron backing-sheet, either, and the welds that held it to the older ironwork looked recent as well.

Petronilla Ehrenberg – according to Jamie's pilfered counterfoils – had arranged for the purchase of this place two years ago, in the spring of 1909.

Lydia moved off to the left, trying to remember whether it was bad luck to walk around a church to the right or to the left – *does a deconsecrated monastery count as a church?* – towards a tower-like irregularity of the wall, hoping to find another gate or door. The place was much bigger than it appeared to be, sprawling away into what looked like it had been another orchard, the trees now mostly cut down for firewood. A stagnant canal bordered it on the north – Lydia recalled passing a disused watergate just beyond the big Naval stores factory – and, even at the distance of many yards, the stench was overpowering. On its bank, as in the field opposite, a couple of dirty camps had been set up, but the sheds seemed empty, trails of looted trash seeming to ooze from their grimy entrances. 'The monks have to have kept farm animals,' said Lydia to herself, 'and that means . . . Ah, here we are.'

The remains of a ruined barn – picked nearly clean of its planking by the frozen poor in wintertime – backed against the monastery wall. Stepping cautiously into the dilapidated shadows, Lydia saw at once the smaller gate, which led through, presumably, from the kitchen quarters. It, too, was locked – the lock also new – but above it, where the loft floor had been, another door pierced the wall. A little searching revealed the remains of the steps that had once led to the loft, and Lydia climbed up and made her way – keeping warily to such flooring as remained over the huge beams, since the planks elsewhere looked rotted and treacherous – to that upper entrance.

It was closed, but the rusted lock had been broken. A hinge had been loosened as well, making the off-balance door hard to push, but the door of the bicycle shed at her Aunt Faith's country place had been similarly crippled, and Lydia remembered the knack of lifting and pushing. Once she got it open enough to slither through, the smell inside was worse than the sewer stink of the streets, a miasma at once metallic and chemical. That much struck her instantly – that, and the fact that the single window which once had lighted the round, bare little chamber immediately within had been boarded over, rendering the room pitch dark.

Only the bleak light of the open doorway showed her a second door on the far side of the round room, leading into the monastery itself.

Beyond that door she heard the scuff and pat of footsteps, fleeing down stairs.

Lydia called, 'Hello?'

You imbecile, whoever's here probably doesn't speak English . . .

'*Alors? Qui est là?*'

Would Russian monks speak French? Father Gregory certainly didn't . . .

She fished in her handbag for the stub of a candle she'd formed the habit of carrying, lit it. By the dim yellow glow she saw that the inner door wasn't locked or bolted. When she pushed it open, it was to find herself on a spiraling staircase, rising above into blackness, descending before her feet into an abyssal night.

Dark or light, vampires won't even be awake at this hour . . .

Through her collar lace she quickly touched the heavy silver links of the chain she wore around her neck. The footfalls might, of course, be one of those horrible bearded factory-workers she'd seen in the streets outside. But if Petronilla Ehrenberg slept in the crypts here, even part-time, Lydia was willing to bet that the dispossessed of Petersburg gave the place wide berth. She descended the stair, left hand pressed to the central column of moist stone, candle held high in her right. '*Qui est là?*' she called out again, and her voice echoed in the low vaulting just over her head. Despite the relative warmth of the lengthening days, in here the damp cold was arctic. '*Je m'appelle Madame Asher . . . Je cherche Madame Ehrenberg . . .*'

Another small round room; a door firmly locked with a new American Yale. The walls here had been painted at one time, a hideous procession of peeling faces and boneless bodies in the stiff, unreal style of the old Russian icons. Only somber eyes and upraised hands remained. After a bare yard of landing, the stair continued down, and the smell that breathed from

below was rank with the seepage of half a million slum
cesspits.

Curiously, Lydia saw no rats.

The yellow light glinted on water below. An inch or so
deep, she saw as she neared it, over a floor of broken brick.
A door stood open to the blackness of deeper hell. She gathered her skirts, elevated the light.

I'm only going to have a look inside to tell Jamie . . .

Eyes flashed in the darkness. Reflective as a rat's, human-
high in the ghost-white blur of a human face.

Lydia's breath froze in her lungs.

It must be later than I thought . . .

She'd seen vampires before, had also seen what she thought
of as partial or incomplete vampires: horrible unfortunates in
whom the process of physical change from human to vampire
had gone appallingly awry. The thing standing in the doorway
bore the signs she'd seen in poor Dennis Blaydon: the
grotesque growth of the teeth – three of them, in this case not
the eye teeth, but cuspids and bicuspids, grown out long enough
to shred the lips – and the erupted, blistered look of the skin.

This earlier experience was the only reason she neither
screamed nor ran.

And, as with the case of poor Dennis, the horror was made
worse by the fact that she recognized the boy. He was the
dark-haired youth – or, at least, he wore the same red-and-
blue striped shirt, the same second-hand American boots –
who had been speaking so earnestly to the so-called Madame
Ehrenberg at the clinic. Who had gazed after that lady with
his young heart in his eyes.

It was clear that he recognized Lydia.

He stretched out his hands, mumbled something around his
outgrown fangs that could have been, 'Gospozha,' as Lydia stood,
staring at him in shock and pity. 'Gospozha, *pomogitye*—!'

'It's all right,' said Lydia steadily. 'Don't be afraid – blast
it – *N'ayez pas peur. Je vous aiderais*—'

She took a step closer, held out the candle to better see.
Whether it was this gesture, or whether the boy heard something in the inky blackness behind him – or whether, at that
distance, he somehow sensed the silver she wore around her
throat and wrists – she didn't know. But he flinched from
her, beating at the air with his hands, and seemed to drop back

into the darkness. She reached the inner door in two strides in time to hear his footfalls splashing, the candle's tiny gleam touching black water underfoot, threading with an edge of light the stumpy groins of cistern or cellar . . . '*Attends!*'

Her voice echoed in some great space, like the midnight of the inter-dimensional abysses that Madame Muremsky and her friends were always talking about, but far smellier . . .

She stopped, heart pounding. James *might* have sanctioned her entry into the monastery from the ruined barn, on the grounds of seeing what was there. He might even have agreed that an investigatory probe of the stairway was allowable, to ascertain whether a second, more serious, and better accompanied visit would require a rope ladder, for instance, or a hammer and spanner.

But he would unhesitatingly have ordered her not to go through this door and, worse, her friend Josetta Beyerly would have looked down her nose and said, *Oh, Lydia, that's PRECISELY the sort of thing those birdbrained girls are always doing in novels! Come out of there at once.*

Lydia backed to the stairway, hoping that someone else hadn't come and shut one of the doors behind her.

They hadn't.

She didn't start shaking until she was halfway across the creaking weather-savaged beams of the old barn, in the cool milky light of the disorientingly endless afternoon. Her trembling, and the panicky sense of having only narrowly averted death, persisted all the way back to Krestovsky Island.

Stillness fell on the cells, on the day room at the end of the corridor, on the whole – Asher thought – of the Köln police station, at two. Even in the depth of the night this was unusual. In the cells there was always some sort of sound, and the previous evening a socialist student group had been taken in, young men who argued incessantly as to whether syndicalism could be trusted not to hand the whole of the movement over to the stinking bourgeoisie lickspittle pigs and abandon the true principles of anarchy . . .

They didn't drop silent one by one, as they had in the small hours, but all at the same moment. The sudden hush seemed to echo: no other sound stirred from the watch room, or from anywhere in the building.

Asher – head throbbing from the fourth or fifth dose of Solomon Karlebach's powder – felt the hairs rise on his nape.

The powder was almost gone. He scraped his finger around the sides of the tin, reapplied it to his tingling gums, hating its taste as he'd hated it through three nights already. Hating the ache in his bones, the hollow pain in his skull from trying to sleep in the daytime with Tweedledum and Tweedledee shouting at one another about *l'Affaire Dreyfus* and the Rape of Alsace and Lorraine. At the same time, he felt a gray, buzzing pressure on his mind, like a warm weight smothering him . . .

They're here.

He got to his feet, swaying a little. He'd been searched when first arrested, and the guards had relieved him of the silver chains that protected his throat and wrists, along with his watch, Karlebach's pincer band, and the silver-bladed knife. He stumbled to the bars and leaned against them, forced his attention to focus on the watch-room door at the end of the corridor. Thus he actually saw them come through it, a man and a woman. The man was small, sturdily built, and dark, dressed with the usual German dearth of fashionableness. The woman was taller, lush-breasted and striking, though she had never been pretty: heavy chin, hooked nose, large somber eyes, darkness reflecting light. They saw him waiting for them at the bars, and the pressure against his mind was like being drowned in laudanum. He knew he should back away and couldn't. The woman – suddenly close – took his wrist through the bars as the man unlocked the door with one of the guardroom keys; she held him until the man was inside the cell, then came in herself while the man shoved Asher around with his back to the bars.

His mouth barely able to frame words, Asher managed to say, 'Petronilla Ehrenberg has sold her services to the Kaiser.'

His mind cleared, sleep draining off as if from an unstoppered basin. The male vampire's hand tightened on his shoulder, long nails digging through Asher's shirt; his other hand gripped him by the hair at the back of his head. 'Where is she?'

'St Petersburg, I think. She's working with a man in Berlin.'

'His name?'

Asher shook his head. 'I need to talk to him.'

It might have been the reflected gleam of gaslight in the corridor; it was as if fire flickered in the deeps of those dark, reflective eyes. Though the vampire's face was a young man's face, it was wrinkled all around the eyes and eyelids. His mouth was nearly lipless, curiously puckish, with an evil sidelong smile.

'We'll talk to him.'

'After I do.'

Close by his ear the woman said, 'T'cha,' and he felt her nail trace the skin of his throat, but the man sniffed with laughter.

'You're going to *bargain* with me?' He sounded incredulous. *As well he might*, Asher reflected.

'It can't hurt to try.'

The man's grip tightened on his shoulder, in his hair, drawing him closer. Fangs glinted in that little smile. 'Oh, but it can. You have no idea how much it can hurt, Herr . . . And whom have I the honor of addressing?'

'James Asher.' Night after night of incomplete sleep, of exhaustion, had put a dreamlike haze on everything, as if he were short of oxygen. 'And you are—?'

'You may call me Todesfall. And where is your Spanish friend?'

'I don't know. I hope he reached Berlin safely—'

'If he did it was two days ago, and he has not troubled to return for you.'

'I think he would have done – one way or the other – had he found the man we sought.' This was in fact a lie, since Asher hoped – and guessed – that Ysidro had gone straight on to St Petersburg to protect Lydia, possibly without even lingering in Berlin long enough to look for Colonel von Brühlsbuttel. He could feel his heart hammering and knew that the vampires could as well; was acutely, overwhelmingly conscious of the woman standing at his shoulder, watching the beat of the pulse in his throat.

Todesfall said softly, 'We can make you tell.'

'Could you trust what I said?' And he saw the dark eyes flicker, gauging that thought.

'More importantly, could you trust what *he* will say . . . *if* you find him. Do you know enough about the workings of the Auswärtiges Amt to be able to distinguish lies from truth? Do you really want to have the Kaiser recruiting fledglings—' He gritted his teeth against the angry clench of the vampire's fists, and kept his voice steady with an effort. 'Or have Petra Ehrenberg running those fledglings as her own?'

'Bitch.' Todesfall rammed him back against the bars with a violence that knocked the breath from his lungs. 'Sly whore. I never trusted her—'

Asher had the good sense not to wonder aloud why, in that case, Todesfall had made her vampire, if in fact he had. He rubbed his shoulder and held his peace.

The vampire woman stepped around to the other's side, and the two of them traded a glance; it was like feeling the cold wing of Death's shadow cross his face. Then Todesfall grinned his sidelong grin again and nodded towards Asher's two sleeping cell-mates: 'Which one of these two do you want me to kill? Don't look away like that,' he added, catching Asher's jaw in his hand and turning his face back, so that their eyes met again. 'If you don't choose one I'll take both: two widows, how many orphans . . .? How many children do you think that one has?' He poked the German with his knee; the man didn't even move. 'Five? Six? Maybe a widowed mother and a couple of ugly sisters depending on his support? What about our skinny friend over there on the other bunk? He's older . . . Maybe his wife is in poor health? Or perhaps she minds her grandchildren . . . Little babies crying for the supper he brings—'

'Stop it.'

'Which one?'

Their only crime was sharing a cell with him. And keeping him awake.

He could tell Todesfall would really kill them both if he didn't choose.

'The older one,' he said, and he turned his face to the wall.

NINETEEN

L ydia spent the following morning writing up a report of what she had seen at St Job's. She made neat sketches – as if she were illustrating a dissection – of the layout of the monastery, insofar as she had seen it, and of the thing – the boy – she had encountered in the crypt. To these she appended an account of the meeting between the unfortunate youth and 'Petronilla' in the sun-drenched hall of the clinic.

Obviously, Horace Blaydon wasn't the only man in the world who had had the idea of producing artificial vampires. And, by the look of it, Benedict Theiss had had the advantage – which Blaydon had not had – of finding a true vampire willing to work with him . . .

But if Theiss had a vampire working with him, why go to the clumsy expedient of producing them by artificial means? Especially when the result – or one of the results – was so disastrous?

She sat turning her teacup for a time, gazing out into the light-filled woods beyond the veranda.

To prevent Madame Ehrenberg from holding over them the power that a master held over her fledglings?

But, in that case, why would La Ehrenberg go along with it? In Lydia's experience, no vampire – not even Ysidro, in so many ways atypical, (*no, he isn't!* she told herself) – yielded a finger-breadth more control than he or she had to . . .

Or was there something amiss with the vampires that La Ehrenberg made? Like the late Master of Constantinople, who had been incapable of getting fledglings? Were they all turning out as monsters? Had she come to Theiss to be *cured*? Lydia's mind toyed with the idea even as she rejected it. No matter how badly Benedict Theiss needed money for his researches, she *could not* see that gentle, kindly man agreeing to help a vampire produce better fledglings.

What, then?

At one in the afternoon, the Baroness Sashenka put in an appearance, dressed to the nines in lavender Poiret that made

Lydia feel gawky and schoolgirlish, and carried her off for luncheon at the ultra-stylish restaurant Donon with assorted members of the Circle of Astral Light. (*My darling, you can't abandon me, that frightful Muremsky woman is going to be there, going on about the instinctive wisdom of the Russian peasant, and I need to have someone there whose husband has actually* spoken *to peasants . . .'*)

While being waited on by the ubiquitous staff of Tatars (Sashenka was quite right about Madame Muremsky's conversation), Lydia inquired about the monastery of St Job and received a torrent of conflicting information, involving spectral lights and noises, secret rituals of the Illuminati, corrupt medieval abbots, eighteenth-century scandals, and the plain financial mismanagement that had eventually closed the place down. It was very difficult to sort out useful facts which could apply to vampires from mere gossip – or even to ascertain which pieces of gossip might have a basis in truth.

'There were supposed to be just miles of secret passageways, between it and its little priories—'

'When the heretical sect was cleared out of there in the time of the Empress Elizabeth, I'm told all its adherents were bricked up in underground cells—'

'They can't have been terribly far underground, can they?' Lydia looked up worriedly from her mushrooms and toast points. 'I mean, it's rather close to the river.'

'That's just it, darling.' Madame Muremsky laid a delicate hand on Lydia's wrist, gazed into her eyes. 'They were bricked up *alive*, and when the tide came up the Neva, the cells would flood, drowning them—'

'Honestly, dearest, the same could be said of my cellar,' retorted the Baroness Sashenka, which got a general laugh.

'Scoff if you will, darling.' Madame sampled a dab of Donon's extremely tasty kasha. 'But the Common People, in their wisdom, avoid the place . . .'

'The Common People avoid the place because someone is paying the police a truly startling sum every quarter to keep people away from it,' returned a Commissioner's pretty wife.

Not much more success attended Lydia's efforts to pick up information about Madame Ehrenberg, aside from the fact that the woman was generally disliked. (*'She's so* intent, *you know, dearest – and the way she runs poor Dr Theiss's life for him is positively obsessive! One used to see him everywhere – always so charming – and now that she's taken to supporting him he's always either at the clinic or his laboratory . . .').*

So, obviously, reflected Lydia, the woman that the real Petronilla was using as a stalking horse had come to Petersburg with her . . . which meant it would probably be impossible to find out anything about her true identity by making enquiries here.

'Are they lovers?' The question would have been unthinkable in Oxford or even London, but was commonplace around the Petersburg tea-tables.

'Oh, I should think so,' replied Commissioner Tatischev's wife, and she licked crème fraiche from her fingers. 'At least, when I encountered her at the Kustov's, where that *handsome* Burenin was reading some of his poetry . . . Burenin has invented a *totally* new language for his poetry, to free the heart from the *bondage* that old meanings and old ways of thought have imposed upon words . . . Well, she – La Ehrenberg, I mean – got up to leave, saying it was a waste of time. Why seek new meanings for Love, she said, when the old one works quite well, even in this day and age . . . *Quite* missed the point, of course . . .'

'I thought she spoke like a woman who was in love,' said Sashenka.

'Or what we were taught to believe was love,' threw in a very advanced young Countess, 'by priests and parents and *men.*'

'What does a German know of love?' Madame Muremsky waved a scornful and heavily jeweled hand. 'What can one expect, of such a people? They have no understanding of the Russian Soul.' And she clasped her hands upon her heart, as if her Russian Soul were about to leap from her breast and manifest itself, in all its glory, to the assembled ladies.

Two hours' discussion of the Russian Soul ensued, and Lydia hesitated to bring the conversation back to Petronilla Ehrenberg, lest word reach her that Lydia Asher had been asking about her.

Jamie, thought Lydia, jotting a note in her memorandum book: *labyrinth, crypt, police protection . . .*

Jamie needs to know about all this . . .

There was no note from Jamie when she returned to the *izba* for dinner. Nor had there been one yesterday, nor the day before. She tried to tell herself that this was only some disruption in the German postal system, though given the renowned efficiency of the Reich, she was aware that this little self-deception was whistling in the dark. Not that any of the notes he'd sent her, daily, from Warsaw, from Berlin, from Prague and all those German cities had contained a word of information: he'd written in the name of a fictitious Aunt Caroline and had clearly striven to come up with the most absurd trivialities imaginable about the weather, the accommodations, and the obstinate refusal of Polish and German shopkeepers to learn the English tongue.

The message was in their arrival. The message was that he was alive and in good enough spirits to invent Aunt Caroline's petty diatribes in that rounded, schoolgirlish writing, studded with underlinings and ellipses so unlike his own dark, jagged hand, knowing that it would make her laugh.

He was traveling with a vampire, in quest of other vampires: creatures who would kill to preserve the secrecy in which they lived. Creatures who existed on death.

She sat motionless in the little study, gazing at the darkening twilight of the woods beyond the window.

He was traveling with Ysidro . . .

She thrust the ghost-white, elegant image of the vampire from her mind.

Any vampire. They are creatures who kill those who serve them, for learning too much . . . or because they grow bored.

And though Ysidro had befriended and protected them so far, she knew nothing of the vampires of those cities whose brightly-colored stamps enlivened the one-way correspondence . . . except that they were vampires. *Dear God, don't let him come to harm . . .*

From the age of thirteen, Lydia had had a physician's clinical and rather mechanistic view of God – awe at His works, but too deep an awareness of the physical limitations of flesh and fate to hold much belief in the efficacy of individual prayer. Lately – after Constantinople, and a deeper acquaintance with vampires – her views had changed, leaving her confused about who she was praying to or why.

Her prayer was a child's prayer:

Don't let him come to harm . . .
Make it be all right . . .
The prayer people prayed all over the world.

There was no more reason to think God would grant that one than He'd granted her desperate plea of six months ago, that by some miracle her bleeding would stop, and her baby would live.

The blackness beyond that door in her mind was worse than the crypts of St Job's, and as she had yesterday, she mentally backed from the thought of that lost child, mentally closed the door. *Stay out of there . . .*

Even as she had backed away already, a dozen times, from the whispered suspicion that had begun to cross her mind, that she had conceived again and might be carrying a child. *Stay away from hope, if you would stay away from despair . . .*

'*Pardonnez-moi,* Madame.'

Lydia almost jumped, as the maid Alyssa came in with a lamp.

'*Ce ne'est rien.*' Thanks to the government's sincere and widespread education program over the past few decades, large numbers of young Russians could speak French, an accomplishment particularly valued among the girls who hoped for employment as maids. One might have to put up with the Madame Muremskys of the world, Lydia reflected, but having seen the St Petersburg slums – having heard from Ivan, and Razumovsky, about the conditions a young girl would encounter in the average factory – Lydia could understand the attraction of picking up someone else's stockings and cleaning someone else's chamber pots if it meant a decent meal every night.

'I'm sorry.' Lydia stood up, realizing she had a headache from missing the supper that Rina had said she'd set out for her . . . Good heavens, when was that?

The windows were inky dark. Drat these endless afternoons, one never had the slightest idea of what time it really was . . .

'Time got away from me. Please apologize to Rina for me.'

The maid grinned quickly, 'Oh, Rina knows not to put food on the table until Madame is actually sitting down . . . It is not that. There is a young lady to see you. It is urgent, she says.'

'A young lady?' Lydia gathered her spectacles inconspicuously into one hand, followed the maid into the long front room. Tried to think of which members of the Circle of Astral Light Alyssa wouldn't already know . . .

The girl in the lamplit parlor dipped a curtsey as Lydia came through the bedroom door. Nothing about the heart-shaped face or thick mass of dark hair seemed familiar, so Lydia put on her spectacles again for a better look: dark eyes, full lips, delicate features that spoke of some southern strain in the blood . . .

'May I help you?' Lydia asked, in French. 'I am Madame Asher . . .'

'Yes, ma'am, I know.' The girl looked up at her, and with the motion of her head the lamplight flashed in her eyes, like yellow mirrors.

Lydia felt for a moment that she'd stepped from the warmth of the room back into winter. Cold and disoriented . . .

'I heard you say so in the crypt at the monastery,' the girl went on, 'when you called out to Kolya. And they said in the street that your coachman's livery was that of Prince Razumovsky. Someone said, there was an English lady staying with him . . .'

For all their sweet fullness – even in the warmth of the oil lamp's golden glow – the girl's lips were not so much as a half shade darker than her marble-white face. When she spoke, Lydia could see her fangs.

Oh, dear God . . .

'Madame, please . . .' The girl held out her hand. 'My name is Evgenia,' she added quickly, seeming to remember her manners. 'Evgenia Greb. I live on Politov Court, near the railway works – that is, I did, I used to . . . That is . . .' Grief twisted her face for a moment, grief and terror that it took her the space of a few breaths to master. But Lydia could see already that this girl did not breathe.

'Madame, what's happened to me? What's happened to us? You said to Kolya that you could help him. I . . . I know we're not supposed to leave the monastery, I know God will strike us down, but Kolya . . .'

'Kolya was the boy at the door of the crypt?'

Evgenia nodded. She was trembling; her dark eyes, with their eerie reflectiveness, swam with tears. Lydia swiftly assessed the girl's clothing: faded hand-me-downs spruced up with cheap ribbon, itself already starting to discolor and fray. She'd seen the same on hundreds of girls as the carriage had passed through the slums, in Petersburg, in Paris, in London.

'He's changed,' the girl whispered. 'And now *I'm* starting to change. Look.' She pulled off her mended gloves, held out her fingers to show the claw-like thickening and lengthening of the nails, shiny as glass and harder than steel.

'Madame said—'

'Madame who?'

'Ehrenberg. Madame said that we were chosen, we would be transformed through our faith, that we would be fitted by God to battle demons.' She put her hands momentarily to her mouth, to still the shaking of her lips – maybe to cover what she'd seen already in a mirror. If Madame Ehrenberg let them have mirrors . . . 'But Kolya . . . and Kolya isn't the only one. I've been there three weeks, and Madame and Dr Theiss swear that all will be well, that we are in God's hands, but some of us . . .'

The girl's voice sank lower, as if to hide from the very shadows of the room. 'She says that we will be able to fight demons. That we will be able to save our families and make the world whole again. But, Madame, I think that some of us are becoming demons ourselves. Do you know what has happened to us? What we have become?'

'You don't know?'

Tears running down her face, Evgenia shook her head.

They took the night train for Bebra, where they would arrive at two thirty in the morning, Asher and the vampire woman Jacoba. She had been a moneylender's wife and a scholar in her own right in the days when Köln had been a Free City under the Empire. From the jail they'd taken him to a tall half-timbered town house, where they'd left him chained in a sub cellar; among the boxes and barrels around the walls there, before they'd taken away the lamp, he'd seen wall niches, as in a catacomb. They were empty, but he'd wondered how many vampires used the place as a nest. Sitting with his back to the wall in the darkness, he had not dared to sleep, which was just as well. Had he dozed off, he knew he would quite likely have seen the dead Frenchman lying in the jail cell, with a slashed throat in a pool of not quite enough blood, and the knife that did it left curled in the sleeping German's hand.

I couldn't have saved them . . .

He knew this to the marrow of his bones, but the fact remained that if he hadn't been in the cell with them, they would both have lived.

'Is that part of the hunt?' he asked, when she took her seat on the hard bench in the third-class railway carriage at his side. 'Part of the game?'

Jacoba raised her eyebrows, surprised that the matter still troubled him. 'Bread without salt will keep you from dying,' she said, in a marvelous alto that was like an intimate caress. 'One savors chocolate, and French cheeses, and good wine.' Her smile was sleepy and amused. She'd woken up the gray-haired French prisoner before she'd killed him and had made sure he'd known that he was about to die. He had not died well.

The way her eyes rested on Asher in the rattling dimness of the smelly train-car, he guessed she was looking forward to killing someone she had come to know.

'I hope I come up to your expectations, when the time arrives,' he said politely, and she was surprised into laughing, which changed her whole stern face. 'One would hate to find oneself no more than a *vin ordinaire*. Tell me about Petronilla Ehrenberg.'

And, because he had amused her, she complied. 'A little bitch,' she said, 'as Brom – Todesfall – called her. Always her eye was upon the main chance.' Her German was old-fashioned and echoed, more than a little, the native Kolensh that the workmen had spoken on the tram three – or was it four? – days ago. The words she used for simple things like salt and wine were not German at all, but a Gothic Rhineland French. 'Had I known he was going to bring her into our circle, I would have killed her myself. Shallow as a donkey's hoof print, but very good with money and credit – her husband was high in the Deutsches Bank – and with a mind for investments. Brom respects that. And pretty, in that pink-and-golden candy-box fashion . . . something, alas, Brom is also a trifle too taken by.'

She folded her hands, square and short-fingered in soiled and mended gloves. At Asher's insistence, they had disguised themselves in the shabby garments of the poor. 'Why take the trouble to avoid the German police by a ruse, when I can turn their eyes away with a thought?' she had asked him, when after his deliverance from the Köln jail he'd asked for workman's clothes and boots, and a razor and basin to trim the whole of his head down to the stubble that now fuzzed his crown.

But his reply, 'Because if the Kaiser is recruiting the Undead you may not be able to turn away all eyes,' had brought results, and on the night train there were few enough to share the accommodations. In faded black, with a shawl over her head, Jacoba looked like any other Jewish matron, unless she smiled, or the flicker of station lamps through the windows happened to catch the unholy luminosity of her eyes.

'Once she understood what Brom could do for her,' she went on now, 'of course she was a lover of Jews. But that was a lie, and she and I have never gotten along. I thought at the time, it was why she left Köln. That she sought only another city, where the master would allow her to hunt. I should have known there was something else afoot.' The dark eyes narrowed to an ugly flicker.

'What would she get from it?' asked Asher, hoping that he could remember the way her speech wrapped around the words, somewhere between German and French. He wondered if, before they reached Berlin, he could get this woman to speak to him in the language of her long-ago childhood . . .

Or was that something else, as Ysidro had said, that had faded with the preoccupation with the hunt?

'What could the Kaiser give her?'

'Give her?' The beautiful dark brows arched, barely glimpsed in the sickly wisp of moonlight that penetrated the unlighted carriage. 'Power, of course. And Brom.'

'Does she love Brom?'

Jacoba sniffed. 'Brom has power,' she said. 'Power over her . . . which she cannot abide. So she convinced Brom that she loved him, in order to get him to make her vampire – I think she may have convinced herself at the same time. She is that sort of woman, who needs to think "love" exists. We – the Undead – we do not love one another, Herr Vin Ordinaire, but we do understand one another, better than the living could ever hope to do. As for that woman—'

Asher could almost hear the capital letters in her voice, more pronounced in German – That Woman – and was hard put not to smile.

'—I suspect that even in her lifetime, for all her romantic moonshine, she loved nothing, and no one, that did not in the end somehow profit herself.'

TWENTY

E vgenia whispered, 'It isn't true.'

'What did she tell you,' asked Lydia, 'that you would become? And what did she do to you, to make you this way?'

The servants had gone. Lydia had sent them up to the main house, not daring to let even a whisper be heard. Gossip in the streets had directed this girl here. Clearly, the woman she thought of as the Daytime Petronilla – the one everyone in Petersburg knew – knew enough people to eventually hear of it, if servants started whispering about a vampire visiting the English lady at Razumovsky's *izba*.

The girl pressed her hands to her face, shook her head violently. 'It isn't true. I am not a *vampir*, I have killed no one—'

'Have you drunk blood?'

She looked up, from the peasant bench where she sat, her dark eyes desperate. 'The blood of rats and mice only, Madame. Madame would bring them in, show us how to slit their throats with our nails and drain the blood into a silver cup. Later, she said – when we had grown, nurtured in the darkness as God nurtures up seeds in the ground – she said we would be as the angels are, able to live upon nothing but air and God's light.' Her whole body trembled as she spoke, and she gazed at Lydia's face as if seeking some clue there that what Lydia had told her was a lie, or a test of some kind.

God, please make it be all right . . .

Lydia closed her eyes, breathed for a moment, trying to find some tactful way of saying what she had to say and knowing, firstly, that there wasn't one, and secondly, that if there had been, she, Lydia Asher, who for all her social adeptness was as tactless as the average house-pet, was the wrong person to entrust with the task.

She opened her eyes at the cold touch of those dead hands upon her own – cold as Ysidro's were – and saw that Evgenia had sunk to her knees in front of Lydia's chair, clasped her hands—

And flinched back in pain, rubbing her fingers even at the proximity of the silver chains Lydia wore on her wrists.

'Madame Ehrenberg was lying to you,' Lydia said, keeping her voice steady with an effort. 'Madame Ehrenberg is a vampire. She lied to you – probably sent you dreams or visions in your sleep—'

The horrified widening of the girl's eyes told her she'd guessed right about that.

'—and now she has made you a vampire, too. Tell me about—'

But, with a cry, the girl flung her arms around Lydia's skirts, buried her head in her lap, and Lydia fumbled the chains free from her wrists, dumped them in a deadly, gleaming pile on the stool beside her chair and stroked the dark, thick hair.

'It can't be!' Evgenia sobbed. 'It can't be, I have killed no one! I didn't want it – and now you tell me I have lost my soul! I am damned, and I will go to Hell, and I have done nothing! *Nothing*! I didn't want it—'

Did Ysidro want it, when his long-vanished master had taken him, in the dark of some London churchyard? Did Ysidro consent, as his life ebbed away, knowing what lay beyond the gate through which he was being drawn?

'I will go to Hell—'

'You won't.' Lydia wondered if she herself would go to Hell – always supposing there was such a place – for telling the girl this. 'You say yourself, you have killed no one – you are a maiden still in this respect.'

'It's what she calls us,' whispered Evgenia, her voice breaking on the words. 'Her maidens.'

Lydia did not say that this was how Ysidro had referred to fledglings who had been made vampires, but had not yet made their first kill. They were most vulnerable then, he had said, lacking the psychic powers that were fueled by their victims' deaths, and utterly in the command of their masters. Instead, she urged, 'Tell me about her. Tell me what happened.'

Like Ysidro, Petronilla Ehrenberg lured her prey through their dreams.

She clearly – Lydia thought – didn't have the Spanish vampire's skill in reading the dreams of those he sought to manipulate, but her methods were similar. Evgenia's poverty, her pity for her family and friends in the bleak slums, the deep Slavic mysticism that provided the only comfort that the poor could afford: these were answered in dreams of voices, of a radiantly beautiful woman who said, *You can strike down this evil. You can save and remake the world.*

'She said, it isn't mankind that does these terrible things to their fellow man. God made man good – even my father admits that – so how could men be truly behind the evil of the factories and the foremen and the landlords? They are demons, she said, that wear the form of men. Demons that whisper to men and make them do the terrible things they do. Papa said this was ridiculous, but the dreams did not cease. Usually, I never dream about the Vyborg-side; I dream about the village where I was born, before Papa came to Petersburg. We were cold so often, and so hungry, but I could walk in the fields there, and in the birch woods . . . But in my dream I could see exactly where she would be found, at Dr Benedict's clinic. It's just along the Prospect from my school. I went there looking for her, three, four times . . . The others say the same.'

'Others? Like Kolya?'

Evgenia nodded. 'They would see her at a place in their dreams and go to seek her. And one day she was there at the clinic. She was standing on the steps as I came up the street. Our eyes met, like they do in books . . . I knew it was she, when I was still a block away. It was like meeting someone I had known all my life, someone who loved me . . . Someone I had forgotten. She said she had been waiting for me. That she needed me. That God needed me.'

Of course. Lydia shut her eyes again, this time with anger at the woman – the same flush of fury she had felt at Ysidro, when first Margaret Potton had come up to her in the dining room of the – *of all things!* – Hotel St Petersburg in Paris. *Don Simon told me I'd find you here . . .*

Lydia thought, *That's why she targets girls and boys of fourteen, fifteen . . . A younger child probably couldn't survive the transition to the vampire state. An older one would not be taken in by so simple and comprehensive a lie.*

Lydia had seldom hated anyone in her life. But for this thing, this terrible lie, this theft of life and hope and faith – *this is what it is, to be a vampire . . . to take these things from a well-meaning child because they suit your convenience* – she hated Petronilla Ehrenberg with a hatred that made her tremble.

'It is the blood of the saints, you see,' explained Evgenia, sitting on the floor at Lydia's feet, her arm resting confidingly across Lydia's knees. 'Papa says, the saints were all just busy-bodies who poked their noses into other peoples' affairs, but there's more to it than that. I know there is! There has to be! And Madame said that St George – the slayer of devils – came to her in a dream and opened the vein in his arm, as she did to me, and had her drink of his blood, as I did hers . . . His blood became hers, she said. As hers became mine. She held me . . .'

Tears flooded the girl's eyes again. 'She held me in her arms, and it was as if she held my soul inside her soul. I felt her mind in me, through me, like a burning light, terrifying and beautiful and filled with love. I was like the clearest water, inside a crystal vase, only the vase was a living heart that loved me. I thought my old body died, and a new one was born, with the blood of St George in its veins, that would transform me and let me see which men were actually demons. Let me battle these demons, these evil things that bring sorrow and pain to the world.' She raised her face to Lydia's, and the light of the hearth lent a deceptive whisper of color to skin that Lydia knew was like white silk.

'Afterwards, she said I had to stay at the old monastery, because we had to grow in the darkness, like wheat or roses grow, until we were strong enough to come forth and live on light. But that isn't going to happen—' Her voice faltered like a child's. 'Is it?'

Lydia said, 'No. That's how vampires are made.'

There was an old hunting-lodge in the wooded hills behind Bebra. The cab from the railway station – as the hub of a

dozen railway lines Bebra was amply provided with cabs –
reached there as the fragile sliver of the new moon set. 'The
train for Eichenberg leaves at ten minutes of ten tomorrow
night.' Jacoba steered Asher across the pitch-black hall – her
hand cold on his wrist, her arm across his back, gripping his
other elbow – to the door that led to the cellars below. This
was, he knew, for guidance rather than restraint, though he
could no more have broken free of her grip than he could
have broken the chains that he carried in their mutual carpet-
bag. An attempt to flee, either here or on the station platform,
would have been plain and simple suicide. Her interest in
escorting him was marginal at best, a task she would cheer-
fully abandon, if he gave her the excuse to do so, to kill him
out of hand.

'Tonight, I should say,' she added, and then stopped. Asher
heard door hinges creak, smelled the moldering rankness of
a cellar. 'It will be dawn in less than two hours. There are
stairs here.' She guided him down. He could feel the coldness
of her hands through her gloves, of her body through their
clothing. At the bottom the floor was brick, so worn and pitted
as to be like a broken honeycomb of dents.

'Listen to me, my friend,' said her voice out of the darkness. 'We will remain here for a day, and then travel to
Eichenberg tomorrow night and remain there also for a day.
But the train that leaves Eichenberg in darkness does not reach
Berlin until the sky is growing light. So this is what you will
do. Tonight I will give you the address of where you are to
go in Berlin. You will go straight from the station; I have ways
of learning where you go and how. Remember that the Master
of Berlin knows you are coming; maybe the police as well.
When dark falls I will meet you, and you and I together will
go calling on this man that La Ehrenberg is using, to connect
her with those on the Wilhelmstrasse. You will not go sooner.'

She released him, stepped away, but he did not move. He
knew she was very close, somewhere in the abyssal dark. Had
she breathed, he thought, he would have felt it on his cheek.

Her voice went on, 'Do as I say, and afterwards we will go
our separate ways. Cheat me, and we will find you, wheresoever
you may hide.'

'I won't cheat you.'

The cold hand rested on the side of his neck, ungloved, so

that he could feel the claws. 'And what else will a man say, who is alone in the darkness with Death? Just see you don't.'

She put her hands on either side of his face and kissed him, her body pressed to his, and such was the power of the vampire that he yielded, as if to a drug – knowing in any case that it was impossible for him to physically thrust her away. Then she pinched his ear, hard enough to draw blood, and chained his wrists together and drew him back to what felt like a pillar. The chain clinked coldly as she locked it around the stone. 'There's water and bread to your left, a bucket to your right,' she said. 'I'll return, when it is time for us to depart.'

'I shall count the hours,' said Asher politely, though the kiss had left him shaking. It was, he knew, what vampires did, to cloud the minds of their victims . . . and it certainly worked, at least for a time. He wondered if he dared sleep, not so much from fear of other vampires – he couldn't imagine a town as small as Bebra would support them, even with the constant stream of birds of passage that the railways brought through – as from fear that she might remain close enough to read in his dreams precisely how he planned to get away.

He did not hear her leave.

'I wrote a letter to my parents,' Evgenia said softly, after a long time of silence. 'Telling them that I was well. She said she'd see they got it . . .'

'They never did.' Jamie had told her about his conversation with the Okhrana, and about the missing young people. 'Were there others there, besides you and Kolya?'

'About six of us. Maybe more. Tasha Plek – she was in the room next to mine, and we could sometimes speak – said there had been others before. Dr Theiss looks after us, or M'sieu Texel. It is Dr Theiss who will come in and take some of our blood in a syringe, to study it, I think. If Madame Ehrenberg is a *vampir*, why would Dr Theiss – who is a good man, and gives of his time and talent to work with the poor – why would Dr Theiss be helping her?'

'If she lied to you,' said Lydia slowly, 'and sent you dreams to make you believe her lies, I'm sure she lies to Dr Theiss as well. God only knows what she's told him.' She got to her feet, helped Evgenia up; the girl seemed calmer, but still dazed, as if she had only begun to take in what had happened to her,

which could never be undone. 'Come,' said Lydia. 'We need
to find a place for you to sleep . . . Do you sleep in the
daytime?'

'I don't know, Madame. In the dark of the crypts one cannot
tell.'

And when the sun didn't set until ten at night, and twilight
lingered for hours, what constituted 'night' anyway?

Lydia took her by the hand. 'Vampires burn up in the sunlight,'
she said. 'Your flesh will catch fire, at even the tiniest ray of
its light—'

'Then how can Madame Ehrenberg be a vampire?' Evgenia
pulled back against her leading. 'Are you lying? Have you
been lying? I've seen her outdoors, in full daylight—'

'I don't know. I think there must be two of them – that the
real Madame Ehrenberg has gotten another woman to pose
as her during the day—'

'No!' Evgenia shook her head so violently that her dark
curls bounced. 'The woman who met me at the clinic, she is
the same one who . . . who drank of my blood, who gave me
hers to drink! There was no trickery! There were many lamps
in the room, the light was good, I saw her. And I know her
voice . . .'

*And if she has a vampire's ability to subtly distort human
perceptions, could she make you think her almost-double was
herself?*

Or was it . . .? The alternative possibility turned her almost
as cold inside as the girl beside her.

But it makes more sense . . .

Shock flooded her; not with panic, but with a queer icy
calm as she understood at last what it was that Petronilla
Ehrenberg had done. 'He needed vampire blood,' said Lydia,
speaking almost to herself. 'Dr Theiss . . . Heaven only knows
what he thinks he's doing. But he needed vampire blood, to
distill in some way to make a serum or a medicine that allows
Madame to walk about in the daytime.'

After all, she thought, *wasn't that what Horace Blaydon was
trying to do? Wasn't that the sort of thing that poor Dennis
was supposed to become? A day-walking vampire, loyal to the
British Empire?* The thought of the horror that he had turned
into still gave her nightmares.

'Instead of trapping vampires for their blood,' she said

slowly, 'she simply made them. He must be testing his serum on them as well. I think that must be what happened to Kolya. One of the experiments went wrong. Maybe more than one . . .'

'No.' The girl's voice was pleading. 'No, you're lying to me . . .'

'Why would I lie?'

'You might be a demon yourself. The demons Madame told us about, that one day we'll be able to defeat—'

Lydia put her hands on the girl's shoulders, looked into those tear-filled, reflective eyes. 'Do you think that's true?'

For answer, Evgenia only sobbed and turned her face away.

'Listen, Genia. Two of Madame Ehrenberg's maidens escaped her: one last year, the other just a little more than a week ago. She hadn't told them anything, they didn't know enough to take refuge from the sun's light. One of them – a girl – went to sleep in an attic on Samsonievsky Alley . . .'

The girl stared at her with horrified eyes, filled with shock and despair. 'The girl in the attic. The girl who burned up—'

'You heard about that?'

The cold hands clutched her, their desperation giving them the first forerunners of the terrible vampire strength.

'I think that has to have been one of them,' said Lydia. 'We have a cellar here.' She guided the girl to the kitchen and opened the half-width door of the narrow stair. 'There's a cupboard; it's not large, but you can remain there, during the daylight hours. Tomorrow – today,' she added, realizing that it had to be well after midnight, 'I'll—' She stopped, the words sticking in her throat at the sight of those terrified eyes. *What on earth CAN I do today?*

I need to speak to Jamie.

I need to speak to Simon.

I need to find some way to help this poor child . . .

CAN a vampire remain a maiden? She recalled how Ysidro's powers to influence dreams, to blind and alter the awareness of the living, even to keep people from seeing his extremely disturbing true appearance – everything a vampire could do, to protect himself as well as to hunt – had waned, during the weeks they had traveled together and he had fasted from human kills. Was it the sheer accumulation of centuries of kills that let Simon – the oldest vampire she knew about – linger awake a little longer before the deathly day-sleep overcame him? Endure for a few seconds the pallid whisper of earliest dawn?

New-made fledglings, he had once told her, were fragile. Most – even those willing and eager to hunt – didn't survive their first half-century.

Standing behind her on the stair, Evgenia gazed at the dark doorway of the cupboard, hand pressed to her mouth like a frightened child. 'It's like a grave.'

'I'll find somewhere else that you can go,' Lydia promised. Razumovsky would return the day after tomorrow. Could she trust him not to ask questions?

She didn't know.

As they reascended the stairs, Evgenia ventured, 'Can you bring me a priest?'

Lydia winced at the thought. To bring a priest to comfort this poor child would be to sign the man's death warrant, if the Petersburg vampires – *when do they all leave on holiday?* – came to hear that the living had proof of their existence. As it was, she knew that Evgenia's continued presence at the *izba* would put the servants – and herself, for that matter – in terrible jeopardy.

I need to speak to Jamie . . .

There had been no word from him for three days, and panic twisted somewhere behind her sternum; *adrenalin flow increased by anxiety*, she noted automatically, and glanced at her watch to time the duration of sensation . . .

For that matter, she reflected as she knelt to prod the coals in the parlor stove back to life, there was no guarantee a priest wouldn't compound poor Evgenia's wretchedness by recoiling from her in horror and telling her that yes, indeed, she *was* damned. Many years ago, Lydia had protested in disbelief when her friend Josetta had said that, by and large, most men would blame a woman for being raped. *Getting herself raped*, was how they'd put it . . . *A normal woman WANTS to be dominated* . . . And fairly recently, she recalled, one of Jamie's scholastic colleagues had broken off his engagement with his fiancée on precisely those grounds. She could easily see one of those bearded, solemn Orthodox prelates – men who not only didn't speak against the periodic pogroms that the government encouraged, but approved of them – reacting to the news of Evgenia's hideous situation exactly as Evgenia had.

That she was damned, through no doing of her own.

Simon will know what to do.

The thought came to her unwillingly, but she had to admit that she had never seen the Spanish vampire at a loss.

But if Jamie is . . . is in trouble of some kind – she refused to look at the darker alternative – *would Simon not have written to me? Or let me know . . .?*

How far away did he have to be, not to be able to read her dreams?

Or was that not something he would do, after their parting in Constantinople?

She walked to the door and opened it, letting the cold flow over her face and trying to gauge by the thin wedding-ring of the new moon how much of the night was left. At this time of the year – it was the twenty-second of April by the Russian calendar, and the sixth of May (if her calculations were correct) in England – barely any actual darkness lay between the last fading-out of brightness from the sky and the first glimmers of dawn. In a few weeks the sky would be soaked with eerie radiance all night. Evgenia had been here—

'Do you hear that?'

Such was the terror in Evgenia's voice that Lydia swung around, to see the girl standing by the stove.

'Calling to me,' whispered Evgenia. 'Like the voices in my dreams. Coming for me . . .'

Oh, God . . .

Lydia turned back to the door, her heart in her throat.

Motion in the starlit screen of trees.

The gleam of eyes.

TWENTY-ONE

'Don't let them take me.' Evgenia's hands clutched Lydia's arm. Lydia could feel her body trembling, pressed against her in the dark doorway. 'They'll make me one of them. And then I will be lost indeed.'

'I won't let them take you.' Even as she spoke, sleepiness rolled over her mind like a drug. She backed into the cottage, bolted the door, and ran to the bedroom. From her luggage she yanked the spare garlands she'd woven, garlic and wild roses, as if she were a peasant girl in the sixteenth century instead of a scholar and a physician and a modern young woman of the twentieth. 'Put these—' she began to say, but stopped herself, as Evgenia backed away, face twisted with repulsion and fear.

'It hurts . . .'

'Good. It'll hurt them, too.' Lydia wrapped one of the garlands around the door handle, hung another over the door. There weren't enough of them, so she ran into the bedroom again and pulled in half the garlands that she had hung above her bedroom windows every night she had slept in the cottage, so that there would be enough for a little to hang over every window in the place. She was so sleepy she blundered into the walls as she moved, her brain fighting the relentless pressure of the vampire minds.

How can I be this terrified and still fall asleep? 'Who is it out there? Is it Madame?'

'I don't know who it is.' The girl pressed her hands to her temples, her eyes. 'Voices – it isn't her. When she held me – when I changed – it was as if she was a part of my thoughts, a part of my heart . . .'

Lydia staggered into the kitchen, pulled open the drawers of the sideboard. *Thank goodness His Excellency would be ashamed to have less than the best silver in the* izba *for his guest.* She fumbled with the kitchen string, dropped the silver forks and spoons as she bound them onto the ends of the broom handle and the poker from the stove. 'Take this . . .'

'It burns!' cried the girl. 'It burns my eyes, like smoke—'

'It will burn them where it touches their flesh,' said Lydia. 'Can you endure it?'

'I think so.' Evgenia looked disoriented, her eyes starting to wander, as if she were having trouble understanding.

'Listen to me,' said Lydia. 'Focus your mind. Try to push past the voices, try to close the door on them.' She yawned hugely, shook her head in a vain attempt to clear it. 'This may be your only chance. Remember, it's not for long.' She threw a glance at the very un-peasant-like clock in the 'red corner.' It was just past two. She took a deep breath. Whoever these were – Golenischev or his rival or those angry young rebel fledglings Jamie had told her about – they would have to leave soon, if they were themselves to reach shelter before the first stain of dawn in the sky. If they were only here to observe, to keep an eye on—

Glass shattered with a splintering tinkle in the bedroom. Lydia dashed in to see shadowy forms draw away from the window sill, unable to bear the proximity of the garlic. At the same moment she heard windows break in the parlor behind her . . . *four rooms, eight windows, two defenders* . . . and Evgenia screamed. A long pole – from the boathouse, Lydia thought – probed through the bedroom's broken window, the hook on its end groping and scratching for the garlic wreath. Lydia strode up to the window, stabbed into the darkness with her own silver-ended makeshift weapon, and as the boat pole drew back she snatched down the swags of herbs from that window and the other, threw herself back through the door into the parlor.

'Gospozha!' Evgenia was jabbing and thrusting through the window with her own weapon, trying to parry another boat pole. She was too far away to use the weapon effectively – Lydia wound one of the half wreaths around the bedroom doorknob, snatched up her heavy skirts, and crossed the parlor in two bounds. In the dark beyond the window she glimpsed a white face, like a corpse's, but mobile and soft . . . A woman's, she thought, as the reflective eyes caught the light.

'Bitch!' yelled a voice from the darkness, and another called out something in Russian; Evgenia fell back behind Lydia, clinging to her – another window shattered, at the far end of the parlor, from a billet of firewood thrown like a spear. Lydia ran to the place, jabbed into the darkness, struggling with the near-conviction that this was all a dream and it didn't matter if she defended the house or not.

'You have to get close!' she shouted back at Evgenia.

Grimly, the girl ran to parry the groping boat-hook when it came in again, first jabbing with her silver weapon, then reaching up to grab the boat hook, to try to pull it away from the attackers. The force with which it was jerked back made her cry out.

'They're stronger than you!' Lydia fell back, grabbed the second fragment of wreath and wrapped it around the door handle of the study. 'We only have to hold them off for a little while—'

A man's voice called out in Russian again, close this time – *he must be standing on the veranda*. Evgenia shouted something back, then whispered over her shoulder, 'He says that you will betray me. That, because I'm already vampire, you'll wait till I fall asleep . . . He says I must, I will, soon. And then you'll drag me outside, to burn up when it gets light . . .'

'I won't.'

Tears were running down the girl's face, crumpled with grief in the dark frame of her hair. 'Even though I'm damned? He says, nothing can save me.'

'You don't know that,' said Lydia desperately. 'A priest will know—'

Another jeering shout from outside. Lydia almost didn't need the translation.

'He says, priests lie. All of them.'

'Do you believe—?'

Something crashed against the door from the bedroom behind them; Lydia swung around. A woman's voice cursed, cold and silvery – in Russian. Then a third window broke, and Lydia rushed to parry the long hooked pole that came through—

She didn't know how it happened – true accident or clumsiness engineered, like the sleepiness, from outside – but her feet caught on one of the low peasant stools and she fell. Her head hit the corner of the table with a sickening crack on the way to the floor. At the same instant she heard more glass break somewhere – *the attic*, she thought, *the windows upstairs*, but she seemed to be viewing the room and herself through the wrong end of a telescope. *Get up! Get up!*

She managed to roll over, and the pain that axed through her head brought on a spasm of vomiting, excruciating in her corset. Gray swam down over her senses, and she heard Evgenia scream despairingly. Then cold hands dragged her up; she saw eerily glowing vampire eyes as claws ripped at the collar of her blouse.

'*Vyedyma!*' The vampire – thin and cold-faced with a cruel slit of a mouth – threw her down, clutching his hand where the welts were already ballooning on his fingers from her protective silver chain. Beyond him, Lydia could see Evgenia backed into a corner by two others, woman and man; the cold-faced man drew back his foot to kick her. '*Gryazn—*'

Wait, no, don't I at least get to see Jamie again before I die?

Something – a shadow – flickered in the deeper shadows of the parlor, and as Lydia's vision fractured away to nothing she saw what seemed to be a pair of disembodied white hands appear out of the darkness behind her attacker. One – connected by a wrist like whalebone to a grimed and smutted shirtsleeve – wrapped neatly around the vampire's jaw, while the other molded itself over temple and forehead, but she wasn't sure.

She recognized the ring on one finger, as with a neat twist Ysidro snapped the other vampire's neck.

That scene repeated itself for her a half-dozen times, it seemed, in various forms of dream, until she came to in blackness illumined by a single tiny flame. Damp chill lay clammy on her skin, where her torn blouse exposed her throat. She smelled coals and wet earth. Her feet were raised and lay on what felt like someone's lap – Evgenia's, she realized, when she heard the girl speak. *We must be in the cupboard in the cellar, in the safety of the darkness . . .*

'Then there is no hope for me?' the girl pleaded.

Ysidro's voice – light and soft and disinterested – replied from just behind her head. 'It depends upon how you define hope, child. Can you become human again? No. No more than you can by effort of will return to the flesh you wore as a child of two. This is not possible.'

'Am I damned? You who are one of them – you who are *vampir* – you would know—'

'I regret to say that I do not, Evgenia. I have been vampire for three hundred and fifty-four years now, and never have God or any of His angels appeared to me to inform me of whether I am damned or saved, or if I am able to alter my state, or even if they care, about me or anyone else. There is no way for any of us but forward, and none – living or Undead – can see through any gate before its portals are passed.'

Very light, very chilly hands passed across Lydia's forehead. She was lying, she slowly came to know, with her neck and shoulders propped on something – a folded coat? – and her head resting against, but not directly on, Ysidro's narrow thigh. She groped for his fingers, even as Evgenia whispered,

'And the one you killed?' Her voice was thick with sleepiness, already drifting away. 'Is he now in Hell?'

'Mistress?' Ysidro's grip tightened gently around Lydia's fingertips.

Silver, she thought. *I still have silver on my wrists . . . Or did I take it off?*

'No, child,' Ysidro went on, 'my strength is enough to snap our friend's neck, but not tear his head off – at least, not quickly. But it rendered him unable to move, giving his colleagues the choice of carrying him away to safety – they had bare minutes of true darkness left – or leaving him to burn up where he—'

Ysidro's voice broke off. Moving her head – Lydia felt as if her own neck had been broken, and she fought to keep from throwing up again – she saw that Evgenia had slumped over in the corner of the crowded little cupboard where they huddled. The girl's eyes were shut, her pale mouth hanging slightly ajar, like any sleeping fifteen-year-old's, except for the fangs.

'Is vampire sleep that much like real sleep?' she murmured.

'No, Mistress.' Ysidro moved the candle. 'How many flames do you see?'

Lydia flinched, turned her head away, the light painful. 'Too many.'

'Then how many fingers?'

'How do I know?' she said, her mouth feeling like it belonged to someone else. 'I don't have my spectacles. My head hurts.'

'I have no doubt of that, Mistress, and had I a spare one for you in my pocket you should surely have it. Did you take any other hurt?'

'I don't know.' Lydia groped for fragments of recollection about the last minutes of the fight. Moving her hand was an agony – any movement, in fact – but she felt at where her shirtwaist had been torn, touched the skin of her throat. The chain was still there. 'I wasn't bitten, was I?'

'No.'

'Is Jamie all right?'

For a moment he was silent. Then: 'Was he with you?'

It took Lydia a few moments to reason out this question, wondering why he would ask that . . . Her mind seemed to be

moving very slowly, and her memory would not release that
last image, of Ysidro's strong white hands wrapping themselves like some sort of prehensile sea-life around the face of
the cold-eyed slender vampire who had called her a *vyedyma*,
whatever that was . . . She'd have to ask Razumovsky . . .

As if putting the words together from several different note-
books, one at a time, on a table, she managed at last to say,
'He wasn't with you?'

Did I miss something?

Another long stillness. Then: 'I had not thought him a man
to betray me, yet I knew he had plans of his own. I woke in
the lodging I had arranged in Berlin, but when I went to his,
he was not there. I thought the way the luggage was laid down
was not as he was accustomed to do it. There was neither
note, nor message . . . I walked about Berlin until nearly dawn
and found no trace of him, not even in the jail or the offices
of the Foreign Service in the Wilhelmstrasse. What became
of him, I know not.'

'Jamie—' And because her head was pounding, and dizziness was making the room rock beneath her in wide, sickening
arcs, she clung to Ysidro's thin hand and began to cry.

It wasn't like Ysidro to offer comfort – in three hundred
and fifty-four years it seemed to have faded away, along with
all expression and most gestures, and perhaps he had learned
that, contrary to the usual assurances in times like this, everything would *not* be all right . . .

But he did brush gently at the hair that trailed over her
forehead, his claws light as butterfly feet on her skin, and
said, in a voice no louder than the flicker of wind, 'Now,
Mistress . . .'

Weeping still, she asked him, 'Why did you kill her? Why
couldn't you just let her go?'

Silence again, longer, and so deep she wondered in terror
if he, too, had been struck by the vampire sleep. If she would
have to lie here, buried in this grave with him until—

Judgment day?

At last he said, 'And where would she have gone, Mistress?'
It was as if he had known whom she meant – had known for
the past eighteen months, that this was the question she was
going to ask when next they met. Slowly, and only after long
silence, he went on, 'In truth, I think it was one of the

vampires from the old Harem in the palace, who saw Margaret – perhaps spoke to her – when she became lost there, the night of the rioting in the Armenian quarter. I do not say I would not have killed her in time,' he added, as Lydia clung harder to his hands, sobs shaking her as if all the griefs since that time – the child she had lost, the wrenched and wretched sense of having been betrayed not by the world, but by her own heart – were cracking apart. 'But another was before me . . . There, there, Mistress, what is this? James is a man of great resource—'

'Why did you lie to me?'

'Because no good can come,' said Ysidro, 'from the friendship of the living and the dead.'

Lydia blinked, struggling to bring his face into focus. His smudged and filthy shirt, open at the collar to show sinew and collarbone, told its own tale, of hiding and dodging – how had he traveled, without the watchful protection of a living man? Or had he lured another to him in Berlin and convinced him – through dreams or money or blackmail or all the other methods the vampire employed – to act as his bodyguard and baggage handler, until Ysidro was done with him?

In the frame of his long white hair, the vampire's thin face was calm, but filled, she thought, with infinite regret.

'It is best that their ways remain apart. When one or the other attempts to cross that barrier, there is always pain, and sometimes evil worse than pain. Mistress—'

She opened her eyes with a start, aware that she'd been drifting into darkness that she sensed was deeper than sleep, an abyss from which she could not surface.

'Do not sleep yet,' he said gently. 'Someone will be here soon.'

'What time is it?'

'Not long past four.'

'I have a concussion,' said Lydia, 'don't I? Is that why I must stay awake?'

'For a time.' He stroked her forehead again, cold flesh and claws like steel and glass. 'I would have left you in the cottage above, save that I misliked how you breathed. It were best that you were watched for a time. The vampire princes have both left Petersburg; those who remain here are the scaff and raff – students, and a man who was a priest, and another who worked for the Third Section. Fledglings who hate both the master who made them, and the other master who would take power in this impossible city where only the weak take refuge.'

'Would you have made me a fledgling,' asked Lydia, feeling a little as if she were drifting in a dream, 'to keep me from dying?'

'No.' Don Simon gathered the thick pottery-red swags of her hair in his hand, ran them through his fingers as if savoring the touch. 'James would not thank me for it; nor would you.'

'Because vampires do not love?'

'I have known those who do,' he said. 'No, Mistress. I do not make fledglings because of what fledglings are: the hand of your hand, the heart of your heart. What the fledgling was in life, the master understands, as if the events – joy or sorrow, coupling or cheating or the glazing-over of the heart – had happened to him, over and over again. There are masters who enjoy this. To them it is a triumph akin to the kill. Myself I find it distasteful, both to hold that kind of power, and to partake of that . . . knowledge.'

Lydia felt her eyes slipping closed, and she struggled to remain awake, as she had earlier in the night – not against the vampires now, but against the velvet weight of pain. Her head throbbed as if her skull had cracked, and she feared to move, knowing movement would bring on nausea again. It was a comfort, she thought – looking at the tiny flicker of reflected yellow light on the narrow wooden shelves, the glass jars and pottery crocks of Rina's faithful housekeeping – to have Ysidro with her, when she felt so cold and dizzy and frightened.

'I've missed you.'

'And I you, Mistress.'

'I thought of you,' she murmured. 'When I was ill last year. I miscarried. I wanted – I thought I was dying, those first few days, and I wanted to speak with you . . . because if I was dying, what I said wouldn't matter. It was silly . . .'

'Not silly at all, Mistress. It only grieves me, to hear that you were ill.'

'Jamie—' she began, and then fell silent again. Then, 'It's been three days since he's written. Four, if nothing comes today. Tonight – when the sun sets – will you come back here? We have to—'

She moved her head a little – at the cost of vise-like agony – but found that his fingers had slacked in her grip. She saw that he sat back against the corner of the wall, his eyes closed, his face relaxed in sleep. And as with Evgenia, the illusion of humanity was so strong – as if the care and grief that had been washed away were only the care and grief of a day – that she wondered how much of a soul remained to him, even after all this time.

What WAS a soul, anyway? The child she had lost – the child she was trying so hard not to hope too much that she might be carrying now, Jamie's child . . . *Who WERE they?*

Who was he, this young man who'd died before Queen Elizabeth had come to the throne? Who if he hadn't been Undead and damned she'd never have met, never have known, never have . . .

Footsteps creaked on the floorboards overhead. Her heart leaped. *Jov, Ivan, Rina . . .*

'We're here,' she called out, and even the effort of speaking was like having the bones of her skull pried apart with iron and wheels. 'Close the door, close the cellar door—'

She heard it close, and footfalls descended the stair. *All right*, she thought, through a thickening fog, *just how are you going to explain who these two sleepers are, and why they have to remain here, and how can I find some other place for them to stay when even moving my head hurts so much . . .?*

I mustn't fall asleep now. I have to make Jov and Rina believe me . . . What if they think I'm delirious . . .?

The thought of further explanation – of any further effort of any kind – brought on another wave of feeble nausea and the desire simply to sleep and let things take what course they would.

Splinters of gold lamplight shone beneath the cupboard door, in the darkness seeming to go through her optic nerves and straight to the back of her brain like needles. A woman's voice – *Rina's?* – said, quite close by, 'We have to hurry. They'll wake at the house soon.'

Shadow moved across the lamplight. Lydia called out weakly, 'Is the door closed?'

The cupboard door opened. Lamplight outlined the three who stood in the narrow opening. They'd closed the door at the top of the cellar steps; no flicker of the rising dawn filtered through.

The gold light outlined the grave countenance of Dr Theiss, the restless, bony face of Hugo Texel framed in his ridiculous whiskers. And highlighted the curved pale lips, the triumphant smile, of Petronilla Ehrenberg, holding aloft the lamp.

TWENTY-TWO

*A*t least I've done what I've done for a good cause, Horace Blaydon had said, when Asher had brought up the subject of the man's turning loose his artificial vampire to feed in the backstreets of London and Manchester . . . cities of the country he claimed he was working to protect.

And yet, Asher reflected, wasn't he one of them himself? *Every kill he makes henceforth will be upon your head . . .*

In the endless darkness of the crypt, Asher could barely tell where memory ended and dream began. Only the fear remained, of what Benedict Theiss might be doing, and what would come of it, during the coming war, and after. Did they think a living weapon like that would not acquire a life of its own?

I had to do what I did, what I am doing, for the common good.

He drew a breath, trying to keep his mind clear. Leaned his head back against the pillar behind him.

They all said that.

I know what I'm doing, Blaydon had said.

They all said that, too.

God preserve us, Asher reflected wearily, *from people who 'know what they're doing'.*

Myself included.

The crypt was cold, as if all the winters of all those years in which it had been in existence had sloughed there and pooled. Despite his shabby jacket he shivered, unable to truly sleep. Yet he knew each waking hour filed something from abilities he'd need in two days' time – if his calculations were correct – when he and Jacoba reached Berlin. He guessed how she'd try to control him in the daylight hours and knew he'd have to move very quickly, or he would be a dead man indeed.

Charlottenstrasse. That would be out towards Potsdam, one of those handsome brick villas that the Junkers who ruled the country built for themselves, for when they came into town to attend the opera and marry each others' sons and daughters: feudal nobles despite the pretense of a parliamentary Reichstag, warriors whose whole souls were invested in the Army.

Soldiers who could not wait for the War they were certain they would gloriously win.

And who did not consider what that War would make of the world that would come after.

They ruled the country, those landowners for whom the only honorable profession was that of arms. Like the French, who considered it appropriate for ladies to get off the pavement to let brilliantly-uniformed officers pass. Of course they could not conceive of a world in which war had become too devastating, too beastly, to be waged anymore. The answer was always more courage: the intuitive depth of the pure-blooded German soul.

He had no idea what he'd do when he reached Colonel von Brühlsbuttel's doorstep.

But whatever it was going to be – and he was almost certain it would involve killing the man, if Ysidro hadn't done so already – he would have to do it swiftly, to be out of Berlin on the noon train.

Lydia whispered, 'Don't hurt them.'

Even the smooth-running motion of Madame Ehrenberg's motor car made her so dizzy she feared she would faint.

'Hurt them?' Petronilla Ehrenberg raised one beautifully-shaped brow. 'My dear child, Dr Theiss will guard them as if they were his own children, until Texel returns with coffins and a cart. Thank Heavens he had his medical bag with him, to keep the servants at the house from waking before time.' The green glance slipped sideways to Lydia, the pale gleam of early morning flashing in Madame's eyes. 'What happened? And how is it that you, Frau Asher, have the acquaintance of not only what appears to be a mature vampire – who is he, by the way? – but also one of my little maidens?'

Lydia thought it wisest to drop her head back against the elaborately-tucked plush of the car seat – she didn't need to conjure up the effects and appearance of a splitting headache – and mutter again, 'Don't hurt them . . .'

The car went around the corner, and Lydia, jostled, felt a surge of nausea sweep her, and despite the agony of throwing up while wearing a corset, she didn't hold back. It earned her several violent slaps, but convinced Madame that she was too weak and disoriented to question – something she certainly was after being slapped with a vampire's terrifying strength. She was barely conscious of the car turning into the court-yard of St Job's, and of the chauffeur – after locking the gate – carrying her to what had been a chapel off the main monastic church.

When they woke her later Dr Theiss was there, and the angle of pallid sunlight through the single arched window was close to seventy degrees towards the perpendicular. The light fell full on Madame Ehrenberg, resplendent in several shades of rose and watching with sharp impatience while Theiss peered into Lydia's eyes with his bright little mirror, and gently felt her neck and the back of her head. 'How many fingers?' he asked, holding up two – mightily blurred, since her specta-cles had been left behind at the *izba*, but distinctly two.

Lydia made a show of blinking, squinting – would a doctor be fooled as easily as her Aunt Faith? – and mumbled, 'Three? No . . .' She reached clumsily to touch his hand, making sure that she missed. Her head still felt like someone had forgotten to remove the ax blade from her skull, and even the attempt to grope for Theiss's hand made her feel faint, so she dropped back to the pillow – which seemed to date from the original monastic establishment, she thought – with a piteous cry. Behind Theiss, a whole array of mildewed Byzantine saints glared from the wall, as if about to chorus, *She's making it all up . . .* 'I want Jamie,' she whispered and began to weep, needing very little effort to sound as wretched as she felt. The tears flowed easily.

'Give her something,' snapped Petronilla Ehrenberg. 'I need to know who that vampire is, and what he was doing there.'

'Madame, there is nothing to give her,' explained Theiss, with a patience in his voice that told Lydia he'd explained this two or three times already. 'She is suffering from a severe concussion—'

'How soon will she be able to talk?'

'I don't know, Madame. One never does, with head injuries.'

With the swiftness of a striking snake, Ehrenberg was at the doctor's side, leaning over him to catch his lapel, jerk him towards her. From where she lay, Lydia couldn't see the details of her expression, but the woman's sudden rage flowed off her like smoke from ice. 'And what kind of doctor are you, not to know that? If you *are* as ignorant as you—'

'Petronilla.' Theiss laid down his mirror, looked up into those gleaming eyes. There was not the slightest trace of fear in his body or his deep, calm voice. 'My beautiful one. No doctor knows these things. You know this – of course you do . . .'

She released her grip, fell back a half step, her lace-gloved hand to her temple.

'You are exhausted.' Theiss quickly got to his feet, took both her hands in his. 'And it is no wonder. The latest injections—'

'I am well.' She straightened up, smiled a smile that Lydia could feel, a warm loveliness . . .

It is our lure to be attractive, Ysidro had said once to James. *It is how we hunt.*

And Dr Theiss was in love with her. Drawn, as James had been drawn – in spite of himself – to the vampire Countess of Ernchester eighteen months ago.

As I am drawn to Ysidro?

For a moment she thought she could still feel the light touch of his claws on her forehead.

'It doesn't matter who the other vampire is,' Theiss went on, 'nor how Evgenia encountered Madame Asher. It makes no difference in the quality of their blood. By the look of those makeshift weapons we found, Madame Asher was clearly fighting against vampires: either Evgenia and this other man, or the vampires of Petersburg . . . He is not one of them, is he? I know you have nothing to do with them, but have you seen—?'

'If he was one of them, he would have killed her,' she snapped. 'What I fear most is what he may have told poor Genia. We shall need to keep her separate from the others – right away from them – until I've had a chance to speak with her. It's too bad we have to keep him in the chapel.' She glanced over her shoulder at the door. 'Genia's cell in the crypts is too close to the others. Their hearing is sharp – some of them already have worked out how to whisper through the old pipes. The last thing I need is for the others to start becoming restless, before their systems have evolved past the point of a physical craving for the hunt.'

He nodded gravely. Lydia wanted to shake him and demand, *Is THAT what she's told you . . .?*

It evidently was, because he asked with great tenderness, 'And your cravings have never come back?'

'Now and then. A twinge.' She shook her head, produced a gallant smile, and brought her hand to her temple again, with considerably less realism, Lydia thought, than she had after her fit of rage. 'I find that prayer will lift all thought of it from me . . .'

Theiss clasped her hands to his chest.

As Mrs Grimes would say – Lydia took strange comfort in the recollection of her cook's sharp little face – *arhh, why don't you go pull me other leg?*

Theiss guided Madame Ehrenberg from the room, closing the door behind them. Lydia heard the lock click, but listened in vain for the sound of a bolt. Their voices retreated across the chapel outside.

Was the chapel she dimly recalled being carried through, Lydia wondered, the same one in which Ysidro was being held? *In a coffin or box, presumably . . .* She recalled windows. Light.

Petronilla Ehrenberg's golden hair catching the light.

Carefully – trying not to sit up until she absolutely had to – Lydia drew up her skirt and petticoat, to feel for the small, flat packet buttoned to the bottom of her corset.

The picklocks were still there.

The cot where she lay was a low one, set crosswise on what had been the altar step of a smaller chapel that in later years had been walled off from the main sanctuary. From the ceiling above her, ranked choirs of soot-darkened angels dimly chorused a silent dirge. Lydia rolled gingerly off the cot, the floor swooping horrifically beneath her; she knelt on all fours for a few minutes, as if clinging to the uneven stones, fighting not to be sick again. *You can do this. You can get to the door . . .*

Trembling, sweating, and repeatedly tangling her knees in

her skirt, she crawled. The lock was a simple Yale tumbler model, the kind Jamie had taught her on. *Thank you, God . . .*

It still took her what felt like hours to pick, clinging now and then to the handle of the door, fighting waves of faintness. *I'll never do it . . .*

You will. You've made it this far. Simon is the only one who can find Jamie, help him . . . If he CAN be helped . . .

She pushed open the door. Afternoon sunlight drenched the chapel, red and gold and gorgeous with serried lines of, presumably, saints and angels, though for all Lydia could make out details they might have been a line of chorus girls at the Palace Theater. The altar and iconostasis had been removed at some time in the past. In their place, on a low trestle table, lay a coffin, its lid criss-crossed with chains.

I'll have to stand to reach it. The thought of picking another lock – or more than one – made her want to weep. *And I'll have to figure some way to make it look like the locks are still in place, in case someone comes through later.* Moving as slowly as she could, she propped herself against the door jamb, pulled up her petticoat hem and found where Ellen had repaired it: carefully teased out two feet of thread. This she wound around her fingers, then crawled – it felt like miles – the thirty feet or so across a floor wrought of slabs of green and brown onyx, worn to uneven ripples by the bare feet of pious men long dead.

Whatever you do, don't faint now.

It was eerie, how still the monastery was. As if the slums of the Vyborg-side, the Putilov Steel Works, had ceased to exist. *Everybody must be at the clinic,* thought Lydia as she bent forward, probes still in the lock, to rest her forehead on the black oak of the coffin lid. She was willing to bet that Ehrenberg's chauffeur wasn't in on the secret . . .

Give me enough money and it's not my business.

Or maybe he was in love with Petronilla as well.

And poor Dr Theiss thought this was all about Petronilla's redemption. That this desire of hers to become human again was a way of saving her soul. Ironic that her pretended goal was so real and deadly serious to poor Evgenia.

Dear Heavens, what will she do to Evgenia, now that Evgenia knows the truth?

I should find her next . . .

Lydia knew that would be utterly beyond her strength. Her vision was already blurring, her eyes going in and out of what focus they had. Twice, and three times, the thin hooks slid and fumbled in the old-fashioned padlock . . . Even when it dropped open, when the slant of the light through the barred chapel windows – silver bars, Lydia could see – showed her there was another yet to do.

Theiss will have to come back before it gets dark and move the coffin elsewhere, if he wants to draw Simon's blood . . .

Or does Petronilla want to speak to Ysidro first?

The thought occurred to her that if Don Simon proved recalcitrant – and Recalcitrant, not to say Ornery, was the Spanish vampire's middle name – it was herself, Lydia, who would be used to convince him to cooperate.

When the second lock came off, Lydia's hands were shaking so badly that she had to sink to the floor, lean against the trestle, and rest, before she was capable of tying the ends of the chains together with knots of thread, with the closed padlocks bound into the knots to give the appearance – from a distance, to someone not paying much attention – that the locks were still in place. *Please, God, keep them both busy with something else until dark . . .*

The outer door of the chapel was bolted from the outside. Lydia almost wept with gratitude that it wasn't possible to go rescue Evgenia, a task she knew herself utterly incapable of. Amid their clouds of gold-and-crimson splendor, the saints and angels watched impassively as she crawled the length of the chapel again, back to her cell. She opened an inch of seam at a corner of her pillow – Jamie had taught her to be thorough – and slipped the picklocks inside, before she laid her head down.

God, please don't let this start me bleeding. Don't let this hurt my child.

Because she knew there would be a child. The certainty of it was the last thought that went through her mind before she passed out as if she had been drugged.

TWENTY-THREE

L ydia dreamed of twilight. Somewhere near at hand men argued drunkenly, children cried. She smelled smoke, sewage, dirty clothing. All the stinks of the clinic. People weary, with the blind weariness of frustration and exhaustion, shouting at one another . . . in Russian, which she thought was most curious, since she didn't know any Russian except, *I will not be back for dinner*.

She dreamed about a grandmother. Evgenia's grandmother? Somebody's – and certainly nothing like the well-starched matriarch of the Willoughby family. A tiny bent woman with white hair, moving painfully about the filthy streets of the slum with a basket of scarves to sell. She had a tall staff, like a mast with five crosspieces, also decorated with scarves: red, purple, blue, pink, like a gaudy tree with all its leaves fluttering in the wind. This she used to support her steps, and Lydia felt the pain in her legs and her back as if it were her own.

For some reason Lydia knew her name was Ekaterina, and that she'd been beautiful when she was young.

Ekaterina had a regular route, like the peddlers in Oxford and London – up the Samsonievsky Prospect, along the Putilov railroad spur (*how do I know all this?*), back by way of the canal. Other vendors, pushing carts of old shoes or carrying trays of hot pies, greeted her: *Zdravstvooytye, babushka*. She'd had four sons, two of whom were in the Tsar's army and the other two were dead, killed in accidents at the Navy Yard, but their widows – and her many grandchildren – called to her outside the tenements where they lived. One of her daughters had saved a little bread for her.

Only on this day – and it was daylight now, Lydia saw, the gorgeous golds of the long arctic dawn and not the deepening twilight of evening – Ekaterina followed the tracks past the steelworks, moving like a small gray fish against the jostling groups of men who passed wearily through the gates for another day's toil. Before her, the walls of an old monastery rose, soot black and somber among the wooden tenements. Somehow the old woman knew that she must walk a circuit around its walls and along the path of the old Putilov canal, and on the side that faced the waste ground – the side over-looked by the broken windows of the old chapel – something pale fluttered among the new little weeds; something pale that, as it moved, revealed the gleam of gold.

Ekaterina crossed herself and kissed her knuckle for luck. Witches and demons haunted St Job's these days. Her daughter's friend Tonya had seen one, flitting about the ruins of the stables on that side . . .

Yet an angel stood beside that fluttering scrap of paper; an angel with a thin scarred face like a skull, framed by long colorless spiderweb hair.

God wishes you to send a telegram, Grandmother, said the angel to Ekaterina.

The old woman crossed herself again. 'I cannot read, Master Angel; I cannot write. I am an old poor woman . . .'

This is why God asks this of you and no other, replied the angel. *Take – obey*. And he pointed with a long thin forefinger to the paper lying on the ground. His nail was as long as a claw and gleamed like polished glass. *You see that he will pay you, for he has heard your prayers and given you this way to earn your due reward*.

Then the angel smiled, warm and gentle as spring sunlight after bone-racking cold – a smile that would lead anyone to do anything for him, even perhaps go down a dark alleyway with him in the night, believing that they would come to no harm.

Ekaterina hobbled forward, steadying herself on her staff of bright scarves, and the angel seemed to drift off a little distance in his garments of light. She saw that the paper did indeed contain several lines of writing in some foreign tongue, (*it's German*, thought Lydia, *why am I dreaming about telegrams in German?*), and that the paper was rolled up and thrust through a fire-blackened gold ring, which bore in its bezel a heat-cracked pearl.

'Where is he?'

Lydia plunged from the dream as if falling from a height into a vat of pain. Hands crushed her shoulders, jerked her

upright – she had never felt pain like the pain that ripped
through her skull, and she cried out as she was shaken like a
doll in the grip of a demented child.

'Madame, stop—!' Lamplight tumbled into the room from
the open chapel door, making all the frowning saints on the
walls seem to fling up their hands in alarm. Behind silver-
barred windows the night was not black, but royal blue.

Petronilla struck her, brute viciousness in the blows; shook
her again as her consciousness reeled. 'Little slut! Carrot-
headed whore! Where—?'

'Madame—' Theiss caught the vampire's wrist, and
Petronilla threw Lydia to the floor, turned upon the physician
like a mad beast.

'You helped her!' Her voice shrilled into the thin wild
registers of madness. Gold hair fell undone around her shoulders, and her eyes threw back the lamplight like a rat's. 'You
came back, unlocked the door . . . You hoped she would come
to you!'

'My darling—' He retreated before her, his whole body
stooped, silhouetted against the lamplight from the door, ready
to dodge or flee—

Does he REALLY think he can outrun her?

Lydia wondered with a sense of detached calm whether Dr
Theiss had ever considered wearing silver around his throat
and wrists. With that many vampires under the same roof,
maidens or not, it might be something to consider. *If I live
through this I'll have to suggest it to him . . .*

'Don't speak words of love to me!' She almost spit the words
at him. 'Not when you've been making eyes at that skinny red-
haired bitch – I've seen you! And that tramp Genia as well!'

'You know that's not true.' Theiss's voice was completely
steady. Floating like a grass blade on top of a blood-lake of
pain, Lydia didn't know how he faced her . . . except that he
must really love her.

'Liar!' Her hands flexed open into claws. Her back was to
Lydia – what her face must be like, Lydia could barely imagine.

Theiss walked forward calmly, his eyes – Lydia thought –
holding those of the vampire. When he came near enough, he
took Petronilla's hands.

'My beautiful one, it doesn't matter. It doesn't matter.
The man cannot escape. Every window is barred with silver,

as are the grilles over the outer doors. We have Madame Asher—'

'Kill her!'

'He will come out, if we have her.'

'Kill her!' Petronilla jerked her hands from his. 'Or do you think you'll keep her for yourself?' She swung back around to where Lydia lay, half-propped against the wall like a broken rag-doll, and her fangs glinted in her drawn-back lips. 'Show me how much you love me, Benedict—'

'I am showing you.' He took her hand again, turned her to face him, hazel eyes calm and filled with love. Suddenly, the tension went out of Petronilla's body, as if her soul had been hamstrung. She almost staggered against him, put her hand to her head—

'Petronilla,' he whispered in that deep strong voice. 'You know you don't mean it.'

'No,' she whispered. 'No. You're quite right, Benedict – forgive me . . .'

She stepped back a little, so that the lamplight fell on her, face veiled in hair like a shimmering cloud. A beautiful face, vulnerable and delicate as a young girl's. Theiss brought up her hand to kiss, frowned, and asked, 'What's this?' and she drew her hand from him. But he turned it, so that the palm faced the lighted door. 'Did you burn it?'

'I – yes, in the kitchen,' she said, in a voice that told Lydia that she had no idea where or how she had burned her hand. 'It was clumsy of me . . .'

But Lydia knew that no vampire is clumsy.

She's having blackouts.

And doesn't want him to know.

Theiss came over to Lydia, gently lifted her back onto the bed. 'Are you all right, Madame?' he asked, and Lydia thought it would be politic to burst into tears again – not difficult, considering how badly her head hurt.

'I didn't do anything,' she sobbed, showing the very genuine terror she had felt a few moments ago. 'I was asleep—'

'Don't lie, little bitch.' Petronilla stepped forward, and Lydia cringed down behind Theiss, clinging to his arm.

He rather quickly disengaged her hand, turned to Petronilla. 'Please—' And to Lydia, 'Who is he? The man we found you with.'

She almost said, *I don't know*, then realized that anything she would say could be checked against Evgenia's story, and she couldn't recall enough of the attack on the *izba* to know what Simon might have told the Russian girl. She remembered only his hands, cold on her forehead, and how light his claws had felt. *He didn't kill Margaret . . .*

Did I dream that?

Did he tell me that because he thought I was dying?

Because he thought HE would die?

Did he tell me because it was a lie, or because it was the truth?

She stammered, 'He is – he is a vampire—' and wilted artistically back against the wall, her hands to her head, as if in a faint, which was not far from being the truth. She heard the violent rustle of Petronilla's silk petticoats and braced herself for another blow.

But Theiss said, 'No, Petra, please. She needs to rest. You can speak to her in the morning. You must forgive her,' continued Theiss softly, as Petronilla's shadow momentarily blotted the lighted doorway into the gaudy chapel beyond. 'She isn't like this as a rule. The strain of what she is going through, coming back from the darkness, learning once more to live in the daylight—'

Lydia whispered, 'Is that possible?' and put her hand over Theiss's wrist. 'How?'

'It is a series of injections.' The tone of his voice, full of grave joy, told her worlds about his love for research, his dedication to what he was doing. 'Distilled from the blood of vampires whose systems have never been polluted with human blood. Who are in their pure state, as Nature made them. Madame Asher, you must rest—'

'Please—' She clung to the warm hands that tried to bring up blankets over her again. 'What will happen to Evgenia? She said – she said Madame told her they would become angels.'

'Not become angels,' he corrected her gently. 'What she said was probably that they are *helping* the angels – that their lives were saved so that they can help in the battle against evil. I'll explain later,' he said kindly, tugging the blankets into place. 'But Petronilla Ehrenberg is engaged on one of the great crusades against evil in this world: a soul dragged

halfway to Hell, she has turned her back on the world of the
Undead, dedicated herself not to their eradication, but to their
salvation. Please believe me, Madame Asher. If your friend
should speak to you – should try to return to you – please
assure him that he has nothing to fear from us. Nor have you,'
he added, and he pressed her hands.

Lydia, whose neck had almost been broken by the violence
of Petronilla's rage, widened her eyes and did her best to look
as if she believed him. 'Truly?'

'Truly. She is . . . The injections have irritated her, made
her short-tempered – as you must know, the Undead have a
truly fearsome strength. But the effect is temporary. In time,
I know, she will grow used to the daylight – will learn to
come back to the world of the living. As will they all,' he said
softly. 'As will they all.'

Bebra to Eichenberg, a journey of barely ninety minutes. Then
nearly twenty-four hours, chained in the blackness of another
cellar. Asher slept the sleep of exhaustion on the stone floor,
but kept waking in panic, thinking he felt Jacoba's cold hand
on his face, the touch of her fangs on his throat. Then he
would sleep again and dream of his old friend Horace Blaydon,
bluff and arrogant and confident in his research and his skills,
reduced to uneasy terror as he saw the fearful changes that a
serum of vampire blood had made in his son.

*I had to do what I did, what I am doing, for the common
good.*

Other times he would dream of Lydia and would wake in
a sweat, wondering if she were all right. If she were guarding
herself, keeping her distance from Theiss and Ehrenberg . . .

If Ysidro had gone to her, or if he were waiting in Berlin.

But remaining in Berlin until nightfall to look for him was
out of the question. Tired as he was, it was going to be difficult enough, to do what he had to do.

The train left Eichenberg for Berlin at ten, with full dark
barely settled on the land. Jacoba, in the faded dark dress of a
workingman's wife, sat beside him in the third-class compartment without speaking, through hours of darkness with Prussia's
endless pine-forests flashing past under the light of the waxing
moon. The compartment – indeed, most of the third-class car
– was empty; only at the far end had a child cried, on and off,

for the first part of the night, barely audible over the thrumming of the wheels and the small clatter of the window glass. In the swaying orange stain of the oil lamps, he'd seen Jacoba's lips curl a little, smiling with no kindness at the thought of that infant in its mother's arms.

She stayed where she was, however, and made conversation about the inconveniences of rail travel in her medieval-tinted German, until the moon set and the linked pentagons of the Maiden hung low over the dark wall of trees. Then she rose from the hard bench and opened the compartment door. Night wind whipped away the scarf she wore over her dark hair; she seemed to hang in the doorway for a moment, weightless as a demon, colorless lips smiling in the dirty light. 'Do not betray me, Asher,' she said, and then let go. The night whirled her away.

She would find, Asher guessed, a root cellar or a trunk in someone's attic in which to pass the daylight hours, and would come on to Berlin once darkness fell. He had seen vampires run and knew their speed: tireless, inexorable, like monstrous half-glimpsed moths.

She would reach Berlin well before dawn. And he, James Asher, had better not be anywhere in that town.

It had been well over a decade since he himself had had occasion to drop out of a moving train-car, and he wasn't looking forward to the experience. But he had a good idea of how Jacoba intended to keep him where she could find him in Berlin, and knew – as he watched the dawnlight slowly strengthening beyond the windows of the car – that it was jump or die. Wantzig flashed by, Beelitz, Potsdam – little platforms never touched at this hour of the morning, though the first workmen were already to be seen moving about in the early light.

And if I break my leg, Asher reflected, gauging the thickening agglomerate of sheds, warehouses, disused rolling-stock and piles of spare ties and extra cinders that trail like dirty spoor along rail lines everywhere as they near their termini, *it really WILL be all up for us. And for England – and the world – as well.* He did not want to think what the world would be, if governments got into the habit keeping and paying coteries of vampires in the only currency they would value.

He had trained himself, years ago, not to think of Lydia while Abroad, rationing the vision of her to those times when it was safe to relax, the way he would have rationed liquor. But he thought of her now, as the tracks and sidings doubled and quadrupled in the clear new sunlight and the train neared the Potsdamer Bahnhof, and he prayed that Ysidro had had the good sense to go on to St Petersburg from Berlin, without even stopping to kill Colonel von Brühlsbuttel in passing . . .

Whatever was going on, Asher wanted a word with the man before he killed him.

And he knew in his heart that if von Brühlsbuttel was Madame Ehrenberg's connection to the Kaiser, killing him wouldn't matter. She'd only find someone else whose whereabouts they *didn't* know.

The train was slowing. Beyond a doubt, a welcoming committee of police waited for him on the platform, alerted by a telegram from the Lady Jacoba that the man whom the Köln police had arrested as Professor Ignatius Leyden, otherwise known as Mr Jules Plummer of Chicago – dressed in such-and-such a fashion and minus the mustache and extravagant American whiskers – would be on the 7:49 from Eichenberg.

Damn her.

She probably assumed she could retrieve him from the jail that night – not knowing that he'd be immediately transferred to a military prison, prior to being hanged as a spy.

Ysidro, he thought, *if I ever see you again I will drive a stake through your heart for getting me into this* . . .

He opened the door, estimated his speed, tossed out the small bundle of his possessions, and dived.

He made a rolling landing down the cinder hill of the tracks, taking the impact diagonally across his left shoulder and back; he scrambled to his feet (*good, I didn't break my leg* . . .), and jogged towards the nearest shelter, a tool shed by a siding. When he'd got his breath back, he jogged down the track to pick up his bindle, as American hoboes called it – a change of linen almost as dirty as what he had on, and the shaving kit Todesfall had procured for him back in Köln – then headed, at once and by the most circuitous route possible, for a bookstore in the Dorotheestrasse. It was in the opposite direction to Charlottenstrasse, but he knew that if he wasn't to be found on the train, the police would immediately figure out what he'd done and begin the search for him, and he'd better not look like his description. *Auf Golden Tintenfaß* was – *thank*

God! – still in its old location – as far as Asher knew the place had been a bookstore since the time of Fredrick the Great – and still under the proprietorship of old Bickern, a little grayer and more stooped than he'd been when Asher had last seen him, but reassuring as the gates of Heaven.

The little bookseller looked up as Asher limped in – probably the least prepossessing-looking traveler since Odysseus had woken up on the beach at Scherie – but said, politely, in his heavily Saxon German, 'Might I help you, sir?'

Working for the Department, one never knew which storm-battered tramp might turn out to be the King of Ithaca, down on his luck.

In English, Asher said, 'I'm looking for a copy of the *Hypnerotomachia Poliphili*. I'm afraid it's rather urgent.'

Bickern's green eyes widened, but as there was no one else in the shop he said, in the same language, 'I may have one here in the back.'

Asher said, 'Thank you,' and meant it as he seldom had in his life.

'Mother Mary, that's never you, Asher?' The bookseller pulled a wooden chair up to the table of the little rear parlor that lay behind the shop's second – inner – room. 'McAliester said as how you were back in the game—'

'I'm not.' Asher winked.

'Oh, yeah.' Bickern nodded. 'Now you speak of it, Mac told me that.'

'Good. And I'm not being followed, by the way – or, if I am, the Berlin police department has improved mightily since the last time I was in town . . . And I'm not going to sit in your chair until I've had a bath, if you can provide me with the facilities for such a thing?'

'Christ, yes, help yourself.' He waved to the old-fashioned stove, beyond which – through the spotless windows – could be seen a pump in the narrow yard. 'Bath's under the stairs—'

'I remember.' Asher had availed himself of the facilities at the Golden Inkstand before.

'Where've you been sleeping, man?' Bickern flipped open the door of the stove, thrust half a shovel-full of coal into the grate as Asher collected the pail from behind the door. 'You look like a fugitive from the soup line.'

'I would commit murder,' replied Asher, 'for the privilege of a soup line at the moment . . . Do you have the doings to get me up in a full beard and some decent clothes? They're looking for me as I am – I'll need money, too. I have to be out of Berlin by nightfall . . . And I need to see a man about a dog.'

TWENTY-FOUR

As a general rule, the Department didn't go in for disguises. Most of its employees were long-timers like McAliester and Bickern, permanently part of the local landscape. Their disguise was simply that they *were* the Germans they would have been, had they been born and brought up in Germany rather than Britain. If an alteration in appearance was rendered necessary by circumstances, it was usually effected by simple change – standing differently, a different mode of speech and behavior: *I know I look a little like the person you're looking for, but as you can see I'm really not anything like him . . .*

Nevertheless, a great deal could be accomplished in an emergency with a change of raiment and accent, and one of Bickern's jobs was to provide the wherewithal, if needed, for quick exits. This could extend to hair dye, eyeglasses, spirit gum, and what Shakespeare referred to as *'an usurpéd beard.'*

Resplendent in the most nondescript of German suits – and no German's suit ever fit him the way a Frenchman's or Englishman's did – and a close-cropped beard reminiscent of the Tsar's, Asher took a public tram out to Potsdam and walked to the Charlottenstrasse at about the time when the maidservants in those handsome houses – behind the sandstone porters'-lodges, the sweeping brick driveways – were 'doing' the bedrooms and their smooth-haired mistresses were embarking on the third cup of after-breakfast coffee. An occasional Palladian facade or Mansard roof spoke of landed wealth, of Junkers who controlled the peasants on their land exactly as if those peasants were still the medieval serfs they had been up until the days of Napoleon. But, for the most part, these were the houses of the wealthy industrialists whose

factories worked day and night to provide weapons and muni-
tions for Germany's armies, and the marketable goods for the
colonial empire that Germany intended to enlarge with victory.

Carriage horses, matched down to the height of their white
stockings, drew shiny victorias under the new-leafed trees:
young ladies in stylish furs, rigidly guarded by chaperones,
on their way for an 'airing'. No vulgar motor cars here. Nannies
in black marched well-mannered toddlers firmly along the
paths. Asher heard one admonish her charges not to dawdle,
though what was the point of taking children for a walk if
not to let them linger over tadpoles in the ditches or unfa-
miliar flowers by the wayside? Nevertheless, he recalled his
own nanny had had precisely the same attitude about walks.
*We must step out quickly if we are to reach the park in time
to turn around and come home for lunch.*

Kleinerschloss was an ostentatious brick villa set back from
the road among elm trees. Through ornamental metal railings,
Asher glimpsed stables in the back. There was no porter in
the lodge, however, and Asher, finding the gate closed but not
locked, pushed it open and ascended the graveled drive to the
door. As he neared it, the porter, uniformed in dark blue livery,
emerged from around the corner of the house and begged his
pardon with polite suspicion: could he be of assistance to the
gnädiger Herr?

'My name is Filaret,' said Asher – that was the name on
his new set of identity papers, at any rate – 'and I have a
message for Colonel von Brühlsbuttel.' The man wasn't in
mourning, he observed, so at least Ysidro hadn't murdered
the head of the house.

'You may give the message to me, Honored Sir.' The porter
bowed with military precision. *Ex-cavalry*, Asher guessed.
And not long out of the service, either. 'I will see that he
gets it.'

'A thousand pardons.' Asher, who had taken the precaution
of actually writing out and sealing a completely meaningless
message in the back room of the Golden Inkstand, returned
the bow. 'I have been commissioned to place it into the hand
of Colonel von Brühlsbuttel only.'

The front door opened; the butler came out, who was likewise ex-cavalry, and the porter's height to an inch. Someone
must have matched them like the carriage horses, except that

the butler was adorned with a moderate-sized paunch and an enormous fair mustache. 'I am afraid this is not possible, Herr Filaret. The Herr Colonel has gone.'

'Gone?'

'This morning.' A look of concern clouded the man's blue eyes. 'He had a telegram, which he showed to no one, but which upset him very much. He packed a few things and left by the early train.'

'Left for where?' asked Asher, and he managed to radiate the air of a man vexed by additional difficulties in delivering his letter, instead of confronted by potential disaster.

The butler shook his head, baffled, and replied, 'St Petersburg.'

'Are you feeling better, Madame?' Dr Theiss took her wrist gently in one hand, angled his little mirror to the window light to peer into her eye. 'Very good – how many fingers do you see?'

Though she was, in fact, feeling considerably better, Lydia made a show of flinching from the light, whispered, 'I don't know – three? Four? My head . . .'

'It's all right. Can you not eat?' He looked at the untouched porridge, then poured her out a glass of the weak lemonade that had been left with it.

Lydia shook her head. Though profoundly queasy, she could have done with the lemonade, but feared it might be drugged. Or worse, she thought, remembering the vicious glint in Petronilla Ehrenberg's eyes.

Theiss, she thought, was remembering it as well, to judge by the hushed tone of his deep voice and the way he kept glancing back at the door, which he had, she noticed, shut carefully behind him.

'Do you feel strong enough to speak with me a little?' he asked. 'Tell me, please . . . This vampire who was with you in the cottage – who is he? Why did he come to you there? Genia Greb tells me that the *izba* was attacked by the other vampires of St Petersburg, three others, she says, and that this one – your friend—'

'He isn't my friend.' Lydia turned restlessly under the light blanket. She saw that she now wore a man's loose nightshirt, and that her hair had been taken down and brushed. She wondered if Theiss had done that, and she shuddered at the thought that it might have been pale fishy-eyed Texel.

'She said that he bore you down the stairs to the cellar when you were hurt. That he spoke to you – behaved towards you – with great tenderness. Is this man English? Did he come here with you? How is it, that you know one of the Undead? It is imperative that I know these things,' he added urgently, taking her hands. 'Imperative that we bring him in. Petra –' he hesitated on her name, then corrected himself – 'Madame Ehrenberg mistrusts him – fears him. I think she must be shown that his intentions are as good, that his heart is as pure as her own. Otherwise—'

'Otherwise she'll kill him,' Lydia murmured weakly. 'The way she killed Lady Eaton?'

The physician's face hardened. 'Lady Eaton, as you call her,' he said, 'was a murderess. A common vampire, who has killed her way down through the years—'

'And Madame Ehrenberg has not?'

For an instant shock and anger made him draw back; when he leaned forward again, his voice was pitying. 'Ach, how should you know, Madame?' he said. 'She has turned her back on all that. It has been twenty years since she has drunk human blood—'

'Is that what she's told you?' demanded Lydia, struggling a little to sit up. 'And have you known her through that twenty years? Have you been with her every minute of that time?'

'I know her as I know myself,' replied Theiss gently. 'No, I have only known her these two years. Yet I feel that we have known one another for decades. She is not an untruthful woman – she has grown past that. I know what she is capable of, and I would trust her with my life.'

'You do,' said Lydia. 'Every time you are together.'

'As you do your vampire . . . acquaintance?' He gave her a quizzical look. 'Perhaps we should not have killed Lady Eaton. Perhaps if we'd had the serum in its completed form then, we could have injected her with it, and after a time her own cravings for the kill would have subsided, as Petra's have. But she was intransigent. Like a wild beast, Petra said. She broke free of her restraints, attacked Petra – Madame Ehrenberg . . .'

'Were you there?' asked Lydia. 'Or is this only something

Madame told you?' And, when Theiss stammered a little, she
laid a hand on his wrist and went on: 'What has she told you
she wants, Dr Theiss? Is it only to be able to walk about in
the daytime? Can she still affect the minds of the living?
That's something vampires can only do if they're feeding on
human blood – on human deaths.'

His eyebrows dived down over his nose; even without her
spectacles she could see that. 'Who told you that?'

'Who told you it was otherwise?' she returned. 'Go down
to the canal some night, by the old watergate, before the tide
scours it, and drag in the shallows, if you think she isn't still
killing . . .'

He was shaking his head, the same look in his eyes that
she remembered had been in Margaret Potton's, when the little
governess had been under Simon's spell.

She went on: 'And Lady Eaton may have been *intransigent*
because she had the idea that since you're a German, and
Madame is a German – and since Madame's been in correspondence for the past three years with some Colonel in Berlin
– her desire to appear more human, while keeping the powers
of the Undead, had more to do with getting on the good side of
the Kaiser than with feeling the sunshine on her face.'

He jerked to his feet. 'That is outrageous! Petra feels as I
do about the "Kaiser" and his so-called "Reich"! All she wants
– all I want – is to have human happiness, human love . . .'

Lydia sat up, though her head throbbed abominably, and
she had to catch her balance against the wall with one hand.
'And is that what comes next?' she said. 'You make it possible
for vampires to walk around in the daytime, then she makes
you a vampire and you live happily forever and ever?' She
couldn't see his face well enough to know what effect her
words had, but he stood frozen, a massive blur in his white
coat. 'Dr Theiss, they are seducers. That is their power. It's
how they hunt. It's how they work. The man I was with – the
vampire . . . I've seen him do it. I've seen him get into peoples'
dreams, the way Madame got herself into Evgenia's and
Kolya's and probably those of all the other poor children she's
been turning into vampires so that you have a source of vampire
blood—'

He put his hand quickly to his temple. 'Who said anything
about dreams?'

Lydia only sat, looking up at him. 'Ask her about her friend in Berlin.'

He took a step forward, reached out. 'You poor child—'

'No.' Lydia pushed his hand aside. 'You poor man. And while you're asking her, ask her how it is that a member of the German Intelligence Service ended up knocking on your door asking for a—'

She stopped.

Petronilla Ehrenberg was in the room.

Lydia hadn't seen her enter . . . Not that one ever did. She couldn't make out her face, but didn't need to. The anger that radiated from her rigid body was almost palpable, like waves of heat. Lydia's face must have told Theiss what was behind him because he turned swiftly, held out his hands . . .

'Dearest one.'

Deadly quiet, she asked, 'Did I not make it clear to you that you were not to see this woman – nor the girl Evgenia – without me being present in the room?'

'I searched for you, my beautiful one, and I am sorry—'

'I told you to wait.' There was an edge to Petronilla's voice that prickled the hair on Lydia's head.

'Indeed you did—'

'If I cannot trust you, who can I trust?' she cut in shrilly over his words. 'I placed my life in your hands, Benedict, because you assured me that you loved me . . . Were you lying, then? I turned against my own kind for your sake. Am I next to find out that what you say is in the serum you're giving me is something entirely different than I think? Is that what's causing this?'

With a swift gesture, she ripped open the top of her dress, claw-like nails shredding the fawn-colored silk to show mottled red spots on her breasts' perfect whiteness, as if Satan had pressed his burning thumb into snow and left blisters behind.

'Petra, please—'

'Or this?' As casually as one of Lydia's aunts ripping up a piece of notepaper, she tore her sleeve free, to show more marks. 'Is that the reason for the voices I keep hearing? For the lights?'

'My beautiful one.' Theiss stepped over to her, and she was close enough that Lydia could see the queer gleam in those terrible eyes; the fixed stare that gave her the feeling that

Petronilla's words were not addressed to the man before her, but to someone entirely different. Like a husband confronted with a beloved wife's temper tantrum, Theiss pulled the torn silk back up over Madame's shoulders. 'You said you burned yourself on a lamp. When did—?'

'Are you calling me a liar?' She slithered from his embarrassed, fussing touch. 'Are you planning to turn me into a – a *thing*, like that latest boy, or like that silly girl whose skin all came off—?'

'*Liebling*, no, of course not. Those were mistakes, terrible mistakes! But I do see now that the serum overexcites you sometimes—'

'*Don't touch me!*' She screamed the words, rounded on him, struck him full force, sending him sprawling like a rag doll, and the next instant she was on him.

Lydia heard his shirt rip; he screamed 'NO!' and she buried her fangs in his throat.

Nothing exists but the kill, Simon had told her once, and Lydia hoped that was the truth as she rolled from the cot, gathered up the baggy nightshirt in hand, and ran – stumbling, reeling, every second terrified that she would collapse, still in the room or in the chapel or somewhere Madame would see her. Behind her she heard Theiss scream again, and this time there was nothing human in the sound.

Simon, she thought, *I can't leave Simon behind in this place—*

And the next moment, in her mind, she heard Ysidro's soft calm voice saying, *Don't be an imbecile, Mistress . . .*

She found a flight of stone steps, railless, steep . . . *Whatever you do, don't fall . . .*

The last of the milky summer twilight was visible from the bottom, and she crawled, clinging to the wall. *An open door*, she prayed. *Please let it be an open door . . .*

The arched door that led into the flagged central courtyard was open, but a grille was locked over it, gleaming silvery in the dusk. Through it, across fifty feet of open flagstones, she could see the iron sheeting of the front gates, which faced towards the railroad tracks. She rattled the silver-plated grille, but it was locked.

Picklocks. In the pillow. If I can remain hidden till she leaves . . .

The floor dipped and swayed beneath her as if she were in an earthquake, as if the whole monastery were a very small box adrift on a rough sea. She clung to the stones of the archway, forced herself to breathe deeply. *There has to be a way down to the crypts somewhere. Genia – or maybe it was Madame Muremsky – said there were miles of rooms and hallways and vaults down there . . .*

She waited until her balance returned, then hurried along the corridor, bare feet patting the stone. *Thank Heavens it's summer and not the dead of winter . . .*

She was reaching for the handle of the nearest door when it was opened suddenly from the other side, and she found herself face-to-face with young Mr Texel.

'Mrs Asher,' he said, with no appearance of surprise, and caught her arm in a brutal grip as she turned to flee. 'You're just the woman I wanted to see.'

TWENTY-FIVE

'Just as well,' was Texel's only comment, when Lydia gasped that Madame Ehrenberg was – as far as she was able to tell – killing Dr Theiss. 'She stays quiet for two or three hours after she kills.'

'She has been killing all along, then, hasn't she?'

He looked at her as at an impossibly naive child. 'What, you think I'm as stupid as old Theiss? *Herr Gott!*' Holding one arm pinned agonizingly behind her, and his other hand gripping her hair, he pushed her through a sort of gaudily frescoed vestibule and into the long whitewashed room that Theiss used for his laboratory.

Lydia recognized the equipment immediately, as she had the smaller version at the clinic: filters, separators, the blue flicker of Bunsen flames, long coils of distilling equipment. A giant rack of reagents, and another of phials, carefully labeled, of dark liquid. There was a safe; on top of it, a couple of bright-colored candy-tins, of the sort Jamie had described as containing poor Lady Irene's severed fingers. Beside the safe, in a tiny silver-barred alcove barely larger than a closet, was a device that nerve doctors called a 'tranquilizing chair', fitted up with not only straps, but also chains.

'So poor Dr Theiss didn't know why she wanted all this?'

Texel sniffed. 'If you mean, has she been lying to him from the start, the answer is yes.' He pulled open the dimly shining grill-work of the bars, jerked Lydia into the alcove and pushed her into the chair. When she made a move to twist free, he caught her by the throat and, shoving her back into the chair, leaped with sudden litheness on top of her, straddling her hips and grinning down into her face. 'And you sit still, Madame,' he said nastily. 'I don't think, dressed as you are, you really want a wrestling match with me – do you?' His eyes glittered as he stroked the torn nightshirt down from her shoulder. 'It's just a pity we have so little time.'

Lydia forced herself to sit still. 'What are you going to do?'

'What I've been trying to do since the start.' He swung his leg back over her as if he were dismounting a horse and, standing again beside the chair, jerked the straps tight over her wrists and around her upper arms. 'Serve my country.' He pinched her breast through the thin cotton, then turned to take a hypodermic and a tourniquet from a nearby drawer.

'What is it?' The liquid in the syringe was clear, not the brownish color of the various serums in the rack on the wall.

'Something that will kill you.' He plunged the needle into the vein of her arm before she could cry out. 'If proper countermeasures aren't applied quickly enough.' He unbuckled the straps, pulled her to her feet again. 'You don't think I'd be fool enough to tell you what it is, do you? It would be signing my own death warrant. This way.'

Since it would be, at this point, lunacy to flee from him, Lydia followed, heart hammering with panic and despair. A door at the far end of the laboratory opened onto a circular stone stairway; Texel took an oil lamp from a table, lit it from the gas jet. Outside the windows, the long twilight was dwindling at last to darkness, though the glow from the steelworks still silhouetted the towers of the monastery wall. Night seemed to rush up from the stairway as he pushed Lydia ahead of him down the lightless brick treads.

'Are you a biochemist as well?' asked Lydia, struggling to keep her voice calm. 'Is that why you were assigned to him?'

'I've taken enough chem classes to know what to look for.'

Texel shrugged. 'Mostly they sent me because I speak Russian. All they knew was that Theiss was onto something that would render a man immortal . . . and able to slip past the closest guards unseen. And that it had something to do with the properties of the blood. I didn't believe in Madame myself until I saw her in action – and saw what happened to her friend Lady Eaton when Madame dragged her body out into the light, when we were done with it. Madame's a cagey one,' he added, opening the doorway – its planks overlaid with a netting of silver wire – at the bottom of the stair. 'She only picks the weak ones to turn into vampires . . . Through here, quickly.'

'Does the serum let her touch silver as well?' Lydia was trembling as they crossed the darkness of an underground vault, her fear having given way to a strange cold sensation, at once dreamy and very clear.

My child, she thought. *Whatever is happening, let it not hurt my child . . .*

She stumbled on the rough floor, and Texel dragged her upright again. 'Stay on your feet, *Leibchen*. There are at least two of Madame's little maidens wandering around down here: one from some of the early test batches, before Theiss got the proportions right . . . and then that other one a few weeks ago, God knows what went wrong there. Maybe more. Yes, Madame can touch silver, or thinks she can. Myself, I think Old Theiss's serum just postpones the burns, and the welts show up elsewhere. He's been pretending all along that he knows what he's doing, but personally, I think half the time he's just guessing. It's why he was so wild when Madame killed Lady Eaton – if she *was* dead, when Madame got me to drain off her blood and slice her up. He knew he really needed to test these things on a true vampire, not those deluded little grubs Madame keeps making . . .'

She was finding it harder and harder to follow his words. 'Is that why Dr Theiss wants Don Simon?'

'That's your sweetheart, is he? Don Simon?'

Lydia bit her lip. 'He's not my sweetheart—'

'I heard you talk in your sleep.' Texel's grin was ugly in the yellow flare of the oil lamp. With his free hand he took her left one, raised the thick gold wedding-band to his lips. '*He* know?'

Lydia tried to pull her hand back, and Texel laughed, grabbed her arm again, and shoved her before him down a short, straight flight of stairs. Even in the summer heat, the small chamber at the bottom kept the clammy chill of autumn. There was a well in the center, covered with a grille of silver bars. Texel handed Lydia the lamp. 'Hold this. Don't drop it – and don't get cute with me. I know what I gave you. You don't.'

He bent, to unlock the grille and move it aside. Lydia crept close, aware that she was getting sleepy – *opiate of some kind?* – and that it was becoming hard to breathe. The lamp-light didn't penetrate into the darkness below, but she smelled water, and the cold seemed to flow up over her. One of the tide-flooded crypts Madame Muremsky had talked about? 'What's down there?'

He took the lamp from her, set it down carefully, then with a quick move grabbed both of her wrists and kicked her legs out from under her so that she staggered. Before she could regain her balance, he swung her over the edge. 'You are.'

Lydia screamed as she fell, tried to get one foot back up onto the rim of the pit, and Texel shook her violently. 'Hold still, you silly bitch—'

'Don't! Please, don't! I'm with child—!'

'It's only about ten feet, and that water's six inches deep. Down you get . . .' He knelt on the edge of the well, lowered Lydia by the wrists as far as he could. 'Oopsy-daisy, *Liebchen* . . .'

She still fell hard, crumpling to her knees in the water, unable to catch her balance. Above her, she heard the grille clank back into place and the grate of the locks. Texel's shadow moved across the lamp. 'Eleven thirty. Go ahead and scream if you want to, *schatzie*. Your boyfriend should be up and about by this time. Just remind him when he shows up that unless he meets my terms you're going to be in a coma by sunrise, and dead by noon. And I'm willing to bet that even if he finds the key, and gets the grille up, he's still not going to be able to figure out what I injected you with in time to do you – and that little bun you say you've got in your oven – any good.'

Lydia sank down with her back to the wall, wanting to remain on her feet – the water was icy cold, and there was no telling what else might be swimming around in it – but unable to do so. Her breath was slow, and waves of dizziness lapped over her, but she couldn't seem to inhale any more quickly or deeply. The water seemed to chill her to the marrow of her bones, then the core of her heart. *Simon*, she thought. *I can't let Simon be captured. Not if they'll use him . . .*

Jamie, where is Jamie?

Even Don Simon didn't know.

He could be dead. They could both be dead . . . Well, she reflected, *Simon already IS dead, and has been so since 1555 . . .*

She wondered again what it would have been like to know him while he was alive. *No good*, he had said, *can come from the friendship of the living and the dead . . .* Because the other vampires would have none of it? Because such friendship put each of them in danger?

Certainly, poor Theiss had found it so.

Because the blurring of that line blurred others? Because of the vampire's seductiveness, which drew the living man or woman into excusing whatever the vampire chose to do, to survive?

She felt herself slipping sideways and thought, *I have to prop myself in a corner . . .*

But the well was round, no corners.

If I fall asleep I'll drown . . .

My child. My poor baby. Jamie, I'm so sorry . . .

Somewhere in the darkness – or she may already have been dreaming, she thought – a soft voice asked, 'And what are your terms, Herr Texel?'

'Where are you?' In spite of his earlier bravado, panic edged his voice like the rim of a rusty can-lid.

'Close by. What are your terms?'

'Show yourself.' And then, after long silence . . . 'I would have you make me into such a one as you are.'

Another stillness, like the smooth patch in a river, deadly and deep. Lydia remembered Don Simon's thin face, like a skull's within the long wisps of his colorless hair, the eyes like sulfurous jewels.

'I can turn you into a vampire, if you so desire it; yet not into such a one as I. Time only can do that. And, indeed, I would advise against it. Once through this gate, there is no turning back, unto death or Time's conclusion.'

'Don't play your little games with me – Simon is your name? Don Simon? You are Spanish?'

'I was Spanish in life.'

In a dream she saw them, facing one another across the silver grill-work of the well, Texel in his rough French tweeds, Ysidro as he had been in the cellar, a white face and white shirtsleeves banded by the black stripes of braces. His long pale hands had been burned – *silver?* – and the old claw-rakes that he'd taken in Constantinople stood out like dribbled lines of sealing wax, as colorless as the rest of his flesh.

'Do as you're told, and when all is over, I'll bring the girl up.'

'Bring her up first. You'll sleep afterwards.'

'Then you'd better hope I wake up quickly, hadn't you? And that the Ehrenberg hag doesn't walk in on us. A hundred times over the past two years I've asked her, but it's something she wants to keep for herself . . . and for children who think she's some kind of angel. There's a laugh! She won't thank you for giving her real competition to worry about.'

'I doubt she feared your competition.' In her dream Lydia watched Ysidro walk towards him, with the weightless drift of a dancer or a ghost. 'To make a fledgling is to make love, to take the whole of what you are and who you are into my soul—'

'Do whatever you have to do,' snapped Texel. 'But do it quickly, before the Ehrenberg quits sniveling over her kill and comes looking for your girlfriend down there. I doubt *she'll* bring her up.'

They stood almost breast to breast; Lydia could hear the German's nasal breath, see every lineament of his face with the always-startling clarity as if she wore her spectacles. She suspected he'd taken his first experience of sexual intercourse the same way. *Give it to me, and let's have it over, girl . . .*

Ysidro's voice was so soft she wasn't sure if he actually spoke the words, or if she heard only in her mind, as one hears in dreams: *When you feel me draw you, let go, and follow. Hold fast, for your body will try to drag you back into death.* As if she were Don Simon instead of herself, she felt the slit of his long talons down the vein in his wrist. *Drink it . . .*

And when, repelled by the taste, Texel tried to draw back—

DRINK IT! Ysidro's hand gripped tight in the German's mousy hair, forced the man's lips against the bleeding vein.

A plunging faintness as the blood poured out, like teetering over a cliff's edge in darkness. The horror of falling, in the second before balance is irretrievably gone. Then, like a violent kiss, Ysidro planted his lips on the young man's neck. The taste of blood, the white cataclysm of the soul rushing out.

Lydia thought, *Is it like that, then?*

TWENTY-SIX

Asher reached St Petersburg at 7:55 in the morning of Wednesday, May tenth – the twenty-sixth of April by Russian reckoning – and took a cab straight from the station to Krestovsky Island.

He'd cabled Lydia from the train station in Vilna, hoping against hope that, after a week of hearing nothing from him, she had not undertaken some investigation of her own.

Ysidro might have stopped her – or helped her . . . If Ysidro had gone on to Petersburg.

He didn't know that, either.

Prince Razumovsky's *izba* was shut. Not even servants moved around its closed-up doors, its tightly shuttered windows.

Damn it. Damn it . . .

'Jamie!' The Prince sprang up from his desk when Asher appeared in the study's French doors. 'Good God, man, where have you been? Madame Lydia—'

'Where is she?'

'They have been searching Petersburg for her for four days!'

The *izba* had been cleared up, the broken glass of the windows removed and the windows themselves replaced. 'Zudanievsky said they found a little blood on the wall of the pantry cupboard in the basement,' reported the Prince, as Asher turned over the two makeshift pikes that the police had left lying on the long parlor table: a broom handle and a kitchen poker to which silver knives and forks had been roughly lashed with string. 'There was a man's jacket there also: light gray wool, rather small, from a tailor in Jermyn Street—'

Ysidro's.

Asher's heart seemed to pound more heavily as he looked around the dim room. The police had piled the twisted garlands of garlic and wild rose stems on the table as well. He wondered what Zudanievsky had made of them. The bespectacled officer had impressed him as a quintessential city bureaucrat, but one never knew, with Russians. In any case, there wasn't a Russian in Petersburg who didn't have relatives still on the land. Despite the ramshackle tenements, the gritty factory-smoke of the industrial slums, over two-thirds of its people were villagers, straight from the wheat fields and birch woods. They would know what all this meant.

Four days ago. He must have made his way straight here from Berlin.

Strain and exhaustion had left him numb, perfectly calm, and cold inside.

The Petersburg vampires attacked . . . Probably as soon as Count Golenischev left town.

Why? How would they have known who Lydia was, or where she was?

Or was it Ysidro they were after?

He said, 'No bodies.' He felt he was viewing all of this as if from a very great distance. As if it were someone else he was looking for, and he himself was someone else as well. 'No sign of burning?'

'*Burning?*' The Prince's heavy eyebrows knotted, but he'd been in the business of secrets for a long time and did not ask further. 'No. Rina – Madame Lydia's cook here – said that a young girl came to see her that night, a dark-haired girl dressed like a lacemaker or a milliner. Madame Asher sent the servants away at once, back up to the house. Jov says they all of them woke up the next day where they'd dropped off to sleep, all at once, still in their clothing, like the castle of Sleeping Beauty. The men in the stables as well. I think someone must have introduced something into the tea in the servants' hall.'

Asher went to the corner of the table, touched the three little heaps of silver there: the chains Lydia had worn around her wrists, and on the other side of the table – as if it had been taken off later, or by someone else – the longer chain that had guarded her throat. Beside them lay her spectacles, like a killed daddy-long-legs of silver and glass.

Lydia.

Someone – not a vampire – must have taken the protective chains off her. That would mean Texel or Theiss.

He was aware of the Prince's cornflower gaze on him, not only troubled but probing, questioning . . . Reading – as Zudanievsky had read – in Asher's silence a knowledge of precisely what was going on. *What is it that you can tell from these weapons, these chains, these herbs, my friend, that we do not know?*

'I'll send for Zudanievsky. He should be at his office—'

'Not yet,' said Asher. He took a deep breath; it cleared his mind. 'There's something else I need to see first.'

'*What?*' The Prince grabbed him by the shoulder, almost shouted the word at him. 'Good God, man, if you know anything, I can have half the Okhrana out—'

'And it only takes one second for someone to panic and cut his losses.' Asher stepped from his grip, gathered up the chains and the spectacles and slipped them into his pocket. The butler on the shallow front steps of von Brühlsbuttel's house in Potsdam had said, *A telegram that seemed to upset him very much. He left this morning . . . St Petersburg . . .*

The German would have only a few hours' start on him.

'I should be back this afternoon,' he said at last, as they stepped out onto the veranda, locked the door again behind them. 'Yes, please, get in touch with Zudanievsky, tell him to have some men ready. But he is to do nothing without my express orders.' Asher blinked, seeing Razumovsky's bitter grin, and corrected himself: 'Without *your* express orders.'

'As it little behooves an officer of the Okhrana to be taking orders from Mr Jules Plummer of Chicago . . . Is there anything that you need? You look like you've spent a night in the train station—'

'On the train.' They walked up the path to the main house again, and he rubbed his face, unshaven and still itching from the spirit gum of the now-discarded Berliner beard. 'And I'd probably better not be Mr Plummer anymore. He's wanted in Germany for murder and espionage. You'd better explain that to Zudanievsky. I'm Jean-Pierre Filaret from Strasbourg—'

'I doubt he'll care. When did you last eat?'

'Nineteen oh-seven, it feels like. I'll need a pistol – an

automatic, if you've got one – and something to eat, whatever you've got in the kitchen.'

He stepped through the French window again and stopped beside the study desk, looking down at the newspaper lying on the corner of that handsome plain of inlay and ebony.

There was a badly-printed photograph of Dr Benedict Theiss, above the headline: SLUM CLINIC DOCTOR BRUTALLY MURDERED.

'Just give me the pistol,' he said. 'I'll return as soon as I can.'

The town house of Petronilla Ehrenberg, on the Sadovaia Oulitza, reminded him a good deal of Lady Irene Eaton's, which lay only a few streets away, and even more of La Ehrenberg's house in Neuehrenfeld. Expensive, stylish, it was situated on the end of a short row of identical expensive and stylish town houses; there was no mews behind. Not for people who kept their own carriages, or who were in Petersburg for long enough at a time to want to be troubled with the upkeep of animals or permanent servants on-site. A pied-à-terre, for Moscow industrialists with business connections in the capital, or the mistresses of men in the Court or the Army.

Small gates opened into an alley behind. The lock on Number 12's was surprisingly expensive, for where it was, but Asher had little trouble climbing over. A narrow yard, like Lady Eaton's: kept up just enough not to look unkempt. Upstairs and down the rooms were showier, with the expensive and rather heavy-handed taste – and many of the same prints on the walls – he had seen in the Köln town-house. But it was a house designed simply to establish the fact that the occupant lived in a house like other people, and slept in a bed.

A crypt had been walled off the shallow basement, its door concealed behind boxes that cost Asher a struggle to shift. Like many basements in St Petersburg, its walls were clammy and everything smelled dimly of sewage. The coffin – mounted on trestles – was empty.

When Asher sprang lightly down from the top of the rear gate of Number 12 again and started back up the alley, a man stepped out from around the corner and held out his hand to him. 'Please, *mein Herr*, ten thousand pardons—'

This didn't sound like either the Okhrana or the St Petersburg police, so Asher stopped and waited while he approached. He walked like a cavalryman, though he was a man in his fifties. His cavalry whiskers were grizzled silver, and his tall, thin form was rather stooping in a baggy but expensive suit as travel-creased and soot-smutted as Asher's own.

'Please, I beg you, forgive me,' the German gentleman went on, with a formal bow. 'I am not the police. I saw you come over the gate – I am trying to find the lady who lives in that house, for I fear she is in some terrible trouble. I do not ask questions, but please, as you are a gentleman, tell me . . . Did you go inside?'

Asher almost retorted, *Of course not, what do you take me for? A burglar?* but something in the man's pleading gray eyes stopped him. Instead, he asked, 'Who is it that you seek, mein Herr?'

'Madame Ehrenberg,' said the German promptly. 'She is – a most dear friend. On Sunday I received a telegram that horrified me. I do not like to go to the police. One hears such frightful things of the Russian police. Yet when I reached Petersburg last night it was to hear the news that the physician who was treating Madame's nervous condition – the man I was directed to see – has been murdered, and I find now her house locked up . . .'

'And have I the honor of addressing,' said Asher gently, 'Colonel Sergius von Brühlsbuttel?'

With a startled look, von Brühlsbuttel replied, 'You have.'

'Is he a vampire?' Lydia whispered, as air – sweet as a thousand kisses – seeped back into her lungs, cleared her mind, though she found herself still unable to open her eyes. It didn't matter. The room, wherever it was, was dark, and she knew it was Simon with her.

The glassy claws – like the angel's, in her earlier dream – brushed her cheek. 'He is, Mistress.'

'I'm sorry.' Her fingers closed around his, thin and strong and familiar, though she thought, *They should feel colder . . .* Her own hands must be icy, though she felt dreamily warm. 'He's won, hasn't he? He'll go to the Kaiser now . . .'

'Do not concern yourself with it, Mistress.'

'You should have let me die . . .'

'Do not concern yourself. I would not let you die by the hand of such a one, and a heretic at that.'

Her head lay against his thigh, as it had in the cupboard at the *izba*. Under her cheek she felt rough cloth worn threadbare, and she remembered – a dream? Dreaming of being carried to a room in the crypts, a monk's narrow cell. When she opened her eyes – or thought she did – by the faint glow of lamplight, leaking through the judas in the door, she saw he'd clothed himself in a monk's black robe, retrieved from some catacomb and rotting to pieces around his body, splotched with cobweb and dust. His shirt and trousers lay folded on the floor in front of the cell's door – *why there?* she wondered. She wondered, also, if she'd have the strength to put them on, then thought about Texel and told herself she'd find the strength somehow . . .

The memory brought others. 'She's dead,' she whispered. 'Irene. Lady Eaton. I'm so sorry, Simon. He said . . . It sounds as if Petronilla killed her.' When he looked aside from her, and did not speak, she said again, 'I'm so sorry.'

'It is as I had thought. It is nothing.'

'You came all this way. That isn't nothing.' Jamie had told her of finding two of Irene's fingers in a tin box, and had said that Simon had cared for her, though he didn't say how he knew this – she knew enough to know Ysidro would never have told him that.

'In the end it is.'

'Texel wanted to get Lady Irene to make him a vampire,' she murmured. 'Only he couldn't find any way to force her to do it; a way that he'd be safe. I think that's why Petronilla killed her. Before he could figure one out. It's why you said there couldn't be friendship between the living and the dead, isn't it? Because someone could use me . . .'

'As did I,' he reminded her, with the palest wisp of amusement in his voice, 'to bend James unto my will. 'Twere best the dead were dead utterly and life left to the living, Mistress. In any case, 'twould have been foolish in him to have dealings with Irene, or indeed with Petronilla. 'Tis not only the blood that the fledgling needs, to become vampire – as James saw, in the case of those two poor maidens, who knew not even enough of their own state to seek the safety of a chamber without light, and as you found with little Genia. If he thinks

Petronilla will instruct him in all those matters of which he is clearly ignorant, of what it is and means to be vampire, he had best think again. 'Tis clear he thinks he knows everything about it because he has observed Theiss's experiments. Yet Petronilla is the only vampire to whom he has spoken at any length. We are an untrustworthy breed.'

'The others will have gone, won't they? The Petersburg vampires.' She shivered, remembering the white faces swimming in the darkness outside the *izba's* broken windows. The horrible strength that had wrenched at hers when she'd slammed and locked the doors . . .

'I think so, yes.'

'Is that why Petronilla picked Petersburg in the first place? Jamie said she only made her fledglings in the spring, when there was enough light that she knew they couldn't escape—'

Her hands caught at his fingers again, strengthless. Even the time-smoothed gold of his signet ring didn't feel cold. 'Will he kill me?'

'Not if he hopes to go on controlling me through you.'

She clung tighter, whispered, 'What he did – what he injected me with . . . Did it hurt my baby?' The thought that she would lose yet another child pierced her, and rather than go through that again, she thought, it would be easier to simply die herself. 'I – I'm carrying Jamie's child . . . You can hear heartbeats. You can feel dreams . . .'

'I can,' murmured Ysidro. 'And I tell you, your child lives and is well.'

'Can you—'

The crash of a gunshot woke her. Lydia gasped, jerked upright, alone on a cot in the cell. Shadows flickered by the judas in the door, and she stumbled towards it as a second shot echoed in the corridor outside. The next moment the door was flung open, Texel's tall form silhouetted against the dim gaslight as Lydia staggered, dropped to her knees.

A dark smear of fresh blood trickled down the outside of the door, just beneath the judas. Texel strode in, caught her arm, dragged her to her feet: 'Was he in here?'

Lydia stared at him, managed to collect her thoughts enough to gasp, 'Who?' even though she knew perfectly well who.

The judas grille was made of silver. So was the handle of the door. All he could do, she thought, was stand pressed to the iron-strapped wood, reach through into her dreams . . .

Texel shook her, the strength of his grip terrifying, and flung her down again. In the near-darkness of the cell his eyes seemed to glow, from the reflected gaslight of the corridor. His hand was as strong as granite, and as cold, and she could feel his gaze on her through the thin cotton of her nightshirt. Not nastily lustful now, as he had been – that had been forgotten, with the sloughing-away of his body's life.

What he smelled was her blood.

'Call him,' he said.

Numbly, Lydia shook her head, and Texel pulled her to her feet again, pressed the muzzle of the pistol he carried against her back.

'Call him. The bullets in this are silver, but they'll make just as big a hole in living flesh as in dead.'

He dragged her to the cell door. The corridor outside was narrow, low-roofed, and puddled with the perpetual trickles of water that crept into every Petersburg cellar. The smell was the smell of the river, sewery and foul. Spots of blood were dispersing slowly into the water for a little distance on the floor, then lost themselves in shadow.

She managed to say, 'If the bullets are silver, he's probably unconscious. Silver does that to them.'

By the shift of those feral eyes, the movement of his head, she saw that he didn't know if she was speaking truth or not.

Simon was right. Petronilla is the only vampire he's ever spoken with about the vampire state . . . and she probably didn't tell him the truth about anything.

We are an untrustworthy breed . . .

And he's afraid to go after Simon into the darkness.

After a moment he pushed her back into the cell and slammed the door. But as she heard the key turn in the lock – the lock she guessed to be silver – she thought of the serum Dr Theiss had made, the serum Texel had to have taken now. *Whatever Simon says, the Kaiser has his vampire.*

Jamie . . . Her mind reached out to him as she sank down to the wet floor again. *Jamie, be careful . . .*

TWENTY-SEVEN

' I met Madame Ehrenberg in Berlin three years ago.' Von Brühlsbuttel settled back into the cushions of the cab as it jolted along the Sadovaia towards the river, folded his long, awkward hands on his bony knees. 'At the Opera. She was alone, and I invited her to my box – not out of any impropriety, please understand, but because I feared she was lonely. She was in mourning, and I observed she had no son or brother or friend . . . She said she had almost lost interest in music, though once, she said, she had loved it very much. I asked her to join me again a week later . . . and so our friendship grew.'

Friendship? Asher wondered. Or simply seduction, which Ysidro had said the vampires engaged in as frequently as they could. This was not often – the Long Game, they sometimes called it. Luring over months, indulging in dinners, meeting at balls. Establishing the semblance of a romance, getting to know their victim – as Jacoba of Köln had gotten to know him – to increase the excitement of the final kill. To add the 'kick' of shock and betrayal to the savor of despair and death.

Maybe it had begun that way. For the most part the vampires lived upon the poor, whose families would not miss them; one reason the masters were so jealous of keeping interlopers out of their territories. The Long Game was a treasure, a treat, indulged in seldom because one time too many would endanger the whole nest.

And, of course, if Petronilla Ehrenberg were particularly fond of that particular game, she might very well slip away from her home territory, to hunt elsewhere . . . like Berlin.

'She said that she suffered a nervous disorder, which made it impossible for her to endure sunlight,' the nobleman went on. 'I felt deeply for her, for of course such a disability would cut her off, almost completely, from the normal joys of human existence. When she came to Berlin – she is a native of Köln – I would do all that I could to accommodate her infirmity;

and we began a correspondence. I had retired by then from the Army – I was myself only relearning the pleasures of civilian life.'

Asher glanced at his hand. The mark of a wedding ring was barely a ghost on the tanned flesh, visible only by the strength of the late-afternoon sunlight through the window of the cab. Five years at least since he'd taken it off, and who knew how long before that, that his wife had died? Prussian Junkers, Asher was well aware, did not get divorces.

Hesitantly, the former Colonel continued: 'I suggested a number of nerve specialists, both in and out of Germany, who might help her. The fact that she suffered from this affliction, I said, did not mean that it could not be somehow helped. Medical science has made great strides in the past decade. At first she seemed to think that nothing could be done for her, but I begged her not to lose heart. I would love her—' He stopped himself, his cheekbones staining a little pink at the admission.

'I would love her both in daylight and in darkness. Yet, I said, where there is life, there is hope.'

He showed Asher the telegram he had received, sent from St Petersburg on Sunday, the 7th of May – April 23, by Russian reckoning:

Petronilla Ehrenberg Benedict Theiss engaged in murder in Petersburg stop they are monsters stop you must come

It was in German, but there was no signature.

'I don't even know what this means. Madame Ehrenberg—' He paused, groping for words. 'It is simply not possible. She is a strong woman, a passionate one, but . . . This is inconceivable. Benedict Theiss – the doctor, she said, who is effecting the cure of her condition – has a clinic here in Petersburg. It was the first place that I sought news of her this morning. It was closed up, locked . . . Yet only last week she wrote to me to say that they had made great strides towards a complete cure. When she is cured, we have talked of coming here to Petersburg to live permanently.'

'Do you dream of her?' asked Asher.

'I beg your pardon, sir!'

'No, I have a reason for such a question,' he said quickly. 'It is none of my business, and I would not ask otherwise: do you dream of her?'

Von Brühlsbuttel frowned, casting back in his memory . . .
In a way that he would not, Asher knew, if Petronilla Ehrenberg
were trying to seduce him, lure him, as vampires lured their
victims to them. 'I have,' he finally said slowly, 'once or twice.
Foolish things, you know . . .' He ducked his head shyly. 'About
six months ago I dreamed she was helping me tie fishing-
flies, although we already had a mountain of them. Then I
think, one other time, I dreamed she took me along when she
was buying shoes.' He shook his head, smiling at a private
memory. 'My sisters used to do that – take me along when
they shopped for shoes . . .'

For a moment more he savored that small recollection,
gazing out the window at the gray Neva, glittering a little in
the late slant of the sinking sun as they crossed over the bridge.
Anything or anyone farther from the sinister spymaster of
Asher's imaginings could hardly have been conceived. *Not
war at all*, he thought, *but simple love* . . .

'Nothing out of the ordinary.'

Above the water a flock of gulls circled, dark against the
red and yellow glare of the factory smoke in the sky.

'At first she did not seem to mind it,' he went on after a
moment, 'that we could meet only by night. Yet I think –
because of my own love for riding, for the woods, for the
beauty of the daylight world . . .' Years fell from his lined face,
giving him the appearance of a handsome schoolboy. 'It sounds
childish in a man of my age, does it not? Yet the beauty of
the world has always been a touchstone to me, everything in
it: a blade of grass, the difference between frog and frog, bird
and bird . . . I would *like* to think that my love for these things
drew her back towards the world on which she had long ago
turned her back. Like music, she said she had almost forgotten
what it was like to care about the world of the light. The world
that she would share with me, if she could.'

Where there is life, there is hope.

And so Petronilla Ehrenberg had started on her private quest
to have it both ways. Letting nothing stop her . . . *No wonder*,
thought Asher, as they climbed from the cab under the gray
walls of St Job, *the Auswärtiges Amt sent someone to watch
Theiss's clinic, if a private citizen of Köln sent fifty thousand
francs to a man as outspoken against the German government
as everyone says he was.*

And once the German agent had arrived, he would have remained . . .

Asher paid off the driver, led the way around the corner of the building to the wasteland of weeds and cinder-piles and disused railway sidings along the canal, which would shelter burglars from investigation. The body had been found in the canal, the paper had said . . . He wondered if Hugo Rissler – the thin and drooping Herr Texel – had murdered Theiss.

Why? Because he was no longer of use? Or had there been orders of some kind from Berlin?

Or had it been one or the other faction of the divided Petersburg vampires, seeking to cripple whatever advantage La Ehrenberg might be offering to their competition?

He descended the low areaway behind a buttress, examined the lock on the deep-set door. New, like the sheeting behind the ironwork of the front gate.

If Theiss had been working on some kind of serum that would allow a vampire to walk in daylight – for whatever reason – it was well that he had been stopped. Was that what they had been testing, those two who had gone to ground without even checking to see that their refuges were windowless? Yet it seemed absurd and foolhardy. But if Theiss had succeeded in his quest—

Beside him, von Brühlsbuttel turned sharply and looked up to ground-level. 'Petronilla!' he cried, a lover's joy in his voice.

With a sharp clack, the lock inside was thrown, the door before Asher opened from within to reveal Texel with a revolver in hand. 'Do not even think,' said Texel, 'of putting your hand anywhere near your pocket.' Daylight showed his face; the ghastly, marble white of vampire flesh gleamed shockingly in his reflective eyes. 'Inside – both of you . . .'

When he spoke, Asher could see the length of his fangs.

Only when they were within the lamplit vestibule did the woman who must be Petronilla Ehrenberg descend the outside steps down into the areaway and follow them inside, locking the door behind her.

For a moment she stood, gazing into von Brühlsbuttel's eyes. Then she whispered, 'Oh, my darling . . .' and the two of them stepped together, wrapped tight in one another's arms.

*   *   *

There was a burial chapel in the crypts, with a dais at one end; the walls down its narrow length were lined with niches in which – to judge by the filthy tangles of bones and half-rotted black robes that lay beneath them on the floor – the bodies of the monks had once been laid. Even now, decades or centuries after the last corpse had rotted to its component bones, the walls stank of decay.

Each niche held a sleeping youth or maiden, wax-white faces stained a little with deceptive warmth by the orange flare of Texel's oil-lamp as the German led the way down the length of the room. Asher counted ten of them, dressed in the faded hand-me-downs of the poor. Clawed hands folded on motionless breasts. Here and there a mouth had fallen open, to show the fangs.

Lydia lay on the dais before the altar, clothed in a grimy nightshirt, gentleman's black trousers, and, over all, a man's white linen shirt. Her face was scarcely less pale than those of the other sleepers against her tangled red hair. Her wrists were bound. She bore no wound.

Completely disregarding Texel and his gun, Asher ran to her. He was half the length of the chapel when he heard his captor laugh nastily, and the lamplight disappeared, followed by the clank of the closing door. Asher cursed, dug in his pocket for the candles and matches he'd gotten from Razumovsky, strode the rest of the distance, and dropped to his knees. 'Lydia!' She was warm. He felt her breath as he brushed back her hair, looked first at her throat and then at her wrists. She stirred when he touched her face.

'Jamie? Ow!' she added. 'I hit my head—'

'Are you all right?'

She started to laugh, weakly but with genuine amusement. 'As compared with *what*? Oh, you darling!' she added, as he fished her spectacles out of his other pocket. 'I'm better than I was . . .'

He was already tearing at the knots in the cord on her wrists.

'And Texel gave me veronal – a lot of it – and told Don Simon he wouldn't give me oxygen or digitalis, or anything to keep me from dying of it, unless he made him a vampire . . . I gather he'd already asked Madame and she'd refused.'

'I don't blame her,' muttered Asher grimly. 'That's a man who'd betray you for the price of a tram ticket. And did he?'

Asher recalled Ysidro's words on several occasions, about the making of fledglings. 'Completely aside from the fact that Texel wouldn't want to place himself in the position of being *her* fledgling—'

'I don't think it was that.' Lydia sat up – rather carefully – and held her wrists steady. 'He doesn't seem to know a great deal about being a vampire, except that he wants to be one to assist the Fatherland . . . and to get on the Kaiser's good side. He thinks it's all like in the penny dreadfuls, that they're just like the living. They held Lady Eaton here for a time, before they killed her, but Madame Ehrenberg seems to be the only vampire he's spoken more than a few words to. Nobody seems to have told him that once he actually became a vampire, he'd probably lose all desire to help the Fatherland or anybody else . . .'

She pulled her hands free of the ropes, threw her arms around Asher's neck, and kissed him, her body shivering against his in its thin habiliments. 'What happened to you?' she whispered. 'Simon said he woke up in Berlin and couldn't find you anywhere in the city—'

'I was arrested in Köln. I think someone must have recognized me. It happens. The town's filled with Foreign Service men, on account of the new fortifications.'

She drew back, put on her spectacles, and studied his face and cropped head. 'I don't see how they could have, but all right, if you say so. Jamie—'

She gripped him again, tighter, more desperate, and for some minutes they clung together like drowning swimmers in the candle's wavering glow. Then the light jerked and dipped with a sudden draft, and Petronilla's rich contralto laugh shivered the darkness. 'Well, 'tis an evening for journeys' ends and lovers' meetings, isn't it?' Asher saw their eyes flash in the gloom.

'Herr – Filaret, I think you told Sergius your name was? Though I imagine it's really Asher, isn't it, unless our good little English virgin is a great deal naughtier than she's painted herself. Whoever you are, if you'll be so good as to take off those silver chains you're wearing. And don't make Texel shoot you,' she added. 'The fact that the bullets in that gun are silver doesn't mean they can't kill you just as dead as lead— *Verdammung*!' she added, clutching at her wrist as if at the bite of an insect.

She fell back a pace, kneading at her arm as if in sharp pain. Texel did not take his eyes – or the gun – from Asher. After a moment, unwillingly, Asher complied.

'Have the lovely Frau Asher put them in my pocket,' ordered Texel. 'Silver doesn't burn the way it did – poor old Theiss really was onto something there. Not that anything would induce me to take that filthy serum four times a day the way Madame does—'

'It's only the after-effects of the first batches,' Petronilla retorted, with a glance of contemptuous loathing. 'Benedict told me it would fade.' She rubbed her shoulder, kneading as if at a violent itch.

'But what did he know about it, really?' demanded Lydia. 'The man wasn't running any sort of controlled tests. For all you know, you could start turning into one of those things like that poor boy Kolya, and I don't think even your poor sweetheart is going to be able to overlook that—'

'You,' said Petronilla quietly, 'keep your tongue between your teeth, girl. There's a little debt owing to you – and to your sweetheart – that it will be a pleasure to pay out.' She moved forward, and Asher fell back a step, shielding Lydia with his body. 'Oh, don't be melodramatic. What on earth do you think you can do against us?'

She was perfectly right about that, but at that point Asher could think of very little he had to lose. He dove at Texel, twisting sideways to avoid the gunshot that echoed like thunder in the crypt, hoping Lydia had the good sense to run for the door that the vampires had left open behind them. It was, he knew, madness to take on a vampire physically; the strength of Texel's blow sent him sprawling against the wall, stunning him, and he heard the tiny pat-pat-pat of Lydia's bare feet stumble, heard her cry out.

Texel caught him by the throat, and he felt the rake of the vampire's claws, on his chest, on his hands; Texel tore away his jacket, thrust him against the wall, and clawed him deliberately, back and forth across his ribs and on his back. Then he stepped away, and Lydia was flung down beside him, gasping, bleeding where her flesh, too, had been gashed.

Petronilla licked the blood from her nails. 'I'm going to enjoy this.' She glanced around her at the half-seen forms, sleeping in their niches in the darkness. 'In an hour they'll be waking. My little blood maidens. They usually don't open their eyes until it's full dark outside. If we can ever locate that *beschissen* Spaniard –' she threw another murderous glare at Texel – 'I shall have to ask him if that's an effect of their maidenhood.'

'I think we'll find that out,' responded the German, 'a good deal quicker than we'll be able to flush him out of hiding. I put one of these into him.' He gestured with the pistol. 'He can't stay hidden forever. And in a few days –' he gestured, as she had, back towards the unseen niches, the pale sleepers – 'these will be strong enough to help us bring him in. Do you think they'll know by instinct how to kill? Or will you have to show them?'

She smiled. 'I look forward to finding that out.'

TWENTY-EIGHT

Texel took the candle, just – as Ellen would put it – to be bloody-minded.

The moment the door closed Lydia whispered, 'Do you have anything else in your jacket?'

'Some twine, the rest of the matches, and about seventy-five roubles.'

'Can you make a picklock out of the frame of my spectacles?'

'Not for the lock on that door. Stay where you are for a minute.' He groped on his knees, feeling in the direction of where Texel had thrown the rags of his jacket, until he found it. Returning to her, he wrapped it around her shoulders, her flesh cold to his touch and her blood sticky on his fingers. Then he took her hand and edged cautiously to the left until his other hand came in contact with a wall, then followed it, passing the niches where the blood maidens slept.

Lydia whispered, 'Is there anything we can do?'

'Not much. Stand here, by the door, and hope it's thick enough that she doesn't hear us breathing through it. If she doesn't have Texel with her when she comes back, one of us may have a chance. We slip past her – if we can – and split up—'

'Here.'

He heard the rustle of her fumbling in the dark, and a moment later she pressed a handful of roubles and half a dozen matches into his hand.

'We try to find Don Simon,' said Lydia firmly. 'He's out there somewhere, and if he's on his feet, he'll be looking for us.'

'How badly was he shot?'

There was long silence. Then she said in a tiny voice, 'I don't know.'

Then silence, dense and endless as the night after Judgment Day, when all the living souls have departed and the dead world is left to its long emptiness. Asher put his arm around his wife, felt her trembling with cold or exhaustion or fear.

Even he could smell their blood.

A voice whispered somewhere in the darkness, 'Yuri?'

Damn—

'Sonia?'

'What is that?'

'There's someone here. There by the door.'

'Blood—'

A girl's voice said – like the others – in the rough peasant Russian of the slums, 'Don't.' And then, in French: 'Madame Asher, is that you?'

Besides the voices there wasn't a sound, but Asher knew, as if he felt it through his skin, that they were moving up the room towards them. Lydia said, 'Genia, it's me.'

And then, shockingly close, the voice of Genia said in Russian, 'Don't, Alexei, stop it!' There was a sharp rustle, like moths – Asher felt the stir of air, movement, as if someone had been pushed away.

'It's all right,' whispered a boy's voice, almost in Asher's ear. 'It will save them from their sins, the same way the Lady saved *us* by drinking *our* blood.'

'That's what she said.' Another boy, terrifyingly close. 'In my dream St Margaret said so. She appeared to me, Genia! She had the Lady's face! They are sinners, they can only be saved through us—'

'It's a lie!' cried Genia desperately, and Asher nearly jumped out of his skin at the brush of a death-cold shoulder against his arm. Another almost soundless rustle, the movement of bodies.

He could smell their clothing, old sweat and carbolic soap, though their flesh was odorless. 'If we drink their blood we'll be damned!'

'You've got it wrong, Genia,' said Alexei, and now there was frantic urgency in his voice. 'You've got it backwards. *Everyone* is damned. It's the blood that damns – and the blood that saves . . .'

And someone else, another girl, very young by the sound of her voice, echoed fervently, 'It's the blood that saves . . .'

Behind them, the door fell suddenly open and lamplight streamed through. Asher barely had a moment to glimpse the ring of white faces, gleaming vampire eyes, less than two feet away from them, before he grabbed Lydia and dragged her through the door, almost stumbling into Sergius von Brühlsbuttel on the threshold. Lydia caught the lamp as von Brühlsbuttel dropped it; Asher slammed the door to, shot the bolt, twisted the key.

The gentle nobleman seemed paralysed with shock at what he, too, had glimpsed in the lamplight beyond the door. Then he seemed to rouse himself, stammered, 'She's on her way.'

'Help Lydia.' It seemed a safer division of labor than trusting him with the lamp. 'Do you have the key to the front gate?'

'Here—' Von Brühlsbuttel reached out, as if to pluck at Asher's sleeve as he led the way through the corridor he remembered, up a flight of steps. 'Those things in the chapel – what are they? What is *she*? I had never seen her in daylight . . . *Herr Gott*, when we crossed the courtyard—!'

'They are vampires,' said Asher grimly, counting doorways, counting turnings, as he had counted them when Texel had brought him down. At least, as a *Junker* – a country aristocrat – von Brühlsbuttel would have grown up with the legends. '*She* is a vampire—'

'And is making a damn good attempt,' added Lydia thoughtfully, 'at taking over the position of Master of St Petersburg. I'm Mrs Asher, by the way, sir . . . Jamie, I don't imagine any interloping fledgling has ever come up with the idea of creating ten fledglings of her own all at once before. They'll immediately outnumber both local nests put together, even if Golenischev and Prince Dargomyzhsky weren't gone for the summer—'

Von Brühlsbuttel halted in his tracks, staring in horror at

this matter-of-fact recital, and Asher caught the man's arm in his free hand, dragged him on. 'We know the Undead,' he said. 'We've fought them for years.' Which sounded better, he supposed, than saying, *We've had a vampire friend since 1907 . . .*

'*Du Gott almachtig . . .*'

Wide stairs debouched into the covered walk that surrounded the courtyard. The silver-barred grille that guarded the archway stood open. Even in the lamplight Asher could see Lydia's face was chalky under the streaked blood, and von Brühlsbuttel looked scarcely better. The German whispered, 'How could I have been deceived in her?'

Checking the courtyard, watching for signs of movement – not that anyone could see a hunting vampire move – Asher replied, 'Deceit is what they do.'

'And even they, like everyone else,' said Lydia, 'have two sides to their souls. You were her friend in Berlin?'

'I was.' Von Brühlsbuttel let his breath go in a little sigh. 'I thought . . . She has changed. She was not like this a year ago.'

'It's the serum, I think,' said Lydia, and she leaned back against the frame of the arch, struggling to get her breath. 'Dr Theiss said so, anyway. The serum they were working on, so that she could walk around in the daylight. It's why she made new vampires – to get vampire blood. I think it affects her mind. And it's had some shocking effects on some of the maidens he tested it on. Texel keeps away from it, but he'll go back and get some if he has to, to pursue us into daylight. I'm all right now.'

She was lying, thought Asher, but it was a gallant lie. The moon had set. The sky above the walls was not black, but a velvety blue, a few shades lighter than royal, and pinned with stars that barely showed against the atmosphere's ambient brightness. She was right. Dawnlight wouldn't save them.

He took her hand. 'Let's go.'

The courtyard was about sixty feet by a hundred, and from where they stood in the arch it seemed like a mile and a half to the gate.

They ran.

And Petronilla Ehrenberg dropped from the balcony above the outer gate, weightless, like a great pale bird.

For a moment she only stood facing them, the lamplight glowing back from her eyes. Then she stretched forth her hand and said, 'Get away from them, Sergius.'

'And what?' Sergius von Brühlsbuttel stepped out from between Asher and Lydia and stood before them, between them and the vampire. 'Watch you kill these people? Petra—'

'You don't understand.' She flinched, clutched at her arm again as if the pain there had returned. In the wavery lamp-light Asher saw the small red spot he had noticed on her neck had widened to the size of an American dollar, and her whole body gave off a strange, sulfurous smell. 'I swear to you I don't do this often . . .'

'Petra,' said von Brühlsbuttel gently, 'I think I do under-stand. Your heart longs for the daylight – you remember what it was like, to love. As I remember. You wanted to open up the door again into the world of the living, and to pass freely back and forth. To have sunlight and love in the world of the living . . . and power in the world of the night.'

She turned her gleaming eyes on him, and Asher saw some-thing change in them, as she looked back through the door of which he spoke. Tears of regret filled her eyes, for all that she had lost, and she cried, 'Is that too much to ask?'

'Yes,' said von Brühlsbuttel, his voice infinitely sad. 'Yes, my love, I think it is.'

Lydia shouted, 'Look out!' and Asher saw movement in the central doorway of the monastery: Texel raising his gun. Who his target was Asher never knew; von Brühlsbuttel gasped, 'Petra!' and seized her, thrusting her out of the line of fire, just as the sound of the shot split the night. The German let out a cry and crumpled into Petronilla's arms.

'Sergius!' Petronilla held him up easily, but Asher could see the wound was mortal. He caught Lydia's hand, ran two steps towards the gate, but Texel was suddenly in front of him, covering the distance with a vampire's eerie, floating speed. Blind to everything around her, Petronilla sank to her knees on the pitted brick pavement, Sergius von Brühlsbuttel's body in her arms. 'Sergius!' she called again, pressing her hands to the wounds where the silver bullet had torn through his body, blood pouring out over her white fingers.

Blood streamed down her shoulder where the exiting bullet had struck her as well, but for that first moment she seemed to feel nothing – *as I would feel nothing*, thought Asher, *if Lydia had been hit . . .*

Von Brühlsbuttel's hand groped for a moment; Petra's met it, clung to it. He whispered, 'I am sorry, my love.'

She called out his name one more time, then her whole body shuddered, and she let him slide to the pavement as she clutched at the wound in her own shoulder, sobbed once – twice—

Then screamed, as the stench of burning suddenly filled the court.

Asher caught Lydia, dragged her a step back from the vampire and her lover; Texel only stood, staring in shock. It seemed to Asher that the flame started from the dark sore on Petronilla's neck and from the one on her hand, as much as from the wound in her shoulder where the silver bullet had gone in, as if all the stored combustion of weeks and months of accumulated daylight were reacting at once. Petronilla screamed again and tried to rise, beating at the flame with her hands, and this time Texel leaped back, face aghast—

Another thing, Asher found himself thinking, *that he hadn't bothered to learn about the vampire state, the powers of which he had so coveted.*

What it was like when they died.

Her skirt was burning – beneath it her legs must have erupted into flame – and she fell, crawling, rolling on the courtyard bricks. Oily smoke and the abominable stench of roasting flesh. Even when her sinews were consumed to the point that she was unable to crawl she was still conscious, screams transmuting into noises more horrible . . .

Did the ancient man who first invented the concept of Hell do so after seeing a vampire burn?

Somewhere the men and women she has killed down through the years are watching.

When at last she was silent, Asher looked up and met Texel's eyes across the flickering pile of ash.

The German's face hardened, and he gestured back towards the monastery door with the gun. 'Get inside,' he said. '*Herr Gott*, that I only took one dose of the stuff . . .'

'Yes,' said a quiet voice from the dark archway of the monastery door. 'Do come inside James, Mistress. I think it would be best, though, Hugo, if you remain outside till daylight – drop the gun. Drop it—'

Hugo Texel stood trembling, the pistol leveled at Lydia's head; then with a clatter the weapon fell to the ground, as if his hand had opened of its own accord. Asher stooped at once to pick it up. In the archway he could just make out Ysidro's pale face and colorless hair, and the cold gleam of his flesh where it showed through the holes of the decaying black robe.

'She didn't tell you about this part of being a vampire, did she?' Ysidro's voice was so soft that Asher, when he and Lydia reached the Spaniard's side beneath the dark archway, could barely make it out, but Texel screamed at him:

'*Teufelschwanz!*'

'I don't suppose she was ever willing to admit that that old Jew in Köln had the power over her, to make her come and go at his bidding . . . or stand still.'

Texel's face worked indescribably, his mouth like some gaping theatrical mask. He tried to move, clawing all around him with his widespread hands, but when he took a step he fell to his knees, as Ippo the student had in Lady Eaton's house, when his master had so commanded. 'When the light comes up you'll burn, too, you devil!'

Ysidro only folded his thin arms, never taking his eyes from the man in the courtyard – and Asher knew that Ysidro, in fact, would have several minutes in which to find shelter in the dark of the crypts. The new-made fledglings were fragile, as he had said.

'I've taken the serum as well! The sun will do nothing to me . . .'

Ysidro made no answer.

Softly, Lydia said, 'He's bluffing. I don't know how long a single dose lasts—'

'Then be sure to make notes, Mistress. Yet I would ask of you, whatever else you choose to do here after full light comes, destroy this serum that Dr Theiss has made. All of it, every drop. Burn his notes. Fascinating as it may be for you to study his experiments, yet I have a grave mistrust of fate. Only in the flame is there safety.'

'For God's sake, man, come to Germany with me!' Sheer panic at what was coming – at what he had seen coming – edged Texel's shriek. 'The Kaiser will cherish us both! Anything we ask for, out of the world that will be Germany's—'

Ysidro lifted his voice just slightly, still without change of expression. 'Think you I do this for power alone?' He asked as if he genuinely expected an answer, and as if surprised at his fledgling's naivety. 'Friends among the Undead are rare enough, in all the centuries of living in darkness. You have killed one of mine. I expect you to make her your apologies, when you see her.'

There was a scent in the air, the wind turning over the Gulf of Finland; seagulls set up a great yammering in the paling sky.

Texel screamed, 'I am of you! I am in your soul as you are in mine! You will feel it – inside, you will burn if I burn!'

Whether he spoke true or not, Asher didn't know. When Texel's flesh first spotted with flame, then surged into a blazing torch, his eyes were drawn to the shrieking, staggering thing in the courtyard; it was some moments before he thought to look back to see Ysidro.

And when he did, Ysidro was gone.

TWENTY-NINE

There were ampoules of silver nitrate in Dr Theiss's laboratory. Asher injected the nine maiden fledglings he found asleep in the crypt with it before he dragged them, one by one, out of the darkness. They all caught fire at the top of the steps, without waking up, the moment he pulled them through the door into the vestibule where the gorgeous brightness of the dawn sky glimmered. Ysidro had been right about how fragile they were.

Lydia said, 'It isn't fair. They never harmed anyone.'

'No,' agreed Asher. 'Can you guarantee that they would not?'

She, too, seemed to hear again the whispering voices in the dark of the crypt and said no more, even offering to help him drag them. He refused. Exhausted as he was himself, Asher did not like the whiteness of his wife's lips and the way she sat down quickly on the steps. When he had dragged out the last of them she said, 'That's only nine. There were ten in the crypt.'

'I know.'

'I didn't see Genia. The girl who tried to keep the others from us. She was the one who escaped and came to Razumovsky's *izba* Friday night – who inadvertently led the others to me.'

'We need to find her,' said Asher wearily. 'But first let's deal with the laboratory. The police will be here—'

'Actually, they won't,' said Lydia. 'Petronilla was paying someone high up in the police for protection. But you're right. Let's not push our luck.'

It was full daylight by that time, and Asher worked quickly, breaking up the equipment and piling it in the sinks. Lydia poured away every phial she found – blood, serum, filtrates – and combed both the laboratory and Theiss's little office in the chamber next door for notes. These she heaped in another sink and set fire to them.

'I'd rather we didn't have the Fire Brigade to deal with,' said Asher.

Lydia didn't ask him why. By her silence, she knew.

They took lamps and searched the crypt, and around noon they found Ysidro.

He'd taken refuge in one of the inner catacombs, where the bones of long-dead monks still occupied the low brick niches along the walls; skulls grinned from ossuary lofts overhead. Through the torn black robe he wore, Asher could see the bullet-wound in his shoulder, black, burned-looking, and oozing, but because he had not – unlike Madame Ehrenberg – been accumulating the effects of repeated exposures to sunlight in his flesh, the damage seemed to have gone no further. Nearby Asher found a gold penknife monogrammed IE, clotted with blood, and the silver bullet he'd removed with it before sleep had claimed him.

His face was relaxed, enigmatic in sleep as in waking. He had taken off his gold signet-ring and laid it on the stone beside his head, as if he knew they would come.

And so here we are, Asher thought.

There were two syringes of silver nitrate in his jacket pocket, and he carried a hammer and two hawthorn stakes he had found in a lower drawer of Theiss's desk.

Where we all three of us knew we would one day be.

He glanced sidelong at Lydia's face, white with exhaustion,

spectacles reflecting the lamplight like insectile eyes and hiding whatever she felt.

Were it not for Ysidro, she would be dead. And with her – she had said – the child she carried.

Lydia's child. My child.

He tried not to hope, or to feel the delirious joy he'd felt last time and the time before . . . and failed in the attempt. It was apparently the province of the living to hope.

It seemed that the Dead did indeed have gifts to give to the living . . .

He will kill when he wakes. Asher looked down at the calm, sleeping face, the straight white eyelashes, the waxen, awful scars that nobody saw when the vampire was awake to trick their minds. He would have to kill, to speed the healing of his wound; to renew those mental powers that gave him mastery over the minds of the living. That let him seduce through dreams.

Asher knew what needed to be done, as if he had sworn an oath to that old man in Prague. Yet – feeling stupid even as the words came out of his mouth – he asked, 'What do we do?'

Lydia turned her face away. In a small voice she said, 'He didn't kill Margaret Potton.' As if, out of so many, that mattered.

'I know.'

She looked back at him, lips parted to speak, and he went on, 'He asked me not to tell you.'

She didn't ask why, but he saw her brown eyes swim with tears.

'He is what he is, Lydia. He cannot be other than that. More than anyone, he knows that that door is shut.'

It was her turn to say, 'I know. But more than anyone – of all the vampires, and I think of anyone still living as well – I think he was the only one who understood – or *would* have understood – that Petronilla Ehrenberg did what she did because she was in love with a living man. That she wasn't working out of . . . of loyalty to the Kaiser or desire for an unlimited supply of trussed-up German Socialists or whatever the Kaiser would have paid her with. Simon was the only one who knew that the way to stop her was to break the tie between her and her dream. Her hope of being able to live with the man she loved.'

She wrapped her arms around herself – it was cold in the catacomb – and looked down at Ysidro's face again.

Asher wondered if the vampire could hear them, sunk in the sleep that he had often said was not like the sleep of the living. *And what*, he thought, *does HE hope?*

''Twere best the dead were dead utterly, he said, and life left to the living,' she went on after a moment. 'It was he who telegraphed poor von Brühlsbuttel, you know. Or, anyway, he got some poor beggar-woman to do it . . .'

'The way he got me to come with him here.'

They are seducers . . .

Every kill he makes henceforth will be upon your head . . .

A lake of blood indeed.

Asher felt numb inside, and cold to the core of his bones.

'You decide,' Lydia whispered. 'I'll be upstairs.'

'Will you be—?'

'I'll be all right. It's not far.'

It wasn't. It was the searching that had taken time, back-tracking with the aid of Asher's twine, seeking out the hidden crypt.

She picked up one of the lamps, the shadows moving over Ysidro's sleeping face like half of a ghostly smile. 'There's nothing in the darkness now.'

She was sitting in the covered walkway around the courtyard when he came up half an hour later, in a patch of sunlight, like a ragged beggar-child in her grimy nightshirt, his bloodied jacket, and Ysidro's trousers and shirt. Her arms clasped about her thin knees, she gazed through the nearest archway into the courtyard, where two grisly piles of ashes still smoked.

I should never have dragged her into this. Asher leaned against the archway, shivering with fatigue, wondering how it was that they had both survived this. *It was inexcusable, to expose her to this. To put her in danger as I did.*

Even the Department never asked me to use those I loved.

In fact, it discouraged us from loving anyone at all.

You cannot serve God and Mammon . . . and if someone could identify which of those two one serves in the Department, would any of us be happier?

Nights without sleep, days without rest or food, had left him feeling bludgeoned, weary beyond reckoning, and he knew that down in the dark of the crypt there had been no right choice. He owed Ysidro Lydia's life, and the life of their child. Lydia had put the decision into his hand, loving them both, knowing what Ysidro was, and accepting whatever his choice would be. But it was one thing to accept, and another, what she would feel, and dream, and wake up sobbing out in the dark of the night. The Germans weren't the only ones who gave no thought to what the world would be like after the battle that they so much wished to win. He remembered the pale stillness of her days of grieving for their lost child, knowing it could have been no other way, but so frighteningly distant . . .

If she cannot forgive me my choice . . .

He had literally no idea what he would do then.

Lydia raised her head as he came towards her, got shakily to her feet. She was always thin; now she looked as if he could pick her up in one hand, like a red-and-white lily. *I could have returned to Petersburg and found her gone, dead . . .*

There was more than one gate through which one could pass, never to return.

He said, 'I couldn't.'

And Lydia flung herself into his arms, kissed him feverishly on the mouth, and burst into tears of relief.

When Asher returned to the monastery two days later – twenty-four hours after notifying the Okhrana that he had 'heard' of fearful things done there, and on the same day he got Razumovsky's order to destroy the contents of Theiss's laboratory at the clinic – Ysidro was gone from the crypt. Nor did the smallest whisper of the vampire's presence trouble his dreams, though for weeks – as he and Lydia journeyed back through Europe – his dreams were not pleasant ones. They stopped in the smaller towns – Minsk and Cracow and Brno – for Asher had found himself uneasy at the thought of spending the night in cities such as Prague or Warsaw.

Of the girl Genia, no trace was found.

AUTHOR'S NOTE:
THE RUSSIAN CALENDAR

When Pope Gregory XIII mandated the switch from the old Julian calendar to the astronomically more accurate reckoning of the Gregorian calendar in 1582, because of religious enmities neither Protestant nor Orthodox countries would follow suit. England and the British colonies in America did not switch over to the Gregorian calendar until 1752 (with the result that most of America's Founding Fathers have two recorded birth dates, one 'old-style' and one Gregorian about eleven days later); Sweden did not make the change until 1753, and Russia did not start using the Gregorian calendar until after the 1918 Revolution that ended the rule of the Tsars. Thus, in 1911, when this story takes place, all dates are different depending on whether the action is taking place inside or outside of Russia, the Julian date being two weeks behind the Gregorian.

Greece did not switch to the Gregorian reckoning until 1924, and many Orthodox churches still use the Julian calendar to calculate the date of Easter.